Joyce Cary was born in Londonderry on 7 December 1888. His father, descended from an Anglo-Irish family, was a civil engineer in England, and at the age of seventeen, Cary embarked upon his studies of art, being based in both Edinburgh and Paris.

In 1912 he served as a Red Cross orderly in Montenegro during the Balkan Wars, and in 1913, joined the Nigerian Political Service. During the First World War he served with a Nigerian regiment, but was wounded and later forced to return to England. He settled in Oxford, and this was where he began his writing career.

Cary struggled for many years to translate his experiences and views into the novelistic form, and it was not until 1932 that he completed his first novel, *Aissa Saved*. Once this had been published he wrote with great fluency, drawing on his African experiences and life in Ireland for inspiration. He developed a highly-individualised 'trilogy style' where each main character narrates one volume in turn. This he used to great effect in The Horse's Mouth trilogy featuring the artist Gulley Jimson. Cary's strengths lie in his credible characterisation, his concern for artistic and political liberty and his skill in producing great comic effect.

Cary was married and had four sons. He died in Oxford in March 1957.

Joyce Cary

Prisoner of Grace

Joyce Cary's 'Second Trilogy'

PRISONER OF GRACE

EXCEPT THE LORD

NOT HONOUR MORE

HOUSE OF STRATUS

This edition published in 2000 by House of Stratus, an imprint of Stratus Holdings plc, 24c Old Burlington Street, London, W1X 1RL. UK.

www.houseofstratus.com

Typeset, printed and bound by House of Stratus.

A catalogue record for this book is available from the British Library.

ISBN 1-84232-039-4

For
MY CHILDREN

AUTHOR'S PREFACE

The difficulty of a book about a politician is that people will tend to read it as a book about government. But politics is the art of human relations, an aspect of all life. That is why I wanted to tell the story through the eyes of a wife whose marriage needs a great deal of management. I wanted to give the complete political scene.

Nimmo has been called a crook. He is not meant for a crook. A crook is essentially a man who is out for himself, who has no principles. Crooks are uninteresting people because their range is so narrow. In state politics they are especially dull. The question had to be how does a real politician, the handler, the manager of people, who is also a man of principle, keep his principles? How far do his ends justify his means?

Cripps was one of the honestest men who ever went into politics, but when he was asked if it was proposed to devalue sterling, he answered that there was no immediate intention to do so. At that moment it was already arranged to devalue sterling within a few days.

Technically he did not tell a lie, but this is not the point, the point is that he had to deceive. Of course any mother will lie to a nervous child about the doctor or the dentist. She will say that a dangerous painful operation will prove a trifle, that the dentist won't hurt. She has to do so for the child's good.

I am not pretending that Nimmo was a completely

admirable character. There are few such anywhere in the world. He is an egotist like most successful politicians. Probably no man would give himself to that craft, certainly he would not succeed in it, without a great deal of conceit. Politicians need great self-confidence. Nimmo was a man, too, not very scrupulous in his eloquence. But the modern leader of the people needs to be a spell-binder, and poets have never been very scrupulous in getting their effect.

An acute American critic said that Gully Jimson of *The Horse's Mouth* was a politician in art, and Nimmo an artist in politics. This is true and penetrating in so far that both are creative minds in the world of a perpetual creation. They are inventing unique answers to problems that are of necessity always new.

The same critic, to my surprise, said that Wilson was a greater man than Roosevelt. To me Wilson has always seemed like a stiff, dogmatic person, applying formulae to life; Roosevelt, the artist creator, improvising as he went, a genius in handling the ever-changing complexities of human affairs. What Wilson lacked was precisely the creative imagination, and the want of it ruined his policy.

The book was called *Prisoner of Grace* because Nina was held to her husband by her sense that he was on the whole a good man. She recoiled from destroying his career because she felt that he was trying to do right. It has been objected that she was not a prisoner of grace in any true sense, because her motive was selfish, she was afraid to spoil her happiness by a crime. But, after all, this means that she is the kind of person who is afraid of guilt, and such people are not in fact bad people. You may call her a pleasure-lover, played upon and used by a clever adventurer. But everyone loves pleasure, everyone who is worth anything is an adventurer. The question is what pleases them and what they risk themselves for. Nina would not get pleasure by giving pain, and Chester was an adventurer not only for his own career but for a cause that he thought good.

Another question was, how could Nina, with her very slender grasp of religion, be described as subject to grace? But grace is not a rare and strange visitor from the mysterious depths of things, invoked only by special exercise, it is an influence as common as the weather and persistent as the heart muscle. It operates, they say, by revelation; but a revelation happens every time we see the meaning of a poem, grasp the beauty of a picture, recognise and respond to kindness or feel sympathy. Grace is so ordinary and common that it is not noticed in its true quality. A man who thinks of himself as an agnostic, or even an atheist, will declare, "I hate cruelty," and explain his disgust by saying that it is a natural thing. "Cruelty is unnatural." And he imagines that he is getting rid of anything like grace by calling his feeling natural. But what he is really affirming is that his feeling is part of nature, that grace therefore is as common as hydrogen gas. In fact we know it a great deal more easily and directly than hydrogen gas.

A last point which is perhaps worth making: some critics objected strongly to the brackets. The history of the brackets is this. The first scene finished was that at the railway station where Chester plants in Nina's mind that fear of guilt which drives her back to him, which makes her a prisoner of grace. This scene worked and so I saw that the book could be written.

But when I began at the beginning in the first person I ran into a great difficulty. Nina telling on her husband, analysing his motives, appeared mean and small, and therefore an unreliable witness. Of course she had to have her own point of view, she could not know all Chester, but she had to be trustworthy in herself or the book became an essay in the cynical and told nothing true of the political experience.

I began again in the third person and found that the scene at the railway station would not come through. In despair I tried the false first, I gave Aunt Latter a brother, a retired civil servant devoted to Nina, and made him tell the story. He ran away with the book and ruined it, everything was falsified and cheapened, the acuteness of the observer only emphasised his lack of real understanding, as sharp arrows will go right through a target and leave no mark.

I was ready to throw away a year's work when one night, I don't know why, those brackets occurred to me. Nina, I said, is essentially a woman who can understand another's point of view, she has to be so to tell her story. All her judgments are qualified. And qualifications go into brackets.

And when I tried the brackets they did make Nina a credible witness. They enabled her, even in the first person, to reveal her own quality of mind. She had, in short, a brackety mind. The brackets made the book possible, without the brackets there could have been no book.

J C

1 I am writing this book because I understand that "revelations" are soon to appear about that great man who was once my husband, attacking his character, and my own. And I am afraid that they will be believed simply because nowadays everyone believes the worst of a famous man. The greater his name, the worse the stories.

And first of all, it is not true, as people say, that I was trapped into marriage, when I loved someone else. If there was any deceit, it was on my side. But I was barely eighteen at the time and did not know what love was; I don't believe, in fact (as I look back on the creature that I was then), that there was any I to be anything for more than ten minutes at a time.

But it is true that all these different I's (the one that loved, as well as the one that liked reading) were determined to enjoy themselves, and that they were also in very close family relations with my cousin Jim Latter. We were like brother and sister, and yet we were not so; and this situation is always dangerous for a girl, because she is drawn into very particular – I mean very confidential – relations with a young man: and always has something to talk about interesting to them both.

My cousin Jim and I always had something to talk about. Even at ten, when I was six, he would bully me, but also spoil me. We were together for weeks during his holidays, and on cold nights he would take me into his bed to keep me warm and comfort me when I was frightened of bats or ghosts. It was he, of course, who first of all told me about bats that stuck in girls' hair and bit into their brains, and ghosts that crept upon them in bed and strangled them with fingers that were like chicken bones.

Jim was a great excitement in my life, but I had other great excitements. I was already a passionate reader and loved to wander about in what my family called a "murky" state but which was really an intense realization of some tale. Jim gave me acute joys, but also he interrupted other joys and tortured me with his furies.

I was far too young and scatterbrained to manage our relations or even to know (as some children with brothers and sisters know quite young) that relations need managing. I can still remember the strange feeling of terror and thrill (which was itself alarming) with which I waited for each of his holidays. Aunt Latter, with whom I lived, would take me to meet him at Queensport station (it was four miles away) and tell me in the cab, "Now, Nina, you're not to be a nuisance to Jimmy these holidays. Remember he has no proper home, poor boy, and we must make this a home for him. If he wants to do things with you, do them willingly. Don't ever forget that Jimmy is very proud. He does not like to be under obligations – especially to silly little girls."

I knew her opinion of Jim: that he was a true Latter, which was high praise; and that he had character, which was higher – in fact almost the highest thing that Aunt Latter could say of a man. For Aunt Latter, the world was divided into people with character, who were rare but immensely precious, so that nothing was too good for them; and the rest, variously described as the mob, the crowd, or the loomp. These terms, I may say, were not class distinctions. The loomp included everyone who at the moment was under Aunt Latter's scorn as a person of no character; that is, one who did not have very decided opinions of which Aunt Latter could approve. And she adored Jimmy.

It would be quite wrong to say that Aunt Latter would, if she could and if it seemed necessary, have cut off my head and roasted me and served me up for Jim's dinner with breadcrumbs (as my nurse would grumble), but she had for Jim not only great love but the deepest compassion. Jim was the second son of her brother, Sir Brougham, who, when his wife died, had gone to live abroad and wandered about the continent with various women. He was a great connoisseur of the arts and wrote expensive books about them which no one read – because he used to abuse Ruskin in them and praise the new French painters. I only saw him once, and then he was so charming to me that I rather loved him. He was a tall thin fair man, with a rather mad expression (his eyes looked frightened and his mouth twitched) and a high voice like a woman's.

But Jim had always hated him and had been such a trouble to him that everyone was glad when Aunt Latter arranged to take him for the holidays. Jim's elder brother, Bobby, on the other hand, always went abroad to his father, with whom he was a great favourite. Everyone liked Bobby, including Jim himself, for though he was like Jim to look at only much uglier, and with the most minute eyes, he was a quite different character, gay and friendly. He never encroached. No one could help loving Bobby Latter, unless determined (like Aunt Latter) not to. I have never enjoyed any holiday so much as the one he spent with us at Palm Cottage. It was only a week, but in memory it seems like a year. I think I was really in love with Bobby (I was only ten, but rather precocious in some feelings) when he went away. I wept for some hours and wrote to him three times – but he never answered. Bobby was a most charming generous soul, but he forgot you as soon as you were out of sight. He kept only the memory. When he met you again, he startled you by remembering all you had talked about with him, and even your prejudices and tastes. But all this knowledge was stored away in some brain cave, and he never took it out till he did see you again. In fact, Bobby could not possibly have remembered all his friends all the time, for he had thousands; and did not really need any at all. Whereas Jim never had more than one or two – I mean real friends to whom he told his private thoughts and who were always very close to him and whom, too, he needed badly.

2 But it is quite untrue that he "adored" me as a child, and was robbed of his "only joy" when I was "snatched" away from him. He often hated me and we fought savagely. We were, in fact, always carrying on a kind of war to dominate each other or to stop being dominated.

For instance, I remember one occasion when we went to picnic at a place called Rockpit, a little beach down the cliffs under Staplehead. There were big waves roaring in and I said that I'd never seen such a rough sea – it must be a full gale.

At that moment we were good friends, standing pressed together and enjoying the noise which shook the whole beach. But Jim, only to contradict me, answered at once that it was only half a gale. "That isn't a rough sea – it's only an ordinary Atlantic swell."

I said that we had often bathed in the swell. And he answered promptly that we could bathe in this sea. It would be a good idea. He liked waves.

I said I had no idea of managing our relations. And I answered at once that if he bathed in a sea like that he'd be drowned. Besides, we had no towels.

"Oh!" he said. "If you funk it!"

Then, of course, we both undressed (but I more slowly); and Jim, to my rage and horror, stalked into the sea. He disappeared at once in a mass of foam.

I lost my nerve and ran to pull him out, but was at once knocked down. It was Jim who dragged me out, and I shall never forget the agony of the long minutes while he hauled me through the surf by the arm and hair and propped me on my feet.

I hated to be handled, and I hated myself naked; and even while I was shivering and spitting salt water I was hating Jim's nakedness. At thirteen he was still a skinny child; like me, in fact, for at ten I had shot up to five feet one, a knobby skeleton, and almost my full height, and he did not begin to grow fast till a year later. As we both had the same fair colouring, strangers took us for twins.

Now both of us had turned green, in blotches, the horrible colour of very white skins in an east wind. But Jim had the Latters' bad circulation, his lips were bright blue, his nose magenta, his eyes and cheeks had shrunk right in. He looked starved with cold and his teeth were chattering the whole time. And though I was even skinnier than he, I was much the tougher. I never had even a cold – he had had pleurisy twice.

And it was quite as much in indignation (though I, too, was trembling and shaking) as sympathy that I said, "You're freezing. Hadn't you better dress?"

But Jim was now well started on the spite game – he would have thrown away his life to get a single cry of fright out of me. And he answered, "That wasn't a swim. Come on, I'll show you how. You put your head under and let the curlers break down your back."

I was terrified for him, but (because that was just what

he wanted) I disdained to protest. I said only, "You know it's dangerous. You just want to show how brave you are."

Then, of course, he went straight in – out among the biggest waves. Once I could not see him for at least a minute.

And when at last he came out I would not speak to him. We dressed in silence, sat down shivering in our wet clothes, on separate rocks, to eat our sandwiches and went home ten yards apart. I was so enraged against Jim (thinking how happy I could have been alone with a book in front of the nursery fire) that I should have been quite glad if I had fallen off the cliff on the way up and killed myself.

We did not speak to each other all the evening. We were hating each other, and I was still hating Jim when I went to bed. But in half an hour I felt him slipping his cold legs down between my sheets, and he said sleepily (but he was not sleepy – he was pretending, in order to hide his embarrassment), "Tell me a story, Nina." But I could not speak. My throat felt stopped up.

Aunt Latter used to say I was sulky, and, indeed, gave me the reputation. But I truly do not think I was a sulky child. For it was not spite that kept me silent; it was a kind of heavy mass of tangled feelings which surrounded me and tied me in on all sides, so that even if I could have spoken I should not have known where to begin.

Jim, raging against me, would ask what was wrong with me – had I got the pip? Then he would be suddenly kind and say, "Cheer up, Rabbit; what's wrong?" and hug me and even (what was very rare), kiss me. Then he would rage again and tear at me as if he wanted to kill me (and I really think he did – I mean, it was the same rage that makes people do murder, and in the most cruel ways); but however he beat me and whatever he did, I would stay limp and not say a word. This, of course (because he realized that he could do nothing to me except batter me or kill me and that even then I should not care), made him still more furious, especially as he thought I was doing it on purpose; though, in fact, I could not help it. All I could do was to try to ignore the whole horrible situation, and I was quite ready to be killed if only it would stop. And it would go on sometimes till I wished I were dead. But in the end Jim was sure to start abusing me again, and then sooner or later he would use some words like sulks (or spite or silly), which I could not bear, and I would find my voice and say that it was a lie. Then we would argue for a time and accuse each other; and Jim, wanting to make peace, would withdraw all his charges and I would be moved to remorse for defeating him, and the end of such a quarrel was always that we swore eternal devotion to each other, agreed to be married as soon as possible, and often, in fact, fell asleep in each other's arms.

Fortunately my nurse generally overslept herself in the morning, and Jim, who all his life was a very restless light sleeper, used to wake up at the least sound and stroll (he did not condescend to hurry himself in escaping from a nurse) back to his own room, next door.

3   This habit of Jim's of coming to my room or taking me to his did not stop till just before I was married. In fact, it became an open recognized practice, and as young people rather than children we would stroll in and out in our dressing gowns, at any hour of night or morning, whenever we fancied a little conversation. You may wonder that we were allowed such liberty, and I have sometimes wondered why Aunt Latter always put Jim to sleep in the next room to mine. I have asked myself if she were simply indulging

Jim with me, not perhaps deliberately, but from that passion for Jim which gradually took hold of her and made her rather blind to other people's dues.

But, in any case, households were just as different then as they are now. Some cousins of ours, the Legh Boles, two brothers and two sisters, were quite as free, and they were rather a strict Low Church household. But they were encouraged to love each other, and so they did, especially the elder pair, who, when the boy was sixteen and his sister fifteen, were rather tragically in love. But, of course, being brother and sister, they got over it. They had to.

At Palm Cottage we were not evangelical, or even very religious. Aunt Latter, indeed, took me regularly to church, sent me to Sunday school, and had me confirmed; but I had heard her say at different times to some of her cronies that if God did exist he ought to be shot for inventing people, and especially children and fools, and that religion was kept going by the bishops to give them something to do. And in her gloomier moments she would declare that the Church really couldn't go on much longer talking such ridiculous nonsense about everything and making such muddles in people's heads. For Aunt Latter, not only the Church but the State and the Empire were at their last gasp – and at that time, of course, a good many people agreed with her.

Everybody remembered the Fenians and the Anarchists who had just been throwing bombs among perfectly innocent harmless people sitting in restaurants, and recognized a kind of violence which could make civilization impossible.

Aunt Latter expected the revolution almost every time there was a big strike and she was sure that nothing could stop it. Not that this prevented her (as a woman of character) from fighting against it. She sat on numberless committees and was always pulling strings to get certain people, whom she called the right people, elected to them, so that they might vote for the right side – that is, Aunt Latter's, the sensible side.

Aunt Latter has been blamed in the family for neglecting me, but this is unfair. I had a good education and books and peace; and also I had plenty of freedom, which I certainly knew how to enjoy.

All my youth, indeed, especially when I was alone, seems to me to have been marvellously happy, and Palm Cottage was exactly suited to make me so, for, apart from the books and the grown-up conversation, the house seemed made for all my moods. It was a small white house, perched on a little plateau of its own, halfway down the road from Slapton moor to the north shore of the Longwater, where there was a little beach and a ferry.

One could climb up, therefore, out of some romantic tale and be almost at once on the moor in a real Lorna Doone country; or, in a different and social mood, go down and be on the beach, which was very civilized and select, with some white villas on the shore, and some fine boathouses, and many yachts anchored.

But the cottage itself, on its triangle of ground against the cliff, with its little wood, its half-tropical garden, its mass of flowers, belonged neither to the fashionable sporting beach just below nor to the bare romantic moor just above; it was like something from a thousand miles away, from the south of France or Italy in spring. I always think of it (or rather feel it) as sparkling in all its walls and windows, in windy sunshine, or in mists of light rain, which made even the grass sparkle and which were so full of sun that they seemed like a liquid light poured out of the sky and blowing about as it fell.

People will tell you that Palm Cottage was relaxing, that no one could be awake there. What nonsense! Who was more awake than Aunt Latter? We were not sleepy at Palm Cottage; but I do think that it made me grow (like the flowers) rather luxurious in my sense of pleasure. It is not true, I think, that everyone has the same capacity for being happy – I mean apart from what happens to them. I do think I had a special power of enjoying just what Palm Cottage could give.

4 I was just seventeen when I first met Chester Nimmo. He was then a clerk in Bing's estate office, and I used to see him when he came to do my aunt's accounts and discuss local affairs, especially church affairs. He did not belong to our church (he was chapel), but he sat already on several committees and could bring information to Aunt about any shift in the balance of power – for instance in the Tarbiton town council, where Aunt Latter was always working to get somebody appointed to something, and Nimmo would bring her reports about who was likely to vote for her man, and whose husband had been trying to make her change sides.

I found such conversations boring, and even exasperating (for I had always something better to do or at least to read). And I would find myself gazing at Aunt's round affronted face and shining forehead (she always had a shining forehead; I used to think as a child that it was due to the activity of the thoughts that went on behind it) or Nimmo's strange neckties in indignant trance. Nimmo at that time was Aunt Latter's chief pet. She always had pets among local young men, generally poor ones. One, who was musical, she had sent to London for lessons. Afterward, I am afraid, he always abused Aunt Latter as being an unmusical person who had ruined his prospects by sending him to the wrong teacher. Most of Aunt Latter's protégés managed to fall out with her sooner or later, and she would say that she didn't expect gratitude.

But Nimmo at this time was still a pet and was always grateful. He certainly owed much to Aunt Latter. He was the son of very poor people and he had educated himself mostly from books. Aunt Latter had got him his first job at Bing's. She had even provided him with suitable clothes.

He was a radical, rather an extreme one; but Aunt Latter, though she abused the radicals (the Latters were all Liberals), often supported them when she was annoyed with the Liberals.

Nimmo was then a very good-looking young man, who appeared about twenty-six or seven (he was really, as I found out afterward, nearly thirty-four), with a pink and white complexion and thick curly brown hair. His eyes were a true brown, as brown as peat water, and he had a very good mouth and chin. His figure, too, though small, was very well made, and he had beautiful hands. People used to laugh at him at the yacht club and call him "Pretty boy" and "The maiden's prayer", and it was the thing to say that his good looks were vulgar. It was an idea at that time that a high colour was bad form unless perhaps it had been caused in Government service, like an admiral's.

I had in the ordinary course of things often been left to entertain Nimmo, when I would make the usual conversation, asking him if he had done any preaching lately (he was a lay preacher) or if he liked gardening, or if he had read any interesting book. But on the whole I avoided these occasions, because I had been startled by the animation of his response; and when I began to find him gazing at me with what I called a languishing expression, I was in an agony to hold my giggles. His admiration, that is, had its usual effect on a young girl who was quite heartless and silly in that relation, I mean in that special relation with that young man. For, of course, I thought of Nimmo as absurd, because I was used to think so, and because he was nervous of me, and because in that congested air of politics I felt I could not bear to be admired even from a distance.

But it was on just such an afternoon, after tea, in the passage outside, that he proposed, and I was still so oppressed that I simply pretended not to have heard him properly and said, "Excuse me, Mr Nimmo," and rushed upstairs. I was not even astonished till he had gone away. The second time I was shocked and said, "Don't be so ridiculous, Mr Nimmo. You know you don't mean it." I was frightened of something new and something that seemed to make a demand of me, and, like a child, I wanted to put a stop to it by a word. I wanted to crush Nimmo quickly and for ever.

But he was not crushed. Again, to my surprise (since I knew how nervous he was) and great dismay, he burst into impassioned and fluent speech. He said that he knew his unworthiness, but love was his excuse and he had always worshipped the "very ground I trod on", that I was the "queen of his soul", and so on. I had never dreamed that young men could use such words except in rather bad novels which Aunt Latter despised so much, and they filled me with scorn. But also, of course, I saw that Nimmo meant every word of them. His voice trembled; there were tears in his eyes; and when he rushed away from me at last as if his ridiculous coat-tails were on fire I found myself also rather shaky and tearful.

This, of course, was the effect of the words. Even bad hymns make me tearful; and Nimmo, with his bad poetry (just as I had feared), upset me so much that I was furious with him and avoided him for several weeks. But it is too troublesome in a country place to avoid people, and after that I met him quite cheerfully, and when he went on proposing I grew quite friendly and told him quite reasonably and politely that I was sorry but I could only be his friend.

5 Aunt Latter, of course, knew all about this affair. She knew most people's affairs. But though she laughed at Nimmo and rather disliked him (she did not need to like her pets, and, of course, if she had not had to forgive them a good deal she would not have felt how much her help was necessary to them), she would say to me, "Don't be too unkind to him, Nina; he is much too useful. And, besides, he really has the gift of the gab. I shouldn't wonder if he gets on the county council some day. He has character, too; he sticks to his radical nonsense even with me."

And when the disaster came to me (if, as I say, looking back on it, you can call it a disaster) and Jim (having for once, poor boy, lost his head with me), and we were both completely at a loss what to do next, she said to me one morning, "You're looking very green, miss. What's wrong with you?"

"I don't know exactly, Aunt," I said, trembling all over.

"And what's wrong with Jimmy? Why has he rushed off like this in the middle of his leave?" She banged down the top of the coffee pot (we were at breakfast) and said ferociously, "I shouldn't even dream what I suspect if you weren't such a dawdling idiot."

"I'm most awfully sorry, Aunt; I can't really believe it myself – perhaps it will be all right. And it's not quite all my fault."

"How dare you blame Jimmy! But, of course, you would put it on anyone but yourself."

"Oh, Aunt, I'm not blaming anyone – I'm only explaining. He thought it would be all right for once – he told me so; and he was in such a state of mind."

"You know perfectly well that Jim can't marry you. No subaltern in the 14th is allowed to marry. You don't want to force him out of the regiment."

This, of course, was just what Jim and I had been worrying about, for I was absolutely determined not to drive him out of his regiment which he was so proud of. He would never have forgiven me; or, worse (as I felt then), he might have forgiven me and then I could never have forgiven myself. So I said I would rather anything but that. "And besides – "

I was going to say that, in any case, I did not want to marry Jim, but I saw that this would only make Aunt Latter still more angry with me.

"Besides what – ?"

"I don't know, Aunt."

"In fact you aren't going to do anything, as usual – except drift."

I thought that this was not quite fair. What I really felt was that I was not going to be driven to desperation. I daresay plenty of girls in the same bad hole make the same discovery. I mean, they find that, once *in* such a fearful situation, it seems quite different and they can bear it after all. Not that it is less awful, but you simply don't have to do anything except bear it, and just by bearing it you get a special sort of power to go on; you even feel a little sorry for people who haven't been through the same awfulness and don't know what it is like.

In fact, if such girls drown themselves, I thought, it is

only because people will not let them bear their troubles in peace. But, of course, Aunt could not have left me in peace; it would have been impossible for her in her responsible position to do so.

6 Besides (a thing I was only just beginning to understand), Aunt Latter was often devoted to me. And seeing that I came to her unwanted at four years old (my parents had both died of cholera in India) as a very serious burden, which she did not deserve (she had greatly disliked my mother's marriage to a poor man in a commercial firm), this was very much to her credit. And I was not only an anxiety but a great expense. It was not until I was sixteen that I had that famous inheritance (it was only five thousand pounds after all), which has caused me to be described as an heiress, and Aunt Latter never touched a penny of it. And as I look back I see what a nuisance I was to her – dreamy and spoiled, always in the way when I was not wanted, and out of it when I was. Above all, I was not at all interested, even as I grew up, in what was so important to her – parish affairs, committees. I felt (which was shocking to her) no responsibility toward society or the Slapton-Latter dynasty to which I owed my position (and several of them had married only to keep up the family) as well as my five thousand pounds.

In fact, I loathed politics, which seemed usually to put Aunt in a bad temper – it was the enemy of all peace and comfort.

That is to say, Aunt and I were highly incompatible, and I have every reason to be grateful to her that she gave up one of her sunniest rooms for my nursery (a boon no child would notice) and that she taught me with a good many slaps (which, for all reward, made me hate her) my manners.

JOYCE CARY

Aunt understood me very well (from her own "practical" point of view) when she accused me of drifting. "And what do you mean to do *next*?" she demanded. Quite appreciating the force of this *next*, I answered that I meant to keep it quiet.

"My dear fool!" she said. "As if you could even keep it flat! There's only one way out – you'll have to marry Nimmo."

"Oh, Aunt, how could I marry Nimmo, or anybody?"

"Of course you can marry Nimmo. He'd thank his stars to get you in a wheelbarrow – and quite right, too. It would be the making of him – and well he knows it. Your five thousand pounds and connections would give him just the start he needs."

"I'd rather drown myself."

"Of course you would; you're a thoroughly spoiled selfish girl. Go on, then, and make the biggest scandal you can. Wriggle out of everything. I should like to shake you."

And now Aunt was in such a rage that I saw it was useless to argue with her. So I went to my room and lay down and actually fell asleep. For I was relieved that Aunt knew the position; and as for myself, I was still in that peculiar state which I can only describe as being "inside" and knowing that it was not nearly so terrible, at least to me, as people "outside" imagined. I thought cheerfully that Aunt would arrange something as soon as she got over the shock.

But only an hour later Aunt waked me up to tell me to wake up and get up at once and tidy my hair and wake up and come downstairs because there was a visitor; and before I was half awake she hustled me downstairs, where Nimmo, lying in ambush in the back part of the drawing room, sprang up and seized my hand before Aunt was even out of the room.

20

7 I had not even thought of accepting Nimmo. And I had no need to say anything, because he kept holding my hand; and when I tried to speak he said quickly, "I know, dear, dear Miss Woodville; I know how you feel. Only let me prove to you how a true man can love." And then he kissed my hands and said, "You don't need to speak – let silence give consent. Oh, my dearest, my beautiful queen – let me take care of you and give you the happiness you deserve."

Of course, he did not want me to speak in case I said no. He was a very clever and sensitive little man, as I soon found out, and he knew very well what was going on inside other people.

And before I could say no (or decide what to say) Aunt popped in again, rather breathless, and said that she was glad that we had made up our minds and that she was sure that we should be very happy.

Then Nimmo wrung my hand (he was too clever to kiss me) and darted away, and I asked (not bothering to say that I wouldn't marry him) if he knew about my condition.

"Of course he knows."

This did interest me (since Nimmo was supposed to be so respectable), and I asked what he had said. But Aunt grew furious again and said only, "He's not a fool, and you can thank God for it; and keep quiet and let him do the same."

I tried to imagine the conversation and thought once more in my strange "philosophic" mood (and perhaps my "condition" had something to do with it) how interesting and different the world was on the "inside". And when exactly (or how) I accepted Nimmo (but I remember a violent letter from Jim accusing me of "daring" him had a definite effect) I don't know. It simply came to be understood in the next few days.

And whatever I thought then of Aunt with her rages and schemes, looking back now, I can't help admiring her strength of mind. It is quite false to say that she sacrificed me – she thought of my "good" as well as Nimmo's. And if her idea was to rescue me from a careless existence, to save me from myself, this was a perfectly respectable idea at that time, and not at all a stupid one, for heaven knows what would have happened to me with my power of dawdling (or obstinacy – there was something in Jim's charge that I had "dared" him; we were quarrelling at the time and I had certainly refused to defend myself) if I had been allowed to "drift". I think I was probably capable of anything because I had begun to suspect that I could reconcile myself to anything.

And this was a very dangerous discovery, not so much for me (since I daresay I should have been happy in the gutter) as for my relations and the "political" world generally. It is just those people, I suppose, who make that discovery young who become "problems" and even criminals.

How bold, then, Aunt was in seeing what "could be done" with both Nimmo (given my five thousand pounds) and myself. It was really a triumph for her and her "political" sense, when a fortnight later (I was married by special licence) I found myself in a train with Nimmo going away for our honeymoon.

And already I was able to reflect that, though I did not like the man, I was not suffering any intolerable burden in being married to him. It was quite easy to sit in a luxurious train and enjoy the view, and delightful to be going to Venice, which I had never seen. As for "getting on" with my husband at this stage, I had only to be polite (and I felt, naturally, immensely polite to such a stranger), while he at once was enormously considerate. And politeness itself

22

makes a situation which is very like affection and much more manageable.

In fact, as I realize now, Aunt's stern training in manners was my salvation. For instance, I had read a great deal in French novels about the private agonies of girls married off without love, and I was a little apprehensive, but I certainly felt nothing even very uncomfortable. In fact, I can't remember anything except my anxiety not to upset the little man in any way (he was obviously even more nervous than I was) and relief that he took all the responsibility and managed so well.

8 Indeed, one of Chester's clevernesses was to take responsibility for everything. He even did my packing and unpacking for me, and (having the lightest and neatest fingers as well as being a man of tremendous energy) would act as my maid, and help me to dress and undress (but only to a point; he was very respectful of my modesty), and even sew on my buttons and brush and comb my hair and plait it for the night. I had never been so coddled. He treated me like a princess, or rather as a princess is reported to be treated. He even saw (and this was wisest of all) that I liked to be alone sometimes, and (though I declared I adored being with him all day, he was so good with guide books) arranged for me to have the mornings in bed, so that I could read my novel, or simply doze and enjoy the feeling of being by myself.

In all this he was like another woman in his tact; I mean, in feeling what I really wanted and arranging that I should have it, without spoiling it, perhaps for ever, by bringing it out into the open and pulling it all out of shape in a contest of manners which would have been, of course, a special danger to us, when we were both so anxious to be "nice".

It is true that in our religious ideas (if you can call mine religious) we did not agree. I had been a little startled on our first night together to hear him murmur (but we were both so nervous at the time that I was not sure if I had heard him properly or if he knew what he was saying) something like a prayer for God's blessing on our union, which seemed to me so comic at such a moment that I had almost laughed. But luckily I was so shy of him it was only afterwards I realized that he had really meant to pray and that what he had meant by our "union" was just what I had thought so unsuitable for prayer. I was, I think, even a little shocked.

And there was a time in the next few days when I did say to myself that religion was going to be the big trouble (for, of course, we were both expecting unexpected trouble – that was why we were both so polite), for Chester prayed aloud night and morning (and though I had always said prayers at night I said them to myself) and used what I called fanatical language. He would pray, for instance, that we should be saved from forgetting our call to holiness in greed and low ambitions and the lustful appetites of the flesh, words which (like that first unexpected prayer for our "union") gave me a very uneasy feeling, so that sometimes I felt angry with him and sometimes I wanted to laugh, which was equally unpleasant because the laughter was, like the disgust, something which I couldn't help, like a schoolgirl's giggling. And I could not let him hear me laugh at such a time. In fact, I had already found that laughing at anything was dangerous because we laughed at such different things.

He roared with laughter one day (and when he laughed, he laughed till he cried) when a rather important gentleman, dressed to the nines, in the piazza, had his new top hat blown into the lagoon (I was sorry for the poor man because he looked so foolish, and, after all, he had dressed up for some important occasion, and it is right to dress up for them); and when I looked at Chester without laughing, and he saw that I was not at all in sympathy with him, he became red and said, "You must admit the gentleman was a little too pleased with himself," with a faint emphasis on the gentleman, as if to say that I had certain prejudices which reflected on his own origin. And for some time there was a feeling as if we had quarrelled, which was very unpleasant, for it made me feel constrained.

Then he detested Italy (which I adored – it was so warm and full of colour), and was shocked by the poverty of the people, which to me at that time seemed as "natural" as the richness of millionaires; that is, simply the customary state of things and certainly not a good reason for spoiling a honeymoon. Above all, he loathed the churches, which seemed to me so beautiful, saying that they were even worse than he had expected.

He meant that they were full of saints and candles. For he had a horror of the Roman religion and said that wherever it had power you found ignorance and oppression and dirt and poverty. I said that perhaps that was because miserable ignorant people needed a nice rich artistic kind of religion, but this also shocked him and he said with his religious voice, "Artistic religion isn't religion at all – how could it be? There is only one true religion – between a man's own soul and his God."

This remark, made in a peculiar tone (afterward I knew it was used by lay preachers) and the man's very solemn expression, again gave me one of those mysterious fits of wanting to laugh; and though I took care not even to smile, he said at once, "I beg your pardon, but I can't help my opinions." I said hastily that I was sure he was right. But he was very much disturbed, and for a long time, though we made conversation, we were both offended.

But suddenly, after a rather difficult lunch (he had eaten nothing – he had a very nervous digestion), he turned into a jeweller's shop and insisted on buying me a garnet necklace; and when I thanked him with all the warmth necessary to hide my feeling that, after all, the marriage would be impossible (I should never be able to stand his aggressive religion), he said, "I know you have been brought up to have different religious ideas, and I hope you will be true to them and never pretend to agree with me unless you really feel agreement. Everyone must be true to what he believes – at least that is the central principle of religion as I see it."

And when I said that of course I agreed with all his ideas except that I thought that Roman Catholics were also partly Christians, he said that of course I was right, that in the house of God there were many mansions.

And afterwards I found that I did not mind the prayers, even when they were long and emotional, because I felt that Chester was not going to make any attempt to alter my ideas or to convert me and change me into a different person, a thing dreaded even by wicked and unhappy people.

9   All this time I was so pleased with myself for making a "success" of my "difficult marriage" (though really it was Chester's cleverness and consideration which made us both happy) I was growing more furious with Jim. For he had written me nothing but abuse, so that I had had to answer that I would not read his letters and that I did not want to see him again. And what was unexpected (but quite reasonable if you think of it) was that my indignation grew

with Jim's baby, for I found, of course, as I might have foreseen if I hadn't been a very young and silly girl, that having a baby is an experience that goes on for a very long time and occupies one's mind even when one is not thinking about it. It is, as it were, inside one's mind, as well as one's body, and keeps pushing at both, and altering their shape, especially after it begins making unexpected jumps and kicks at them. These jumps were all like prods, saying, "This is perhaps one of the most important things in your life, and Jim has spoiled it for you as well as himself by his selfishness and cruelty."

And here again Chester showed his cleverness, for he was most sympathetic to me, most careful and attentive. And he arranged quite "naturally" that when the baby was born, in June, we should be abroad again, in France, and should go on being abroad for another ten weeks, so that there was no local announcement till then and the date was not generally known. Of course, it was announced that the birth was premature and had obliged us to stay abroad, but the whole event passed off so quietly at a distance that only the worst gossips were curious. What alarmed me at first was that the baby itself, a boy, was just a miniature Jim, even to the arrogant look of the eyes and the "you be dashed" expression on the little tight mouth. So I was surprised and relieved that no one said more about it than that the child took after my side of the family.

One day, indeed, when I was nursing Tom, and Chester was watching me (as he loved to do), I remarked rather thoughtlessly, "He's going to have Jim's nose, too"; whereupon Chester jumped and turned quite green and said, "I don't see this Latter likeness. Most people say he is the image of me except for the eyes; they, I agree, are absolutely yours." And then he went out.

This startled me very much. I had heard a good deal all my life (in Aunt's political conversation) about the "trickiness" of people like Chester, and for a moment I felt very uneasy – it was very much as if, in the words of Miss Braddon, a "gulf opened beneath me". It seemed all at once as if Chester's considerateness were the mask of something very ugly and dangerous.

But perhaps just because I was so startled I hastened to tell myself that I had been tactless. Indeed I took so much pleasure in the boy (even though he did remind me of Jim) that I was not going to spoil it by worrying about anything at all.

And altogether apart from the general interest of a first baby, and the charm of its smallness (which is charming in all creatures, and even toys) and the pleasure of nursing it (which was quite unexpectedly pleasant – at least to start with), I did feel a very strong affection for Tom. I quite delighted in him. Why this should surprise me I did not wonder, though I suppose I had heard of women, especially young women, who don't like their babies, and some who even hate them and want to murder them.

10 Even before we came home, Chester had startled the neighbourhood by "going on the warpath". He wrote a letter in the *Courier* which was the radical paper, calling the town council a super-mutual admiration society, he put himself down for election, and he bargained for a "good" house, the Orchard, just up the hill from Palm Cottage.

Of course, he proposed to buy the house with my money, but I quite approved of this. My view was from the beginning that he had married me for (or at least, because of) the money and ought to have it, especially as he had been so tactful about the baby.

Besides, he gave me something I had always longed for – my own sitting room, where I could gather my books together, have a really comfortable chair, smoke an occasional cigarette and, best of all, wear my spectacles. At that time no lady under fifty ever wore spectacles in front of people, and neither Aunt nor Jim, nor even Chester, for their different reasons, could bear me in spectacles.

Aunt would say, "Take off those nasty things – they make you look like an owl" (in her practical and positive way, she had worked it out that my face was too small and my forehead too large for spectacles); Jim would take them off with his long neat finger and thumb as if rescuing me from an unpleasant insect; and Chester would gaze at me with a look of alarm, and fidget, and say at last, "Do you know how those things mark your nose? I am sure they don't fit you properly."

So in my new sitting room I enjoyed many hours of peaceful bliss, for which I did truly thank Chester. I had learned already how much, in such a complicated and "political" (I was soon to understand what Balzac or perhaps it was what Vauvenargues meant by calling matrimony a political education) relationship as marriage, one should be grateful for simple thoughtfulness.

In the same way he arranged, after Tom was born, that I should sleep alone for the night nursing. My life, indeed, at this time was separate, a life within a life, or rather beside it. Of course, this happens to most wives when they have their babies. They begin a separate life on one side, and are busy all day with things which are too many and small for their husbands to know about; their timetable becomes quite different, and it is quite right (I should think) that it should be so. For then each has his own life, and is a real person who can enjoy the other.

But I can't say that I did enjoy my husband at this time, because I was quite as much shocked as other people by his letter to the *Courier*, and still more by his plan to send out a circular, through all Tarbiton, still more violent and abusive.

He spent several days composing this circular and then brought it to me for criticism. He had great faith in my grammar because I was supposed to be good at "English".

As I have realized since, there was nothing very unusual about this circular. It was only a little better written than most, and something new in a place like Tarbiton.

But I had never seen such a thing. I thought, "It's all lies from beginning to end. Fancy saying that the policy of the council is to 'keep the poor poor'."

And, in fact, from a non-political point of view it *was* all lies – and also a savage attack on several of my friends, like Major Freer who was mayor that year.

I was frightened at the idea of the storm it was going to make (I thought it would ruin Chester before he began), and I could not understand how my five thousand pounds had changed the nice quiet respectable and very proper little clerk at Bing's into this aggressive firebrand.

But when I began to question the circular, he took it away from me, turned very red and tore it up. "I shouldn't have shown it to you," he said quite coolly (but I saw his hands trembling); "but I think those slums are a public disgrace."

I began to explain that I was only objecting to the statements in the circular, because everyone would know they were lies and they would be denounced and give Chester a bad name. But instead of answering, he apologized for bringing me into it, because naturally my "sympathies were all the other way".

At first I thought that this was the "wounded martyr"

game I suppose everyone plays, more or less politely, when they want to show resentment and keep their dignity. But when I said indignantly that he had no right to say such things, he suddenly grew very excited and said that he was not blaming me, but "of course" I was on the other side – my whole life and education had been different. I had never been poor.

"You don't know what class is," he said (and I saw him shaking with excitement). "You don't know how different you are. Why, you would have more in common with a Negro – I mean a Negro gentleman – than with Bill Code" (Bill was our gardener for one day a week). "You think me a cad" (and he made a face as if he were going to burst into tears). "No, no, that's not fair – not true" (he put out his hand and just touched me on the breast, as if to say, "Forgive me"). "You *feel* me a cad."

Of course, I wanted to deny all this as absolute nonsense. I specially hated (because now I felt how true it was) to be put in another "class".

But before I could speak he rushed out of the room (still grasping the fragments of the circular which had caused all the trouble), and I saw that he had really been on the verge of tears.

But when I came to dinner, I found him in his most charming easy mood (though he was watching me all the time). He complimented me and made jokes. It was I who was embarrassed.

I was, however, determined to have an explanation with him. It seemed to me impossible that we could live together as husband and wife while he thought that I despised him. And thinking that it was now safe (that he would not get excited), I ventured to say that he was quite wrong about my ideas – I did not feel this difference of class.

31

Whereupon he answered very seriously, "Perhaps not – but it's there or I shouldn't have wanted you. None of your back-lane girls for me. I always swore I'd get a lady and I have."

And when he saw that I was embarrassed again by this queer remark, he said (and he really seemed to be laughing at me), "That's another thing I couldn't say if I were a gentleman – but I have a fancy for the plain vulgar truth."

The next week the circular went out exactly as it had been written, with all the lies in big letters; and it made a bigger storm even than I had feared.

But it put Chester on the council and caused a local committee to propose him as a candidate for one of the new county councils.

11 "Class" at this time was an obsession with Chester. On the smallest excuse, or none at all, he would grow furious and talk of the "silent conspiracy to keep people like me in our places". And he would say that in his case it had nearly succeeded – he had had to wait till his middle thirties to get his chance.

I learned to dread the subject, and at last we nearly had a quarrel. That is, I thought we were quarrelling. I had not discovered how hard it was to quarrel with Chester. When I accused him of nagging me about class, he apologized at once – but began again the very same day.

I should have thought that he hated me, if I had not had good evidence at the same time that he was very much in love. He would lie in my arms while telling me how he had wanted to "strangle that old hag at the Court" when she had come to his mother's cottage with the "Christmas dole". And he knew, of course, that the "old hag" was my cousin Mary Slapton – "Aunt Mary".

And I thought he did this on purpose – he liked the tension. It excited him. And looking back I see how naive it was of me to expect an exceptional man not to be exceptional.

The effect then was to make me feel that I had to do with a very odd man (even allowing for his class) who was slightly mad and also pitiable like an invalid.

I felt, too, as everyone seems to feel when accused of being in a superior class, very uncomfortable and even guilty, and so I was very eager to help him. I was delighted when he asked me to "vet" his speeches for him and when he rehearsed them to me.

He would ask me if I thought they would "go over", especially his similes. He said that I was better at judging a speech than Aunt Latter, because she was too instructive in her ideas. "A speech," he said, "should never instruct; it should rouse people up."

12 Nothing is more exciting than to be mixed up with a beginning of a public career (I mean a career like a singer's or a politician's, where people have to be impressed, and no one ever knows quite how an audience will behave or what will please them); and now, when Chester did stand for the county council, and spoke to quite big meetings (county councils were still quite new, and the elections were almost like parliamentary elections), I used to find myself trembling in my chair as I listened.

Of course, it was just this tension between us, my feeling that Chester felt himself among enemies (including myself), that made me so anxious. What despair when he tried a joke (which we had carefully thought over beforehand) and no one laughed! I would feel myself so hot and red that I had to bend down my head in case someone noticed it. And what agony at the end waiting to see if anyone would clap! I think it was because of this very agony that when people did clap and cheer (and it was already becoming obvious that Chester was a very good speaker) I was ready to cry, and also, what is really strange, to throw myself into his arms and tell him how wonderful he had been.

Indeed, on the day when he was elected, and there was a special meeting in Tarbiton to congratulate him and both of us were rather drunk with all the cheers and speeches and more cheers, I did really believe that I was growing into a kind of love with him. And perhaps I did love him that evening out of gratitude for rescuing me from the agony of fearing for him.

Certainly I was delighted by the notion that now he was successful he would stop being nervous and "difficult".

And Aunt Latter, who did not even like Chester, was wildly excited by his success. After all, she had done more than anyone else to start him on his career, as Chester always acknowledged. He was not only her great success, he was her only one. And already she was dreaming (for we all thought it a dream, even Chester himself) of getting him into Parliament. She was very eager to persuade Cousin Slapton, and also another cousin, Wilfred Connybeare, to propose him to the Liberal leaders as a candidate. She even hoped, I think, to get him a directorship through their influence with the Battwell Land Company, where they were both directors.

I mention this here because of the legend that Chester even at this time had "sold himself" to the capitalists, and especially Connybeare. But the truth is, on the one hand, that Wilfred was then very much against Chester, and, on the other, that Chester absolutely refused to have any dealings with Connybeare on the ground that he made money out of drink (he was a brewer); and neither could he bring himself to pay his respects to Slapton, because he was a landlord and owned half Tarbiton. He refused all invitations to Slapton Court and I did not care to ask Slapton to the Orchard just then, because Tom was teething and used to cry a good deal.

But this attitude toward my family no longer alarmed me; I had found it was quite easy not to worry about it. I had, in fact (how I did not quite know), come to accept the "impossible" situation that Chester looked upon me, even in his most affectionate moments, as a class enemy.

As I say, just then I sometimes thought that I was growing to love the man, and this pleased me very much because, though I had been so relieved to find that marriage was possible with only politeness, I was now (which was unexpected, but perhaps Chester by stirring up all my nerves had made me less contentable) much greedier for happiness. I thought how nice marriage must be for people who were "really" in love.

And it was at this time that Jim chose to come on leave from his regiment to Palm Cottage.

I met him there by accident (but he was lying in wait for me) and detested him at once. He had grown, I thought, into the worst type of smart soldier, fearfully pleased with himself and not at all ashamed of it.

He had grown fat (he was already quite tall; he had shot up to nearly six feet in a long illness during his teens), his eyes seemed minute, and he had a big yellow moustache that spoiled his rather sensitive mouth.

He attacked me at once for marrying that "tout" and told me that he could prove that Chester had looked up my Uncle Woodville's will at the lawyer's to make sure that I really had an inheritance, due at twenty-one or marriage.

He had only "taken me on" because my "cash would give him a start in his filthy job of stirring up trouble". He would tell Chester as much.

I defied him to do so and went away in a rage. But, of course, it was mad to dare Jim to anything. The next afternoon he came up to the Orchard, right into my room where I was dozing over a book, took off my spectacles, and said, "Where's that son of mine?"

I saw that he was in a furious mood and that he wanted to make me equally furious, so I pretended (though I could not see the print) to go on reading and said nothing.

He accused me then of jilting him for that "dirty little snake".

I told him that he was the jilt – he had never wanted to marry me. He had preferred the idea of going to India and playing polo.

But, of course, Jim (after the disaster) had spoken of marrying me (without making any attempt to do so); and now, having succeeded in putting each other in a rage, we were both ready to exaggerate and make the worst of things. Jim began to shout, and possibly he did believe just then that he had been ill-treated.

Suddenly we heard a step outside and I said, "Be careful; that's Chester. He must have heard you were here."

Chester knocked at the door (as he usually did at my door), and I called, "Come in." But at that moment Jim deliberately caught hold of me and kissed me – he wanted to make a scene.

I tried to pull away, and Chester said quite calmly, "I beg your pardon – I didn't know Lieutenant Latter was here."

Chester always called Jim Lieutenant Latter at this time and one could not tell him it was wrong. It was too small a thing and it was never certain that he did not do such things on purpose to show his contempt and hatred for "shibboleths" of class. That is, what seemed trifling to me might be, after all, something important to him and even something which he was quite ready to be difficult about.

Jim turned on him and said, "Excuse me, but I always thought I was going to marry Miss Woodville."

"I certainly did not understand that," Chester said. "I thought that you had gone away on purpose not to do so."

"You didn't think anything of the kind," Jim said. "You took your chance to get hold of her, but what you have really done is to buy her with her own money."

Chester turned pale and pink in blotches, which was his way in any distress, and said that he did not propose to argue about such a matter, and that Jim might at least consider my feelings.

Jim said then that his feelings had to come in, too, considering what I had been to him, and that Tom was his son.

Chester answered that Jim had better be careful of the law – he was uttering a criminal slander. And Jim answered that he did not know anything about the law; it was no slander, but a fact, which he, Chester, had known all the time when he was collecting that five thousand pounds.

"And you knew you could get round Nina with your religious soft soap."

Chester, who behaved with great dignity throughout, said to me then, "You needn't be afraid. I don't believe a word of this wild nonsense."

"Damn it all," Jim said, "we all know the facts. There is no need for play-acting. It's not a public meeting. Nobody is going to be impressed."

Chester then took me by the arm and led me out into the bedroom, saying, "Perhaps you had better go, dear. I'll deal with this."

And he did deal with it. He left Jim alone in my room and sent in a note to say that if he had any further communication to make it would have to be in writing; and meanwhile, if he did not leave the house at once, a policeman would be called.

13 Jim then went away without any more trouble (as he told me afterwards, there was nothing else to do except break the windows, and he thought that beneath his dignity as a subaltern in the 14th) and Chester at once came in to tell me so.

"I have taken steps to make sure that you won't have any more trouble" (in fact he had complained to Aunt, who turned Jim out on the spot; she had a certain amount of power over Jim then because he depended on her for his whole allowance), "and I hope you aren't too much upset by the scoundrel's lies."

I said that *he* must not be upset – Jim had always had a violent temper.

Chester then looked at me with a sympathetic expression and said in an indignant tone, "I'm sure he hadn't the least excuse for such a suggestion – I mean that he had taken liberties with you."

I could only answer that, of course, he had taken "liberties" – as Chester knew.

"How could I know – no one told me. I had no reason in the world to suppose anything of the sort."

I was absolutely astonished by this declaration. I knew it to be a lie, and if I had not I might have suspected so from the very cool way in which Chester made it.

I answered at once that, of course, he knew – he had arranged for Tom to be born abroad and for all the confusion about the announcements.

Chester had now changed his sympathetic expression for a peculiar look that I had not seen before – not so much "hard" as fierce. It seemed to say, "No nonsense, please – I won't stand it." There was a pause while he seemed actually to be letting me feel this threat.

Then he said in the same cool voice, "We both know very well that Tom was premature – the doctor himself can testify to that. And it was on the doctor's orders, too, that I took you abroad for your health." As soon as he said this he went out of the room.

I was left very angry and also rather frightened. I was quite astounded that the mild and loving Chester could dare to threaten me.

As soon as I could leave the house unnoticed, I went straight to Aunt and told her what had happened. I pointed out that it was impossible for me to go on with Chester unless he admitted the facts.

"Impossible?" she said. "What's impossible?" and she shook her enormous scissors at me (she was cutting up newspapers for her scrapbooks, as she did every evening) and said, "What does the idiot mean?"

"I mean that I can't live with a man who deliberately accuses me of the meanest kind of trick when he knows very well I didn't deceive him at all."

I had seen at once that Aunt was in a very bad mood. The quarrel with Jim had been very violent, and all quarrels with Jim made her wretched. She was not merely cross but rather shaky in her hands and very sarcastic.

"Why not?" she said, snipping at the paper very quickly and carefully as if she were dissecting my argument. "Who told you this stuff? Why should he admit anything?"

This really frightened me. "But, Aunt, you don't mean he didn't know about Tom when I married him?"

At this Aunt grew still redder and angrier and said that, of course, Chester knew – she had told me as much. But she hoped I didn't suppose they had discussed the matter in "so many words". Did I really expect any decent man to take Jim's leavings if it was admitted they were leavings? "It would have been asking too much of Chester with all his pushingness. After all, the man is a cut above the Hottentots."

In fact, what exactly was understood between Aunt and Nimmo in this negotiation has never come out and never can come out, for it was never put into words, which, of course, was exactly what these two clever people wanted. They simply agreed together without anything that could be "pinned down" to make trouble afterwards.

But to me, at that moment, this understanding seemed worse than none at all. I found myself all at once put in the place of a criminal who may be accused any day – in everlasting uncertainty and insecurity. I should not be able even to defend myself. And I said at once that I couldn't go on like that; it was an impossible position, absolutely impossible.

"And why can't Chester admit the thing if he knows it's true? It's a perfectly stupid idea unless he simply wants to humiliate me, and that's not very clever either."

"I should think you were a good judge of stupidity, but Chester may have a better idea of his own business."

"It's my business, too."

"I tell you what, miss. I should think him the fool if he admitted anything whatever. Suppose something came out – there's been gossip enough, goodness knows. He's got to be in a position to deny everything."

"But what about my position? How can I go on living with him?"

"Your position? Here, stick that in the Local Government book under Licensing, and don't use too much paste. That Parks section you did last year is mouldy already. It's a double bed; isn't that a good enough position?"

"Oh, Aunt, I meant without mutual confidence."

"Mutual confidence! So that's the position – like Stanley and Livingstone on the missionary posters. And how long do you propose to stick in that position before the kettle boils or Tommy wants his supper? For goodness sake, child, don't drive me mad. I seem to remember that you put yourself in a position – and you can thank your lucky stars and Chester and me for getting you out." And then she did lose her temper and say many rude things, such as that Chester had pampered me up like the Queen of Sheba till I did not know myself from the Queen of Sheba.

Aunt Latter was always enraged against people (husbands or wives) who failed to "get on", and also she took a very low view of marriage, probably because her own love affair had gone wrong.

I stayed to supper with her, but she did not console me at all. And I came away in rather a desperate frame of mind, determined to have a "final explanation".

And as soon as Chester came to the bedroom (he was very late – I daresay on purpose, and I was already in bed) I said that now we were alone together I hoped he would admit the truth. "Don't you see," I said, "that you are putting me in an impossible position by making me responsible for such a mean act? And how can I ever trust you if you do such things?"

And when he simply made no answer at all, I was so enraged by what I thought his impudence that I threw back the clothes and was trying to jump out of bed on the other side to run away from him, when he caught me by the arm and said in an anxious voice (but I thought it also sounded cunning), "I see now, of course, how you could make such a mistake. There were misunderstandings on both sides. Perhaps neither of us has been in a condition to face the truth. And as for blaming you for what has happened, that would be stupid as well as cruel." Then he went on describing my unhappiness, deserted by Jim, and how he had known that I was ill and unhappy and had taken advantage of it. This, he said, was a very great wrong, because he had done it deliberately, knowing that I did not love him. And so on. And then he excused himself on the ground that he had loved me so much. He said that if I could not forgive him, of course he could not ask me to go on as his wife, but that if I left him it would break his heart.

14 And these speeches, in Chester's "thrilling" voice, had a very strange effect on my nerves. I write "thrill", because as soon as I heard this description (not by a woman, either, but by an enthusiastic young man) I felt how right it was. Chester's voice was one of his great gifts – it made him a power. And now when his voice shook, I felt myself shaking all through my body (as I say, I was really worn out with feelings already), so that I wanted to scream, "Stop, stop!" I would have done anything to stop this frightful quivering which seemed to shake my ideas and self-control to pieces. It seemed that I was two women, one of them quite furious still and watchful of every move by this cunning enemy, and one of them so close and sympathetic to him that she felt all his feelings like her own. And this was the most agonizing sensation I had ever known. It seemed that I was being torn apart (though I was told only the other day by a very intelligent and happily married woman that she had felt just the same on the honeymoon, and that she believed most women were more or less "split personalities"); so that when Chester went on telling me of his love I was angrier and angrier, and yet when I felt his hand tremble as well as his voice this love seemed to fly all through me, so that I was all a tension of anger and pity at the same time, and all my arguments seemed to fall apart into dry dusty fragments which were quite contemptible. I tried to stop him by saying that he must not blame himself for everything, but he began to kiss my forehead, and to my horror I realized that I (at least the second woman) was growing almost as excited and tearful as he was. And I begged him, "Don't, don't; you're too tired!"

But instead he asked me to pray with him; and though I was surprised (and all the time the top woman, the angry one, was more and more determined not to be "drawn in" by his tricks), I was quite glad to do anything for peace and jumped out of bed at once and knelt down beside him. He took my hand and prayed for a long time. But what astonished me was that he prayed against lies, and especially what he called the lie in the soul. "Help us not to deceive ourselves about the wickedness and evil, low ambitions and fleshly lusts of our own hearts."

I thought again, "Good heavens, *he* is the liar, and I haven't any ambitions or fleshly feelings either – I'm very glad I haven't."

But his voice went up and down (sometimes he was so loud that I was afraid the servants would hear); he was what they called wrestling in prayer. And as his voice broke, I realized that the man was not just performing a part – he really was in a kind of agony; his hand kept gripping at mine so that I thought he would break my fingers, and his breath came in sobs and groans.

So though I was cold and in pain, with my hand and my knees, which were practically bare (I only had my nightdress), on the carpet, I kept still and bowed my head in a reverent manner. And when my nose began to tickle, as if I were going to sneeze, I pressed my left forefinger (he was holding my right hand) against my top lip and prayed, really prayed, on my own account, from my heart, for him to finish quickly. But he was still more moved and excited. "Oh, God," he said, "who lives in our breasts, God of understanding and mercy, teach us to *live* in forgiveness; send us *Thy love*, and the power of *Thy Wisdom* which is to renew every day, every hour, in love. Send us the life of the *soul* which is to be born again every moment into a new world of life and love."

At this point, in spite of everything, I did sneeze. And I mention it (just to show how queerly things work in this difficult world) because it had quite important results. It overwhelmed me (that is, the second me) with shame. I felt as if I had dropped an umbrella during a funeral sermon, or the Jewel song. I could not even apologize at such a moment. But when, after a moment's pause, he said to me, still in the voice which he used for prayer, "Are you cold?" I answered very eagerly, "No, no – please don't stop." And he did go on. But only for a moment, to finish the prayer in the proper manner. And I could tell by the way he held my hand (taking it deeper into his) that he was thinking more of me. And the moment he had said "Amen" he took me up and lifted me back into bed, and said, "I should have put something over you. Now you have caught cold." And when I answered him that I never caught cold, he kissed me and said, "That is like you – you are too good. You are the one who really understands how to forgive." Of course, the top woman saw very plainly the danger of this argument (every woman knows that compliments lead to obligations), and I said at once that he was quite wrong about my virtues. I was not so much a forgiving person as a lazy one who liked to be comfortable and peaceful in her mind, and that was why I could not bear any "mysteries".

But Chester interrupted in a very excited way that I undervalued myself; I was a wiser and nobler person than he because I lived in forgiveness. "To look forward – that is the only way, that is the true forgiveness. The forgiveness of God is in the life of the soul, the everlasting fountain of His grace, renewed every moment. Yes, my darling, we must look forward to the new life of our spirit, to new joy in our love. We must begin again, from this hour – do you understand?"

And he was so moved and excited (and it was a true feeling even if he had given it to himself) that, of course, I said that I did understand, that the only way truly to forgive (which is, of course, quite true) was to begin again, and I said that I was grateful for all that he had done for me. It was the least I could say after the sneeze.

And the moment I *said* this, I felt all that Aunt had said about Chester's special position and his goodness to myself; I saw why with his feeling of being surrounded by enemies (including myself) he was so careful about what he admitted even to me.

It happened so suddenly that I was quite startled by my denseness before. It was, I suppose, just what Chester's chapel friends called a "conversion". And I suppose, too, there was nothing extraordinary about it; every young married woman has them, when she sees things in a new light.

Certainly I had had a whole series of conversions that year, so that I was quite a different kind of person. And so, far from life being "impossible" that night, it was all at once surprisingly happy (though still with rather a special tense kind of happiness). I showed Chester that I was repentant and he was very fond.

15 Of course, each time life became more "possible" again it was also more complicated. There were more "dangerous" subjects. I knew now and never could forget that Chester, with all his affection, was playing a kind of political game with me. He was taking up a strong position and thinking of his career.

I could not help being watchful of his tricks – I was always ready to say, "There, he's cheating again."

But now I know I was often wrong. For men of imagination (and imagination was Chester's great strength; it enabled him to enter into other people's feelings) are very easily entered by imaginary anxieties, and even wild fancies. Their strength is their "weakness".

For instance, in the Lilmouth riot, where two people were killed and over twenty badly hurt, most records accuse Chester of deliberately breaking his word and risking loss of life in order to get into the papers. And I myself was ready to believe this at first, but quite soon I did not know what to think, because the more you know of the facts the more uncertain they seem.

It was, of course, the pro-Boer agitation that gave Chester (and so many other young radicals) a real start. This was the time when Lloyd George had just begun his attacks on the war; he was defying the mobs that wanted to lynch him, and the very mention of his name was a thrill to radicals.

Nobody now can have any idea of how Lloyd George was hated at that time. Our soldiers were being defeated and massacred and everyone felt ashamed and guilty toward them as if they had been betrayed. But no one could say so; even to think it seemed like encouraging the enemy.

I, too, hated Lloyd George. I should have been glad if he had been lynched; and yet (which is the strange thing about this special hatred) I was also afraid of his getting killed, as if that, too, might make me feel guilty and put God on the enemy's side. And I resented this feeling, too, as if Lloyd George had deliberately risked his life in order to torture people with this very fear and hatred.

Of course, this was not "really" true, but I felt sure, all the same, that the fact that Lloyd George did risk his life made all these agitators discover in some secret part of their imagination *how people could be tortured and confused in their minds by this tremendous bravery and self-sacrifice.*

I don't mean that all the pro-Boers who got chased through the streets and pelted with stones and thrown into ponds during those years were copying Lloyd George, but that they were encouraged by the discovery that governments simply do not know how to deal with martyrs.

Yet I dared not even hint such a thing to Chester, for he would have thought me simply "low-minded", and perhaps he would have been right, because he took care not to know why he took such risks.

How disgusted I was with him when, in spite of warnings, he held a meeting in Chorlock. The hall was wrecked, and a young boy was very badly hurt; and Chester himself had his head cut open with a stone.

But furious as I was about the whole affair, I thanked heaven afterwards I had not told him that he had only got what he deserved, because he was really horrified by the violence. It was because of this riot at Chorlock and the injury to the boy (who had a fracture of the skull and afterwards became epileptic) that he gave his undertaking to the Chief Constable. In fact when his friend Mr Goold brought him back that night with his head bleeding he was shaking so much that he could hardly stand – I had never seen anyone in such a state of nervous excitement.

While I was washing his cut, he kept on trying to tell me what he had really said and how the riot had started, but every time he began to speak he shook so violently that he had to stop to explain he was not badly hurt and he did not know what was wrong with him. I could not persuade him to go to bed.

Mr Goold, meanwhile, was doing everything possible (as I thought) to make him worse. He was walking about the room all the time saying that he knew who had started the riot and they had been paid to do it. And when I asked who would pay village boys to throw stones, he said he was going to find out, but that the Government was behind it. "You noticed," he said to Chester, "how it started all at once – somebody at the back gave a whistle." To my surprise, Chester said that he had noticed it and that there had obviously been a plan to wreck the meeting.

I was just going to say that it was natural for people with relations at the front (one of my cousins was killed in the first month, and we had just heard that week of Jim's being wounded) to feel the same indignation at the same remark abusing the troops. But I did not, because I knew that Goold would have some rude retort, and that Chester would suspect some "class pact".

For instance, when letters began to come to me from Jim (Jim in hospital had begun to write to all his relations, rather good letters, describing the bad management of the war), and I read them to Chester (in case he wondered what was in them), he had said, "I wonder what his object is in attacking the Government." And I could not convince him that Jim was writing only what he thought, without any special purpose. Afterwards Mr Goold said to me, "I hear the officers are getting up an agitation for more troops." And when I said that I had letters only from one officer (who was, besides, critical rather of his own colonel than the Government), he only glared at me as if to say, "You're in with them, too, of course."

And he persuaded Chester that Jim's real motive as an officer was to enlarge the army and so to increase his own chances of promotion. It seemed to me, in fact, that this man Goold was always planting new suspicions in Chester's mind, which was already much too ready to find plots everywhere. I detested Goold so much that I was always very careful to be especially polite to him. I knew that he was Chester's closest friend, and I said to myself, "No one shall say that Chester's wife deprived him of his friends."

But, in spite of all my resolutions (and just because I *was* a foolish young wife), I did begin, in those agitated days after the Chorlock riot, the quarrel which made the man so dangerous an enemy.

16 Goold was then a man of nearly forty; he was one of the chief members of the chapel, a great preacher, and chairman of several important committees in Tarbiton, including the pro-Boer committee. He was a short red-faced man, very spare, with a long neck, a long nose, a receding chin (Aunt Latter called him Gooseface), and curly hair bursting out of the top of his head as if pushed up by some violent force. And he did seem always full of violence. Even when he was sitting still you felt he was only just managing to "hold himself in".

His father was a Tarbiton grocer, also very religious (but

rather a bad sly old man; he had been fined for some trick with his scales, and also he had been in prison for misbehaving with young girls), whose shop was in a back lane at Tarbiton – a miserable sort of place. But two years before this he had retired, and the son had at once bought two more shops, very good shops, one in Tarbiton High Street and one in Chorlock.

He had bought these shops (both established groceries) partly with money lent by Chester, that is, my money; and though I had agreed that this was a good investment (Goold paid ten per cent), I had really hated it because I knew that it would bring Goold and Chester still closer together. In fact, Goold from that time was always in our house, when he behaved to me, not exactly rudely, but as if I did not matter.

On this evening, of course, he was quite triumphant about this meeting. He was delighted with Chester's speech, and said over and over again that it was the best he had ever made, especially the bit about the troops. "That got 'em – that started it. They couldn't stand that. That's the stuff for Lilmouth. And what a bit of luck that London reporter was there; it's the very first time any London paper has sent a reporter. But probably someone gave them the tip that the Tory gang was going to make trouble." I asked what Chester had said about the troops; and Goold, looking at me with his big dog's eyes (his eyes protruded, and always had rather a mad look as if to say, "You won't like it, but who cares"), said, "He called them murderers and cowards, as they are."

I said nothing, for I was too angry, and also that critical part of me was waiting to see what Chester would do.

"Murderers and cowards," Goold said, "and their churches pray for them."

Suddenly, to my own surprise, I asked him how he knew there was a plot. "If Chester's words started the riot, it couldn't have been done by a plot."

Whereupon Goold grew furious and said that the plot was common knowledge, and that he knew I wanted to drive him from the house, but that some day Chester would realize which of us was his real friend. And then he strutted out of the room.

I asked Chester at once to notice that this quarrel, if it was a quarrel, was none of my making, but he answered only, "Yes, but he knows you don't like him in the house," which, of course, was true, but only made me more indignant.

"What I don't like is him talking about plots and trying to make you go to Lilmouth. You know there would be a much worse riot there." Chester made no answer to this, and I really think he was hesitating. But the next day the London papers came out with violent attacks on him, calling him a traitor, and saying that he should be arrested; and Goold rushed round in triumph to congratulate him on becoming a "national figure". Lilmouth, he said, was now his great chance – a turning point in his life.

I said that if Chester went to Lilmouth he would be arrested. But Goold cried, "So much the better"; and Chester (seeing that I was shocked by such "tricky work") said quickly, "You see, Nina, we have no right to consider a personal risk – the matter is too serious. This war is a crime."

And when, after Goold had gone at last, I reminded him that he had promised the Chief Constable not to hold a meeting in Lilmouth, he said only, "Yes, hold – I'm not going to hold one."

"But you know what he means."

"I know that his only object is to stop free speech."

And just when I was thinking that, of course, he would find some excuse for breaking his word, he turned on me and said, "You think it's because I'm tricky that I'm always looking out for tricks."

As I say, Chester practised this kind of unexpected remark to throw me off my balance and he usually succeeded. Before I could even say no, he went on, "How do you know it isn't a plot? They don't need even to speak. It's understood – they start at your *gentlemen's* schools." And I saw that his face was shining with sweat. He was in such a rage of resentment that he could hardly speak. He came quite close, as if he were going to bite me, and croaked, "What you call the team spirit – playing the *game*."

Then he rushed out of the room, as he always did when he had given way to such a fit – he hated me to see him lose his dignity and show his spite. But after that how could I blame him for being tricky if he *felt* that he was surrounded by tricks and bad faith?

Of course, he meant to confuse me about his trickiness; but his rage was a real rage, his suspicion a real suspicion. I could not even say that he had given way on purpose, for he had really given way. The sweat on his face was real sweat, his hatred of my "gentlemen" real hatred.

I could not even resent his attack, because if he felt like that you had to excuse him. I could not say another word, and that, too, was somewhere in his purpose.

17 I don't know if it is worth telling the whole story of the "Lilmouth plot" which is now probably forgotten. Put simply, it was secretly arranged that Chester and Goold and two others, members of the pro-Boer committee, should come by the back door to a big meeting in Lilmouth for the African Missions and be given places on the platform. Then Chester was to get up and testify to the good work of the missions and contrast it with the action of the Government in making war – and in fact to make a speech against the war.

As everybody knows, this plan worked even better (or worse) than could have been hoped for. I know, for I saw it. I had been forbidden to go in case of trouble, and did not mean to. In any case, I had determined not to go, on any account.

And this was not only because I was so disgusted with the whole plot, but because of something said to me by my old friend Major Freer at the yacht club. "You're quite a radical nowadays, aren't you?"

Of course, I denied this (I was astonished at such a charge), saying that I simply was not interested in politics. But he smiled sadly and said, "Well, I suppose it's natural – now you've married into the cause."

This made me very indignant. But also it gave me a very uneasy feeling. I realized how much I had got "mixed up" with the politicians, and how much I had been worrying, not so much about politics (except that I hated them more and more) as about their effect on Chester's moods and prejudices (such as his "class" obsessions). I saw that the Major had not been so stupid, that I really was getting "involved".

And this was a horrible feeling. It seemed all at once that I was, after all, being changed (for the worry was real), that I was being turned into somebody else.

And so at that time (it was one of the reasons why I was so angry with Goold) I was very strongly against political entanglements. I was determined to have nothing whatever to do with the Lilmouth plot.

I was quite glad, in fact, when Aunt (who was one of the platform party, as a strong supporter of missions) asked me to come in to Lilmouth with her on the day. It enabled me to *show* how firmly I stood aloof. I said yes, I should like to go – I had to do some winter shopping.

And when we arrived I said goodbye to her and went to buy a warm dress for myself and woollies for Chester (he was a chilly little man in spite of his high complexion and always needed the heaviest combinations in a frost).

And all the time I was trying on dresses I was saying to myself, "The whole thing is absolutely disgraceful – simply a mean low trick. And if he gets killed it's absolutely his own fault. I needn't even be sorry, and I won't. I'm not tied to Chester, I should hope." But I kept on feeling odder and odder, as if I were going to be sick. In fact, I was full of odd feelings which kept dashing about inside me so that I could not concentrate even on woollies (much less the dresses) and at last I went out of the shop to walk on the front and look at the sea and get cool. When suddenly I saw a poster of the meeting on a lamppost, and all the feelings rose together in one enormous wave and whirled me away like driftwood. I rushed to the hall actually in terror that I should not get in, and I thanked God when I not only squeezed in but got a seat in a very dark back corner, between two young men whom I knew quite well, a young Tarbiton butcher who was a chapel member, and one of Goold's grocery assistants. They were both very polite, really more than polite, kind and thoughtful.

Chester's chair on the platform was empty when the meeting began (this was because Chester and Goold were both sure that there would be police spies in the hall; and in fact, as it turned out, luckily for us both, there *were* detectives there), but after a Baptist minister had spoken a few words about the mission of Christianity in Africa, Chester suddenly appeared from the back and walked right across the whole platform to his place. The result, of course (and I felt sure it had been all thought out), was that the whole hall noticed him, and there was at once a rustling noise while people were saying, "That's the man who called the soldiers murderers, and made that awful riot at Chorlock."

And you could feel at once what is called "electricity" in the air, and it is really like the feeling after a flash of lightning when you are waiting for the thunderclap. Some woman behind me said (not very loudly), "Oh, it can't be," and at once dozens of voices began to shush with noises like small waves going back on a shingle beach.

All this, however, made me feel still more determined *not* to get excited. I said to myself, "The whole scheme is simply to make people excited, and it's based on a thoroughly low view of human nature. It's disgusting and humiliating." And I felt more and more angry with Chester himself.

I could see by the way he was sitting, very stiff, with his hands clasped tightly together in his lap, that he was in his worst state of nerves (he was clasping his hands like that to keep them from shaking); and I thought, "He pretends to love peace and truth, and there he is working himself up (or letting his own nerves work him up) to cause as much trouble and tell as many lies as possible." The woman behind was still muttering, and someone in the gallery made an exclamation which started another explosion of hushes, and it was a great relief when at last the missionary sat down.

But at that very instant Chester jumped out of his chair as if on a spring and began his speech, and his voice was so quivering with excitement that I was at once terrified of his losing his thread or his grammar. But Chester even then had a power, not, as people say, of "letting himself go", but of keeping up with his own excitement; of thinking so fast that he went with the crest of the wave and did not sink into confusion.

Only when he did this he was apt to forget prudence, that is, he was more violent; and on this night he did almost at once begin to attack the Government, and used some words about the Government selling its conscience for gold, which were afterwards improved into the phrase (I read it in a history book only the other day) that England had sold Christ to the High Priests of the Rand for gold. Also I believe he did speak of the troops as butchers in the pay of Pontius Pilate.

But I did not hear this, because almost as soon as he opened his mouth (I can swear to this) men and women from all over the hall began to shout and within a minute there were dozens of fights going on. People (not by any means all hooligans, but there were some very rough young men there, on both sides) were climbing on the stage, and Chester himself was struggling with two young men (they looked quite respectable people, clerks or shop assistants, in neat dark suits) who seemed to be trying to throw him into the pit.

As for those round me, a few were still sitting in their places and looking stupid, but most of them were standing up and screaming "Cowards!" and "Brutes!" and "Down with the traitors!" and "Throw them out!"

And, what is extraordinary, I, too (as I was told afterward, for I have no recollection of it, and in fact for a long time I wouldn't believe it), was shrieking "Cowards!" – and even "Kill them!" I suppose I wanted to kill the people who were attacking Chester; after all, he was a small man against hundreds. It was in fact (so they say) these ridiculous shrieks on my part, and my getting up on a chair to see what was happening to Chester, that attracted attention to me, so that I was recognized and attacked. But how that began is also quite mysterious to me. I remember only falling off my chair and hands seizing me as if from all sides and everywhere, all over my body.

The end of it was simply that nearly all my clothes were torn off, somebody smacked my face so hard that both my eyes were blackened, and after a confused foolish struggle I found myself (I have no idea how) wrapped up in a very prickly overcoat with metal buttons (it was a soldier's coat), being carried down a long dim corridor full of little tables by one of my friends from Tarbiton (it was the butcher and his nose was pouring blood over the coat), a tall man in a blue uniform (he was a Marine, the owner of the coat), and a strange youth, an extraordinary young man with popping blue eyes and an immense mop of yellow hair, who kept saying that he was absolutely ashamed of the whole thing, that he had been all against the Boers until that evening, but now he thought he would really go and fight for them; so that in the state I was in, quite distracted with rage against everybody, including myself, for behaving in such a senseless manner (I was, of course, especially furious with Chester for being the cause of it all), I very nearly burst out at him, to tell him to stop being so silly. But thank goodness I managed to remember that he was saving me and that he was obviously a nice young man, and to hold myself in.

And he went on talking about his shame till they put me suddenly into an ambulance, which drove off at once into a dark street, where it stayed until, after what seemed like several hours, the door was opened and two policemen lifted in a stretcher covered with a blanket. And before I could even feel the shock of having a corpse put in with me we were driven away at full speed, with our bell ringing.

There was almost no light inside the ambulance cart, but the street lights kept flashing through the little windows at front and back, and suddenly to my horror the corpse sat up and threw off the blanket.

But before I could cry out to the driver I saw that the corpse was Chester (and in spite of my indignation with him I can't describe what a relief it was to see that he had not been killed), and before I could speak to him he burst out furiously, "I hear they insulted you – Nina."

"But how are you, Chester? What have they done to you?" (I could see that his clothes were torn, but, in fact, thanks to the police and their stretcher, he was not hurt at all.)

"Never mind about me – thank God you're safe!" And he went down on his knees beside the bunk. He was almost crying with excitement, and it was impossible to quarrel with him. In fact, we were both in such a queer state of mind that we began to laugh at ourselves and our rags. In a drunken kind of way we were suddenly drawn together, and yet all the time I was feeling in some deep place, "He did it all on purpose – and now he's going to be a hero."

18 And this Lilmouth affair, just as Goold and Chester himself had expected, did put Chester "on the map". He became from that time a known man, and people for the first time began to say that he ought to be in Parliament. He had more invitations to speak than he could accept; and though there were no more riots as bad as the Lilmouth one, the police were always in force. There were always interruptions and fighting and booing in the streets. And the London papers would report that "Mr Nimmo gave his usual performance and repeated all his most virulent slanders on our sorely tried troops."

Such attacks gave Chester a particular kind of pleasure. He would read them to me and say that if "they" thought they could "put him down" they were much mistaken.

Often they were read out at what Aunt Latter called Chester's "belles assemblies"; the gatherings of his supporters and local agents and chairmen of committees who often came together at the Orchard, and the more violent the words, the more they seemed to enjoy them, just as they never forgot the Lilmouth riot which had made Chester's name.

I don't say that they said openly what a good thing it was for them to provoke violence and get people killed. In fact I don't believe for a moment that they even thought it. It was at this time I began to feel among "political" people the strange and horrible feeling, which afterwards became so familiar to me (but not less horrible), of living in a world without any solid objects at all, of floating day and night through clouds of words and schemes and hopes and ambitions and calculations where you could not say that this idea was obviously selfish and dangerous and that one quite false and wicked because all of them were relative to something else. The lies were mixed up with some truth (like Chester's belief in a class plot), and the selfish calculations (like Goold's planning to make trouble at Lilmouth) melted at the edges into all kinds of "noble" ideals (like Chester's passion for freedom and free speech).

So that even while I heard the "belles assemblies" denouncing the "jingoes" for provoking the riots I dared not think, "Good heavens, what cant!" And when I felt their triumphant joy after a riot (because they felt that it would lose the Government some more votes) I knew it wouldn't be fair to say that they were simply hypocrites who thought they had hit on the right way (as indeed they had) to get back into power.

And it was now much harder for me to "live my own life", because since the Lilmouth "outrage" (it was no good telling them that I had done nothing but disobey Chester's orders) I was looked upon as a "heroine of the cause" and I was received with bouquets and cheers when I went out with Chester.

I don't mean that people like Goold "really thought" that I had become a good radical, but that they pretended to do so on the general political principle of not seeing how anyone can fail to agree with them. And this system did work quite well, because I could not seem critical all the time without feeling cantankerous and therefore in the wrong.

But I did avoid, as far as possible, receptions and presentations – I was embarrassed by congratulations that I had not deserved. I confined myself to acting as Chester's secretary and hearing him rehearse his speeches and playing the hostess at the assemblies. But even so much (and Chester's praise – he praised everything I did to make me do better) gave me a high reputation as a good political wife.

19 But if they had known it, the reason why I worked so hard at the letters and speeches was that I was afraid of being a very bad wife; or, to speak more truly, I was afraid of what would happen to me, if I came to hate Chester. My devotion, in fact, was like those embraces and kisses I had used to give Jim as a child when I met him at the station and remembered all our fearful quarrels. They were a kind of incantation to make me love.

For what frightened me was that all this time while I was

working for Chester that critical piece of me, a very strong and active piece, was criticizing everything he did. For instance, it absolutely detested the way he and Goold, and all the radical set, were attacking the Government, and having the best of it. It seemed to me as if some poor helpless creature, very big but hopelessly weak, like a whale among sharks, was being tortured and snapped at and driven to its death.

Of course (what I did not know then), this is the case with all governments; it was the same with the Liberal Government afterwards when it was attacked by all the other parties and at last simply torn to pieces. When people attack the Liberals nowadays, and jeer at them, I feel just the same indignation. I am one of those people (I expect because I am rather timid by nature) who naturally hate tramplers, and am especially frightened of lies, of anything cunning and malicious.

And so I dreaded those evenings when Chester would come in after some successful meeting and begin to tell me about it (even when I had been there) all over again. He used to be so excited that he was like a small boy who has gone a little mad at the end of a party. He would walk round the room hitting himself on the chest and rubbing himself behind, and telling me how he had been inspired to make fools of the hecklers, and how cleverly he had turned everything against the Government.

And I would admire him all over again and tell him how clever he had been, just because that little spiteful voice within me was saying all the time how mean it was to make some poor young man, who had tried to ask an honest question, seem silly; and yet by a trick of speech not really answering his question at all; and it would say, "But none of these people care one penny for truth or honesty; they are simply clever cunning agitators who would do anything for success and power."

Sometimes, indeed (when Chester had been unusually clever and made a devastating answer), I would feel a real hatred, which is quite a terrifying thing. It is more like an illness than a thought. And I never knew when it was coming. All at once, even when I was telling Chester how brilliant he was and how he was bound to be Prime Minister one day (at which he would laugh, but he would not quite disbelieve it either), I would feel a kind of chill in my whole body, which made me actually shiver and set my teeth, and then a sudden hotness, like a flush of fever (I used to get red at the same time because Chester noted it, and he would stop and gaze at me), and simply not know what he was saying.

And this hatred would be so terrifying, I would be so frightened at what it might do to me, that I would say to Chester, making use of the blush, "Isn't it time you came to bed?" in a way that was an invitation, so that I could hide that feeling of loathing and get away from that dangerous place of hatred, that great hole which I could not see to the bottom of and which was always threatening to swallow me up and destroy my happiness forever.

But still I could never control that angry critical part of me, so that even when he was in my arms I would look down on his thick crinkly hair and detest it (it always seemed to me too curly and shiny, coarse and common hair, such as would naturally belong to a cunning, greedy creature with no honest true feelings) and the little frightened soul inside me would think, "Look at him now, how ridiculous he is really, almost crying with excitement and greed; here is your prophet of the Lord" (for you may be sure that the more excited Chester was the more certainly he would begin with some "religious" words – it was like grace before a meal), "your great man, wriggling and panting and sweating like a nasty little animal." Even while I was thinking this I knew how wickedly unfair it was, because, of course, it so happens (which *is* very unfair) that a man has to be rather ungraceful in that proceeding, whereas a woman can be as calm and dignified as she likes; she need never do anything absurd.

But for this mean part of me, the very unfairness of my criticism was an attraction, because it would say that unfair people, cunning greedy people, like Chester, have no right to consideration. And this was the most frightening thing, that there seemed no cure for these disloyal spiteful feelings; for the more I devoted myself to Chester, the more I would criticize. I was quite furious when, at the election of the County Radical Committee, he was beaten (quite unexpectedly) by a Liberal who actually supported the Empire. Yet I was feeling all the time a secret satisfaction and comfort, for I could not help the thought, "You see, after all, trickery doesn't always have its own way."

20 As I say, I did not go often to Chester's meetings; and one reason was that on these days I could escape to the peace at Palm Cottage. I began to have, in fact, a kind of nostalgia for my happy times there. I suppose everybody, even the happiest wife, feels at some time this homesickness, and everybody knows how very strong it is when it first takes hold. It is like an infection, a nervous fever. And what made it especially strong with me just then was that Jim's letters from hospital (he had remembered our picnics and sails far better than I) brought back to me all those pleasures in which Jim had had no share, the joy of reading some forbidden book (forbidden only because the print was too small), the delights of escaping by myself into the moor or to some hidden beach under the cliffs.

Jim's letters, too, were full of homesickness. He was counting the weeks till his discharge from hospital (he had nearly died of enteric after being cured of his wound), when he hoped to be given long leave at home and to see us all again at "dear old Palm Cottage where we had such glorious times". And that winter when his father (he had been ill for years) died at Cannes he resolved suddenly to leave the army (of which he wrote so critically, obviously he had not been a success as an officer) and settle at Buckfield, as agent, and secretary to the Hunt. Buckfield was the Latter house. It was only about forty miles away from us at Palm Cottage.

This did not seem a very wild scheme at the time. For Bob was still with the army and talked of making his career as a professional soldier; and though Sir Brougham had left Jim only two thousand pounds and some furniture, he had also asked Bob in a letter to give his brother quarters at Buckfield, at least so long as he was a bachelor.

Aunt Latter, too, was delighted with this plan and suggested that Jim should take a training course in estate management at Bing's office. "He can stop with me at the Cottage and go down with Chester to the office every morning."

When I suggested that neither Bing nor Chester might like this arrangement, she said I was a selfish egotist for not wanting to help Jim in his troubles and that I did not know my own husband "possibly because he was not a fool".

But the scheme fell through when Bing suddenly "sacked" Chester. He had, I think, been waiting only till the war was over. He had not been able to do it in wartime for fear of being accused of persecuting a pro-Boer. But he had sons at the front and he hated pro-Boers, and so he could not bear Chester in the office.

I had never seen Chester look so ill as on the day he came home with this news. His salary from Bing was half our income. "This means goodbye to politics," he said, and perhaps he thought he meant it.

"Good heavens!" I said. "You're not going to let a creature like Bing change all your plans? Bing is nobody."

"But don't you see that if I go on – if I go on giving so much time to politics – we should have to live on capital – on your money. And that's something I couldn't allow."

But just then, of course, because of my secret hatred, I was delighted by any chance to help him. I begged him to think of my money as his own. I said nothing would give me more happiness. And he was so grateful that he kissed my hand and said I was a noble soul and with me by his side he had no fears.

21 In fact he had great fears, and rightly so, for when the radical member for Chorlock died (and Chester had been promised the seat) some fanatic attacked him on education.

Chester was very keen on popular education. He knew, of course, that it was important for a "rising man" to be known for some speciality, and he had chosen education. What he had not noticed was that this was a bad subject, because it attracted all the fanatics and lunatics who wanted children to be taught their special kind of religion.

It was incredible how spiteful the "good Christians" were on this occasion, because Chester had once said somewhere that the Bible needed interpretation. They *invented* lies against him (such as that he had illegitimate children), and when he challenged the lies they said they were justified against so evil a man.

They were terribly in earnest, because they believed that they were fighting God's battle. And Chester lost the nomination.

The letter telling him of this disaster arrived at breakfast time, and for years Chester could not eat a kipper without feeling sick.

Of course, he did not show his despair. He was very proud, and he would have despised himself for being upset by a temporal misfortune. His bilious attack was supposed to be due to a chill, and he made speeches in favour of the candidate. He even prayed for his success – that is, for God's blessing upon the cause of justice and freedom.

And this was the first time since our marriage when he held a prayer meeting in the house, and afterwards what he called (it was Goold's word) a general "stock-taking".

These "stock-takings" or "soul-searchings" were a regular practice among the congregation of Fore Street chapel. They were supposed to be done in private, and were really a kind of private confession to oneself of all one's faults and sins, and a resolution to improve.

On this occasion Chester did, I think (but he didn't tell me what he had decided), find fault with himself for being too ambitious, and too fond of his meals, especially sweet puddings which were so bad for him. He worked harder in the garden, and refused second helps, and asked me as a special favour to stop smoking; which I did willingly enough, for I had only just begun to smoke and did not really care for it. Aunt Latter, too, detested seeing me with a cigarette, for, though she herself smoked fifty cigarettes a day, she considered smoking very unbecoming in women, and also very bad for the complexion. So that her smoking (which at that time I rather laughed at as typical of her inconsistency and "arbitrariness") was really (if I had had the common sense and common charity to see a very plain fact) something which should have made me sympathetic, for it was the plainest confession that she despaired of her own complexion and regarded her womanhood as a failure and a nuisance.

22 Chester, as I say, was anxious and depressed, and this made him more religious. You must never forget that Chester was a truly religious man and always on his guard (perhaps because of his special temptations) against a low idea of human nature and mean worldly ambitions. And I think it was because he was specially religious at this time (when his ambitions had been frustrated) that when, one morning in June, we heard that Jim had actually landed he proposed that we should ask him to the Orchard.

At first I did not understand him. I thought that he was facing a "situation" and treating it as a social problem. I said that it would be bad enough to have Jim at Palm Cottage, and I, for one, meant to avoid him if I could.

"And how," he said, "could we forbid Captain Latter the house?"

"You mean that people would talk?"

This hurt Chester, because it had naturally occurred to him (it couldn't help it) that people would be interested to see how we received Jim (for there was always gossip, probably much more than we knew of, as we both suspected), and he looked at me with a mournful glance (he gave his eyes this expression by opening them rather wider than usual and raising his eyebrows) and answered me rather sadly (which was fair, because he did really despise gossip) that it was not a question of gossip but of common kindness and family duty.

"That should have occurred to Jim," I said, growing a little nervous. (I thought, "Is he going to strike some attitude? Is this going to be another Lilmouth drama?") "I at least don't want to see him again after the way he behaved."

But Chester (obviously full of his idea, he even had his "noble" expression) said that that had been three years ago. "Surely, Nina, you don't bear malice all this time."

"But it's not malice," I said, "it's just a situation, and, after all, it was he who made it so awkward."

Chester thought for a moment and said then, "Yes, but putting it at the lowest, that seems to me why we should do our best to remove any bitterness and establish a proper understanding."

I asked him if he realized how difficult it was to make Jim understand anything that did not suit his own convenience.

"I know," Chester said then, "how much you suffered. I am asking a great deal of you. But perhaps even for you it might be wise to overlook the past. We should at least have to see him when he will be so near, and if we asked him to stay – "

"To stay?" I cried in consternation.

"The bold approach is nearly always the best – especially in a case like this."

"There," I said to myself, "it's the old confidence trick. We are to stop Jim from doing any more damage by trusting him not to."

But just then Chester, as if reading my very thought (and probably he did), said, "And what I feel so strongly is that your Jim has suffered, too – very great disappointments and hardships. We owe him some reparation. I should not feel at all comfortable if we failed in kindness toward him."

Chester said this in his thoughtful and "convinced" manner, and the moment he spoke I felt how right he was, so that I was even surprised at my own small-mindedness. I was ashamed of myself. It seemed to me that Chester's "grand" gesture was only another proof of something not merely "imaginative" and "theatrical" in his character, but true, for he had seen the plain truth of Jim's unhappiness where I had simply overlooked it.

And as for the "confidence trick" (so often made an accusation against Chester with his "trust the people"), what did it mean? That Chester really did believe in trusting people? Perhaps he took advantage of his faith, when it seemed the best policy for him, but still it was his true faith, at least at the time.

So I said at once, "Yes – and he's been so ill. Do write to him."

But Chester answered that I ought to write. "It would look strange if you left it to me – as if I were trying to take up a certain position."

And since I was so much in the wrong and felt so guilty toward Jim, I wrote at once, sending a warm invitation from us both.

And this had at once a most inspiring effect. There is nothing (I found) like doing a grand thing and also a slightly dangerous thing (as Chester said, the bold thing) for making one feel "good" – that is, as if one has had a glass of champagne at an unusual time (say for breakfast) or made a rather daring bet and may either lose too much or make a big sum.

As soon as the letter went we were all very energetic and, as it were, revived. I made a special journey all the way to Exeter to buy new curtains and some Japanese fans for the drawing room and new cushions for my own room. Aunt

Latter made a new plan for getting Jim appointed assistant agent at Slapton (the Buckfield scheme had failed because Bob said – but we thought it was an excuse to keep Jim away – he would have to sell the place), and Chester excelled himself at a meeting in Chorlock where he called the landlords baby-starvers.

Chester and Goold had begun this attack on the landlords some time before, because, as they explained, now that the war was nearly over it was important to find somebody to attack in place of the generals and the War Cabinet. And since Bing's had got rid of Chester there was nothing to prevent him from abusing all their clients (the local squires) to his heart's content. And, naturally, the more he said against them the more indignant he became.

He had, of course, every reason for indignation, for in those days there was great poverty in some of the poorer villages and children of large families were often half starved. So Chester's wrath, which I looked upon then, in my critical mood, as simply a political move (I had heard of plenty of discussion in the "belles assemblies" on the necessity for a "new offensive"; even the anti-war party always used these fierce metaphors), was quite sincere; and his cleverness (taught by experience) was in choosing the right thing to be angry about, that is, not the schools (because no one really wants education except teachers) and not drink (because most of the voters liked it), so much as poverty, which was detested, especially by the poor.

True, Chester was violently attacked for saying that poverty was a preventable curse, but only by a few millionaires and economists, who said that he was an irresponsible demagogue raising false hopes among people who had enough to bear already.

It has always been a charge against Chester that he could

seem to believe anything that "suited his book", that he could always spellbind himself with his own voice.

But this is one of those dangerous "facts" which are so hateful because they are partly true as facts and so hide the real truth which is that Chester's imagination suggested to him every day hundreds of truths and it was always easy for him to find among them one that "suited" him. And certainly at that time (taught by experience) he was very careful in his choice of what to be excited about.

And this fertile imagination was, I think, one reason why he sometimes seemed too rigid in his principles. He lived in such a whirl of exciting ideas that every now and then he got frightened (like a child in a carnival full of monsters) and grabbed at the nearest solid object (that is, principle), however cold and lumpy.

And it had always been one of his political principles (like "freedom" and "peace" and "equal opportunity") that poverty ought to be abolished. Indeed, when (in working himself up for this campaign) he showed me some of the cottages, even in Tarbiton, and told me some of the stories of the poor people, then I was shocked, too. It would have been impossible not to be shocked. So that he really meant that phrase (which seemed so ridiculous applied to old Major Freer or my cousin Slapton, both the kindest and most generous of men) – baby-starvers.

The speech, in fact, was a great success (it caused enormous indignation, and was reported in the *Morning Post*), and on the day Jim arrived Chester was in better spirits than for weeks past.

23 Jim had refused my invitation, because, as he said, he had already promised to stay with Aunt Latter; but, of course, the fact of the invitation by itself made a new and delightful situation, and he wrote most warmly, saying that he would be delighted to dine with us on his first evening.

And Chester welcomed him with such warmth (holding and pressing his hand) that I was afraid Jim would make some caustic remark. It was a relief to see Jim (after a moment's surprise) almost as enthusiastic as Chester. The two men, I thought, might have been long lost brothers in some melodrama. But if I was inclined to see something comic in this dramatic meeting, it was only, I think, for the same reason that I had once been inclined to laugh at Chester's dramatic prayers; because I did not want to be carried away and reformed. And I did not succeed in being aloof, because I was already surprised and troubled by the extraordinary change in Jim.

Why I should have been surprised to see Jim changed by three years, during which time he had been at a war and nearly died, and also made a failure in his regiment, I can't tell, except that young people never expect to see anyone else changed (they say usually, "So and so is going through a 'phase'," as if he would come out like a train from a tunnel, just the same as before); but I kept on looking at him as if I had never seen this Jim before.

And it was true that I could hardly recognize him. He had shaved off his moustache and had a new mouth, not at all a military mouth but more surprised. He had grown so thin and yellow that his very nose was a different shape, sharp and fine, and his eyes seemed much larger, and also much more blue. But he was not only much older looking – he had the air of a disappointed man. He had often that expression which you see in such men when they think no one is looking at them: of anxious inquiry, as if something had just happened to them which it is important for them to understand.

He seemed pleased by the Slapton plan. "It's not Buckfield – and I never cared for stag hunting; but I certainly might consider it if the old man will meet me on the pay."

"That would be wonderful – you would be living quite close to us."

"Nina has missed you," Chester said.

"I wonder," Jim said, and then at once began to talk about the agency and how farms could be improved. "I might ask for ten per cent commission. I have got to pay off my debts, and I can't do that on a miserable five hundred pounds a year."

Jim (and this again shows how much he had changed) blamed himself very much for wasting so much of Aunt Latter's money (she had not only fitted him out for the army but paid his debts three or four times, to the amount of at least two thousand pounds) and said that he was determined to pay her off. "In fact, if that damned brute had run straight" (this was an old steeplechaser that Jim had bought some time before as a speculation) "I'd have paid her everything last winter. But that's only another reason why Cousin Porty" (Slapton) "must give me a decent whack."

And as soon as we were alone together, which happened very soon, because Chester, in his usual fussy way, went to inspect the table for dinner, he said to me, "You won't mind if I come to live in your pocket?"

"You know I should love it" (though I was nervous at this). "But isn't it a pity to leave the army?"

"Best thing I could do for myself; and, besides, I couldn't go on taking an allowance from Aunt Latter. She's quite dipped."

"But, Jim, it wasn't your fault if the horse was interfered with."

"No, but I ought to have remembered my luck."

"Yes, you always had bad luck."

"And I am a fool not to look out for it."

24 Before I could be really astonished at hearing the proud Jim admitting a fault Chester came bursting in to say that dinner was ready. He still could not remember to let the maid announce dinner. Or rather, I think that he found it absurd to leave it to her, having ascertained the fact himself and probably stepped into the kitchen to taste the soup and feel the plates to make sure that they were hot.

And at dinner Jim scarcely spoke to me; he talked about the war to Chester, who was using all his arts to charm, though, of course, he did not give Jim any whisky. And when Jim, forgetting himself, answered the maid who had asked if he would prefer ginger ale or lemonade, that what he would really like was a small whisky and soda, Chester said firmly that this was a teetotal house. He was sorry, but that was a rule that could not be broken for anybody.

Jim apologized at once, and in quite a new way, obviously wishing, that is, to make all well and thinking of Chester's feelings. And afterwards, when we went into the drawing room, he asked me to sing, which he had never done before, for it had always been part of his training of me not to encourage me to be conceited or to "show off". And when I had sung and turned round to see if he liked it, I saw that he was quite tearful, which gave me a strange feeling of confusion and wonder. But I did not even then say, "Jim is in love with me." I thought, "Poor Jim is feeling sentimental after not seeing any women for so long, and it is natural for him to be sentimental about me – he has always fallen in love with married women, especially when they have young babies. He is just that kind of man who rather recoils from getting married because he is fastidious and likes a hard mattress and cold baths, and his own bedroom and his own luggage all to himself. Jim could have been a Jesuit if he had not been so mad about horses and so fond of domesticity – I mean the idea of domesticity."

This, I think, was true. Jim did fall in love with me as a young wife; his voice was different when he spoke to me, and Chester noticed it at once. He, too, felt the difference in Jim; and when we came to say good night he shook Jim's hand again very strongly and said that we were all united in a very deep bond of brotherhood and mutual sympathy. In fact, he made one of those speeches which always enraged Jim and caused me to blush, possibly because they threatened to upset us.

For Jim, as I say, was very easily moved in his feelings. You would say he was a sentimental man, and so he was, but so were most young men in those days. They would cry like fountains at a play called *East Lynne* when a little boy died. Of course, it is sad when little children die, I mean permanently sad; and so I can see why young people nowadays laugh at plays like *East Lynne* – they don't want to lose their dignity. But I think they ought to excuse men like Jim for crying, for, after all, they would not laugh at a Frenchman talking French. It was the right thing, then, for Jim to be sentimental about young mothers. It was (in 1902) a true manly feeling. And when he said good night so sadly and went out into the night, both Chester and I were quite tearful, too.

25 It was Chester's attitude toward Jim's return that set the key for us all. When he urged Jim to come as often as he liked, I felt at once how impossible it was, how mean, for me to avoid him, or even to be on my guard.

And when Jim asked me to go sailing, it was Chester who made it easy for me to go, saying that it was more important for me to sail with Jim, a pleasure I had not enjoyed for years, than to do small household tasks.

Jim had bought a new boat (and he bought it at a ruinous price on borrowed money simply to take me out in the newest and fastest and neatest new boat on the Longwater), and when he took me sailing he no longer used me as living ballast or went beyond Staplehead on rough afternoons to try to make me sick. On the contrary, he would not let me touch a rope. He would bring cushions and rugs and wrap me up and ask me every moment (or at least every half-hour) if I were comfortable. He would say in quite a diffident tone as we came home, deliciously sleepy but not tired, in the evening perhaps very late, "I suppose you couldn't spare the time for a run tomorrow to such and such a beach? It seems a pity to waste this wind." And I would say, all the more enthusiastically because he was so diffident, that I should adore it if only I could get away.

But I knew that Chester would urge me to go, and I could go with a clear conscience toward him (he had been so good about Jim that I felt very conscientious toward him), because, though he was speaking almost every day in the new land campaign, he did not expect me to listen to what he called speeches at the cart tail. In fact, he preferred that I should not do so, because (as I think) he was not very polished at these meetings (which were never reported) and abused some of my relations like Wilfred and Cousin Slapton rather violently. Not that Slapton had any property in Chorlock, but that he owned half Battwell where the sitting member, a Conservative, was said to have lost all his money so that he would probably not be able to stand again.

Chester said, of course, that he had no chance at
Battwell, or anywhere else, yet I could see that his hopes
and ambitions had both started up again from some private
internal source (quite possibly his Christian goodness to
Jim) and so he was full of fight. I know he called Slapton a
drunken parasite and a leech swollen with the children's
blood (Cousin Porty was, in fact, rather fond of his wine
and had a red round face), which he would not have cared
to do if I had been present.

So that three or four times a week I spent whole
afternoons with Jim in his new boat; and to sail on a fine
day (I mean a fine day for sailing, with a right amount of
breeze) even now seems to me a special bliss. There is no
sound but the popple of water against the bow and a deeper
gurgle under the bilge; the boat slides forward with a
motion which is not like any other, even the smoothest,
because in the smoothness of sleighing you feel all the time
the hardness of the crushed snow, and in the rushing of a
motor car you feel the bounce of tyres and springs,
mechanical contraptions. And in the intoxicating dash of a
high gig (much more exciting than a motor) you felt the pull
of the traces and the crunching of the wheels, the whole
vibration and shaking of the thing tilting nervously on the
camber of the road. But in sailing you feel all the time the
lovely touch of the water, bearing you up with its enormous
mild strength. I have no memory of my mother, except one.
I had been in some mischief or other at a strange house, and
had been hiding in terror in some tall hot narrow place until
my father and mother came there, I suppose to fetch me;
and when I heard their voices I rushed out and began to
explain. But what I remember next is simply the feeling of
being carried by my mother, the soft warmness of her body,
and the soft bouncing movements of her walk. Just to feel

it in memory is to feel the immense relief of that moment. It was as if all my tied-up compressed agony of fright (and probably guilt) had suddenly flowed out into a vast calm peace, which was, in fact, nothing but the sense of being carried by my mother. Memory cannot distinguish one from the other; it was a single feeling, and I do not remember any special elation or relief. It was, I suppose, too large and spread out, and too expected.

26 And I was just going to say that sailing on the Longwater with Jim gave me a similar joy and comfort, but, of course, it was only similar in the escape. What is called so often the bosom of the sea is not at all like a mother; it is too cold, too beautiful (or rather a quite different kind of beauty), and its coldness and strength and beauty are an important part of the joy of being carried up on it. You feel it as power, stronger than stone and smoother than snow, the most beautiful and strongest thing in the world; you could see it swinging and dipping and glittering all round you, so that its sparkles seemed to be dancing, not only on the tops of the little waves but right into the air at least two or three feet above; you were all among them, in a kind of gay triumphant procession, a wedding-day procession wherever you went, and there was no noise of engines, nothing smelly or clever pushing you along; it was the wind that did not care whether you were there or not, which had been blowing millions of years before there were any boats at all, which was simply moving on its own way and carried you with it when you caught a little bit of it in your sail.

I felt such joy, a deep peaceful complete joy, that I found myself quite excited with it; with a deep peaceful excitement which did not even want to speak; and a great deal of that peace was from Jim, because I knew him so well, and he was so simple and complete (even his selfishness was on a grand scale) that he was like another piece of nature. All the bumps and hollows, the rocks, streams, chasms of his character were as well known to me as Slapton Moor, and (this was, of course, the most important thing) they were no longer dangerous to me; they were no longer the property of that jealous savage who had allowed me to walk in them only on bare sufferance, and who might at any moment turn upon me with his stick or his gun.

He did not, it is true, invite me to explore these recesses; he told me nothing about his sudden determination to leave the army, except that he had always disliked the colonel, who was, he said, a "half-bredun". "You couldn't trust him not to get the wrong idea." He talked, when he did talk, about our memories together. He would say suddenly at the end of a long beat to windward, "You were a funny kid, Nina. You did what you liked with me, didn't you? Ready about." And when we had gone about, and he had tucked me up again on the weather side, and shifted his pipe to the leeward corner of his mouth, he would say, "All the same, we had some pretty good times."

"Lovely times," I would say.

And after a long pause he would answer, "I was mad about you, but I didn't know it. How could I? You were such an extraordinary kid; all bones and spit. Extraordinary how you have changed; I mean all round."

"I wonder. I don't feel changed."

"You have grown into a remarkably nice woman. Even your voice is different; I love your singing now. But, of course, a lot of things have been happening to you."

"You mean my marriage?"

"I was thinking more of Tommy; nothing like a baby to bring a girl out."

"I am certainly fatter than I was."

"I didn't mean that." Jim did not exactly frown in his new politeness to me, but there was a frown in his mind. He did not approve of what he considered a lack of refinement in my remark, unsuitable to his conception of my new status. "I meant your character," he said severely. "And it has taken the angles out of your temper, too. What a fool I was, Nina, to let myself be swindled out of you. And now I suppose it is too late. I seem to have made a mess of things all round."

And such was the effect of our surroundings, of the glittering atmosphere through which we slipped like dream royalties in Hans Andersen, among a noise like fountains, of the immense calm sky all round us, the fields brought down to the size and brightness of velvet rags heaped in a work-basket, and the villages, even the town of Ferryport, reduced to quaint models such as one might see in some millionaire's nursery, that such alarming remarks came to me without the least shock. It was as if they had been rendered harmless, on the way through this beautiful transparent air full of contemplation as lucid as itself (though, of course, it was my contemplation), so that Jim and I and our private passions seemed also far off, comprehensible, and therefore easily dealt with. And Jim would say in his contemplative tone behind his pipe, "Why did we fight?" And I would look back on those two children as on two strangers in a miniature world (like the figures in a glass ball) crowded close with events, and say, "We were like two cats in a sack."

"I don't think you ever cared for me as I cared for you."

But I would say quite freely, studying the little girl in the miniature, that I had adored Jim. "It was because it was a real passion that I could not manage it; we were too young to be so badly in love."

27 I am not going to pretend that one of us was aware of a "situation". On the contrary, we were all intensely aware of it. But so far from causing us any embarrassment, it removed any anxiety. For it seemed to us all that we had discovered a new kind of social being in which, simply by the exercise of Christian virtues (forgiveness, mutual sympathy, and the scorn of mean suspicion), we could all be not only happy but, as it were, exalted.

There was really an extraordinary sense of elation in the air, at least among us three (for to Aunt Latter everything that happened in the whole world was quite ordinary and unmiraculous); and just as Jim was transformed by his love for me (or at least for the young mother of his baby, whom, however, he hardly looked at), and I was half drunk with sailing, and peace, and the joy of Jim's new character, so Chester had never been so understanding to us both.

Chester, indeed, as his spirits improved on account of his violent speeches against the landlords (it always did him good to fight somebody and to be abused), grew more and more affectionate not only to me and Aunt Latter but to Jim. He and Jim were more than brotherly together, or let us say they were like brothers, who, being different in every possible way, are very affectionate because they have no common ideas. I think, too, that they also found the situation exciting. I don't mean that Chester was glad to see Jim's new passion or that Jim was pleased to see me Chester's wife, but that these feelings, too (as well as the noble brotherliness), gave also a special tension to the air and tension is itself exciting all round.

When Jim would repeat, in Chester's presence, his favourite discovery (to explain to himself why our relation had changed so much; though, of course, he had changed much more than I) that marriage had brought me out, that it obviously suited me "no end" to be married, he caused a sensible pressure in the air, and made me feel that I was turning pink (yet I did not resent it, because I could not quite believe that Jim meant what he might have meant); and when it was time to say goodnight Chester would always, rather ostentatiously, go out of the hall to let Jim say goodnight to me alone.

This was also a little bit of drama; he liked to make a grand gesture, and to know that it was grand (and it *was* grand). And especially on Jim's last night he took care to leave us alone for a long time, and even to tell us that we should have as much time as we wanted, for he said, "I am sorry I must go; I must catch the post with my letters."

We had had the news that week that Major Darty had resigned the Slapton agency to take a partnership at Bing's, and we had been talking all the evening after dinner about what Jim could do at Slapton as soon as he had left the army. What a fine opening it was for an active man. But Jim had seemed more and more silent and dejected, even when Chester now wrung his hand and said that he hoped to see him again soon, settled for life in the dear old home. Chester always called homes dear and old, but it was very effective in his sympathetic voice, and moved us both very much.

As soon as I was alone in the garden I asked Jim how soon he could get out of the army, but he answered that he did not know if he wished to do so; and when I said how absurd that was, and how wrong, after all Aunt Latter's planning, he said, "What is going to happen to us all, Nina, if I come and live here? It is asking for big trouble."

I was surprised, because I knew at once that he was speaking the truth. And then Jim took me by both hands (we were standing at the end of the garden, among the shrubs, in a rather dim light from the half moon) and said, "I have been screwing myself up for this for a week, Nina, but I know I am right; it's only common decency after Chester has been so decent. This has got to be goodbye."

Of course, I said why? It wasn't necessary. Why couldn't Jim live at Slapton? But he kept squeezing my hands and shaking his head. And then he said again in a very thick voice, "Goodbye, Nina."

28 His misery was so fearful (and with Jim it was not acted; it was real misery, and he didn't enjoy any of it) that I began to tremble at the knees trying not to cry. And as I bent down my head, suddenly he began to kiss me and say, "Don't cry, Nina," and then, "So you do care." And I found all at once that I was in love with Jim, or (I suppose I should say) in a new love with the new Jim, who had been so gentle and respectful, and who was so sad to go away from me; and I was in love with all my heart, perhaps with what Chester would have called my soul. I felt for Jim, I loved his gentleness and love for me. I dare say I had been getting into love for six weeks past, but the discovery was a complete surprise – as if the door of a familiar room had jumped open by itself and shown nothing on the other side but the open sky. Or like a fall – what they mean by falling in love. Something, I suppose, not at all extraordinary to those who have suffered it, but which astonished me as if I had been turned into another person, that is, a woman in love. And I was frightened by this queer feeling as if I were a new unknown person to myself. I tried to push Jim away, saying loudly, "No, no, I won't, I won't!" meaning, I suppose, that I refused to be in love.

Perhaps I rather hoped that Chester would hear me calling out and interrupt us, but he did not come out, and Jim drew me down the garden and kept on kissing me and saying that we were made for each other; and he knew I knew it, too. And that the only honest thing was to tell Chester at once.

I asked him how he could do such a thing after Chester had been so good, so trusting, but I asked as if I knew the answer already. It seemed to me completely reasonable and logical when Jim answered that it was just because of Chester's trustingness that we could not deceive him; it would be a most dishonourable thing.

I said then (but this discussion which seemed so short must have gone on for hours, as we wandered from the shrubbery to the little orchard, and from the orchard through the hedge into the kitchen garden, and I kept unhooking my long silk skirt – it was my best evening frock put on for Jim's last evening – from the gooseberry bushes) that it would be a wicked thing to deceive Chester; we must (as Jim had suggested) say goodbye and never see each other again. But Jim answered (and again his answer seemed not only reasonable but noble) that this was just what he meant by deceit. It would be wicked to persuade Chester that I loved him when I did not do so; and on my part it would be a horrible piece of play-acting and impossible for a girl with the least self-respect. He was sure, indeed, that I couldn't manage it now that I knew my own feelings.

What is extraordinary when I remember that night, and how vividly I have remembered it, even the warm damp feeling in the air (it had been showery in the afternoon), is that even when Jim and I were persuading each other to run away from Chester we were living in that strange, rather exalted atmosphere which Chester had thrown round us all. We were using words like love, honour, truth, feeling in his "noble" sense. When Jim, as we trailed for the tenth time through the kitchen garden, said to me, "We can't go on like this for ever, and you know it; it is a rotten situation for all three of us, not to speak of Tom; we have got to get free," the word free, by itself, seemed to thrill in my nerves. And it was Chester's word; I mean it carried Chester's tremendous faith and enthusiasm.

Freedom for Chester was the answer to every problem. It meant for him, Let God provide – don't get in His way. And so, as I looked at Jim's long pale face in the dim light of the sky, which was a kind of luminous cloud, that very word "free" gave me the feeling that we ought to be able to fly away through the air.

We had stopped, not because my skirt was caught again, but because the walks in the kitchen garden were so narrow that I was always a little behind Jim as I held his arm. And so when he wanted to emphasize his argument to me he had to turn sideways and look back at me, which brought us to a stop, and, being stopped, we seemed to be two serious people carrying on a dignified grave debate, so that I answered in spite of the furious joyful excitement in my veins, thoughtfully and even mournfully, that I supposed Jim was right. We must be free; it was the only way that we could put things right. But how should we get free? What should we do in this terrible situation?

And so we walked on again, and went on debating for a long time; or we thought we were debating, when perhaps we were enjoying happiness which (as I dare say we knew in our bones) could never again be that enchanted joy of our first communion. I should have liked it to go on for ever, but nothing goes on even for a short time. And presently Jim became bored with it and wanted to kiss me and tell me how he loved me, and how he had always loved me, and we spoke of our love as children (which we now agreed had been love), and how we had crept into each other's beds. And at last, Jim, growing more and more impatient (though, of course, nothing on earth could have satisfied our feelings at that time – I mean no action possible to human beings), said that we could never go back to the old miserable false life, even for an hour. And he made a plan then and there to call for me next day (or certainly the day after – as soon as he could "make arrangements" – he would go to Buckfield at once and raise the wind from old Bob) in Aunt's trap and take me to one of the small hotels on the moor where we could stay until, as he put it, the whole wretched business could be straightened out. Then he would take the Slapton agency and we would live at Palm Cottage.

As for Chester, he would explain everything to him when he came for me. Meanwhile I must promise not to behave any longer as his wife.

29 I delighted in this plan (it proved Jim's devotion), especially in Jim's resolve to ask Chester for me. I said that this was the proper way to treat Chester after he had behaved so well.

But Jim, for some reason, now became suspicious and irritable. He asked me why I was so anxious not to hurt Chester's feelings. What about *his* feelings all these years?

I suppose all this was the natural consequence of our exalted state before and the difficulty of going on in that vein. But when I swore I loved him more than any quantity of Chesters (which was true – I was quite wildly in love with him) he said that I did not know what love was. So we began to argue, and I was almost in tears of disappointment (not only with Jim but with the whole world), when suddenly he stopped me (we were among the bushes again) and took hold of me, and challenged me to prove my words to him, so that I could not go back on them. At first I did not know what he meant, but when he made me understand (and this shows the strange exaltation at that time) I said yes, yes, anything he liked; didn't I belong to him? And though I was startled when at once he spread his overcoat (with surprising deliberation) on the wet grass (I had not expected to be taken at my word immediately) I could not withdraw. In fact, his promptness challenged me.

But now I must confess something, because it has real importance – I mean, not so much in my life as in Chester's, that Jim, on this occasion, and for the first in my life (I had no idea even of the possibility of such a proceeding) did certain things which at first only surprised me and shocked me a little, but afterwards gave me a most extraordinary experience. So that I seemed (and was) quite lost in it, and said to myself (which was quite wrong, because, as Jim confessed to me long afterwards, when we were really intimate, he had picked up the idea in India where young people actually learn it out of textbooks), "It is because we love each other."

And yet, of course, it's no good saying that all this was a purely physical thing (caused by Jim's new idea), because the physical thing at that moment was so mixed up with the spiritual thing that they could no more have been separated than body and soul. And afterwards I was so moved not only in my body (which felt as if it was *changed* – into another kind of material, lighter and quicker, and, as it were, more living and more eager) but in my mind, as by the sense of a grand event, a dedication and solemn pledge (all the more *serious* because it had come with such an unexpected sensation) that I was a little shocked to hear Jim say in a tone of calm satisfaction, as if he had completed a deal by signing a contract (but Jim had a strong sense of contract), "That's all right then. Now you belong to me, and you can never have anything to do with that poop-stick again – not if you have a grain of honourable feeling."

For the strange thing was that now Jim had forgotten himself so passionately and made sure of me, as he said, he was the old Jim again; he had stopped being respectful to me, or polite about Chester. But in my mood at the moment he could, as I said, have done anything he liked to me, and in fact he had to explain to me twice over (I had such difficulty in thinking about anything while I was all feelings) the new arrangement for me to come to him at a place near Buckfield where we could stay quietly together. And as I had barely any sense of what he was saying so I had none of the time, and was very much startled to hear Chester's voice somewhere in the garden saying, "Are you there, Nina?"

30 I pulled myself from Jim at once and flew toward the house. No one was in the hall, and the hanging lamp (which I had always detested – it was in pink glass, a wedding present from Goold) gave me a feeling, still stronger than before, that life at the Orchard had always been unendurable.

This made me hurry (to avoid Chester) all the faster toward the stairs; but just as I reached the bottom step Chester came in from the back passage and said, "So there you are after all." I said, yes, I was just going up. And he answered, "I see you have torn your frock."

"Oh dear."

"I was wondering what had happened; you have been over two hours out there."

This astonished me and gave me a sense of terror. But Chester was calm and dignified and I saw that he was not going to make even a little scene.

In fact Chester had changed very much in these three years while he had become well known, and so much looked at. He was very much more self-contained, and not so excitable – at least on the outside. I said, "Was it really so long?" and yawned, and said I must go to bed, I was really worn out, and I ran upstairs.

But almost at once, while I was at my dressing table, I heard him come in behind me, so I hastily seized my brush and began to brush out my hair in case he would want to do it for me. But he did not even come near; he said from the far end of the room, "Are you very much in love with Jim?"

"Please, Chester, don't let us talk tonight."

"So there is something to talk about."

"I am too worn out."

"In fact, you are tired of me."

"No, but I am really exhausted. And you know you ought to have a good sleep, too; you have your big speech tomorrow."

"My speech?" he said. And now he really did seem agitated. "Do you think I can make a speech at a time like this?"

"Of course you can; you must" (for as I was going to upset him so terribly, I was very anxious that he should be "sensible"). "It is very important for you. Whatever happens, you must make your speech."

"What is going to happen? Are you going to leave me?" I didn't answer this. He said after a moment, "You know I only want your happiness." This made me tremble, but I did not turn round, and after a moment I heard the door close. Neither did he come to bed, so that I lay awake all night, for I had not expected this (though I was so glad of it); and when I got up I felt already as ravaged as if I had been fighting him for days.

And, indeed, in this house Chester had so pervaded every room with himself, his fits of love or religion, his queer pompous remarks about freedom or duty or goodness, that his nerves and his triumphs pressed upon one from all sides. The very ceilings which he had whitewashed, and doors which he had painted, reminded one of his fearful energy, and his delight in the house. And now the unusual silence (for I could hear nothing but Tommy chattering in the nursery and knocking a brick on the floor) seemed to speak for him, too, as if they were his thoughts brooding over my deeds.

When I felt that weight I fell into a kind of terror, and I said to myself, "What am I doing waiting here for him to invent some new trick to catch me? Am I going, or am I not going? Somebody must suffer, whatever I do." And then I knew I could not wait another moment in that house full of Chester. I packed in a frenzy, and dressed myself in an old summer frock, a printed muslin that Jim had always loved; it had grown rather tight for me, but still I thought that Jim would like it because it showed my figure. And I was keeping my mind on Jim and what he would like. I felt only that I must reach Jim and join myself to him.

31 It was then nearly ten o'clock and the next train from Queensport to Buckfield Junction was not till 11.10 am, but still I was determined to go out of the house at once. So I slipped away by the garden gate (not to give the maids cause to wonder at the bag) and took the next bus to town. When I reached the station, therefore, it was not much past the half-hour, and I went to the waiting room. I thought I should be safer there, because I had a feeling that the town was full of Chester's spies (it was, of course, full of his friends and enemies), who would at once detect my plan and tell him of it.

Yet I was quite stunned when ten minutes later Chester walked into the waiting room and came to sit beside me. I stared at him for a moment and then I thought, "I don't care; I am not afraid of him." And at once I felt quite strong and determined, so that I said quite calmly, "What about your meeting?"

Chester made his little shrug and wave as if to say, "That's nothing to matter," and sat down beside me. He looked quite normal, except that he kept staring at me in a fierce way like a dog at a stranger when he does not know whether or no he ought to bite him.

I asked him, "Who told you I was here? Was it Amelia?"

He made another shrug of his shoulder (I found out afterwards that he had actually suspected what I might do, and had himself been watching the road from the top passage window of the Longwater Hotel) and said, "I am sorry – I only wanted to make sure."

I said, "Make sure of what?" And then added quickly, "You asked Jim to come to the house."

I was seeking in desperation for some weapon against him, and I was going to say that I had warned Chester against Jim, and therefore everything that had happened was his fault. But when I caught his eyes looking into mine, not fiercely any longer, but with a kind of sad wonder, I absolutely could not speak the words. "Yes, I asked you to ask him," he said. "Was that wrong?"

"No, of course not; it was good of you. You have been goodness itself all along, and that's why – " Then there was a little pause while I was trying to find the right phrase.

"Why what?" Chester said.

"I couldn't pretend things to you – it would be too mean."

"So you want to go to Jim?"

"Don't you see I must go?"

"I was putting the emphasis on 'want'. Do you *want* to go to Jim or only to escape from me?"

"Please, Chester, don't cross-examine me – it's too late; it really is too late. You mustn't stop me now; you can't."

"If you really *want* to go I shouldn't dream of stopping you." Then after a little pause he said, "I want you to be happy, my darling; I owe that to you after all the happiness you have given to me."

"You mustn't try to catch me like that. I have not been specially good, as you know."

"Perhaps you haven't loved me – I couldn't expect that. The difference between us was too great – all the differences. I understood at once that for you I was worse than a foreigner – I was a kind of savage; even my religion was repulsive – "

And when, horrified by this charge, I was going to protest that "class" had nothing to do with the matter, he held up his hand and said, "I say that only because it makes what you have done all the finer. You would not sin against love – you set yourself to be a true good wife."

"But all I did was quite easy – it had nothing to do with our difference" (I did not want even to say the word class). "Just being a wife – it's something to do. And what else could I do to fill the time?"

"There's a great difference in the way that people do their duty. You stooped to me, but you might have made it an insult."

"I never stooped. You mustn't say such things – they're not fair. And as for duty, you know very well women are different; they like things friendly and peaceful in the house."

32 Two market women had come in from shopping. They sat down opposite the door, and then recognized Chester and nudged each other and gazed at me as if wondering what sort of a woman had caught their great man. I said to Chester in a low voice, "Must we go on like this? People are beginning to notice."

But he made another little jerk of his head and said, "So you have made up your mind?"

"Yes, Chester – I must. And it's nothing whatever to do with our differences. But I can't tell you how wrong that is with those women looking on. There's only one thing – about Tom."

"Of course, Tom will go to you as soon as you ask for him."

"You are very good."

"No, I am trying to do what is right."

At this I felt a little throb of excitement or fear; I knew that there was going to be a battle. I looked at Chester and found him staring at me with that fixity which meant that he was plotting something and trying to spy out his ground – that is, the state of my mind. Of course, I only felt more determined to fight him. I was bothered only by the women opposite, who had now been joined by a large man in a red neckerchief and a child of about four. The women had now realized that we were having some kind of argument and were staring with all their eyes. The child, too (it was sucking a lollipop and it had half its very dirty hand in its mouth at the same time), was gazing at us, trying to discover what the women found so interesting. So I said, "Really, Chester, we can't go on like this, in a waiting room, with all the world staring at us."

But Chester made only a jerk of the shoulder and came a little closer to me. So I said, "Are you staying just because it worries me?" But he did not pay any attention to this. He repeated, "We have to think what is right for us all."

"It's wicked of you to say that I stooped – I never dreamed of such a thing."

What I wanted to say was that only a man with his obsession about class could talk about stooping; but, of course, that was just what I couldn't even hint.

Chester looked at me as if he knew exactly what I had in mind, and said slowly, "What I'm afraid of is that you may be making a terrible mistake. I know you will say that I would think this, that I am only being selfish, but I can't help that. I must speak out – it's a duty."

"A duty to keep me even if I don't want to stay. I thought you said you wanted me to be happy – that you wouldn't try to keep me."

"No, I meant a duty to our marriage, which has been so fruitful in results – in our work together."

And then he made a little speech, saying how much I had helped him in ways that I perhaps did not realize (class again, I thought, raging at the impossibility of making the man believe anything that it did not suit him to believe), and he ventured to suggest that in a situation like ours it was impossible to decide only on personal grounds, because there was nothing to take hold of. Everything there was simply a matter of feeling, and so the only way for us to come to some reasonable conclusion was to seize firmly on some principle that we could both agree on. And he was sure I agreed that our marriage had been good in its fruits – it had led to good for others. It had been blessed with our work for right and good things. "And now if I do have the chance of the Battwell seat, I can hope for a much wider sphere of action – a much greater usefulness. I really think, Nina, that our life together has had God's blessing upon it, and you might blame yourself if you broke it up."

I felt still more furious at this approach and said that I did not think of God as quite so political; but Chester answered at once that he was sure that God hated poverty and misery. "And I know you do so, too."

"Yes, but there are principles on both sides – and I simply don't know what you mean by stooping."

The small boy had now detached himself from the women and was slowly dawdling himself toward us round the table – that hideous table of yellow oak that they have in waiting rooms. He had reached the near corner, and was leaning against it, dribbling lollipop, with one finger up his nose, and his eyes fixed upon me with a round vacant gaze like that of a very young calf staring at a pump. This stare irritated me very much and I spoke rather loudly, and I dare say the women heard, because they also stared and I thought the flowers in their bonnets seemed quite stiff with curiosity and excitement. The man was staring, too, but with rather a scornful expression as at a foreigner who does not know how to behave.

And suddenly I did begin to argue about religion (because, of course, that was what he was arguing about) and I said that I knew, of course, that Mr Goold would threaten me with some terrible punishment from heaven, but I didn't think that was a very nice idea. "Mr Goold no doubt thinks of everybody as stooping or being stooped to – but I don't like a God that is always trying to put people in their places and to make them suffer if they don't behave humbly."

Chester slightly moved his hand (it was only as if to brush my nonsense away) and said, "All the same, we have to fear Him; or let us say if you like, we have to fear the consequence of doing wrong – the sin against love."

This made that old terror start up inside me; the very word love made a nerve jump. I looked again at Chester and thought, "He can't believe I stooped to him – it's simply a trick," and I said coolly, "I simply don't understand Mr Goold's religion."

"Naturally your ideas are different – I was speaking of our work together. And what I'm so afraid of is that you are being hurried into a decision that will spoil your life – I don't speak of mine or his. Is your cousin a man whose judgment can be relied on? I should have thought that you were the more responsible person. All I beg is that you will take a little time to think things over. You needn't be afraid that I'll try to influence you. If you come back now you will be left entirely to yourself. I could go away if you liked – "

But I could not bear any more argument and said, "Why 'naturally'? My ideas are just my own ideas – it's nothing to do with our difference as you call it."

I suddenly noticed the child's dirty sticky hand on my frock; it had come close up, attracted, I suppose, like all children, by someone in misery (children are like flies for knowing where a wound is and buzzing about it), and it was staring into my face. But I did not care what happened to my frock, even if it was for Jim, or what was overheard. I was thinking that my last argument had been quite nonsense, because, in fact, we were different and the difference was due to our education and the ideas we had been brought up with. And I said quite loudly, "The only difference is that I would never even think about stooping. And as for what we have done, are you sure it is so good – I mean in politics? You know very well Cousin Slapton and poor old Major Freer are nothing like baby-starvers. Is it so good to make bitterness and hatred – even if it has helped you on and even if you do get into Parliament?" (I said this to show that he was not really so high-minded about his work; he was thinking of his career, too, in case my going away should hurt it.) "But, of course, you will say that it's *natural* for me to think like that. *Naturally* I'm different and I stoop."

And when he seemed about to say something, I went on quickly, "And if you think it's *natural* for me to treat you badly – I can't help it. You must go on thinking it. I can't come back now. It's too late."

Then he jumped up, kissed my cheek and walked out on the platform and out of the station.

33 I was astonished at this sudden move on Chester's part and thought, "The confidence trick again with a little bit of trust in God added." But the astonishment remained and it set some nerve tingling which joggled all my inside. I kept sitting with my chin in the air, looking quite dignified (for the man was still scorning and the women were still wondering, and the child in its fascinated state actually climbing onto my lap and dribbling down my front), and saying to myself, "Yes, he used that quiet voice on purpose; he knew that I wouldn't expect it. He has never used that tone before. And to talk about the sin against love when all he wants is to get into Parliament! And why 'naturally'? But that's another trick – like 'stooping'." And these two words kept flying about inside my head like starlings that have fallen down a chimney into a room. It did not matter what I thought of Chester and whether he was playing tricks or not, because I could not think. I only felt a fearful indignation like a violent headache and those frightened words whirling and beating everywhere and knocking fragile things down.

I found myself grasping the handle of my bag as if it were the only clear sensible decision in my possession.

Suddenly the women got up and began to fuss about their baskets. One of them came across the room to give me a last stare, grabbed the little boy by the arm and jerked him almost upside down, saying, "What are you doing, Alby? Didn't I tell you not to go mauling at people's dresses!"

Then the train came in, and the women went out to catch it, dragging the little boy (he was still looking back over his shoulder at me, though I am sure he didn't know why), and I got up with my bag and followed them. But when I reached the door my feet stopped and turned me aside. I simply could not go out, and neither could I make up my mind to stay. I went a step to one side, and then came back to the door, but absolutely stuck there. I seemed to have no will to do anything, or rather I had two wills which were fighting inside me and tearing me apart. I can never forget the agony of that time, which must actually have lasted three or four minutes before the train went out. And really I think it was a kind of relief to me when at last it did so, for it made a decision for me. It ended that agony; and though it ended only in a kind of despair, it was more bearable. It was like the pain after a tooth has been pulled out – an aching pain when you know that you are bleeding fast and you feel weak, and your head is singing with the gas, and the world is only just assembling itself and turning into a really solid world again, but still you know that the crisis is over.

So after a minute or two (for I felt very shaky) I walked out of the station again, giving up my new ticket, which the man gave back to me (I found it the other day after thirty years in an envelope marked with the date, and showed it to Jim; for some reason I had put it carefully away), and took a fly to Palm Cottage.

I went to Palm Cottage, because I could not bear the thought of being in the same house with Chester, even if he did not "influence" me – I knew that he was influencing me all the time. That was what I was fighting against.

I explained to Aunt that I was not well, and in fact when I went to bed I felt very ill and wrote at once to Jim to say that he should not come for me yet because I was not fit to go out. But that I was his for ever. And I asked Aunt Latter at once how long it would be before Chester got his nomination at Battwell, and she said it might be any day now – certainly not more than a week. So I decided to stay in bed for a week.

Aunt Latter, of course, had by that time discovered the whole, or almost the whole, story, and she had never been so furious with me. For one thing, her whole plan for Jim was ruined, because Cousin Slapton had refused him the agency on the grounds that he could not afford to countenance a scandal (the whole county was talking about us) which would infuriate all the radicals. What is more, he blamed Aunt Latter for encouraging Jim to flirt with me. And, of course, Aunt Latter, knowing very well that she had done something stupid, was the more furious with everybody, including herself.

But to my surprise she did not abuse me. She glared – it was obvious that she would have liked to beat me – but she pretended to believe that I was really ill and even coddled me. And the reason was, of course, that she, like Chester, was in terror that I would ruin Chester's chance at Battwell.

She talked to me every day about the situation at Battwell (the member had had a stroke and she was sure he would have another quite soon and die) and how important it was for a candidate in a country place to have a "respectable home life".

All this, of course, made me more wretched. I felt as if I were being slowly pressed to death, like those wretched people who would not tell the judge whether they were guilty or not guilty – I thought that very likely they did not know, the thing was too complicated.

Chester perfectly understood my feelings. He put it about that I was ill and treated me like a sick person. He brought me flowers every day, but even when he came to my room he did not approach the bed, but said polite things from the door, and smiled (an extraordinary "false" smile – a kind of wide toothy grin; it was the kind of smile you see on a child's face when he wants to "get round" you but knows you know it), and suddenly disappeared.

It was through Aunt Latter that he suggested that I needed a change. "Go up for a week or two in town and look at the shops and do some theatres and buy some clothes. You could stay at Johnson's."

I said that I did not need a change and I certainly could not go to Johnson's, which was the most expensive hotel in Britain.

Chester answered (again through Aunt) that Johnson's was my "family hotel", meaning that Bob and Cousin Slapton used it. He added (this was a new idea) that Aunt should go with me – he would be too busy for the moment.

Aunt, who loved Johnson's, at once became very eager,

and at last I agreed, only because it would take me further from Chester.

For though I could not blame Chester for his "noble" manoeuvres, I felt a deep anger against him.

But also I was more and more disgusted. I said to myself, "Everyone is scandalized by my behaviour, but, to be fair to myself, I am not really a bad woman – not very bad. For one thing, I am too lazy. In fact, I am a very ordinary kind of woman who simply wants to be happy without giving too much trouble and can, in fact, be happy quite easily. It is really thoroughly unjust that I should have got mixed up with such an extraordinary person as Chester, who uses his religion to torture me and his class hatred to tie me to him till I can hardly breathe."

It was this idea that I had been picked out by fate for specially bad treatment that filled me with resentment. And, of course, all my anger centred on Chester. I felt for him that special hatred one feels toward people who take up a position of moral superiority and use it to domineer over one. The better they are, the more one hates them.

And now that I had time to reflect on my life with him, I saw very clearly that he had already destroyed most of my happiness, and unless I was absolutely firm and rather hard he would wreck my life.

34 It has been said quite openly and it is passionately believed that I was Chester's ruin: that I not only "corrupted" him morally but forced him into luxury and extravagance; that I divided him from his best friends and destroyed his religion; that, in fact, it would have been much better for him if I had caught that train. But again the truth is quite different from the facts and much more complicated. For instance, in this case it was Chester's own policy to give me this expensive "holiday" and to buy me new clothes. I hated the very idea of either, and I was very much against his proposal to ask Goold for a loan. I pointed out to Aunt that Goold hated me and that we owed him too much money already. But Chester paid no attention to this and went to Goold that same day.

Goold had been a great help to us in the last years. He had made a great deal of money in the war by a lucky deal in tinned meat and now had a new shop in Tarbiton High Street as well as an even bigger one in Lilmouth. And he had always said that anything he had was for Chester, too – his money was the gift of God and should be used for God's work.

But lately there had been a coolness. About three months before, Goold had shocked all his friends by engaging himself to a young farm servant, just seventeen, without education or even looks. She could barely write her name, even in large print, and had a round pink face set, almost without a neck, on a round thick body, and immense legs.

Chester said this disaster had come about from Goold's modesty, but Aunt Latter's view was (and it was borne out later) that he was taken by the girl's extreme shyness and docility. "Gooseface Goold," she said, "is the sort of rat who is terrified of women. That's why he is such a brute to them, and why he has picked this silly sheep."

I had seen the girl on the moor (she worked at one of Aunt Latter's two little farms) and she had often milked me a jug of fresh milk for a picnic. I thought of her chiefly as extraordinarily tongue-tied. She would lean her great cheek against the cow's ribs (it would bulge out sideways and quite shut up her eye, already small enough; she had the smallest little Dresden blue eyes, real "peepers") and present to me her enormous hips in a spotted blue print, while her great pink hands and mottled arms pumped up and down. But she had a shy broad grin (which caused both her eyes to disappear at once) which made one feel suddenly cheerful and also fond of her. So I had not been so much against the engagement, and I had felt, besides, that Goold would be more civilized with a wife who could be asked to tea, and with whom one could make real contact through babies and maternal problems.

But as I say, Chester had said something to Goold about the danger of his marrying beneath himself, and now when he went to borrow there was a bitter quarrel. Goold said that Chester's marriage of which he had been so proud had made him a byword as the deceived husband and that I had led him to the devil. And Chester lost his temper and said something to the effect that Goold was the laughing stock for being caught by a silly lump like Daisy, who had nothing to commend her but youth and fat.

Chester was so furious after this quarrel that he even tried to prevent his friends from dealing at Goold's shops, and did, I believe, actually damage his trade, at least for a short time. As for the money, he borrowed more than a thousand pounds elsewhere, on mortgage, to pay Goold's debt and also to meet the expense of my "change of air", and this debt was the beginning of his more serious financial troubles. But the reason was not that I wanted luxury at Johnson's (he dispatched me there, with Aunt as chaperon, as soon as he had raised the loan) but because his plan was to give it to me, as part of my "cure".

And, of course, I saw through the scheme from the beginning. Chester was playing the great "putting off" trick.

Lots of people, of course, put off some unpleasant moment because simply they can't bear to face it, but

Chester had a regular policy of putting off. He would even put off a meeting to see if things would "come his way" – if the other side would make a slip.

But now, of course, I was only the more disgusted. I said to myself that "putting off" was too obvious a trick – it could never alter my feelings, which were real and true, much less the facts of what had happened in the garden.

35 And now something happened, quite unexpectedly, which promised to make the facts a thousand times stronger. For I began to suspect I might be pregnant (and I knew by certain dates that only Jim could be responsible); and though at the moment this discovery made me still more wretched (because I felt again how weak I had been to turn back from the station), it also settled a big problem – the big problem. "That will decide it," I thought. "Chester won't be able to argue any more."

And from this time, I think there is no doubt that the luxury (and I was too unhappy to care that Chester had planned it so) which I had so despised began to tell on me. It was like an anaesthetic, which changes all your flesh before an operation. I remember that hotel not as a prison where I suffered torture (though my real position grew worse every day as I had more and more reason to fear that I was pregnant) but as a kind of nightmare palace where I was obliged to live in a ritual of majestic calm misery.

And it seems to me that though I was in such perpetual wretchedness, it was more bearable because I had to carry it in a dignified manner (and in new expensive clothes – Chester had instructed Aunt to get me some clothes, and I did not fight her; she was still being very kind, very tactful, but obviously with great difficulty), through padded corridors and past rows of looking glasses, which reflected back to me not an agonized face but simply myself in a rather becoming frock, looking only a little dark under the eyes, which suited them very well by making them look more blue.

It was as though thick carpets, and velvet curtains, and soft upholstery, and deep mattresses, as they took the noise out of steps, and the resonance out of voices, also took the vibration out of feeling. I was in pain, but it was a steady pain – it did not throb.

And the next thing was, after a week, that I began to "take notice", as they say of a sick person who is turning the corner and who would be fearfully bored if he did not begin to "do things". I opened the morning paper (though in a dignified sad way) when it came to me in bed, and at table in my conversations with Aunt I discussed the news from Africa or China quite politely – indeed I began to feel again what Aunt and Chester always made me feel, whether I liked it or not, that a perfect storm of history was raging over us all the time and it was rather weak and small to shut one's eyes to it.

There is no doubt, in fact, that Johnson's made me more "reasonable". I suppose that is why rich people are, on the whole, so reasonable. I know few more reasonable people than my cousins Slapton and Connybeare.

And one morning, when Chester suddenly appeared (Aunt tactfully vanished at once to an "important engagement") I found myself shaking hands with him as with an old acquaintance.

I did not even protest very much when he proposed to take me shopping in Bond Street and bought me still another expensive frock. For I knew already that he grew angry and suspicious when I tried to refuse presents from him. He looked upon it as a kind of insult. And, of course, it was part of his idea of me as a "lady" that I needed a great deal of spoiling and especially loved to have money spent on me.

While there is no doubt that Chester himself loved to spend money. He was not a scatterer like Jim, who never even thought about money, but he loved to feel money in his pockets so that he could dash it down on the counter and feel like a king.

So I did not argue about the frock. I thought, "It is all in his schemes and I'm not going to fight about trifles."

Indeed, I realized that our relations were quite different. For all that had happened to us seemed like an event elsewhere; I mean things that have happened elsewhere and have therefore got rolled up into an event – which is something you have to accept and can talk about.

I even felt sorry for Chester when I thought, "Poor little man! Here he is planning and scheming, and going to fearful extravagance to please me or tie me up in obligations. What will he say when he finds out that, after all, I am carrying Jim's baby – that he will have to give me my divorce?"

36 For Chester, I could see, was now very confident of winning me over. I would catch an expression on his face as he stood before me in the lounge, looking down at me, which was exactly his expression before a hostile meeting; even more, when he walked across the floor to pull the bell (Chester was a great bell-ringer in hotels – he was always rather fierce with menservants) a look at once resolute, but also confident and joyful (Chester had a lot of expression – like lions – in his legs and back and the way he carried himself), as if to say, "They're very sure of themselves, these ladies and their minions; but I'll show 'em – I'll change their tune."

I meant to have a complete explanation as soon as I was quite sure of my state. But it happened that very same evening he became very complimentary. He made me put on his favourite, and the most expensive, of the new frocks, though I protested that it was too elaborate (he liked me in rather bright colours, which was why some people thought his taste vulgar) and also too low especially for a dinner by ourselves in a hotel; and when I came down, he said, "My dear, I never saw you look lovelier – you must agree that we chose the right dress for you – really most beautiful though it is so simple" (it was "simple" only by Tarbiton tastes; frocks from Exeter at that time were covered with frills and flounces). "But, of course, the material is thoroughly good; nothing like a Macclesfield silk, a pure silk. Yes, beautiful; and it suits you to perfection, it has such distinction – such purity of line."

What he meant was not only "You are looking beautiful and distinguished in that frock which I bought at such expense to do you credit" but also he was suggesting to me (or trying to inject into me) the feeling that simplicity, and goodness, and purity, and even perhaps British silk (because it had no foreign insincerity or tariffs about it), were the highest beauty, and that if I wanted to be perfect in beauty I ought to study them.

And this sudden attempt to apply a moral lesson (it was more than a month since he had prayed over me) startled me – I was out of practice in bearing it. Also perhaps, as I was feeling "important" to him, I was annoyed that he did not treat me with more circumspection. In any case, I burst out (but quite quietly – the waiter was close by) and said, yes, it was a nice dress, but I was not feeling so nice myself because of a certain something that he had probably guessed, that would make it impossible for us to keep on putting things off. Unless there was an election quite soon, I should not even look respectable.

Chester, who was eating a chocolate pudding which I knew would upset him (but in our new relation I could not tell him so), simply answered, as if he had not heard me, "Battwell – yes – it's a tricky constituency with all those hill farms and peculiar people. The sitting member was nearly beaten last time because someone saw him at the theatre in Lilmouth." And then he went on to say how important it was for me to visit the constituency with him. "Voters like a candidate to be happily married."

Chester could always astonish as much by a piece of cunning as by seeming to have no tact at all. I was so taken aback by the last suggestion that I looked at him in amazement, whereupon he smiled in a radiant manner (a little too radiant) and said, "You might turn the scale – I'm sure that electioneering duchess was not half so pretty."

I answered, of course, that this was absolutely impossible; but he went on eating his pudding (a second help) as if I had not spoken. And I thought, looking at him, "Does he really think he can treat me like a mouse in a bottle? Does he think me so weak and wobbly?"

I said no more then (I could not argue such a point in front of the waiter), but I sent for him next morning (he had taken a single room for the night) and told him I was feeling sick.

"And I'm afraid, Chester, that is quite definite, because, as you know or perhaps you don't know, that when Tom was beginning I was sickish almost at once." And I was going on to say how sorry I was but at least the situation was now cleared up and we could come to a definite arrangement, when Chester interrupted me, "My dear, this is wonderful news!" leaned over and kissed me tenderly (but in the kiss, a long rather hard kiss, I thought he was trying to warn or threaten), and then, before I could utter another word, vanished out of the room. Half an hour later great bouquets of flowers and a large bottle of scent arrived, and also a note begging me to stay in bed that morning, and saying that he might not be back for an hour because he had an unexpected engagement.

37 But, in fact, I did not see him again till that afternoon, when he came in with Aunt Latter and told me that he had been summoned urgently to an important conference in Tarbiton, so he would leave me in Aunt Latter's "good hands" for a day or two till he could come back. And both of them fussed over me as if I were an invalid, but taking care that I was not left alone with Chester.

I saw, of course, that Chester had brought Aunt Latter simply in order to prevent my confessing anything. And I looked at Chester really with horror; it seemed to me that he was capable of the boldest (but also the stupidest) villainies. I burst out at him, "Really, Chester, you can't shut me up like this. No, it's impossible, and stupid, too – because I can't bear it – no one could."

Chester had to hear so far, but I'll never forget the look he gave me as he made for the door, so fierce, so cunning, as if he would have liked to bite me, but in some place which would not damage his property. In a moment he had gone, and I jumped out of bed to dress (meaning to follow him and make him understand that I was in earnest). Aunt Latter said, only in her driest tone, "Perhaps you will condescend to tell me what all this fuss is about?"

I told her in ten words (though I am sure she knew; her question was only a trick to get me into an argument) and pointed out why I could not stay with Chester.

Aunt Latter said only, "So that's it. You really are quite the most worthless young woman of my acquaintance. But none of the Woodvilles were ever good for anything except amusing themselves at other people's expense." I said that might be so – goodness knows I was not proud of myself. But I was in love with Jim; I had always been in love with Jim. And as for Chester, he had always treated me like a ninny, and I never wanted to see him again. "I don't know why the man wants to keep me when he despises me so much."

Aunt listened to this with a screwed-up face of fearful disgust and said that she, too, could not imagine why Chester wanted me, but she did not pretend to understand men, anyhow, or their tastes, and what he wanted me for was his own business. But as for love, she said (and I can't describe the drawl of contempt and loathing with which she pronounced the word), "What you mean exactly by that I should much like to know. I do know friendship and family loyalty and decent feeling and common gratitude and reasonable conduct and self-respect; and I know, too, what it is for a lazy spoiled creature to read novels and throw herself into the arms of any young fool of an idle young man who has the misfortune to come within reach of her. Why, what would you do with Jim if you got him at last? What have you always done with the poor wretch? Driven him out of his wits with your airs and graces."

Then suddenly coming over to the sofa and fairly raging at me, "And you send Chester off to fight his first election alone! Do you *want* him to lose the only chance he may ever get?" And she added these surprising words, "I know it's useless to appeal to your better feelings, but as you pretend to have some affection for Jim you might have reflected on his very bad position and how important it might be for him to have a friend in Parliament."

Though I did not pay any attention to Aunt's views on love (she had suffered too much in love to know anything about it), I was startled by her vehemence, which stopped my own wrath like one wave hitting another. And I was able for the first time to see the important *fact* that if Chester lost the election I might have to blame myself for it.

How, I asked myself, would I be able to desert a man in such a bad misfortune? "Yes," I thought, "and with nothing to live on but what's left of my money."

And so, though I did not at that time *really* believe in Chester's career (I suppose very few young wives do *really* believe in their husbands' careers, they haven't enough experience to know that even very ordinary young men have careers), I assumed an indifferent air and said that, very well, if Chester wanted me to parade with him I could do it, but it would be his fault if it made things worse for him later. And I absolutely could not go back to the Orchard.

Aunt and Chester at once accepted this plan. Rooms were taken at a seaside hotel (for my "health"), and Aunt was able to put me in the train and carry me off in triumph.

And (except for the fact that my whole motive was to get away from Chester) she had good reason. For the more I thought of it, the more I realized how important it was for me (in the selfish sense) that Chester should have a big success. I was extremely anxious to help him – to be driven through the streets in a landau, with Tommy on my knee, to address letters, to canvass the back lanes and Slapton tenants, and to go to chapel tea parties.

Already we were very busy, for in the same week the Tarbiton seat (not Battwell, where, in any case, Goold, still raging against us, had managed to nominate a Baptist) unexpectedly became vacant; the member went bankrupt and had to retire. Chester, being the most obvious local choice, was nominated and we were thrown at once into the turmoil of a desperate election.

38 I suppose nearly everyone has taken part in an election, but no one who has not fought in one of those "revolutionary" elections at the beginning of this century, when people really thought that they were within reach of a marvellous new world of peace and comfort and universal happiness, can even imagine the excitement of them or how one could be carried away by enthusiasm for one's own side and scorn and hatred for the other.

It may show the kind of atmosphere in which we lived during those three weeks, that when an old family friend, Mr Mockley, who was a Unionist liberal, made a statement against Chester's Irish policy (and the Irish vote was absolutely essential to us), I literally could not speak to him. When he came smiling to shake hands (I meant to be polite at least) my hand simply jumped away from his and then my eyes looked through him and my legs (trembling with shame as well as political indignation) walked past him. And in the same way when Jim wrote furious letters, suggesting that I was being "kept from him", and threatening to come and "have it out" with Chester, I was quite horrified by such a suggestion. I answered by return begging him to be patient (pointing out that, on account of my condition alone, I was absolutely his – it was only a question of time before I came to him for good), with long explanations of the critical position at Tarbiton, and how terribly important it was for both our sakes that Chester should win.

And though it was true that I was "being kept" from Jim, such was the whirl of affairs in which I lived that Jim's indignation seemed a little out of place. "What is he worrying about?" I thought, while rushing from the committee room to the printers to order new posters denying the charge in the new Conservative poster that Chester "stood for nationalism of the land" (he did, but only in private – the Conservative poster was a lie and a dangerous one among our small farmers). "Doesn't he realize what an election means?"

Indeed, the position was very critical – that poster had done a lot of harm. All of us were working from morning to night. Chester himself was speaking ten and twelve times a day, often at meetings which tried to yell him down and threatened to duck him. He showed, that is, all his courage and good humour, his marvellous resourcefulness. The women, especially, adored him and were quite comically jealous of me as his wife.

It was just about then, too (in the last mad ten days), that I found myself all at once surrounded by solicitous looks. I was always being urged to take care of myself, to sit down; being wrapped up in shawls and tenderly inquired for. And I discovered that it had been put about by Chester's agent that I was in a certain condition and that only my devotion to Chester and "the cause" had brought me, at the very grave danger of a miscarriage, to help him in his great fight.

I was quite furious at this low electioneering trick. I knew that only Aunt or Chester could have invented it, for no one could have noticed any change in my appearance yet except that I was apt to be a little pale in the mornings.

I went straight to Chester and asked him if he had put out the story. He was in the street, under the door of the hotel (it was raining), waiting for the gig which was to take him to an open-air meeting. He looked from the sky to me with an air of impatience and said, "Tack" (the agent) "thought it a good idea; it's been noticed that we're in separate rooms."

"But, Chester, you know that we have to be in separate rooms."

"I don't see why – and it's encouraging some dangerous gossip."

This cool remark startled me very much. For the very rush of the election, the daily contact with Chester at his "most political" (and if he was brave, he was also cunning, as appeared at that moment), made me realize even more strongly how false our relation had become, how cynical it was even to think of patching up our marriage while I was pregnant by the man I truly loved, how impossible it would be for Chester and me to have any peace or security together. I felt horror at the thought when I imagined Chester "being nice" to me and playing the "good papa".

And I burst out, "You don't imagine that we can really start again?"

Chester made no answer to this. Then, as the gig came rocking up, he looked again at the sky and said, "If polling day is like this we'll probably lose. Some of the poorer old men can't face the wet – they haven't the clothes for it." And as he climbed into the gig, he called over his shoulder, "Did you get those cards off?"

And when I went to Tack, and he told me that the story (he did not even apologize for it) might bring in a hundred waverers (chapel people who had heard gossip about Chester's marriage), might even "do the trick", I began, much to the man's irritation, to laugh rather wildly, saying that Chester certainly knew how to turn everything to account. Several girls, frantically sorting canvas cards in the next room, then came running with glasses of water, and I had to pretend to be faint or I might have laughed myself silly.

And yet, only a day later (but it was the day of the poll),
I found myself playing this very "low trick", and even more
deceitfully, for I went out so pale (with a little powder
added) and so dark under the eyes (with a little "bronze")
that Chester himself was alarmed for me and wanted to
send me to bed for the morning, when, as I pointed out, I
needed every moment of it to canvass the brewery
workmen, doubtful supporters who might still be
persuaded to vote for our side, because I was Wilfred's
cousin and they had known me all my life.

As you know, Chester won the election by a bare fifty-six
votes on a recount, and afterwards we were carried from
the Town Hall literally head-high among what seemed like
millions of lunatics, yelling and singing and trying to kiss
our hands and clothes and even our boots; so that when we
found ourselves at last alone in the top corridor of the
hotel, we were quite staggering with weariness and drunk
with triumph.

But we were still talking both at once about that
extraordinary last day (we had so much to tell each other)
and I was describing how my shoes had been pulled off
(perhaps for souvenirs), and he was saying that it was the
turning point. But had I seen the printer's bill? And then he
. began to laugh and tell some story about a supporter who
had gone to the wrong meeting with a slogan in his hat and
been chased out of the window. And, holding my elbow as
if to support me (both of us were so tired that we could
hardly stand and yet everything was still happening to us –
the cheers and boos and congratulations were bouncing
about in that fearful tiredness like heavy wreckage after a
storm), he stopped at my door and, laughing still, said,
"After twenty-five years."

And his laugh was different. He had an expression that I

115

had not seen before, naive and childishly frank. "I can tell you what no one else knows – that I promised myself this when I was Bing's office boy in second-hand trousers. I didn't know how it was to be done, but I said I should do it if it cost me my life. And I don't know quite how it has been done. But I do know what to do with it – you'll see."

"Nothing can stop you now," I said. "Oh, how glad I am that you're in." And truly I was glad – it was an enormous relief.

I was pushing the door open, but I now found that Chester was following me into the doorway – we were both halfway through. So I stopped where I was, thinking, "Here's a new trick" (I was quite amused to notice it), "but it won't succeed. I'll simply wait here. How silly he is, with all his cleverness, not to see that the essential situation is just the same – it rests on solid facts."

Suddenly his face changed (and even in that moment I thought he had *prepared* the contrast); he looked at me with such worn and anxious features that he seemed a different man, old and harried, and he said slowly, "Yes, I could do something that matters. It's the biggest chance – if it isn't wasted."

And in that fraction of a second I discovered how wrong I had been to think that nothing could be changed in the "real" situation because it rested on "too solid facts".

When you are dealing with men like Chester facts simply turn round the other way; and as for situations, it is their business to change them.

For one thing, I saw for the first time (feeling its presence for the first time) that though it might have been hard to leave the man breaking his heart, if he had failed, it was even harder to do so when he had succeeded at last "after twenty-five years".

And when, in a panic, I tried to feel again the "certainty" of my new "real" love for Jim, I found nothing but a confused sense, not of passion, but of something that had happened – of something historical – and something, too, that, like old history, had been gathering footnotes and qualifications so fast (such as "Aren't you the more responsible person") that it conveyed no more useful advice than history generally does.

As for being weak or wobbling, I have never been able to tell whether it is weaker to do something stupid because you don't want to seem wobbly or to change your mind because you have been weak before.

I opened my mouth to say something about my "position", but Chester (he knew I was beaten before I knew it myself) had already put his arm round my waist and I knew with real "certainty" that what was "impossible" for me was taking the risk of his being wasted.

I made no protest at all as he drew me into my own room and shut the door; I was conscious of a despair so enormous that I did not want to think.

39 Now I have to explain what happened on this occasion because of this other charge that "I corrupted" my poor husband, not only in soul but body. It is obvious, of course, that people, simply because they are in the same house or family (or only meet once at a dance), do change each other in various ways (and Jim, when I wrote to him explaining why, after all, I could not be his, answered that it had been the worst bad luck of his life to know such an absolutely rotten woman), and especially husband and wife. For they are influencing each other all the time. They make all sorts of discoveries about each other's minds and feelings and accommodate themselves to them, and so they produce a situation which is the marriage; and (I suppose) a marriage is like a climate as well as a tradition – it does change bodies as well as souls.

Now in my despair at what had happened to me so unexpectedly and to my whole future, I was anxious only to "put Chester off", to be "with myself" even if he stayed in my bed. And as I say, I knew Chester for a man (and Jim was the same in this respect but for a different reason – that is, Jim did not have religious feelings but only wanted to be sure that he was a success) who could not be happy unless he felt that I was being happy at the same time (and, after all, it is a great pleasure to know that the other enjoys giving one pleasure); and so in my desperation I was suddenly inspired to show him (with him it needed only the slightest indication which would seem almost accidental) something of what Jim had revealed to me. And the result was even more surprising (but both of us were in such a fever of weariness that we were a little unbalanced), so that Chester was, at first, quite astonished. He was even a little alarmed as if he had upset me too much. But then, he could hardly express his joy and excitement. For (what I had not foreseen) he took this very natural achievement (just as I had done with Jim) as a sign that we were at last "at one".

And how could I have explained to him that my whole idea (completely the opposite of what it had been with Jim) was to avoid "oneness"? I was astonished myself by the result of my inspiration. Besides, as I realized at once, just because of his "religious" view of love and marriage he was very innocent and could not have realized (even if I had tried to explain it, which was impossible – it would have brought down on me all the force of his evangelism) that I had been so responsive simply from a natural cause and that I had led him into my new "Indian" discovery, simply from anxiety to make a success of the difficult new beginning, and to hold him off from digging into my soul.

But it did not happen so with my nervous, passionate, fanciful husband. For it was from this night (I nearly put fatal night, for so it was nearly fatal) that he fell into a real passion of love, so that he even looked at me differently, and he spoke to me in a different voice (two or three different voices), and when he touched even my arm through a sleeve his fingers seemed to say, "my wife."

40 Immediately after the election Chester put me in a first-class carriage (from this time he always took me first, though alone by himself he travelled third) and carried me back to London, to find (as he said) a "nest". But he did not look far. He went straight to a big house on the Embankment (in that imposing terrace which used to be called Grosvenor Parade) and asked me how I liked it.

The house looked enormous and it was in very bad repair. Windows were broken and its ugly yellow paint was falling off in patches as if it had smallpox.

I said at once that it was much too big; we could never afford it. "And isn't it a Slapton property?"

"Yes, but he's going to reduce the rent."

"I should think so. It's been empty for five years, and it's almost a ruin. Cousin Porty calls it the yellow elephant. How much is the new rent?"

"Two hundred a year."

"Good gracious! Chester, how could we pay such a sum even if we let the Orchard?"

"It's the only house I've seen with a river view."

"But, Chester, I should hate the view if it was ruining us – and it's only poor old Thames dirty water."

In fact the whole scheme appeared quite crazy. The election had cost us more than a thousand pounds, which was nearly half our remaining capital. Chester had won by a very narrow margin (against a lot of opposition from the Baptists, who had wanted a candidate of their own), and the next general election was years away. But Chester took the house (ignoring my arguments, as if he had not heard them), and I am bound to admit that I should have hated to live anywhere in the world with no view but the other side of the street and rows of windows staring at me all day, like spies.

But those, like Goold, who said at once that this house was chosen only to please my luxurious tastes, were quite wrong. Chester wanted a view for me and a sunny nursery for Tom, but he wanted also a centre for his own schemes. And, in fact, before we had the rooms half furnished he began to entertain and to hold conferences and committees, which made the house more like a public building than a "nest".

A good many people (like myself) were surprised at the extravagant way in which Chester now, as soon as he was elected, began to "branch out" in all directions. A good many people said that it was a case of swelled head and that he would soon ruin himself all round.

In fact Chester's "mad extravagance" in taking this house and spending so much money on his new committees and propaganda was all deliberately planned; and if you say it was a wild gamble, and (together with my bad influence) did put him on the road to ruin, you will have to admit also that (together with my money and connections) it gave him the chance of achieving that importance which obliged the party, when at last there was a general election, to reckon with him – that the gamble, as they say, "came off".

And when one looks at other successful men, one has to admit that most of them have "taken big chances" and might have been called at some time in their lives swellheads and gamblers.

41 When I first knew the man Bootham (called Chester's evil genius) he was an assistant in Goold's Fore Street shop. He was then a lanky gangling boy, more than six feet high, with enormous hands and feet, a long neck and a long stupid nose. Long noses are usually intelligent, but when they are stupid they are stupider than buttons.

Bootham had a nose like a sheep and the same solemn expression. While he stood quite still (which he was fond of doing, as if in deep reflection) he looked extremely wise, but the slightest call upon his wits, a question about anything (the price of sardines), would cause him to leap into a panic, which was quite justified, for he seldom knew the answer. He was the kind of overwhelmed young man for whom you are very sorry until you have to do with him and find out how slyly and crookedly he does the simplest things.

Bootham was some relation of Goold's, who gave him his place in the shop and then tried to get him into Bing's, who would not look at him.

If you wonder how such a person came to be so important in our household, the answer is that he came in a bargain and stayed as a spy.

I say that Chester had never been so much in love with me and in a most "religious" way. This does not mean that he went on being "noble". It was quite the opposite, and I look back on this time of success and glory when we first came to town as the most terrible in my whole life. For he set to work at once to put a guard upon me and to cut me off from my friends. He was from this time a very jealous husband.

I said that Goold's quarrel with Chester had nearly cost us (to Chester's surprise) even the Tarbiton seat. This worried Chester very much; and on the very morning after our "new beginning" when I waked up feeling indescribably worn and sick (as if all my bones had been taken out and my skin filled up with sour cold porridge), it was to hear him say in an indignant tone that he was bitterly disappointed in Ted Goold. It was shocking that a man in his position should put "a private spite before his public duty" – his public duty (as I thought as far as I could think anything in the midst of my headache) being to make Chester's seat safe for the next election.

But I was quite ready to do my duty as a political wife, when about a month later (we were in the middle of our move to London) Chester came to me and said that Goold and Daisy were to pass through town on their way home from the continent (he knew even the dates and the hotel where they were to stay – he had already his "sources of information") and asked me to call and make myself pleasant to Daisy. I liked the plan all the more because I liked Daisy and was glad to escape from the pressure at "our nest", which was full of Wesleyan ministers and furniture movers.

So when the day came I went to the hotel (a temperance boarding house in Pimlico; Goold was now quite rich but he did not approve of "spoiling" Daisy with luxuries), and after some difficulty in finding anyone to do anything for anybody, got a queer little servant to take up my name; and down at once came Daisy Goold, laughing from ear to ear and declaring that I had come "on the nick", because Ted was out to the barber's and she was just fretting herself to pieces for "summat to do". Daisy and I, in fact, were at once happy together, and this was the beginning of what was called the "wives' conspiracy". But there was no disloyalty in Daisy – it would be even more unfair to accuse her of plotting against her master than it is to say that I "ruined" Chester. And, in fact, when I hear now that so and so has spoiled her husband's life I always wonder how her own life would have turned out with a different husband.

Daisy, in fact, had already been wonderfully "spoiled" by her marriage. She had lost all her shyness and, therefore, most of her manners. She laughed and talked all the time, and in five minutes, as soon as she had put on her hat to come shopping with me, and gone fifty yards in my cab, she was being almost embarrassingly confidential. For (and this is where Chester and Goold were wrong in thinking that I encouraged Daisy in her "rebelliousness") she had from the beginning little respect for Goold. She was a very simple person, and very simple people, I think, do not respect anybody. They haven't enough imagination. Daisy Goold, in short, had the usual idea of the village girl that men were somehow comic, and she was full of stories about Goold's comical ways. Yet she was in the greatest awe of him, and said that his temper "fair curdled her blood".

As for my "rather sudden friendship with that lump", as Chester called it, I myself was surprised by the pleasure I had in Daisy's company. But the men's notion (a pretty common one among Tarbiton husbands, who think that any two wives seen laughing together are laughing at them) that we spent our time planning extravagance and deceit at their expense was just as absurd as the idea among some women that men left alone together talk of nothing but "the sex".

I was delighted in Daisy because she was so frank and amusing; she was like a breath from the moor, and the moor had always meant a special joy of freedom to me.

I think, indeed, that one reason why I revelled in this meeting was simply that I felt so disgraced. As Jim said, I had let everybody down all round. What a joy to be with Daisy, who did not care what I had done!

And at this first meeting as wives (first meetings are the most important – they set the tone for the rest) we were not only both escaping from possessive husbands but Daisy was in her eighth month and I in my fourth (much bigger than I had been with Tom), so that we were at once on special terms – and, to tell the truth, laughing terms. Our own appearance together (Daisy was about five feet high and thick by nature) was a standing joke – quite apart from Daisy's extraordinary confessions about Goold, who was apparently a very "nervous" and "orkard" as well as "cross" kind of partner.

Daisy had Goold's leave to buy some London clothes (and I was buying curtains), and we went to various expensive shops. Like other people who have been very poor, Daisy had no idea of money and put everything on the bill. Neither would she take any advice. She would demand it, but she did not even seem to hear it. When I advised her against an enormously high feathered hat, she said, "Ees, 'tis too gay; they'll never stand for that at Tarbiton," and then at once bought it. She was not so much obstinate as unable to resist her fancy. Yet she assured me that she would not have dared to go into "them nosy shops" without me and made me promise to meet her again next day. "And don't tell your man and I'll tell Ted I've got to get summat private for the lying-in where men aren't allowed."

I promised, but I did not keep the secret from Chester, for

I had already found out how suspicious he was in this new vein and how unpleasant it was to excite the least suspicion. He would become even more attentive and watchful and more passionate. It was as though he wanted to cure his frightful jealousy by "proving" all over again (but even more violently) that I "really" loved him.

42 Daisy, it appeared, had not only told Goold the lie about visits to a maternity stay-maker, but also promised, every time she went to a rendezvous with me, to be back in an hour – disappeared for the whole day and then told more lies and much less plausible ones.

The result was that Goold, who was even more suspicious than Chester, after three days of quarrelling (and on the last day but one of their visit), set up an inquiry, found out from the boarding-house servant about my first call (I had sent in my name) and telephoned to Chester (we had just got our first telephone) to know if Daisy were there. And Chester, who never let me out of his sight without asking exactly where I should be found, answered with a list of shops, including Shoolbreds.

As it happened, we had gone first to Shoolbreds, and in an even more contagious mood (like children toward the end of the holidays) than usual. Almost as soon as we arrived we began to laugh at the unexpected sight of ourselves in a large looking glass. Daisy said, "Well, I never! Look at me – talk of a bluemange!" and giggled so violently that we had to sit on a sofa to let her recover herself. "Oh dear!" she said then, wiping her eyes with the back of her hand. "Now I've give me a pain." And I said, "I hope not." Whereupon Daisy uttered such a shriek (rocking herself to and fro, and putting her face in her hands) that people in the shop turned to stare.

But red and ashamed as we were, we could not stop laughing; we were, I suppose, hysterical in the true sense of the word. And yet, I don't know how to explain it, it was an immense pleasure to feel so helpless and abandoned, so carried away from the proper world (and Shoolbreds, which was a very proper shop) into this free lunacy where there was nothing to do but laugh.

And just at the very moment of this rather disgraceful performance a little plump red-faced man in the middle of the floor turned sharp round to look at us and we saw that he was Goold. And as soon as she saw her husband, Daisy gave a cry of fright, "Oh dear! Look! Oh lordy! Ted! Oh, whatever shall I do?" and scrambled up and actually ran away into a dressing room. I had never seen any grown-up person fall into such a panic or behave so childishly. And the man came rushing up to me, quite crimson with rage, and said, "Excuse me, Mrs Nimmo, but where is Mrs Goold?"

"She went into the dressing room, Mr Goold. Her stocking was coming down."

"I don't believe a word of it. You put her up to it. I saw you laughing."

"But, Mr Goold, we weren't laughing at you. Daisy is absolutely devoted."

"I don't need you to tell me about my wife's feelings."

"I'm most awfully sorry that we missed you. I'll go and see what's wrong."

I found Daisy quite terrified and almost in tears, and had to persuade her to come out; whereupon Goold, without a word, took her by the arm with one hand, with the other in the middle of her back, and rushed her off, Daisy herself wearing the most comical expression of despair. And yet the very next morning she turned up again at the Parade, saying that Ted had given her a proper dressing down and made her cry so much that she was still "so sore as a quinsy", so we should have to be careful he didn't catch us again. In fact, though she was terrified of her Ted, she could not resist shopping with me any more than she could resist magenta silks and gold fringe.

And this is how (quite according to plan) Chester and Goold were reconciled. For Chester sent to ask after Daisy (and to make some joking remark about "these ladies when they get among the shops"); and Goold came to complain of me; and Chester (as Daisy told me), having conceded that I was apt to lose my head in shops, was able to ask Goold how on earth their misunderstanding had come about; while Goold was very ready to have Chester on his side against my "influence" with Daisy. In fact, I think this was part of the bargain (a first clause in the treaty), because Chester asked me that night not to take Daisy shopping again as Ted "was very distressed about the girl – she has run up enormous bills and told even bigger lies about them."

I did not mind this prohibition or even the sacrifice of my character during the negotiations (I did not feel that I had any character to lose), but I was shocked to hear the second clause – that Chester had proposed to take Goold's nephew Bootham as his private secretary. "Ted was delighted," he said to me, "and practically apologized for his opposition at Tarbiton. We can count on the whole Bethel vote. Besides, the boy himself will be an asset – he knows it's his big chance and he's ready to do anything."

I was in consternation at accepting any of the Goold family – I knew that, for Goold, I was the scarlet woman. And I pointed out that Goold was "planting" Bootham on us because he had failed to sell groceries and that he did not like me. But Chester said that I was mistaken; the boy was only shy, and he must give him a trial after his promise to Goold.

So Bootham arrived and proved, at once, even more incompetent than any of us could have dreamed. He could not type a letter correctly or look up a train. Chester, rushing out on some emergency, and hurling himself into his coat (Chester always fought with his coats until he often tore the linings away at the shoulders), would call for me in despair. "Nina, Nina, have you a moment? For God's sake look up a train for so and so this afternoon; Bootham always loses himself in *Bradshaw*." And this valuable secretary would write letters and leave out some important word like "not", or put in a wrong date.

My dislike of Bootham was not prejudice, as Chester pretended; still less was it the more usual coolness of a wife toward her husband's confidential secretary. The man was a danger. And Chester could have had his pick. For what we had not realized in the country was that he was already quite an important person in the party.

It was not only that he had made himself a name by his "treachery" in the war, but also that he represented a whole mass of radical opinion which had grown suddenly strong during the war, either by discovering its own strength or by getting roused up by anti-war speeches (no one could tell which and no one could possibly know – radicals themselves had no idea and did not care either) ; but also that he had already shown his flair for getting in touch with party supporters and subscribers, big manufacturers, and even rich peers, and especially those who *don't* sit much on committees but prefer to make suggestions from the background (which have to be attended to); so that a great number of influential people, themselves not in the public eye, knew of him and said to each other when he was a member, "Chester Nimmo is our man – he'll work it for us."

I never denied that a secretary was necessary, not only to sort out callers (which I could not have done without offence), but to give them the right answers.

You must never (as Chester pointed out to us all) tell an important nuisance that you have no time to see him; you must eagerly fix an appointment at once, but at some rather awkward time, just before lunch or dinner, or at two o'clock on Saturday afternoon, when either he won't be able to come, or if he comes he will have to go away again almost immediately. For the bigger such a nuisance may be the more easily he is offended, probably because (having been put off so often) he suspects that people don't like him and feels a sense of injustice.

Bootham offended one such man, quite a great man but very troublesome, so much that he became a permanent enemy of ours; but he let in some immense bores, so that Chester would be utterly exhausted. I admit that these disasters worried Bootham himself more than anyone else; in fact, it appeared that the poor wretch was terrified of almost everything and everybody (including me) in the world where he had failed even to sell mousetrap cheese.

43 This Bootham spied on me from the first (I knew he was writing to Goold about me, because Daisy warned me in a special note from her hairdresser's – written there to avoid the terrible Ted's eye), but it was not till I had proof – till I came suddenly into my sitting room one morning and found him actually reading a half-written letter from me to my cousin Robert (about Jim who was giving us both very great anxiety) – that I gave an ultimatum and said that I would not stay in the same house with him another day.

I saw at once that there was going to be a big battle, for as soon as I came into Chester's study, even before I spoke, he looked at me across his desk with that expression which I called his glare, and Jim his "point".

But Jim was more accurate. At such a moment (when he was seized with a violent suspicion) it was not only that his eyes suddenly glared at you but his features seemed to take a different shape, his nose stuck out, his jaws gripped together so that the muscles swelled up in his cheeks, and his whole body became fixed and stiff, as if absolutely arrested by the violence of his idea.

I saw at once that Bootham had managed to be before me, so I said quickly, "Not that the letter was so very private – it was only to Robert about Jim. But I'm sure you'll agree that Bootham is impossible." And I sat down carelessly on the couch to avoid the "point".

"He says he only moved the letter aside because he wanted to get at the address book beneath – and it was I who sent him for the book."

"Do you want him to spy on me? Is that why you keep him? Yes – that must be it, when he is so bad at everything else."

Chester got up and came toward me looking severe and also very excited. "I'll sack him this moment if you say the word. But what's this about Sir Robert and Jim?"

"Nothing except that Jim is wasting his life and Bob's money at Buckfield and we are all very worried about him. After all, I treated Jim fearfully badly and – "

Chester made a face as if he had a tic and interrupted quickly. "Do you see much of Jim nowadays?"

"Never." I was quite astonished. "Jim wouldn't see me if I tried; he is absolutely furious with me, and I'm not surprised."

Chester walked up and down the room and then made another "point". It was obvious that he did not believe a word I said. I was obliged to argue with him – to remind him that Jim had not been in town for weeks, that Buckfield was a four-hour journey, that I hadn't a moment to see Jim. I grew indignant and asked him if he thought I would lie to him; and suddenly he came up to me where I was sitting on the couch and sat down close beside me and said, "I shouldn't know if you did, should I?"

And, with a very queer look, "This jealousy is very vulgar. I don't know how to treat a lady, do I?"

"You've treated me with the greatest goodness."

"I wish I knew what's going on in your mind at this very moment – or any other moment."

"But nobody knows that about anybody – not exactly – it's natural. It's nothing to do with me as me."

"You are quite a different person with Captain Jim or even your aunt – you don't bother to be so polite to them."

And this gave me such a startling glimpse (as he intended) of his mind, full of suspicion and uncertainty, that I exclaimed, "But all this is nonsense. People aren't so different. Daisy Goold and I are perfectly happy together."

"Yes, but then I love you – more than you seem to think. And I can't help it – whatever you do."

And suddenly the whole matter was raised to a different plane; and when Chester afterwards spoke of Bootham, saying that he would be sorry to offend Ted again and to hurt the boy's feelings, who was so loyal to him and the cause, still he was completely in my hands, and if I insisted he would turn him off that minute, it was I who begged for a reprieve. We agreed that Bootham should receive a warning and be given another chance.

The truth is that one may complain about a jealous

husband, but if (it is not always so) his jealousy is the consequence of true love, it is very hard to fight against it.

To be loved is an obligation. Whatever you do you can't shake it off. You simply have to deal with it, if only for the sake of your own peace.

And so Bootham was fixed upon me, and Chester accomplished the first stage in my final encirclement. For, of course, Bootham continued to spy (it was his moral duty to spy on the scarlet woman), only more carefully, so that I never again caught him red-handed. But even had I done so, Chester would have contrived to keep him, for he had already come to find his spying indispensable. He would not have had an easy moment without someone to keep an eye on me.

44 That is to say, that Chester, because of his passion for me, had to be my enemy, and it made him a very cunning and relentless one. He never stopped his manoeuvres for a moment; there was trickery in his kindest deed – it was another nail to hold me. And often I thanked him (and almost loved him) for an act which was really wicked in its treachery. For instance, I said that I was very troubled at this time about Jim, and I had been corresponding with Robert about a plan for paying his debts and getting him a post. I had been glad when Robert left the army, some months before, and came home to clear up his affairs at Buckfield, because I was able to consult him about Jim.

Jim had been at Buckfield all this time, buying "wonder" horses (which no one else would have anything to do with), losing Bob's money on them and abusing the country, which, he said, was rotten with money-grabbers and pacifists and little-Englanders.

Bob was very fond of Jim, but he was not at all blind to his faults. He came up to town especially to see me about him. We went to Battersea Park, where we could be at peace (and afterward to a concert to explain what I had been doing), and talked over the whole ground. Bob declared that the only hope for Jim was to get him out of England and into some job. I said that Jim would have to like the job. "Yes, that's the problem. There was an opening on an estate in Ceylon, but he says there is no sport there."

"It would be a waste of Jim to plant tea."

"He ought to have been the eldest son and inherited the place. He would have been ideal as an MFH like his grandfather – that is, if he had inherited fifteen thousand a year." And I had to agree that Jim would have ruined Buckfield and that he would be better abroad.

But the first thing was to pay his debts, and Bob was trying to sell some of the furniture and carpets which Jim had inherited from his mother. He had heard of my new house and now proposed that I should buy in some of the family things, which, of course, I was glad to do for several reasons.

Bootham, at a later date, made a great to-do about this transaction, and in fact the Goold party has put out a story that, as soon as Chester began to rise in the world, my family swept down upon him like a flock of vultures and picked him clean.

For instance, when we were looking for our house it was said openly in Tarbiton that Aunt Latter was trying to plant the "yellow elephant" on Chester, and that the lease was the price Chester had to pay her for bringing me back to him in time for the election.

And, of course, though I am sure there was no bargain between them (people do not make such bargains, they do not need to have anything definite – they just do each other the good turns that are satisfactory to each other), I dare say there was an understanding. That is to say, all the parties concerned "understood" without any need for words that they could help each other. I know, for instance, that Cousin Slapton just about this time wrote off Jim's debts to him and also he gave Aunt Latter a new silk umbrella with a gold band, for she said to me, with her usual frankness, which was her great virtue, showing me the umbrella, "I think Porty owed me that, considering the state of the chimneys alone."

And Chester certainly knew about this "family deal", because one day, when this very umbrella blew inside out, he exploded into a shout of laughter, and (when at last he had recovered himself) said, or rather stammered, still laughing, to me, "Now we'll have to get another house," a joke he remembered for years, and repeated at least until the great quarrel to poor Aunt Latter – and one which always reduced him to the same helpless laughter, even when he saw that I would smile only from politeness.

But what I want to point out is that there was no "corruption" in these "deals", because everybody concerned was simply doing a kindness (or showing gratitude) to a friend. The "facts" are once more quite untrue. Aunt Latter and Lord Slapton between them certainly had the advantage of Chester's taking the "yellow elephant". Aunt Latter certainly counted on Chester's influence to help the Latters generally (and at this very time she was pressing him to get Jim a job as King's Messenger), and Bob did get me to buy a good deal of Jim's furniture. But none of these acts were predatory. On the contrary, they were friendly; they were the sign that Chester was accepted in the family.

And the family was just as much at his disposal as he at

theirs. Apart from what Aunt Latter had done for him (because all my family regarded my money as a kind of investment which Aunt Latter had "placed" in Chester's future), Slapton and Connybeare had been turned on to propose him for a directorship in the Battwell Estates Corporation. True, Chester had refused it, because it owned public houses, but the family had given him the chance of at least a thousand a year.

Chester, on his part, could have refused "the Chelsea elephant"; and no one would have blamed him. In a real family, such "deals" are always being offered and refused. What none of us realized was that Chester had never belonged to a real family, at least one with many connections and the power to exchange favours. He did not understand our kind of world at all. And so in spite of his jokes about Aunt Latter's umbrella, he imagined sinister "arrangements" all round him and he thought it quite fair (as a countermeasure) to take information from Bootham. And Bootharn was more and more audacious. He managed to detect and open "by mistake" in Chester's mail my only letter from Jim in the last three months – a very abusive one telling me not to poke my fingers into his affairs – Bob was quite enough; and Chester knew even that Bob and I had discussed handing Buckfield over to Jim as manager.

He pounced upon me one evening in the drawing room. "So Sir Robert is thinking of the Captain as agent." He liked to take me by surprise with his information, perhaps to show me how dangerous it would be for me to plot against him. And in the surprise, I felt myself blushing, which annoyed me very much. So I answered, "Did Bootham tell you? I saw him listening to me at the telephone."

This made Chester turn red, but also it made him angry. "I beg your pardon," he said, "if it was meant to be a secret."

"Good heavens, no!" I said. "But naturally Bob would like to see Jim settled – so would I."

"At Buckfield. I should have thought Sir Robert would need an experienced manager."

"That's the real – difficulty. Jim has no experience."

And Chester pounced again. "Sir Robert seems to spend a lot of time running up to town for your advice."

"I haven't seen him for weeks."

But I turned even redder, for this was a lie and I hated to tell it. What's more, Chester knew it was a lie. "I'm sorry," he said. "Someone told me he had called on Monday when I was at the House." And I could only pretend to have forgotten the visit.

Why I told such dangerous pointless lies I don't know, but I remember that once when Jim and I were caught climbing into a boatyard to look at a new schooner (we were planning at that time to have our own schooner when we grew up), Jim, who was the soul of truth, at once told an enormous lie (that we were looking for a dog), and I supported him. There is something in being watched and suspected that makes one lie – a kind of instinct to keep things private. Unless I took great care, I lied to Chester about the smallest trifles.

And I discouraged Bob from coming to see me at home, because Chester despised him and I could not bear to have a man so kind and simple despised by a clever "go-getter" like my husband. Chester attacked me at once after Bob's very first official call (he had come to congratulate Chester on marrying "quite the nicest of my cousins"). "What does that fellow propose to do with himself now?"

"He is rather an authority on art – at least on some of the early Italians."

"Oh, he writes."

"No, he hasn't written anything; he says he doesn't know enough yet, but he is collecting materials for a book."

"And he must be nearly forty."

"Only thirty-six."

"What a life!"

"Why, Chester, he is a very nice man."

"Not a very difficult achievement, if one inherits four thousand pounds a year, and apparently no sense of responsibility." And he spoke indignantly of men like Bob, who drew "large incomes" from the land and did nothing for it, and nothing for their country either, at one of the most desperate crises in history. "One has only to meet such men," he said, "to understand the French Revolution and to see how necessary it was. The French nobles were nice men, too; some of the nicest, they say, that ever adorned this fortunate planet, but utterly useless and decadent." In fact, Chester, on Bob, began to fall into his platform style, so I did not ask him if it was right for people to be murdered because they were nice. And I said to myself, "He does not begin to understand Bob's sense of duty toward Buckfield, or his interest in art, because he wants to make speeches against Bob's class. He plays political tricks even with his own feelings."

45 I admit I did see a great deal of Bob at that time, but not because I was flirting with him or plotting against my husband; simply because he was an old friend, and to go with him was an escape from an atmosphere so thick with suspicion and heavy with moral pressure that I could scarcely breathe.

Bob was as clear as glass – he had no tricks whatever. He had grown up like an ugly Jim, with Jim's "light horseman" figure, but too long a nose, and the minutest eyes. And his character, too, was quite different – he had none of Jim's complication. He was tolerant and gentle. He was, if anything, too modest and always laughed at himself. I could easily have loved Bob. I think perhaps he was meant to be my man – if we had met at the right moment and he had loved me. But he never began to love me or need me (he never needed anybody), and I think I am probably a woman who needs to be needed, to get involved.

It was certainly a great happiness to me when Bob came to consult me about Jim and about his own future. For I loved to be with him and to feel that even our thoughts were the same kind of family thoughts, so that, even if I didn't know what he was going to say next, I was always ready for it and something said in me, "Yes, yes; oh, but that is exactly what I was just going to feel myself." And, what is strange, I never felt so with Chester or even with Jim.

Those days still remain with me as something precious, and it seems (but it can't be so) that they were all rather fine spring days when the sky was rather cloudy but the clouds were very white as if new for the season and the sun kept darting down between them the most brilliant clean new rays, and the trees were bursting out all over their heads in a rather ridiculous manner, like little girls with their hair screwed up in paper before a Cinderella dance; and there was always a bright ripple on the Thames, which also seemed to have quite new clean water, and the grass was so new and fresh and soft that it seemed to belong to a special tender kind of world, newly created for sentimental conversation. And I leaned on Bob's arm (I was getting very heavy and had pains in my legs) and we spoke rather sadly about Jim's passion for lame colts and the truly frightful state of Bob's roofs and drains. Bob would say that a family place was a curse, and I would say, yes, if one let it spoil one's life – but he must not do so. And he would say that Jim and the Maries (Aunt Latter and Aunt Slapton) would never forgive him if he let Buckfield go. "And I'm not sure if I would forgive myself. We've always lived there till my father's time and done our proper work. One always feels afraid of destroying something that can't be replaced."

And I knew this feeling so well that we talked of it for whole afternoons and wondered whether we were really "decadent", as Chester and his friends thought; whether perhaps "decadence" was simply a sense of obligation to things that did not matter or had stopped mattering; and Bob would say again that his misfortune was in having been the eldest son, so that he could not become a professor or an artist.

Once, in the park, when I was urging him not to let Buckfield destroy his life (we had been going over the ground for the twentieth time), be said, suddenly laughing, "Shall I toss up?" And he did actually toss up, and the penny came down for selling Buckfield. Then he said, "Best out of three" and it was again for selling. But both of us were very depressed afterwards and wondered if, after all, Bob would not feel that he had committed a crime in destroying a historical connection.

And in the end, of course, he never made up his mind to get rid of Buckfield.

All our talks seem, in memory, to have been rather sad, as if a fate were hanging over us; and, indeed, we were both at an age when one begins to feel what fate is – I mean circumstances that can't be changed except for the worse.

And yet I was terribly startled and distressed when one day Bob wired that he could not come (we had tickets for Pachmann), because he had to go at once abroad "on business" and did not know when he would be back. In fact, I did not see Bob again for years. But I had no idea for nearly a year that Chester had suddenly called him up on the telephone and warned him that he was seeing too much of me and that he, Chester, "would not have it".

46 People who imagine plots always make plots; you might say their whole life is a plot. Everything they do is meant to have some effect beyond itself. Indeed many of the people who came to the house (especially the younger MPs) had got so plotty (or perhaps political people are born so) that everything that happened anywhere was "significant" of some "development". If you only asked them to take an ice, they looked at you knowingly as if to ask themselves what you were "starting" and why. I don't say that Chester was like this, but, as I gradually realized, he did see life largely as relations which (like those between nations) were subject to all sorts of "strains" and "diplomatic action". If he wanted a special favour from me, like going out to a very dull dinner (I did not like dinners just then when I was so big), he would begin, before any mention of the invitation, by bringing me flowers or chocolates.

On the other hand, when I had been "kind" to him he always gave me a treat or present. Of course, many husbands do so; what I mean is that for Chester these attentions not only expressed gratitude and affection – they formed part of a complicated "politique". They were meant to set up moral obligations; they smoothed the way for a delicate *pourparler*; they prepared a *rapprochement* or brought about a *détente*.

It was no good blaming men like Chester and his friends for being artful and insidious; they thought that there was no other way for sensible men to live, at least if they wanted to "keep their end up".

And now when Chester suddenly interested himself in our plans for Jim by offering to take charge of the whole affair, debts and all, he began by going to Aunt Latter and insisting on complete secrecy. His name was not to be mentioned even to me. The hard question with Jim was the debts. He owed nearly two thousand pounds, of which more than a thousand were debts "of honour" to certain racing men and bookmakers.

Jim insisted that these debts were the important ones; the tradesmen and the bank and the stables could wait. And he would not listen to any plan that did not put the "bookies" and his club friends first. They were to be paid in full, or Jim, so he said, would never be able to show his face in England again.

Aunt Latter and Bob quite understood this feeling and were trying to pay a little to both parties, with a promise of more to come.

But now Chester's lawyer proposed a most complicated plan. Chester would take charge of all the debts, provided that Aunt Latter and Bob would give Jim an ultimatum to apply for the African service or they would cut off supplies. Chester on his side could arrange through a Liberal supporter (a very rich man who made soap and had a lot of influence) that if Jim applied he would get a favourable reply, in spite of his rather doubtful record. Then, when Aunt protested that the climate of West Africa (in those days it was called the white man's grave and so it often was) might kill Jim, he took me to Paris for a week and bought me a diamond bow for my hair. This was not only to separate me from Aunt and Bob and Jim, but to win my support.

And he was not merely disappointed when I, too, hearing for the first time of his plan, objected to the climate (how should I have felt if Jim had died?). He was offended as if by a meanness, which he showed by a certain melancholy look and voice and by praying rather more fervently to be forgiven "as we forgive them that trespass against us", which nearly always meant me.

I have never, after so many years, discovered all the ramifications of this Chester plan to get Jim out of England and to keep him out – there was so much interviewing and telephoning and gentlemen's agreeing that even Aunt and Bob do not know who cheated whom. But what suddenly decided the thing was the discovery that Jim was actually in danger of arrest (not without a suspicion that someone on Chester's side had put the police on his track); apparently he had pawned, among other things, a dressing case which had not been paid for.

As all Jim's family knew, this was not a crime in Jim. He never had the faintest idea which of his possessions had been paid for and which not. He distinguished only between what he absolutely needed (like four new suits a year) and what he did not absolutely need (like two dressing cases or antique furniture). But it was no good my explaining this to Chester. It was a moral question, and in all such Chester would listen to me in silence and make no answer, as if to say, "You are hardly qualified to judge. This is a matter of principle and only a man of sound principle can decide it."

And, as I say, Chester was a man of principle – he had to be – or he would have lost his way in his own "diplomacy". And now, of course, he (or rather his lawyer operating on

Bob's lawyer) was able to frighten Aunt and Bob so much (and even to alarm Jim a little) that everything was huddled up in a hurry. Jim took the African post and agreed to pay off the debts at ten shillings in the pound, by instalments. We all subscribed for his kit (except Aunt, who, having sold altogether two farms to educate and support Jim, now quarrelled bitterly with him because he called on Aunt Slapton without telling her), and he went off in the best of spirits with an express rifle, new guns, two saddles, and a dozen polo sticks.

He was happy, because he understood that the "debts" were to be paid. It did not come out for months that by the word "debts" Chester did not mean debts of honour. Also his lawyer had managed to enrage these creditors so much by suggesting that they were scoundrels who had preyed on Jim that Jim really had some reason to be afraid of coming home again. And this, of course, whether he had planned for it or not, was just what Chester had wanted.

47 You may have wondered how Chester afforded to pay even a part of Jim's debts and take me to the Crillon and buy me diamond bows, but already before this time a great change had taken place in our finances; that is to say, it was in this spring that Chester, according to his enemies, "sold himself to the capitalists". For which, of course, I am held chiefly responsible. But you shall judge.

Already in July of that year, after the Christmas bills (and Chester, it is true, had given me a sable cape, but quite against my will; the last thing I wanted was for Chester to ruin himself for me), we had a warning from the bank. And in April the manager suddenly refused us an overdraft. I have never seen Chester so angry and excited as when he got this letter. "It's a deliberate attempt to smash me," he

said, "and drive me out of politics, a typical Tory trick."
And when I suggested that the manager had been very
helpful before and was apologetic now, he asked me why he
had waited till we were at "the critical moment".

I cannot remember what the critical moment was – I
rather think the middle of a by-election at which Chester
had been making violent speeches against the "money
lords". For Chester, we were always at a critical moment;
and I suppose he was quite right – all moments are critical
for politicians.

And I dared not defend the manager, because he might
have had political prejudices (it's impossible to tell what all
his motives were) and because I was feeling anxious about
certain bills which I knew to be pending for furniture and
carpets, including Jim's.

I have said that Chester always rose to occasions (for one
thing, of course, the idea that he was surrounded by
unscrupulous enemies made him always very pugnacious
and wary), but also he somehow managed to profit by
them. There was perhaps some truth in the old joke that if
Chester Nimmo, stark naked, were attacked by two
desperadoes, armed to the teeth, there would be a short
sharp struggle, and an immense cloud of dust, and then it
would be found that the footpads had murdered each other
and that Nimmo was wearing the full evening dress of an
archbishop with gold watches in every pocket.

What happened now was that he used this crisis both to
finish the general defeat of the Latters and to take away the
last of my independence. First he asked my leave to put the
Orchard in the market. "My dearest, I know this will be a
great blow to you – I hesitate very much to suggest it. It's a
shame that my mismanagement should always fall on you."
Of course, I said that I had been the extravagant one and

that the Orchard must go. Then he thanked me very touchingly for my "generous heart", saying that he had never known anyone more free from any meanness about money, and said that if I could bear it we ought to go to Tarbiton at once to arrange a sale. Aunt Latter could come up and look after the house and Tom, in my absence. In fact it would be a good thing if she could stay till my baby was born – it would give me a chance to rest.

I thought this a good plan, and Aunt was delighted with it. She came to town at once with all her trunks and files and seized on the best visitor's room.

But the result was that when I came back I found that the housekeeping and the accounts had been taken out of my hands, and, as all the bills had come to light (they were far more than I had dreamed), I could not answer Aunt Latter's indignant charge that I was not fit to have charge of money and that, in any case, she could not hand the books back until they were "straight". Meanwhile Chester had put the Orchard in the market and "asked the advice" of some of the richer Liberals – that is, showed them that he needed help. And they not only lent him large sums but offered him two directorships, and a share in a syndicate for making electricity.

Even then Chester hesitated to accept – he had so often attacked company promoters and called them bloodsuckers that he felt he would be putting himself in a false position by becoming a director. And as I said, he had always refused to join my Cousin Wilfred's land company.

But even Mr Goold, when we wrote to him, agreed with me and with all Chester's friends that there could be no real objection to a syndicate which intended to make electricity and which had for its motto (it was Chester's own minister at Tarbiton who suggested it – he himself had a share), "Let there be light."

And Chester agreed from the beginning that electric light was a boon and saved the work of servants. But I admit at once that what finally convinced him was the plain fact that if we did not get some money from somewhere he would have to go bankrupt and give up his career, not to speak of the Radical Freedom League as well as the Peace and Freedom Council – that everything he had done would go to waste. And for Chester these were really sacred causes, more important even than Old Age Pensions or Health Insurance. And that is why, in the end, he joined Western Development, and not because, as some of his critics said (including Aunt), that he thought he was going into business with God.

What really annoyed Chester's enemies, perhaps, was that when he did turn his attention to business he was very good at it. The electric syndicate was a great success from the beginning. It got contracts for half Tarbiton and all the big houses round, including Slapton's. Cousin Wilfred lighted his whole brewery with its current, and both he and Slapton were original shareholders. When the works were floated as a company at the end of six months, they went up three times in value in a few weeks.

And I am not going to pretend for a moment that I did not enjoy having plenty of money and a good allowance (even if the accounts were in Aunt's hands). Next to living with the man you love and having good health, it is the most delightful thing possible. Even when you can only esteem your husband and are subject to eye headaches, it is a very great consolation.

48 I said that Chester had brought Aunt Latter to town and put her in charge of the household, on the excuse of my needing rest and peace before my lying-in. I very much resented this plan at the time, for, though I loved Aunt, I had never "got on" with her any more than I got on with Jim. But for some reason, perhaps because she was so happy in seeing Chester so successful and getting Jim settled, she now became much more tactful with me. She suddenly began to tell me stories (some of them very improper but very funny) about the family and well-known Tarbiton characters.

I think this happens quite often to young wives having their *second* baby – I mean older women then accept them (like men elected to a club and properly seconded) as members of the cult and tell them things they would not dream of telling to brides with only a "honeymoon ticket".

Certainly we used to laugh so much sometimes that we must have seemed quite mad. For there was something violent and passionate even in Aunt's laughter, and I laughed all the more because I was so surprised at Aunt's geniality to myself.

Also she was enchanted by the baby, a daughter, born that spring and even more like Jim than Tom had been. She insisted on being an extra godmother, gave her an expensive cup, and chose the name, her own mother's name Sara, which then (though Chester tried to fix *his* mother's name Hester on the child), as Sally, became the name used by us all.

And though even after Sally was born, for month after month (there seemed no reason why Aunt should not stay forever), I was a "cypher" in my own house, that is, merely a wet nurse and a drawing-room entertainer, to play and sing to the gentlemen after dinner (but not too long), I did not mind it greatly. Aunt was like a mother, and there is something specially pleasant for a young wife to have her mother about so long, that is, as she is sympathetic (I mean enjoying the wife's experiences) and not upsetting to the husband.

Also, of course, Aunt's presence often protected me from "moral pressure"; for though Chester did not hesitate to talk about our moral duty in her presence, she would always take it up as a political question (how, for instance, it would affect opinion in Tarbiton if I were put onto the ladies' committee for Sunday Observance – a thing I dreaded), and this, for some reason, made it less compulsive. I actually escaped this committee on the general grounds that the effect in Tarbiton, though good, would not be worth the wear and tear to my milk and the price of return tickets to the west.

But above all (and this, too, was after Sally was born) I began to discover not only my own childhood but a whole new aspect of it from a "grown-up's" point of view. I suppose, indeed, this is another reason why mothers become so important, in a new way, to daughters, after they, too, are mothers; because they not only become confidential in a new way (however discreet they are they have much more meaning to each other) but the mother's experience as a mother is always interesting to the daughter.

49 And now, through Aunt's eyes, I saw myself not only as a delicate child but a difficult one, and how wisely Aunt had dealt with my crotchets. For instance, I had always been very fond of slipping away by myself from Aunt and nurses and grown-ups generally, either up to the moor or into the loft, where there were piles of old books and magazines (turned out from Buckfield at the time of my grandfather's marriage), on which I would browse for whole afternoons; or still more exciting adventure, down the road to the wall just above the Longwater Hotel (the wall was level with its long purple slate roof) in order to watch the guests strolling on the lawns, playing croquet, coming ashore in smart dinghies with white ropes round the gunwales, from their yachts, or moving about in the immense conservatory after dinner, under the Japanese lanterns – especially in Regatta week, when the hotel was crowded with the "big yacht people" and the fashionables, I could not resist the attraction.

Talking now on equal terms with Aunt (who reminded me of the occasions when I had been smacked for it) brought back the very sensation of one of those evenings, dark and clear, and full of soft warmth as if the whole world were a conservatory under an immense roof of clear invisible glass – the very pressure of the wall in my stomach while I hung far out to watch the ladies and gentlemen come out from dinner into the real conservatory right below me. The whole occasion (apart from the joy of being out alone at a forbidden time and place) gave me a feeling which I can hardly describe, a combination of delights including the triumphant sense of being unseen in my dark upper heaven, calm and spacious, and looking down into a brilliant little world, a perfect doll's house, full of the most exquisite mannikins who were, all the same, real grown-up persons.

I could remember even the special ecstasy (kicking my toe against the wall, and making holes in my boots) with which I had watched some couple from the ballroom go to a corner among the palms – the twist of the neck and jerk of the arm with which the lady would throw open her fan on sitting down, and the violent gesture of the man tossing up his coat-tails before taking his place beside her (which, I am sorry to say, reminded me of a familiar gesture with my own skirt in a less romantic situation).

These nights were the reason why in Regatta week I had been so often lost at bedtime.

But when I reminded Aunt of the smackings I had had (sometimes with a slipper), she answered, yes, and did I remember the pneumonia I had caught hiding in the hedge along that wall, or that two of her sisters and one of mine (my elder and only sister) had died of their "chests"? "About the only thing you got from the Latters is your chest and it nearly killed you three times."

And then she said, "You were properly spoiled, my girl, but what could I do with such a brat? I couldn't smack you every day – I didn't believe in smacking except as a last resort – but it was the only punishment that had any effect. If I sent you to bed you would not eat, and you were too thin already. You were always too fond of your own way and quite ready to spoil yourself if no one would do it for you – though there were plenty who did do it for you – from that old fool Freer to Jim and the nurses. Well, I did my best, though no one will believe it. At least I gave you plenty of freedom – too much perhaps when you think of what happened at Exeter (this was where Jim and I had had our mysterious disaster), and I didn't let you die of it."

50 All at once I saw that I had had plenty of freedom, and this had been the background of that happiness which I remember so well. Perhaps it had ruined my character, but how happy I had been, wandering and browsing among the books and dreaming on the moor. My life as a child seemed now like a long trance of contemplative delight.

I was, I know, pitied (that poor little orphan at Miss Latter's) by certain neighbours, and especially by some of my friends at the yacht club like Major Freer, for being so often in disgrace. And I was indeed terrified of Aunt's smackings – very hard ones (but I dreaded even more than the pain the tremendous emotional disturbance, including my own screams); but what I now remember so vividly was not only my happiness as a child (as in a different department from the awful situation of the smackings) but that I had really possessed happiness.

I suppose most children are often happy, but few, it seemed to me, *had* happiness. They lived in their amusements like little fish wriggling in a nicely warmed sea and did not know any more than fish where or what they were. But though I had no idea what I was (and, as you must see, I am not perfectly sure of it now), yet I know I possessed happiness, because I remember it in detail, and we do not remember things as pleasant unless they so impress themselves. When I revelled among the old magazines in the loft (ruining my sight for life, just as Aunt had warned) I knew I was revelling.

And so I remembered now not only important events, such as a blue sash that, quite unexpectedly, my Cousin Slapton gave me for a party, when I was, I suppose, about five, and many times that Jim was cruel to me, or kind, but also, in quite a separate class, my actual delight, not in the sash or anything that Jim ever did to me, but in some glimpse of the garden, in a hole in the wall through which one could see different aspects of the estuary and the opposite shore, and the boats as in a dark frame which gave their colours the brightness of an illumination; or a favourite toy at Slapton House (old Aunt Slapton kept it in her work-table drawer) among half balls of wool and scraps of stuff sewn with odd buttons (I think she used it for darning her brother's winter stockings), one of those glass balls in which, if you turned the thing upside down and

151

back again, a little snowstorm, marvellously real with slow drifting silent flakes, fell upon three minute persons coming away from a grey church, extremely perpendicular, with a castellated tower, just like Slapton Church, and going toward a house with a red roof and two fir trees.

This toy, not even a good specimen of its kind, enchanted me and I would play with it half an hour at a time, fascinated by the realness and the smallness of this world which I could hold in one hand. I could scarcely not believe (the snow was so real, so soft, so slow) that the people (the man wore a black frock coat and top hat and carried a red umbrella) were moving. I hoped every time I turned the glass (knowing perfectly well that the thing was a toy) to see them walk through the snow and go into the little house.

I had often hinted for this ball (I was forbidden to beg), but Aunt Slapton, who was such a kind gentle old lady, also had a great attachment to her "things". And when I hinted she would become deaf. So one day I stole the ball. I still remember the terror of my escape from the house (by the garden door) with this booty under my petticoat. And the secret enjoyment of the wonder in the loft where I hid it under a pile of old papers, trembling all the time at the thought of the hue and cry, the questioning and the slipper.

In fact Aunt Slapton (perhaps pitying the "poor orphan" in the hand of her Cousin Mary, whom she feared and detested) never said a word about the theft. It was my nurse who found the ball and took it to Aunt Latter. But, to my amazement, Aunt simply put it in a drawer and (like Aunt Slapton, but from different motives) also said nothing about it. When one day she caught me playing with it, she smiled in an odd meaning way (but I could not detect the meaning) and said, "Where did you get that? Here, take it away – take it away."

Which seemed then only the kind of incomprehensible thing Aunt would do. But now I saw it as part of her policy of not smacking me too much – as a light upon her problem as an unwilling but anxious guardian. In short, at twenty-six (when many children begin to discover their parents) Aunt suddenly became for me a human being who had loved me and worried over me for twenty years and given me much happiness, and who herself had had very little. Indeed, I realized that this time was perhaps the happiest of her life and that she had never been really happy before.

51 So that when Chester one day remarked that Aunt had now spent fifteen months with us I (who had so dreaded her coming) could scarcely believe it. And I hastened to point out how useful she was in the household – I did not know how we should do without her. To this Chester warmly agreed. In fact, Chester never really seemed to dislike Aunt's presence – and as I told myself, why should he? It was he who had brought her to the house.

It was true that as she settled down and enjoyed herself, happiness (unlike what is usually expected of it), far from making her more mellow, seemed to bring out her tendency to manage people (for their own good) and even sharpened her tongue. She became a little arbitrary in arranging our amusements together (we both liked a musical comedy and an occasional race meeting), not so much to suit Chester's convenience as my pleasure; and her epigrams about Chester's friends or even Chester himself (such as that one about his going into business with God) became still more lively and reckless.

When I gave her a hint that her voice was loud and penetrating and that Bootham was always lurking in passages and listening with his door ajar, she only uttered some louder and ruder things about persons who were cheese-mity in the Lord. Like other impulsive warm-hearted people, Aunt could not resist a joke. I dare say, too, that, like Cousin Slapton who justified some epigram of his own with the remark that everyone who liked port also enjoyed a dry biscuit now and then, she needed to be tart because she was exuberant.

But Chester did not seem to mind Aunt's tongue – he seemed delighted to consult with her. Only once did he seem to find any fault with her, when he remarked to me one day that he admired my skill in "keeping her happy".

I was greatly surprised and said, "But do I?"

"My dear, she clings to you. But, of course, she is a great clinger."

"Aunt seems to me a most independent person."

"She would like to be so, no doubt." And then with another confidential smile which I did not understand, he began to talk of the problem of managing one's relations with people who did not really understand the whole problem of relations.

Chester, especially since he had come into Parliament and begun to take part in making party decisions, had often talked about the difficulty of "managing people" as the ultimate problem of democratic politics. He had, in fact, run up against men who were quite as strong-willed as himself – and often more important. I have heard him speak of several famous leaders as "political problems". And as he spoke now, I did, for a moment, have a glimpse of Aunt as a "political problem". But I was so accustomed to think of her as one who solved other people's problems, as a highly intelligent woman who, so far from being a political problem (and I never could quite get used to seeing any person as a "political problem"; I thought the phrase was

just part of the special language talked by political people),
was herself a politician, that this glimpse seemed a mere
fantasy and vanished at once.

So when Chester paused and looked at me as if expecting
some encouragement or support, I did not know what he
meant and said, "But don't you think it's rather an
advantage having Aunt here? She can talk to you about
politics and she knows such a lot about everything."

And he answered at once, with his usual politeness, "If
you are content, that is all I was worrying about."

So I was as much astonished as shocked when, only a few
days later, he picked a quarrel with Aunt.

I should say here that Aunt had gradually built up a mass
of duties for herself; apart from a lot of secretarial work,
she had organized a regular women's branch of the
Freedom League. And one morning, when I came in from
the library (already anticipating a nice read), I was stealing
past the dining room (where Aunt was sending out circulars
to selected radical wives), when she called me in. I found
her at one end of the table (she used the dining room as her
office) and a volunteer lady at the other, both writing hard.
The atmosphere was full of that urgent importance which
only Aunt Latter could produce. She did not even move her
head when she asked me where "that Bootham was".

"No doubt in Chester's room."

"Then why don't he bring the Tarbiton address book? I
asked him this morning. Ring the top bell like a good girl."

"I don't think Bootham likes being rung for."

"Then why don't he do his job? Ring, ring, my dear;
we've no time to waste on footling."

I rang, but Bootham did not come. Instead he tried to slip
out of the house. But, of course (the poor lad could never do
anything well), he knocked down the volunteer's umbrella

and Aunt Latter bounced out to intercept him. "Where's that address book, Mr Bootham, that Mr Nimmo told you to give me?" Bootham, turning very pale and poking out his neck like a goose, muttered that he did not remember anything about any book. "Of course he told you, and you heard him. What do you mean, Mr Bootham?"

Just then Chester did come, and Aunt at once appealed to him. "Chester, Mr Bootham, for some reason, refuses to give me the address book for the Radical Ladies appeal."

Bootham, looking still more wooden, said that he had no instructions about the Tarbiton address book. "Instructions?" Aunt Latter said, with great scorn. "Are we running a shop? You were told, and I don't know why that should be necessary either."

"Excuse me," Chester said (he was standing with his hands clasped together, and his head a little on one side, and his eyes turned a little upward and sideways, in what I used to think of as his shop-walker attitude). "I am rather at a loss." And when both Aunt Latter and Bootham had explained again, he said in his lightest tone, "Did I say anything about an address book?"

"But I was there," Aunt Latter said.

"Then, of course, it must be so," Chester said. "Though I admit I don't recollect it. But we are all so busy nowadays – Bootham, especially, has really too much to do."

And then Aunt Latter, who was quite as quick as Chester to take a shade of meaning, exclaimed, "I see. How stupid of me. But I will go at once," and began to hobble upstairs (she had begun to have rheumatism rather badly in the winter) before even Chester could grasp what she intended.

Then he ran up after her and offered all kinds of assurances, but she said only that it was not the first indication that she was not wanted, that she had been wrong not to have taken earlier hints, and she begged Chester to leave the room while she packed. Thereupon he walked out, as I thought when I met him on the landing, with quite a cheerful tread.

52 All this had astonished me, and at first I had felt for Chester; I thought Aunt Latter impossibly touchy. But when I went to help her to pack, I found her in very great distress. Her face was swollen as if she had already been crying, and her hands were so shaky that she kept dropping things on the floor.

She told me at once that she did not need any help – would I kindly go away. But I simply could not bring myself to leave her. I suppose it is shocking to any child (and I was still a child with Aunt Latter) to discover that a parent can be humiliated to tears; and now I seemed bound to her by dismay as well as sympathy.

But when I tried to console her by saying that Chester was terribly upset by this misunderstanding, and I was sure that he did not understand how badly Bootham had behaved, she answered in her usual downright way, "Of course he understands. He is jealous of me with you, and the children – you know he hates it when we have our jokes together – he has been looking for a chance to get me out for some time."

I was so startled by her misery that I went to Chester and told him that he must, at all costs, make it up with her. But to my surprise he said coolly that he had done everything possible.

"The truth is," he said, "that she wants to drive Bootham out, and I could not possibly allow that. Besides, she is not a good influence with the children. It is really quite a good thing that she should go."

"But not like this, Chester, in such bitterness. After all, she has done a great deal for us."

I said "us", because I could not very well remind him that I was one of his obligations to Aunt Latter. But he answered that he fully appreciated all that he owed to Aunt Latter, but he could not allow her to dictate to him. And I was so surprised and angry that I burst out, "In fact, it is just what she says – you don't need her any more, and so you are getting rid of her."

Chester said nothing to this, and appeared so indifferent that I went away even angrier than Aunt Latter (who was, in fact, not angry at all, but only wounded) and made no further attempt to keep her. And when she left I went with her, leaving a note to Chester to say that I must see her comfortably settled. For as Palm Cottage was let right up to the New Year, and Aunt Latter had managed to quarrel with Cousin Bob about some debt of Jim's, she was obliged to look for a lodging which had also to be cheap.

Now all this time Aunt was raging against Chester. "He'd sell his soul for office, if he ever had one – or any one of us." And when at last we found a room (rather a poor one, but cheap and close by), she had a drink (she went to the bedroom for it – she did not yet drink in public) and came back still more angry. "And you look out for yourself, too, my girl – he's driving all your friends away – first Jim and then Bob and now me."

"Bob?"

"Yes, you poor ninny – Bob. Didn't you know that he warned Bob off the course? Asked him what he meant by flirting with you; and, of course, Bob, being Bob, took fright and ran off to Rome."

This news gave me a very unpleasant sensation. For the first time I felt (what I suppose Chester had always felt) that things were going on behind my back. "But, Aunt, are you sure?"

"Of course I'm sure. I tell you he's a devil – and a fool, too. They're all alike, these climbers – creepers and bullies. They don't trust anybody. They have only one idea for a friend or a wife – an imbecile like Bootham, who licks their feet, and a slave woman who trembles at a word. You see if he doesn't start on you now – sneaking and hissing and winding himself round you and crushing you into pulp – just female pulp. Take my word for it, my girl, as things are going now, in ten years you'll be a chattering idiot. And that's what I say – the fool, with all his smartness, is making a fool of himself, wrecking his chances, throwing away his true friends who can give honest advice, destroying his own property. For you are quite as good a wife as the little rat deserves – better, considering that you brought him the cash that gave him his start." Then she made another dash into the bedroom (because, I think, she was afraid of weeping) and came back in a still fiercer mood to say she wondered I had stuck to Chester – "the little snake".

And I, too, wondered. The more I thought of Chester's treatment of Bob (I saw Bob's astonishment and I wondered if he thought that I was a party to some treachery against him) the more I was shocked. Shock is the only word for the mixture of disgust and fear and anger (I suppose just what Chester felt against the Tory banker) which filled me. I felt surrounded with treachery. And I said that after this nothing could induce me to go back to Chester. I would stand by my dear aunt. Whereupon she was so moved that at last she gave way to quite violent weeping and said that she knew I was the only person in the world who had ever loved her. Which made me ashamed of not loving her more often, and determined to love her better in future.

It was in the middle of this affectionate scene that Chester walked in, with a large basket of fruit, and greeted us in the most unembarrassed manner.

53 Aunt Latter, who was sitting with me in half the armchair, got up slowly (she was not quite sober and her pince-nez was more crooked than usual) and glared. But she was quite disconcerted – I had never seen her so taken aback.

And I admit I, too, was astonished. I think neither of us had realized how "cool" Chester was getting since his success in town.

Chester put the basket on the table and congratulated us on finding so near and convenient a lodging, and said that he must send round a "better chair".

He had so tactful an air (like the family lawyer at a funeral) that I was astonished when he went on at once to say to Aunt how sorry he was about "this little difference", but he was sure she understood his difficulty. She would be greatly missed on her committee, but at least she had put it on a sound footing.

I thought at every moment Aunt would explode; she actually opened her mouth to do so. But Chester suddenly changed his tone and expression (like one who is willing in pure courtesy to pass over an awkward situation) and asked her if she had seen some letter of Lord Rosebery's to *The Times*. Did she think it should be answered by some member of the radical wing?

Of course, Aunt understood very well what Chester meant – that he would not have her back on the old terms, on any account, but that if she liked to be "reasonable" he would not cut her off entirely from his circle. She turned redder and redder; even Chester, I thought, looked a little uneasy. And I would have welcomed the explosion. I hated to see this smooth man play cat and mouse with my poor aunt.

At last, with a kind of grunt, she said that Chester did not need *her* advice – she knew that he would do what he liked in any case. But Chester paid no attention to this; he went on discussing the letter, analysing it, guessing at its intention and how much support it would get from this and that shade of opinion, mentioning what certain leaders (Mr Lloyd George was very angry about it; Mr Asquith recommended caution) had said about it; though Aunt Latter continued for a little while to grunt and glare (she must have felt like a dog whose master snatches away a steak and then offers it a rubber bone) she soon began to make comments. In fact resentment had become ridiculous. So that in ten minutes from Chester's arrival Aunt was discussing the matter in quite her old style (only a little more downright even than before, as if to say, I'm not going to soften my opinion just to please Chester Nimmo), so that one could have said that they were old friends.

I can't describe my astonishment to see these two people who had just had such a bitter irreconcilable quarrel, come together again without any kind of explanation or forgiveness, and in less than ten minutes start a new relationship at a different level.

But also I was still more indignant. And when Chester said to me on going out, "You won't forget, my dear, that we have the Vidlers (rich party subscribers) coming to dinner," I did not answer. I thought, "You have been too clever for once. My family may forgive, but I can't."

And as soon as I was alone with Aunt (making tea for her – she could not at that time boil a kettle or light a gas stove) I said to her, "I do rather wonder, Aunt, that you let Chester get round you like that." But she answered in her sharpest tone, "What do you mean, get round me, as you vulgarly term it? He was discussing a very important matter, with due respect for it, and me, too."

"Oh, Aunt, he's treated you abominably. You said yourself that he cares for nothing in the world but his career."

"What then – we'll hope he'll have one, in spite of his toadies. It is a good thing that there are some men still who have enough courage and ambition to go in for a real career. We need 'em pretty badly just now. Look at this situation in the East. Do you realize it might mean a European war? But I don't suppose you even listened to what he was saying. If the Archangel Gabriel came in this moment to tell us that Judgment Day was tomorrow, you would only wonder what hat you would wear for it."

This seemed to me very unfair, for I have never thought much of hats and I answered that I saw Aunt was determined to forgive Chester however badly he behaved.

All this time Aunt had been growing angrier, muttering to herself, "Get round me," as if I had insulted her, and now she suddenly screamed at me, "What do you mean, forgive? Do you take us for village idiots like yourself? And what are you doing here?"

"I thought I was staying here."

"Staying here? Have you no sense at all? Pull yourself together, for God's sake, before your husband loses patience and sends you packing. You were lucky that he took you back after that last exploit."

I felt so much astonished that I could only murmur some question about her warnings. But she answered tartly that if I could not manage a husband who was "visibly hanging out his tongue for me, I ought to be poleaxed".

In fact she grew so excited and abusive (I suppose she could not forgive me for seeing her "put upon") that I was actually glad to return home in good time to dress for dinner.

All that evening, while Chester was at his most lively and brilliant and his most polite to me (in public he was even too elaborately polite to me), I could see that he was really full of triumph. He would look at me from time to time across the candles (there were only four to dinner, and he was close enough for me to see his expression), and he had just that joyful glitter in his eyes which I had seen after a meeting where he raised a laugh at the expense of some unlucky heckler.

Everything he did that evening, even the way he swaggered round the room that night in his vest (the one ugly thing about him was his lumpy hairy legs), expressed a delight that he could not hide. And though he pretended that what pleased him was the accession of the Vidlers, "and Vidler's backing is almost worth a place in the Cabinet", and congratulated me on the success of the evening, saying that I had never been more charming or looked more beautiful, it was plain that he was really enjoying his victory, not only over Aunt but over me. For in the very act of paying me these compliments he looked me in the face with the same exultant air as if to say, "Now I've got you – and what are you going to do about it?"

And, what is strange, for the first time I was afraid – not of what he might do, but of something unimagined, as if he still had resources (in his knowledge of "real life", of how people "worked", I could not forget how he had subdued the formidable Aunt Latter) that I had no idea of.

Thus as he grew more and more complimentary and attentive (but still with that touch of malice) my loathing of him passed into a kind of reflective trance; and when, to my astonishment, he had the impudence to make approaches (saying, of course, how he had been adoring me and wanting me all the evening, but seeming to laugh at me, too), I found myself too "scattered" to oppose him. I said to myself (as so often with Jim when we were children), "Very well – do what you like to me," and behaved like a dutiful but rather abstracted slave. But he (unlike Jim) showed no indignation – he behaved like a master who chooses to be a little rough to enjoy his mastery.

And I did not hate him, because it was useless – because it might have pleased him in that masterful mood – a fact that I have no doubt he had taken into account. He knew already (as some journalist wrote about him the other day) a great deal about power.

54 Tom was now six years old, rather small for his age, but beautifully made like his father and with the same fine skin and delicate hair. All his movements, like Jim's, were neat and exact – he never knocked things down. I shall be accused of being a doting mother if I say that even as a child Tom was a fascinating person, but all who knew him afterwards as a young man agree that he had extraordinary charm and his career is proof of his gifts.

Besides, he was openly admired. People turned to look at him in the streets. I dare say this admiration was not good for him, but how is one to prevent it? One can't say to strangers, "Don't fall in love with my child – it is bad for him," because it would be worse for him to hear you say such a thing.

Tom himself, fortunately, seemed indifferent to his admirers. He was much too excited by his own affairs to waste time on other people's. He was very good at playing by himself, acting a porter at the station banging doors, or a high-stepping horse in the park, or Aunt Latter cutting up a newspaper, or Mr Goold preaching.

And he was very good at drawing. His drawings were admired by a real artist, an R A who came to paint my cousins at Slapton. Of course, all children draw amusingly, because they dash down their quaint notions so boldly (and because we know they are children), but Tom had an extraordinary power of composition as well, especially in colour. He would draw scenes full of cows, dogs, and boats (the boats were often higher than the cows), and fill in the corners with people who could often be recognized, at least by their hat or legs; and even single cows, or boats like Major Freer's yawl with a brown spanker, and a cow at Little Tor with a white face.

Chester delighted in these paintings. In fact, Chester was the best of fathers, and I thought sometimes with relief that all my fears about his "special" position with the children turning out a disaster to us all and especially them had proved quite wrong. Indeed, it seemed his special position might actually turn out an advantage, because it made him (with his "noble" principles) try to be a better father than most. He would visit the nursery two or three times a day, and he made painting especially so exciting to Tom by inventing new ideas and telling stories about them that I would find them both shouting with laughter together.

I remember one morning at the Orchard when I went to the nursery and Tom was sitting on Chester's knee as usual, and Chester was painting an elephant and telling a story about it, how this very elephant had gone to a party and eaten not only all the cakes but the table, and finally the house. Tom laughed so much that he got down to roll on the floor, and Chester himself was helpless with laughter.

We were all laughing, because nothing is so catching as a child's laughter. Besides, Chester really enjoyed the rather violent joke of the host's dismay when his guest ate everything.

And when the nurse complained in those early days that Tom would not do his painting for himself, and got too excited, I paid no attention to her. I thought that she was suffering from the ordinary jealousy of nurses. But now soon after the Latter Waterloo (as Cousin Slapton called it), with the complete "rout of the old guard" (that is, Aunt Latter; Cousin Slapton made a joke of something which was very cruel to her), Chester suddenly began to read to him from the Bible, and to hear his prayers, and I noticed myself that Tom would be very excited, so that he could not get to sleep. And when I told Chester that the child was perhaps too young for some of the Bible stories, he said only that he had enjoyed them even younger, and that Tom asked for them. "Because you make them so exciting," I said.

"Do you want me to make them a bore?"

"No, but perhaps not quite so exciting."

Chester said that he would be careful; but it seemed to me that he made no difference. One night, when I saw Tom gazing at him with all his eyes, flushed with excitement and quite absorbed, the thought suddenly came up in my mind, "This is a new plan to fix me down; he means to lay hold of Tom. He will bring him up in his own way and take him away from me." And I had such a bitter feeling that I felt quite astonished and confused.

It was such a terrifying fancy that I quickly put the feeling away. I said to myself, "That is just what I would think. It is absolutely wicked to blame Chester for taking so much interest in Tom. And as for his not paying much attention to what I say, he is so excited and nervous about his political hopes and schemes that he really has no time for bothering about trifles."

But still the feeling would come back to me almost every day at prayer time. The truth was, I suppose, that Chester, having won all his big battles over me (and I was beginning to realize that the last, when I came back so tamely from Aunt Latter, had been decisive), could not help being in a position of a conqueror. However wise he was, like a Christian power that occupies some rather barbarous country and studies the inhabitants very carefully in order to win their allegiance, so that the more intelligent at least give him credit for good intentions (however the mob, I mean my own barbarous instincts, reacted against the stranger), still he was a conqueror.

Everything he did, even in kindness, was under suspicion. Indeed, the more kind he was, the more to be feared, because kindness in an enemy is even more oppressive than cruelty. It threatens the very soul.

And it seemed to me now that Chester used his cleverness with Tom to give the child political ideas. The giant in Jack the Giant Killer was always a wicked Tory and the wolf in Red Riding Hood had a face just like Joe Chamberlain. Of course, Chester seemed to do this as a joke. But when I said that Tom, at six, was too young to be mixed up in political feuds, he said that he hoped I did not want the boy to grow up with the wrong ideas. "He can't be too young to learn to hate grabbers and snobs and to feel his own privileges, as privileges."

I could not argue with Chester on these moral grounds and I suppose it is true what someone said, that no woman can bear to think of her son as a bristly man of fifty with a bald head and a red nose, smelling of whisky and tobacco and complaining about the Government, whatever it is. But I was haunted by a worse picture of Tom: as a party man, ready for any meanness or lie to help on the party, and living all his life in that dirty cold fog of propaganda and bitterness which seemed to go everywhere with many of the people who came to the house, like Goold. I knew, of course, that there must be parties and fighting between parties, and I suppose propaganda is better than murder, but I was horrified by the idea of turning a child into a partisan.

55 One day Chester and I were in an open landau with some East End mayor who was standing in a by-election for the borough, and as we were crossing Battersea Bridge Chester began to tell a story (the mayor, as Chester had discovered already, was a great family man; Chester was wonderfully quick to find out a subject that would "bring him together" with a possible supporter) about Tom's passion for slipping away from his nurse to look at the river, from this very bridge, especially at a certain spot. And as we were passing we all looked at the spot and cried out together.

For there the boy was, leaning over the parapet in a most dangerous position, gazing at some men unloading a gravel barge. I was taken so by surprise and frightened that I called "Stop!" and jumped down before we had stopped; I thought that if I wasted a second Tom would be in the river. And the child was so absorbed in watching that he had almost overbalanced. When I caught him and spoke to him he was quite unaware of me. As I lifted him down, he stared at me with a dazed expression as if awakened from a dream.

Even when we brought him with us in the carriage and

the men laughed at him (the mayor's notion of making himself agreeable to a small boy was to chaff him about playing truant and to suggest that he was taking lessons in "gravelings" which would be useful in his Papa's next election), he still looked bewildered, as if he could not accustom himself to being dragged so suddenly into so different a world.

And Chester began, as usual of late, to "improve" the moment by pointing out to Tom that, though people amused themselves by looking at the bargemen from bridges, they never considered how badly the men were paid or what hard lives they had.

At first I hardly noticed this – like Tom, I was in a different world. It was as though the shock of seeing the child apparently disappearing over the bridge had broken something "set" and "everyday" inside me and let out all kinds of feelings which went dashing and prancing in my darker caves. Tom's hand, clutched firmly in mine as if I were his only contact with reality, seemed to convey a special current, not of sympathy or appeal (Tom was thinking of me as little as of Chester), but of something that I had forgotten and must never forget – the special quality of a child's happiness. And it seemed to me that my own happiness had had something that was being taken from Tom, what I can only call its "pure" enjoyment of feeling.

And all at once I was revolted at the idea of Tom's escape that afternoon being used to give him a political lecture. And I thought, "He simply can't be allowed to stay under Chester's influence – it's a crime."

The whole political atmosphere in which we lived seemed, all at once, so stifling that I could not bear it another moment. And suddenly, to my own surprise (but I was still shaking at the picture of Tom disappearing into the river), I said that I must take the boy home at once.

The men were very polite and sent me home in the carriage. I was ashamed to give them so much trouble and I could see them both thinking that I was a typical lady, spoiled and whimsical. But I had stopped being the correct spouse. I simply had to escape.

56 The only way, of course, to remove Tom from the political atmosphere at the Parade was to send him to boarding school, and I knew that Jim had gone to school at six, when his parents were abroad; and after that to Eastborough. All the Latters had been to Eastborough and assumed that Tom would go there. Aunt had warned me several times to put the boy's name down for a place. But I knew Chester's prejudice against all boarding and public schools and I could not say to him, "Tom must go to a boarding school because it is the only way to separate him from you. You are too much for him." For one thing, he would not agree (or perhaps understand); and for another, he had no family tradition, that is, something that didn't need explanation.

It is, I dare say, good in most families to separate fathers and sons at the awkward age, but (as I realized now so strongly) in families that always send their sons to boarding schools (which are most families with important or overwhelming fathers or mothers) it need not be said or even thought about. In fact, talking or thinking about it might spoil its use. It is like something you inherit, a religion (which quite often won't bear argument either) or a nose.

But with Chester, his inheritance was so different that everything had to be argued, and when at last I raised the question I found the argument was worse than I had expected.

All I said (choosing a good moment – the only possible moment for such a difficult question; that is to say, when Chester had had a triumphant day and was joyfully – not wearily – affectionate) was that we had never yet made up our minds about Tom's schooling.

Chester at once stopped getting into bed (actually he had one foot in, and was holding up his nightshirt in both hands; I had given him pyjamas, but he preferred nightshirts because in some radical circles (certainly by Goold) pyjamas were considered rather snobbish and also a little free-thinking) and exclaimed, "Are you hinting at Eastborough again?" I said that I had not mentioned Eastborough. But he answered, "You have been thinking about it ever since Tom was born."

"But, Chester," I said, "after all, I have to think of Tom, and what would suit him, and I'm not sure that London does suit him with his delicate chest." And I went on to say that perhaps, too, our very busy kind of household was not the best place for a high-strung child.

Chester had taken his leg down again and had crossed his arms, a gesture which meant that he had taken his seat on the bench. He was looking at me so angrily that I saw, at once, how bad a moment I had chosen. For the best moments are the worst if something goes wrong. He said, not at all in his polite tone, but a very brassy one, that I must be mad to suggest a boarding school for a child of six, "unless you think that I'm not anxious to do the best thing for him – is it that you think I'm a bad influence?"

"Of course not, Chester. It's because you've been so good with Tommy that I'm sure you don't want to spoil his chances in life."

"Ah, Eastborough again – I thought we should have it

sooner or later." And I said that he knew very well that if Tom was to go to Eastborough his name ought to be put down at once.

"You are determined to make a snob of him, then."

"No, but not different from other boys in his own walk of life."

I avoided the word class to Chester, because it was apt to excite him so much. "It is bad for people," I said, "to feel discriminated against."

"Exactly. That's why I say, send all the children to the same kind of schools."

"But, Chester, I wouldn't mind if all children did go to boarding school. What I'm afraid of is seeming to discriminate against Tom."

"You mean you want to make a snob of him because all the others are snobs. No, I won't do it."

"I see your point, Chester. Of course, you are right."

"Well then – " He stopped and stared at me.

"But I do think I'm right, too."

"How can we both be right?"

"I don't know, but that's what I feel."

Chester went on staring for a moment, and then turned red and said with great indignation, "But you are not right." He began to march up and down. "It's impossible – even to please you. It would be treachery to everything I stand for. It's a question of the boy's very soul."

"Yes – that's why I – "

"Excuse me," he interrupted, as if I was speaking blasphemy, "the thing is too serious – I cannot compromise. It's not just a question of Eastborough – any so-called public school is out of the question."

And when I tried to speak again he held up his hand as if I were someone brawling in church, and said, "Please,

please, Nina; don't you see I can't do anything else? My mind is made up."

And what made the quarrel so disastrous at this moment (the good moment that had become the worst possible) was that (since reconciliation was out of the question, and we had to be together) we could not even touch one another. So, as the mattress was rather hollow in the middle where we usually lay, I was obliged to balance myself on the extreme edge and hold on with both hands in order not to slip down against Chester. Neither of us could sleep a wink; and when I saw Chester get up in the morning with rings round his eyes, and heard him close the door of the dressing room with unusual care, to show that though I was a criminal he would consider my feelings, I felt like a criminal.

From that moment he would not even hear the word school from me. He had, I saw, taken firm hold of his principles, and they were quite good principles. From his political point of view he *was* right. But so (I thought) was I. Of course, it is quite common for people who are both right to quarrel. One of my cousins married a Latter who drank and treated her badly, and, besides, they had no children and she longed for children. So she ran away with another man. But her husband would not divorce her, and her children were illegitimate, and the new lover's family tried to make him leave her, and they were both very unhappy. But no one could say that anyone was in the wrong. They just had different principles. That was why I was so alarmed by this quarrel with Chester.

57 This news about Tom, as might have been expected, produced a convulsion among the Latters. To Aunt, Bob, the Slaptons, half a dozen cousins, and especially Jim, it seemed that not to send Tom to a "good" school was an act of political revenge against a child, a mean and wicked crime.

I don't think Chester even began to understand this feeling in my family, because he never understood that people like Aunt and Jim and Bob and even Slapton also had very strong and deep ideas about the "soul" (even if they did not talk of them), and that they looked upon people like Goold and even himself as having (perhaps from no fault of their own) rather bad small souls – that is, envious, suspicious and tricky.

Jim, hearing the news from Aunt, wrote me from Africa for the first time in eighteen months – a very sharp note saying that he would hold me responsible for Tom's getting a "fair deal". And what was more remarkable (for he had never before shown much interest in Tom), he wrote to Cousin Wilfred and asked him if it would be safe for him to come home. Of course, this was a hint to Wilfred to clear up the rest of the debts, especially the "debts of honour", that is, the debts that Chester had refused to deal with precisely in order (at least, so we thought) to keep Jim out of England.

Jim had now been in Africa for two years, and I was bound to admit that he seemed to be enjoying himself. He complained only of the shortage of big game and the difficulty of getting any polo at his station, because of its remoteness from a ground and other players.

The station was called Dutchinluga, and Jim was in charge of a tribe called the Lugas, who seemed to wear no clothes at all except a little basket of woven grass shaped like a thimble. They were cannibals, but ate only other tribes, and they rode bareback on ponies over their mountains. Jim wrote that they were "the finest chaps he'd ever met", and that "you could talk of European civilization, but the Lugas had a better one of their own, and lived a better life than any of your professors".

These letters used to irritate Aunt Latter, who said that it was just like Jim to adopt a lot of cannibals in the remote bush, when he ought to have chosen some line which would bring him into notice and get him a foot in a big station. And she pointed out that, whatever he might say about European civilization, he had spent his leave at Cannes. Neither did he seem to mind his "exile" very much apart from an occasional complaint that, though half his pay went on his creditors, he did not see how he was ever going to see old England again, because he did not propose to come home in order to be barred at the clubs, and cut in Tattersall's ring. It was only now (and it shows how strongly he felt about Tom's having a "fair deal") that he made a determined effort to "get clear". He wrote to me, warning me that he would hold me responsible for "the boy" (and indeed I felt responsible to Jim as well as Tom) and asking me what "the cousins" were up to. "They could get me out any day they liked."

I took this letter both to Slapton and Wilfred and pointed out what a scandal it was that Jim should be kept out of the country just *because* he was an honourable man. And I found them very sympathetic. They promised me to "do something" for Jim; not, however, on the grounds of his martyrdom, but because, as Slapton said, he seemed to have "taken a pull at himself".

In fact, Jim had actually paid off some of his smaller debts. His only extravagance seemed to have been buying some old army blankets for "my chiefs" and importing some hunting horns and ponies so that "my fellows" could hunt jackals "in decent style".

And a good many people were now beginning to

sympathize with Jim in his "exile". People always do come round to the exile, and also for the last year there had been articles in the papers about the fighting in Nigeria, and the public, getting over their boredom with heroes after the last war, were beginning to look round again for someone to admire.

So they had begun to make much of the "lonely pioneers of the *Pax Britannica*".

And Wilfred was actually in touch with some of Jim's honour creditors, when something happened that threw out all our calculations.

58 This was the election of 1905, the "disaster" in which the Liberals absolutely overwhelmed the Tories (Chester carried Tarbiton by over two thousand, the biggest majority in its history) and formed a new Government pledged to social reform. And Chester was offered at once the place of Under-Secretary for Mines, a very important place, because the Minister was in the Lords. Chester would have to represent the department and do all the speaking for it in the Commons.

I suppose nobody now can realize the effect of that "revolution" on even quite sensible men like Wilfred. But the truth is that it was a real revolution. Radical leaders like Lloyd George (though Chester was always a little suspicious of him, saying that he was not fundamentally a man of principle) really did mean to bring in a new kind of state, a "paternal state", that took responsibility for sickness and poverty.

And this was all against the old idea of what a state could do or ought to do. Even old Liberals were alarmed and talked of the "slippery slope to economic ruin and dictatorship".

Above all, there was the "feeling in the air" of some big change. I noticed it even in the nursery. My nurse asked me (and she had forgotten to change Sally's wet stockings) if "the army would be stopped". She had a brother in the army and was afraid that he would lose his place.

Wilfred had already arranged to see Chester on "family affairs"; that is, as, of course, I knew, on the new plan for getting Jim clear. Now he sent his congratulations, saying how glad he was at the triumph of a "real westerner" like himself, and the interview took place at once.

And as I discovered (not from Chester but the cousins), it was agreed that Jim should not be cleared, because it was not "in his own real interest" to come home.

Obviously there had been one of those "tacit bargains" which Chester imagined all day everywhere. And, in fact, he and Wilfred did a great deal of business together. For though, of course, Chester had been obliged to resign all his directorships on getting a post in the Ministry, he was still a big investor in the companies and also a partner in two private companies: Goold's Stores (since their reconciliation he had put a lot of capital into Goold's) and a small engineering company making pumps. He saved a lot of money both for this company and Goold's by an agreement with Wilfred that their buyers should not bid against each other for certain properties.

That is, though Chester had resigned from his directorships, he had to keep in touch with business in case the Government was beaten and he wanted his directorships back. And, on the other hand, his advice was even more valuable to the companies (though I need not say he never told them official secrets) because of his new connections.

You may say, in fact (Aunt, disgusted that Jim was not to

177

come home after all, said it with great bitterness), that Wilfred changed his mind because Chester had suddenly become a man of power and his friendship was more valuable than the collective goodwill of a declining family like the Latters. And what I have written about the consternation of many established people at this "revolution" seems to support Aunt's view.

But though I was so furious with Wilfred on this occasion, I should hate to fall into the vulgar trick (which is, besides, very disturbing) of pretending that political people are all self-seekers. I know from my own experience that it is not true. They are only "practical" people who try to "make the best" of things. One brewer who came to see Chester and tried to persuade him to visit one of his public houses incognito was actually a radical himself – even a republican (and rather mad) – but he was anxious that Chester should understand the value of public houses to the poor. He was afraid that Chester would support some "wild theory" about the "wicked brewers" from ignorance of the facts.

And a great number of the people who suddenly became friendly with us at this time and asked us to their parties had no connection with politics – for instance, the children who asked our children to their parties in all directions. Little girls made a great fuss of Tom, and boys would spoil Sally with sweets, who had no idea of what a radical meant.

Aunt would say that the mammas were behind the misses trying to make a catch; and boys had papas in the background, who wanted favours. But Aunt was a professional "clever" talker and I really think (though, of course, some mammas do very early begin to hunt for eligible sons-in-law) that any little distinction (and the name Nimmo was already something to catch the ear) does excite interest and curiosity. Mothers, too, even without matchmaking, do want "nice" friends for their daughters, which is the same thing as eligible ones later on; and little girls had, I know, vague romantic feelings about Tom from hearing their parents discuss his family as well as from his blue eyes. As for the young men, and even old gentlemen, who wanted to take Sally, aged four, to tea at Gunters, I'm sure most of them made much of her simply because, as Chester's loyal supporters, they felt for her something of what courtiers feel for a princess – of course, in a very small way.

I discovered, in fact (and it interested me very much, because I had not expected it from the novels – those rather cynical novels – people usually write about "society" and especially political society), that many people, and especially energetic clever people, high up in business or politics, are naturally attracted by rising young men (and Chester even now was only forty-three) and want to meet them only from curiosity; and would even help them on without the least idea (or not in the first place) of getting any advantage from them.

The truth is that clever people like clever people and society people like interesting people. I have even heard a great Tory leader (the Duke of N) complain that there was no fighting against "these demagogues", because as soon as any one of them got his name in a *Times* leader his duchess asked him down for the weekend and encouraged him to preach his "pernicious rubbish" to the whole county.

It was natural that a successful man like Cousin Wilfred should be attracted by Chester's success, and also for Chester to like a clever well-informed man like Wilfred.

And Chester did like him. He was pleased to find that he agreed with him about the value of public parks, with suitable refreshment, and the need for better housing. He said that Wilfred was a clever fellow. They had a mutual attraction.

And when he said (taking the same view as Aunt) that Wilfred wanted "to get in on the ground floor" and (laughing at me) that this was "what Lord Slapton calls the English tradition of political tolerance and continuity", I tried to make him see this other and fairer (and also much more interesting) point of view.

But he only went on laughing at me and said I was a good cousin, and pinched my chin. He was perfectly sure that all these new friends wanted to "use him" or "rope him into their robber gangs".

Yet he did laugh, and (this was an immense relief to me) he did not dwell on the matter; he did not seem to resent "these little games" so long as he "saw through them".

"I'm not so green as I'm cabbage looking, am I, darling?" he said to me one night after I had showed him an invitation from a coal millionaire who complimented me on my husband's "brilliant grasp of a highly technical and complex industry". But before I could assure him that he was anything but "green" (and even five years before he would have wanted such an assurance) he roared with laughter and became at once particularly affectionate.

And I thought that just as he was not so nervous of "class conspiracies", so he was not so touchy with me. That is, he was more easy and careless in our relations; he did not flash out at me about our "difference of standpoint", or say (as once he had always been saying or hinting), "But then, I'm not a gentleman."

And it seemed to me that when men come into power it is as though they had come out of a tunnel through a mountain (going up all the time, but not noticing it) and suddenly see a whole country spread at their feet, and see it from a point of view quite new and startling to them. For everything has changed its proportion.

Chester saw "the world at his feet". And though he still believed in "class plots", he was confident that he could deal with them. This is why (and not because of the "corruption" of money) we began, from this time, to go to "great" parties and to ask "great" people to our house, and also (which gave much offence in Tarbiton) went sometimes to the opera. For to Chester, now an important man, that is, important among important people, which is the only real importance, all parties and amusements had become of very small consideration beside the responsibilities of his post.

Also we were much better off. We entertained a great deal, and Chester (though he still kept all the accounts, and Bootham paid for my clothes, even my lingerie) insisted that I should be well dressed.

59 For me, of course, the big change seemed to be that I was now the wife not just of a rising man but one who had begun to arrive. I was photographed for the papers, and even painted for the Academy by an enterprising artist who wanted commissions from the "new regime". I dare say I was much envied as the spoiled wife of a brilliant and adoring husband; and, in fact, Chester had never been so generous and affectionate.

But also he had never expected so much from me, not only in our private relations, but especially in public ones. Every day there were visits to pay, receptions, luncheons, official functions at which it was my duty to appear as "the charming and chic Mrs Chester Nimmo", who had been judged a "considerable social asset to the new Government which lacks the big guns and big houses of the Tory hostesses".

I had to do my best to live up to this absurd reputation (largely invented for me by Chester's friends in the radical press and quite probably at his suggestion), because to fail in the role was to "let Chester down" in the public eye – and you can't afford to injure a man with whom you are at war, that is, if it be a "moral war".

Indeed, if I did fail as hostess – and I was not at all suited to the task, I was apt to be sleepy (according to Aunt, lazy), and also I was always very bad at hiding boredom (according to Aunt, too fond of amusing myself, which I could certainly do very well, with a book) – Chester, who had "eyes in the back of his head", would turn round and give me a significant look. And afterwards he would say, "I'm afraid you found old So-and-so a bit difficult."

"Oh dear! I hope I didn't show it."

"My dearest, I was admiring your patience. As you know, he is the most touchy and spiteful old brute in London. He would be delighted to do me a bad turn, and there are several ways to his hand."

This meant that I had affronted old So-and-so (my mind had wandered during one of his immense stories about "what I said to Gladstone in 1884") and that Chester might suffer for it. And for this I not only apologized – I was truly sorry. For the tension between us was always growing worse. In fact, Chester's glory and the pressure of our engagements, far from relieving it, only made us less fit to bear it.

Of course, it was never mentioned between us that Chester had stopped Jim's coming home – he would not have acknowledged it. Such things (like Sally's paternity, never to be admitted) were tacit.

Tacit conflicts, secret reservations did not worry Chester in the least; I think he enjoyed them. He was used (I imagine from childhood) to live in a world of manoeuvres; he was always taking up positions and digging entrenchments. He was very good at the art.

But I could not bear to be always at war; I could not bear to live with a secret enemy, even when he loved me.

And (what I felt even more bitterly than the treachery to Jim) I had lately heard from Eastborough (in private, but very unexpectedly) that now Chester was in the Government it would be not easier but harder to make an exception for Tom and let him in at short notice. The school was obliged to be careful of charges of favouritism. And Tom (he was now nearly eleven) should be entered at once – already he would be lucky to get a vacancy.

And now I began to see that I dared not lose the battle for Tom's soul, as Chester himself called it. I had, I suppose, known that before, but I had been depending on Jim's arrival to win it for me.

But neither did I see how I was to fight Chester, who was just as determined. For him, too, it was a decisive battle which he dared not lose. Besides, he was triumphant all along the line. How many wives, I used to wonder, submitted to having all their accounts reviewed by a secretary or never left the house without writing down where they were to be found? True, I had come to this position chiefly by my own fault, by extravagance and fecklessness, and also by a love of peace (which Aunt called my chief vice – and perhaps she was right); I had no right to complain.

But though I could not complain, I felt a kind of desperation. To quarrel with Chester, to deal with him at all, was like struggling with a shark whose teeth all point the same way. His love and his anger both swallowed me down a little further into a horrible stuffy darkness.

60 And I think it was chiefly despair (though the doctor said it was nothing but "seasonitis") that made me so thin and nervous that summer. I began to sleep badly, and when I did sleep I had terrifying dreams (once I saw Tom dead on a bank of mud by a river – but he was wearing polo boots – all among rubbish, old tins and planks and hats) and I lost my good appetite.

Chester, on the doctor's advice, took me for a holiday to Venice (because I had loved it and he loathed it) at a time when he should have been hard at work in his department. But I was ill in Venice and came back sleeping worse than before. Also I had lost nearly a stone in weight.

Chester was in great dismay at my loss of looks and my sleeplessness (which kept him awake), and kept on sending me to specialists. Then he would stand over me with bottles of tonic, which I detested (I had hated medicine from a child) and which gave me spots that were even more detestable.

Now I will not say that Chester thought I was making myself ill on purpose – the very idea is infuriating to any man (it seems to him a very mean trick, and so it is); but he did at last accuse me of not trying to get well.

This happened one evening before dinner, when he found that I had forgotten to tell him that my latest bottle was finished. He turned very red (the bottle was still in his hand – and Chester had a great faith in medicine, at least in a new medicine) and said, "Did you really forget it?"

"Yes, but it wasn't doing me any good."

"That's what you always say. Do you want to get well?" And he walked up and down, controlling his indignation, but letting me see, too, that he was controlling it. I said that I did want to get well (though I was not really sure of it – I was too tired) but that none of the bottles was any good.

At last Chester stopped at the foot of the bed (I was lying on the quilt, too tired to dress) and made a "point" at me, and after half a minute burst out, "Is anything worrying you – bills – the Aunt – Bootham? If so, for God's sake tell me. I don't care what it is." And again after a moment he added, with a kind of rush, "Jim?"

I said, of course, that nothing was worrying me. Then there was a long silence and we looked at each other, and Chester made another immense effort and said, "The children are all right – I never saw them better." And I answered that Sally was a picture but Tom seemed a little peaky and scattered. I wondered sometimes if he was getting any good out of his present teachers (Tom had been sharing a tutor and governess with a neighbour), if he did not need a change.

But the moment Chester heard the word "teacher" he jumped up as if I had stabbed him, and said, "You're not going to suggest a boarding school for Tom? Surely we had settled that miserable business."

"I haven't mentioned schools for years."

"No, but you think schools, and look schools, and hint schools, and breathe schools, and leave prospectuses and magazine articles about schools on my desk and in my chair."

"But, Chester, I am really worried."

"So am I. You are driving me mad. I tell you that it is impossible. It would be a criminal thing. Think of my position, Nina. You are asking me to go back upon all I stand for, in the most public manner."

"But, Chester, you are asking me to sacrifice Tom. What

shall I say to him when he grows up and finds we have made a difference for him – just because of politics?" And then I saw him turn red – he was surprised by this new idea. I said quickly that, of course, I saw his difficulty, but could he not leave the responsibility to me; it was surely a thing in which there ought to be some free choice?

"Most certainly," Chester said at once. For, of course, he believed very much in freedom.

"But not for me?"

And he was so taken aback at this audacity that I saw my advantage and said (just as if I had been fighting with Jim in the old days), "You always talk of letting me have a free choice, but it really does rather seem that all you mean by freedom is what you think right."

"Excuse me, but that is not so."

"But, Chester, what have we been arguing about, then?"

"Not what I think right, but what *is* right. You are not going to tell me that class distinctions are a natural thing?"

"I don't know whether they are natural, but I do know they exist just now, and we can't let Tommy's life be spoiled by pretending that they don't." But then Chester went into a long indignant speech about what was natural in such a way that I forgot (till an hour afterwards) all about my argument that he wasn't giving me my freedom to choose, or considering Tommy's future.

This, of course, is the usual technique with practised arguers. I had often heard Chester dealing with opponents by leading them right away from their own point and answering some question that they had not asked. And if they protested, he would accuse them before everybody of being contentious, or splitting hairs, or even of trickery in trying to confuse the issue.

And feeling that he was playing this trick on me, I said,

"I see it is no good going on, because you turn everything round to suit yourself," a rudeness which made him furious. But I would not let him go on. I said quickly that I would not say another word; the matter was decided, and would he ring for Molly, because I ought to get ready for going out.

But that night, when we came home from the party, I was so desperate that I felt I could not bear him, so I went to bed at once (he always went first to the study when we came in – to see if Bootham had left any notes about urgent calls) and sent a message by Molly to say that I was so worn out (which was quite true) that I was going to take a sleeping pill. This always meant that I did not want Chester with me and he would sleep in the little room upstairs. But tonight, to my surprise (he felt my desperation), he came in and said, "Are you really going to take another draught? You never take them three nights running." This was true, for I was always afraid of drugs taking hold of me. So I answered that on this night I did not care about the rules, because I must sleep. And Chester went out backwards looking at me really with hatred. For he loved me so much that often he could have killed me.

And I was so desperate, that as soon as he had gone I reached out to the bedside table and took six cachets at once and slept for twenty-two hours. I nearly died, because, apparently, even one cachet was rather a strong dose; and in the morning Molly was so frightened not to be able to wake me that she sent for Chester, who sent for two doctors, and they could not bring me round till the evening.

Chester was nearly mad with fright. I have never seen anyone in such a state. When I came round, he was kneeling beside the bed and staring at me with his mouth half open and his eyebrows raised – it was as if he had had a stroke and his face had gone to pieces. Then when he saw I was awake, he cried out and began to kiss me and said in a furious weeping voice like a child who has been slapped and hates you for it, "How could you do such a thing?" (His cheeks were quite hollow and green as if he had been starving.) "Why didn't you tell me?"

I said that it had been an accident. But he got more angry and answered impatiently, "No, no, no! We can't go on like this – tell me the truth for once."

"I was so worn out with arguing – "

"Arguments? What arguments? You're not accusing me? Do you realize what you've done, and what you might have done? But you never give me credit for any decent feelings."

He was in such misery (and also a strange state of nervous excitement) that I was anxious for him (we were, in fact, both crying together as if some fearful disaster had happened to us) and assured him over and over again that I had no idea of killing myself or anything so exaggerated. I was shocked to think that Chester should accuse me of so mean a trick.

In fact (being rather weak and inclined to "pour out"), I did at last give way to his entreaties and told him the truth, that I had only wanted to sleep and sleep and had not cared what happened to me so long as I did sleep.

And this was a mistake. It was never safe to tell the whole truth to Chester, for he always improved it. He said at once, "But it's the same thing – I knew it." And while I was still secretly contradicting these words, he added, "That's the way you would do it."

He pulled away from my arms and got up, staring at me. "My God! What are you made of? How can I ever understand you?"

He really did believe it was the "same thing", because that was the "way I would do it". And when I protested that if I did not "really" know what I was doing I couldn't be held responsible, he grew exasperated and began to argue the point, saying that I "really did know". I only refused to acknowledge it to myself. But suddenly in the very middle of a word he stopped, and a most queer expression came into his face, of anger and bafflement together (for a moment, in a startling way, I was reminded of Jim's look as a child when he had failed to get what he wanted), then he turned sharply and went out of the room.

61 Chester never forgave me for my "wicked and cruel" attempt to destroy myself (and him, too – for an inquest might have ruined him); but also from that day he had a completely new attitude toward me. He treated me more like a problem and less like a cherished possession; you might say that he used a different diplomacy. I was still the conquered country and one quite unfit for responsibility – but all the more capable of making a dangerous nuisance of itself.

And though he was full of resentment, yet he blamed himself very much for allowing such a "situation" to arise and gave all his mind to arriving at a "settlement".

The very next day he went to see a certain friend in the Education Office, and when he came back to me he asked if I would allow the boy to be "crammed" for a scholarship, for if he turned out to have a classical bent there seemed to be no reason why he should not try for a scholarship at Eastborough. "I understand," he said, "that X (a radical minister) is putting his daughter in for a scholarship at Turton" (a very expensive girls' school) "and I should think Tom has more brains than any of that family."

So it was arranged that Tom should go to a crammer's so that he might try for a scholarship at Eastborough.

And having settled that question, he went on at once to the next. "Now about Jim," he said one morning (but he had had a bad night; his digestion had been very bad ever since the accident). "Is it really the fact that he can't come home till the gambling debts are settled?" (A thing, of course, that Chester knew as well as I did.) "Would you like me to make inquiries? I should be glad to break any deadlock."

Of course, I thanked him very warmly, saying that it was just like him to do better by Jim than Jim's own family.

"Yes," he said (and you could see that he was remembering his "nobility"), "it is men like Jim and their work which are the true justification of empire. A good many of those who criticize our action in Nigeria are completely blind to the human factors involved on both sides – " In fact, he made a little speech, which was, I thought, a good sign – he was feeling better.

And I need not say that as soon as Chester next met Wilfred (they met quite often to discuss their business interests) it was discovered by the family council that Jim's debts of honour could be very easily settled. Wilfred and Aunt took over his IOUs and he was free to come home and walk into his old clubs whenever he liked.

But if you think (as many thought) that it was weak in Chester to give way to me, that this was only another proof of my "malign influence", you would be wrong. For the truth was quite different. Like other men busy in "great affairs", he had a system of answers as well as times, which was a kind of twisted wire defence to keep off small invaders – and it was very hard to break through.

But if you did break through, you found inside always at least some part of the original Chester.

I know that people (especially Tarbiton people) were

saying already that he was "a traitor to his religious principles", and it is true that he no longer had time for preaching or going so often to chapel, but at bottom, as you found in any crisis, he was still a religious man. That is, even if he had stopped taking much interest in God, he still believed in "freedom" and "brotherhood" and the "rights of the individual".

That is why he began now to build Jim up as a hero and to consider Tom's future, even at some risk to himself. He had recollected that Jim and Tom were individual persons. It gave him real satisfaction (quite as much as his success in "settling" my difficulties) to "do the right thing" by Jim and to find a clever way (it satisfied everybody) of getting round the question of Tom's "class education".

For he had discovered by his inquiry that even the extreme radicals did not object to scholarships, because they were open to everybody.

And later on, when Tom went to Eastborough after all (he did not take a scholarship – he never really had a chance), it was because when Chester met the headmaster and some of the boys he did not hide behind any prejudice but allowed himself to see how lively and intelligent they were. His letting Tom go to Eastborough (the school was ready to take him "on the scholarship examination", which was also an answer to any charge of favouritism) was not a weak act but a strong one for which I have always admired him.

62 My Latter relations had no right to say (but one cannot stop them thinking it) that Chester mishandled Tom; and just as unfair to believe (like some of Chester's "faithful") that Tom hated Chester and took every chance of disobeying him and injuring him. The real

truth is that it is always difficult to be the brilliant son of a brilliant father, and even harder the other way round.

I remember too well the day I first realized this. Soon after Sally's birth (much too soon according to the doctor) I got up to go with Aunt Latter and Tom to the Zoo. Aunt Latter had members' tickets for Sunday, and I was very anxious to be at this treat, especially as I knew that while I had been laid up Chester had given Tom many treats.

But just as we were setting off, Chester proposed to join the party, and when he was told that there was no ticket for him, obtained one at once by simply telephoning to one of the Fellows. And at the Zoo (perhaps because he felt that he had defeated our plan to go alone with Tom) he was in his most brilliant form. Indeed, in the monkey house he made so amusing a speech about monkeys, pretending to recognize various famous men (including Darwin himself; Chester, of course, believed in evolution, but somehow he always had a dislike of Darwin and the evolutionists) in the cages and talking what he called monkey (chattering like a monkey but saying real words) that there was quite a crowd listening to him, including Aunt Latter, who was in fits of laughter. Aunt Latter, indeed, was quite elated with pride. But what was delightful to me was to see Tom's enjoyment (as I say, he was a child who was inclined to enjoy everything) as he realized, perhaps for the first time, Chester's unusual cleverness and his success with the audience. He stared first at the people round and then at Chester – he was quite flushed with excitement.

Chester, too, I thought, was excited by Tom's admiration – his sudden shrieks of laughter. I saw him smile in a triumphant way when he looked down at the boy. And when Tom, in his ecstasy, seized him by the trouser leg, he

patted and stroked his head with the spontaneous warm
affection which made him so attractive a man.

But a few minutes later, when we were in the bird house
and Chester was involved in a discussion with Aunt about
the German menace, Tom suddenly grew bored. Then he
disappeared, and when I found him in the grounds he
refused to come home. There was a scene. The boy fought
and screamed like a child of three, and when I said that his
papa would be ashamed of him, he shouted that he hated
Papa. Even on the next day he was jumpy and "difficult".
Chester was like a drug to him (and other people, too, but
it did not have the same effect on Aunt or Bootham) and
too much of it produced a reaction.

And though, at last, Tom was sent away to school, it was
impossible to protect him from Chester's "effects", because
they followed him everywhere. Even if Tom did not see his
name in the papers (and luckily small boys do not read the
papers), other boys' parents and the masters did so, and
spoke of Chester to the boys who talked of him to Tom.

And these boys were often critical, looking for an excuse
to find fault with Tom. For Chester's "atmosphere",
especially now when he was rising into real power, was
rather like a big electric charge – it caused explosive
tensions all round, not only of devotion but disgust. Some
people will detest anyone who has the smallest celebrity,
even heroes. There was a boy of fourteen at Queensport
who rescued a little girl from the harbour, and was given a
medal, and two days afterwards some other bigger boys set
on him in a back street and broke his arm. A prominent
man, even if he is a saint, and never does anything but pray,
must always make enemies. But a Minister who is always
governing people and deciding what they must do or not do
accumulates enemies at a fearful rate, and he does not

gather friends in equal proportion, because the people who get some advantage from him think that it is only what was due to them.

Especially during the fight against the Lords in 1909 (Chester was a strong supporter of Lloyd George's great land bill) I was startled to discover how much hatred was gathering round us (I had some more anonymous letters, one telling me that my new fur coat, which had been photographed for a paper, was bought with money robbed from the people), and found out how hard it is to escape the sense of it. I would feel it in the air whenever I waked up at night – like a special darkness in the middle of the ordinary dark – a weight on my blankets.

But Chester was growing hardened – I suppose it was very necessary that he should be so. He was only annoyed by its effect on the children. Tom, in his first term, at thirteen, actually had a fight with a boy who said that the Government were a lot of robbers and that Chester himself was a low guttersnipe who stirred up trouble in order to make himself known and rich. Tom won this fight (though he got a black eye), but he was very excited about the whole affair, and, when we went down to see him, declared that if he had his way he would abolish the Lords altogether. Chester was delighted with him (and so was I), but managed to persuade him that it was not necessary to fight with anyone who criticized the Government.

"Yes, but you don't know what they say about you, Papa," Tom said, hanging on Chester's arm. "Nobody could stand it."

"I could stand it, Tommy," Chester said, laughing; and, "I'm not going to have you getting killed even on my behalf."

"But I wasn't killed. I won. Of course, he got in one first, but afterwards I simply massacred him."

"It was lost on the second reading," said Chester, laughing.

"I should think so," Tom said, quite seeing the joke. "The noes had it." And then they both laughed so much some of the boys looked at us (we were close to the school and the street was full of boys) in what I thought was disapproval. But Tom didn't care for them; and when Chester said, "We are causing a civil commotion," Tom answered, "Of course, they know who you are, but you needn't mind. I'm used to it," as if to say that Nimmos must expect certain discomforts.

And I think, in fact, that Tom's bad reports that term (he was said to be careless in work and also to show a certain aloofness toward rules) were due much more to the excitement of being Chester's son than to the fight. Though the fight also made him a little too popular with some other energetic characters. For Tom was a sensitive and enthusiastic boy who reacted very quickly to a "situation". Whereas Sally, on the other hand, did not seem at all affected. It was, indeed, only in this year that it occurred to her that Chester was a public figure, when some other small girl at a party pulled her hair and called her a stuck-up thing.

Sally was not, in fact, conceited, but she had what Aunt Latter called the high Latter carriage; that is, she walked very upright (like Aunt Latter and Jimmy) with her head a little on one side, and her chin held rather high. Withal she was a very pretty little thing with great violet-blue eyes, and hair like new wheat straw too pale for artificial light but most beautiful in the sun. She looked, indeed, so pretty and so fragile that people would turn in the street to look at her, and old ladies would sorrow over her as a young angel not long for this world. But, in fact, Sally was very strong, and extremely healthy, and her faraway angelic gaze usually meant only that she was wondering what she would get for her next birthday. She was, in fact, a most practical child, which did not mean that she was not romantic. She had a passion for fairy tales, and her first pantomime excited her so much that she played Cinderella for weeks afterwards. But nothing kept her awake, and she had a very slow imagination. She would look at one with her lovely eyes wide open while one was describing some excitement – a yacht race, or the Grand Canal – and then ask, "Who won?" or "Is the water deep?"

When Sally's hair was pulled because she was Chester's daughter, she was merely indignant and declared that she would tell her papa. She then asked us if Chester was a great man, and how great he was, and concluded with satisfaction that if anyone else pulled her hair she would call the police and have her put in jail.

Sally had always adored Chester, as he adored and spoiled her. He treated her with all that cleverness, that tact, which he had used with me, but without the jealousy and suspicion which had made me suffer by it. He would anticipate her thoughts and desires in a manner which seemed magical to anyone who did not know so well the grooves of a very simple mind. And even Sally, unreflective as she was, would sometimes be surprised, and exclaim, "But, Papa, how did you know that I was going to say that?" And he would laugh, delighted with himself and with her.

63 I said that Tom was extremely proud and fond of Chester. He took the keenest interest in Chester's career; and when in 1908 the Minister Lord B died and Chester (after an agonizing week when we thought an old hack would be jobbed in) was promoted to the place and a seat in the Cabinet, he not only wired his congratulations from school but wrote a very good "grown-up" letter saying how wise it was of the Prime Minister to give Chester the place, because he was not only in the Commons, but had a real genius for debate.

But the difficulty with clever children is that though they grow in all directions at once, they are always getting out of balance. One bit suddenly becomes very grown-up, and another bit stays quite childish. It was only a term (or perhaps two terms) after Tom had fought that battle for Chester that they had their first bad quarrel. I had noticed at the beginning of the holidays that Tom had become suddenly more reserved. He talked politics more (thoroughly approving of the new attack on the Lords and asking the most intelligent questions), but also did not seem so much amused by Chester's jokes.

Chester used to tell stories with great energy and dramatic effect, acting the parts, imitating voices, and bursting into a shout of laughter. One of his favourites was about a new member, who, having made his maiden speech (Chester was wonderful in showing the poor man fumbling with his notes), sat down on his hat. Sally and Tom had always laughed heartily at this story, but this year (and it is true that Chester, since his promotion, had been in very high spirits, which made him laugh even louder at his own jokes) I noticed that Tom did not laugh, but got up quickly (as if embarrassed) to help himself to something.

And the same afternoon, when we had been at a matinee together (he loved going to plays with me as I did with him – his enjoyment was so keen), he said to me, "They rather overdid it, don't you think?" And then before I could answer, "I wish Papa wouldn't squeak when he tells those stories."

"But, Tom, he was imitating some poor man's voice."

"But he does it so badly. It's so exaggerated and he's getting worse. Somebody ought to tell him."

"My dear Tom, your papa is quite famous for his imitations." And Tom only made a face as if to say, "So much the worse." I nearly said that if Tom had known the agony we had gone through in that week when it seemed that Chester would be passed over he would forgive a little exaggeration now, but reflected that this might be rash. To explain a husband to one's children is almost more dangerous than letting them get wrong ideas. You may fix something that would otherwise dissolve away in the natural whirl of their fancies.

But this was not the end of Tom's new critical revulsion. A few days later we had a reception (it was one of a series we gave to celebrate, and emphasize, Chester's new dignity) in the evening, on this occasion chiefly for Tarbiton supporters, what we called locals (Daisy was there in a green frock, which made her seem, as she herself said, like a beetroot in a salad; and somehow her splendid diamonds looked like paste), to meet some "names". We had another Minister, and a judge, a famous but respectable author, two knights from the Treasury and half a dozen MPs and peers. And it happened that Tom was late.

Tom had a good deal of freedom, and, besides, he was not very punctual. He liked perhaps (as Chester did also) to arrive rather late at any party and "make an entry". And, in fact, there were inquiries for him, remarks (in our hearing) on his good looks, his cleverness, and two ladies from Chorlock (not so much malicious as anxious to live up to what they thought a "smart" party) claimed to have seen him from their cab, half an hour before in Chelsea, come out of the music hall with some girls, all smoking cigarettes.

Cigarettes in themselves were considered rather fast in Chorlock and Tarbiton.

This story, of course, made a buzz in the room, and clearly a great many people (they kept looking at Chester or me as if to see how we would take the news) were delighted. It was something new and interesting. Besides, a good many of Chester's Tarbiton friends, including Goold, said that Tom was being ruined at Eastborough; and some others, like Aunt Latter (and I rather think Daisy Goold, and especially her daughter Kate, who adored Tom), were glad to hear of his breaking out.

There was already, in fact (of course, in a small way), what you might call the usual Crown Prince's party ready to encourage Tom against Chester, or simply to encourage him to do what he liked. And, in fact, I had a good idea this evening of how he had come to be smoking with some "queer" looking girls. I was pretty sure that the girls were the Tribes, three "artistic" daughters of a certain "artistic" widow with a little house nearby. The girls all studied various arts and heartily despised "conventional", and especially "political", people. It was the kind of house where there were always odd-looking young men lying about on the floors, and the fireplace was full of dead matches, and somebody was always practicing Chopin somewhere upstairs. The girls were all very earnest about all the arts, and Mrs Tribe dressed in floating garments and had a series of romantic attachments with young actors who came to study their parts with her. She herself had no connection with the stage, but she was the widow of a journalist and critic and was supposed to have great taste.

Chester and I both rather liked Mrs Tribe, though she was always carrying Tom off to her house, flirted with him, and encouraged him to look down upon our "conventional" existence. And I thought Chester suspected that Tom sometimes smoked with the girls, who all made much of him. But if so, he had never said so. He quite understood that Tom needed a certain amount of licence, if only as "Crown Prince".

64 But, of course, when, twenty minutes later, Tom "made his entry", looking I admit, a little princely but not at all too arrogant (he was too pleased with life to be pleased with himself), everyone looked at him in a particular manner. He did not notice these looks – he was looking round at once for someone to share whatever had amused him. Probably he was looking for me, because he and I had been to the Palace together several times, in the afternoons. But before he could find me, Goold (who was his godfather) came in the boy's way and asked him abruptly about his lady friends with the cigarettes.

Tom, who detested Goold, blushed suddenly and answered in a very cool manner, "Ladies, Mr Goold? What ladies?"

"The ladies you were with just now," Goold said, "at the music hall."

"I don't know what you mean," Tom said. "I haven't been out of the house this evening." And then as an obvious afterthought added, "Except to go to the post."

There was already an awkward silence, and Chester now quickly intervened (pretending not to have heard the exchange) to ask Tom to fetch him a certain book. But the moment the boy was gone, Goold and the two visitors who had seen Tom agreed that he had been afraid to confess; and Goold said to Chester, "I knew the boy was running wild. I told you what would happen if he went to that school."

Chester turned it off by some joke about the need of keeping ladies' secrets, but he hated to see Tom cut so bad a figure; and afterwards when we went to Tom's room to say goodnight he told him about the Chorlock visitors, who had brought the report of his being seen, and said, "I hope Mr Goold didn't think you were prevaricating." And then quickly, before Tom could tell a definite lie, "I don't know if you met anyone on the way to the post" (indicating to Tom how he could still make a plausible story), "but if so, it would be quite a good plan to explain the situation to Mr Goold, even now. It's so important not even to *seem* careless about facts – I mean, it is not only necessary to tell the truth but to avoid any doubt about it."

And then (I think as usual when Chester got upon a moral subject he allowed himself to be a little carried away) he went on to say how easy it was to be careless about facts – and how foolish, because, in the end, it defeated its own object. It did not even deceive. Untruthfulness was, in fact, the worst of vices, because it included all the others. It was not only cowardly but self-indulgent (and growing still more eloquent on a favourite theme – he was really speaking to himself and me quite as much as Tom) it might even be called, in the words of a famous preacher, the gate of hell, for it led to self-contempt, which was precisely, in modern terms, a state of corruption and misery – a real hell. Of course, he said, he was not suggesting for one moment that Tom had glossed over anything.

Tom, during this speech, had been looking at Chester with an expression of peculiar intensity. He was very red and I could see that he was very much upset. He had always hated any reproof from Chester. And now he suddenly interrupted to say, "But, Papa, you *are* suggesting it – I wish you wouldn't," and he stopped.

"Wouldn't what?" Chester was startled by the boy's angry voice.

"Wouldn't say such things when you know they aren't true."

"What?" Chester seemed confused. He really did not understand.

I said quickly, "Why, Tom, I believe you have a temperature," for I was frightened. I felt the danger of a quarrel between these two lively people, especially if they allowed their imaginations to carry them away. And I put my hand on his forehead. "You are quite hot. Wouldn't you like a nice cool drink?"

But Tom pushed away my hand and said in a very distinct voice, looking furiously at Chester with an expression exactly like Jim's when he was in his most obstinate mood, "I said you tell lies." And then, getting more angry still (as people do when they begin using violent words), "And so you do. You know you do – beastly lies."

Chester turned a deep pink, and I could see that he was furious, for, as I say, he could never bear the least reflection on his honesty. Of course, that is common enough with men in politics, or the law (which is rather the same kind of thing; they both have to "make a case") – they are apt to get angry if anyone accuses them of trickery or falsehood. And not only those who really are tricky but some of the honest ones, too. So that Chester, with his very delicate conscience, was even a little bit too touchy on the point. He would see an insult where it was not intended.

I kept shaking my head at him, meaning that the boy was beside himself with nervous excitement, and did not really know what he was saying, but the only result was that Tom said, in the same cool voice, "Don't shake you head, Mama; you said so yourself."

"That's absolutely untrue, Tom. I don't know what you are thinking of." But I felt myself trembling at the knees, for Chester was staring at me. "It's very wrong of you to say such things."

What I was afraid of was that Tom had heard Aunt Latter joking to me about Chester's speeches. It is very hard to know what even intelligent boys of fourteen understand, and what they have taken up wrong. But before I could say anything Tom said, "Then you are a liar, too; everything in the house is lies." And now having talked himself desperate (just as a child who starts hitting something, even a dog or a cat, quite gently and experimentally to see what will happen, may easily, if it gets excited, go on and beat it to death), he put back the bedclothes and jumped out of bed as if to escape from the room, but luckily Chester was in the way between him and the door.

And Chester had recovered from his shock. He had always been wonderfully good with excited meetings, and angry opposition, and I dare say his experiences helped him now. He said only, quite mildly, "Do you know what I think, Tom? I think you had better go back to bed before you talk any more nonsense."

"It's not nonsense; it's true."

Chester then turned to me and said, "I think you are right; he doesn't look at all well. These hours are really too late for a boy of his age." He went out of the room. A really wise move. I don't see how Chester could have behaved better. I had never been more impressed by his sense and considerateness.

65 As soon as Chester had gone, Tom would have run out of the room, as he was, in his pyjamas, if I had not caught him. And then we had a kind of struggle. The boy seemed quite mad and kept on saying, "Let me go! How can I stay? How can I stay after this? I must go."

"But where could you go at this time of night?"

"Aunty would have me – or Uncle Jim" (Jim was on leave and had gone to Buckfield for the hunting).

"But, Tom, how could you do such a cruel thing as run away from Papa? You know he loves you."

"It's the lies – everything is lies."

But he was not struggling so wildly, and Tom was still very slight and small for his age. I was able at last to bring him back to the bed, and he let me put him into it. And while I tucked him up, I pointed out again how unfair it was to accuse Chester of being untruthful, and I said that if he was thinking of his speeches it was ridiculous to call them untruthful. "You don't mind when I tell Ball" (Ball was a youth we had just engaged to act as butler) "to say that I'm not at home."

"That's not the same – but I don't care."

"And you don't call barristers liars when they try to make a jury vote for letting off a murderer."

"I know."

"It's really unkind to say that Papa tells lies."

"I know – it's not that," and he gave an enormous sigh. He looked so wretched that I put my arm round him and gave him a kiss.

"What is it all about, Tom? Do tell me."

"I don't know. It's – he never lets you alone."

I pointed out that Chester gave Tom a great deal of freedom. And again he agreed. "And if he is anxious about you and wants you to grow up into a good and true man, you know that's because he is so good."

"Oh yes, I know – I know." And then suddenly he burst into tears, clinging to me and trying to hide his face in the frills of my dress. And I was so shocked, it was so terrifying to feel the helpless desperation in a boy so proud, that, to my horror (in spite of the smile which I had assumed to tell him how absurd he was), I began to cry. That is to say, my eyes began to flow.

"You see," I said, "it's not fair to him."

"Oh, I know – I know. That's just it. It would be absolutely wicked – to – to run away. Oh yes – I'll have to stick it."

"But, Tom, you mustn't talk of it like that. And you know how fond you are of Papa."

"Oh yes, I know he's good. Oh dear, I wish it was school again."

But gradually he became calm, and at last he lay down and said, "I'm sorry I've been such an ass." And he seemed so quiet and resigned (his very patience made me want to cry again; but how could I dare even to show too much sympathy?) that I suggested he ought to apologize to Chester. And he answered, "Oh dear! Must I? I'll try."

But he did not succeed. In fact, on the next day he avoided Chester, and when they met at luncheon he would hardly speak. He was obviously under such constraint that he could not do so. And Chester was both embarrassed and irritated by awkwardness that he was not used to and felt that he had not deserved.

This situation made me very anxious, for I saw no way out of it, and there was no comfort in the house while the two men were at war. But luckily I happened to mention the matter to Jim (he expected me to write regular family letters whether he answered them or not), and he came up at once.

This was Jim's second leave in England and there was no difficulty about his staying in the house. On the one hand, he had made it plain to me that my past conduct was unforgivable. Alone with me he was cool, sad, and dignified (often he reminded me of the boy who had hated me as a child, when I failed to be enthusiastic in his projects), and in company he made it plain that he was Chester's friend. And it was quite true that Jim had now a high respect for Chester. "Wonderful how the chap has come through the crowd – a real winner," he'd say, "and starting with a handicap like that." He had, in fact, the same feeling for Chester as he had had for all the good little horses who had run such grand races for him (never quite winning) or for any ranker who had become a colonel. Jim (perhaps because of his own failures) had a strong sympathy for anyone who had to fight against odds.

And Chester, on his side (especially when he saw Jim's aloofness with me), had welcomed Jim to the house. For Nigeria had been a good deal in the news, and, though some radicals were attacking the Government's policy, some others were supporting it on the grounds that it had left power to the native chiefs (even some of the old slave-trading chiefs) and was thoroughly nationalist. And Chester, who, of course, supported the Government's view, had been very keen to get inside information from Jim about the actual situation in Africa.

66 Jim was extremely popular with both the children, perhaps more so than Chester, even with Sally. They had, of course, much more respect for Chester, but they were more at ease with Jim. This (I suppose) was only to be expected. Jim was just the kind of man that children adore, especially when they meet him only in his holidays, when he has nothing to do but amuse them. He was a hero to them, because he came from wild places, and was a kind of king in Africa (a position Jim enjoyed, in imagination, just in the same way as they did) and had shot a lion. He used to give them riding lessons, and he had promised Tom a gun when he was fifteen. Above all, though he was very critical of them both, especially Tom, and used to speak far more rudely to them than either Chester or myself, they knew that he was not trying to manage them. They knew that if he criticized Tom for wearing his hair too long, or Sally for looking sulky when I asked her to fetch my spectacles, he was not trying to teach them how to make a good impression. He simply thought that long hair and unwilling service were "wrong".

And when I told him the whole story of the scene with Tom he was completely shocked. "My God!" he said. "What that lad wants is a good tanning. But I knew you'd spoil him. And as for poor old Chester, he'd ruin any kid. He's too soft with them. I suppose it's the way he was brought up himself – that class always spoil their kids."

I was startled by his indignation and begged him to say nothing to Tom; but he would not listen to me. "Nonsense, Rabbit; you can't dodge out of a thing like this. You might ruin him for life. It's like breaking in young colts. You don't want to keep pulling them about or you spoil their tempers, but you can't let them get away with anything either, or they'll never run straight again. I'll talk to Master Tom." And he went at once to Tom and gave him a most tremendous blowing up: not only about being rude to his parents, but about smoking. He said that he was ashamed of him; that his conduct was ungentlemanly, and that if he was his son he would give him a good licking.

And Tom was much affected. The fact was that words like gentleman and gentlemanly meant so much to Jim that he put the most terrific force of meaning into them (though I suppose they are quite spoiled and useless now), so that they got right through Tom's self-consciousness and pride (not to say arrogance; he couldn't forget that his name was Nimmo) and I believe (though Jim didn't tell me so – he had a strict code of honour toward children, or at least boys) he was nearly, if not quite, in tears.

And afterwards he did actually go, in quite a grand way, and apologize to Chester, a thing which had a most powerful effect on Chester, who quite understood what it had cost the boy. He was indeed so delighted that he gave Tom (what he had been wanting for some time) a three-speed bicycle, and went specially to thank Jim. He was most enthusiastic about Jim. He told me that night that what he admired in Jim was his loyalty, his dependability, his selflessness. And this last word, which surprised me so much, expressed Chester's highest praise.

67 As for loyalty, since Chester had got into the Government, and been so severely criticized by some of his old supporters for "going into society" and even "revelling in the sweets of office", he had begun to set a high value on loyalty. And he was much struck when he found that Jim was prepared to defend even a radical Government. This came out one night at one of our "heavy" dinners, when one of the principal guests, a backbencher, who had, all the same, a great deal of influence with the extreme left, asked if it were true that the Nigerian Government used forced labour on the new railway.

This was a tricky question, because there was a lot of feeling in the party about forced labour, and Chester (since most of his support was from the left) had been careful not to commit himself in either direction. Besides, in the family, we all knew that Jim was having a quarrel with his Resident (it had gone on for years) about the treatment of "my poor bloody Lugas" in some labour camp and had threatened to appeal to the Governor over his superior's head. As Jim explained, he was not afraid of fighting the "blowhards," because "they can't kick me out – the Lugas would eat anyone else."

I saw Chester give Jim a quick anxious look, but Jim only screwed up his eyes at the questioner, as he does when he is asked to buy a horse (as he says, an offered horse is "usually a stumer"), and said, "That's rather a large subject, isn't it? You are all for roads, are you?"

The MP, a very sharp little man, and a regular fanatic, said rather impatiently, "Roads? What roads?" And Jim answered, "Oh, I beg your pardon, it is only that some people are against the Nigerian railway; though, you know, I can't myself see how we are going to give the people a better standard of living without one. The distances are so big, and head carriage so wasteful. I may be wrong, of course, and I don't know anything about your political angles over here, but speaking purely as a bushwhacker who has had a certain amount of experience in famine conditions – that is, seeing people actually die of starvation." And, in fact, he started a discussion on African poverty which made people rather ashamed of being pernickety (most "political" people can sometimes be moved out of politics; they are never *all* politics. And, of course, clever politicians know how to take advantage of this. It was one of Chester's favourite moves) and quite skilfully dodged the question of forced labour.

Jim always dodged that question, because, as he told me in private, the labour was forced. It had to be forced, because the people had no idea what a railway was, and so they didn't want it, and it was no good paying them even good wages to make it, because they did not want anything that money could buy. Besides, most of them lived so far from any place where the railway would pass that they would never get any direct benefit from it in their own lifetime.

"Damn it all, we have to make them do their bit, or there wouldn't be a hope for a railway, and it's only for two months in the dry season when they've nothing to do on their farms but drink. It would work out all right if it was properly handled on the spot, but the railway chaps don't know how to treat raw labour, especially my poor devils. But what is the use of writing reports to HQ? They stick them in a pigeonhole and give you a bad mark for being a nuisance. Why should they care? No one is going to know that a Luga tribesman is different from a Yob, and what's fair for a Yob is damned cruelty to a Luga. They killed three of my chaps last year. Shut them in a local jug for shooting at some trader and never even bothered to tell me; so, of course, the poor bastards thought they were going to be hanged and they just took on and died. A Luga can die in twenty-four hours if he feels hurt in his feelings and thinks he has not had a fair deal; they are a very proud people."

Jim, in fact, did not approve of the Government of Nigeria, nor of the way raw labour was being managed, but, as he put it, "I twigged that little fox-face was out to make trouble somewhere, and I wasn't going to tell tales out of school."

And he was extremely difficult to draw. Apart from his old prejudice against politicians in general, on any side, and all writers and journalists, he enjoyed, I think, eluding questions. He had a way of assuming the manner of a simple-hearted soldier administrator who didn't understand questions of state, which made people ashamed to pester. When closely examined, he would even look stupid, opening his eyes wide and saying (as to another man who tried to discuss the railway work), "When I mentioned the – ah – expense of head carriage I ought to say that I don't even know the actual figures – and, of course, it varies locally." And so he would get the whole discussion into such a tangle that if anyone should ask him again about forced labour he would say, "Well, that's the position as I see it, though, as I say, I haven't got the actual figures, and they wouldn't really be very much good if they existed." And then he would talk about "the difficulties of government in Africa, the famines, and the disease, and the struggle for life wherever we stop disease, and the population begins to increase".

And Aunt Latter would draw him out, and Chester himself would be excited. Of course, now Jim was at home again and came to the house, Chester was anxious to like him and "build him up". Chester always liked to like people (this was one of the nicest things about him) – especially those (like Jim) who had given him a lot of trouble: and not just to make a good "situation", but because, in some deep place, he really did believe that if you pretend people are good (as he had praised my "goodness" to make me better) they will become good.

He was quite extravagant in admiration of Jim to his friends and praised his work in Luga to the skies, which, indeed, seemed only fair. For Jim, I thought, had had little enough acknowledgment from the Government which he served so well.

So when Chester declared that we ought to be ashamed of our comforts when we thought of Jim's hardships, I did not point out that Jim preferred the hardships in order to save up and have money to cut a tremendous dash when he came on leave.

Besides, Chester would have hated any suggestion that might spoil his enthusiasms. He liked to feel enthusiasm – it seemed to give him a special kind of confidence. I think he felt (without looking into the matter – it was not a thing that he would want to look into) that all enthusiasm came from God.

68 It is quite untrue that the trouble between Chester and Tom came about because Chester oppressed the boy with his moral strictness, or that I took advantage of this to "seduce" him from his filial duty. Chester never even pressed Tom to come to chapel and he was confirmed in the Church of England (it seemed easier at Eastborough); and, indeed, Chester himself, in town, gradually stopped being very particular about going to chapel. He would often come instead to a short service in my church, which was just round the corner.

And this was not due to "laxity" or "snobbery", but simply to the fact that he knew more church people and no longer thought them "impenitent" and "graceless"; and also, as he grew always busier and more harried, he simply had not time to go to long prayer meetings, except, of course, at Tarbiton, when time had to be made for them.

And as for my relations with Tom, it is true that we were on very confidential terms. But the very fact that Tom had such immense admiration and respect for Chester made it difficult for him to chatter "nonsense" in his presence, whereas with me he would say whatever came into his head.

Aunt Latter had accused me of flirting with Tom, but this was her prejudice, it was he who flirted with me and often quarrelled with me, too. He would criticize my clothes (he himself as he grew up was very particular about his clothes and was inclined to be a dandy, wearing the most wonderful ties and waistcoats), laugh at me for this and that, my novel reading and the fact that I was always mislaying my library books (he had no idea how disjointed a woman's life is), and chatter about his friends, his ambitions, the latest play, and, of course, about Chester. He would say that when Chester was Prime Minister he would keep a horse in Downing Street. He would ask me how I should like to be an earless as he called it. He would pick a courtesy title for himself, Lord Grosvenor Parade, and say that it would be a nuisance to him, because it would shut him off from such professions as pavement artist. In fact, he loved to talk nonsense with me and make me laugh, and if, as Aunt Latter said, he did not respect me, I dare say that this was also the reason why he told me his secrets. The truth was that Tom was so naturally gay and such good company that I did not always remember to be matronly with him, especially in the company of some of his artistic friends, like the Tribes, whose family relations were extremely free and easy.

I have to look at old letters and diaries to recall "big" parties in those years, but I remember every detail at the Tribes': the small dark rooms crowded with rickety furniture, the peculiar smell of dust and linseed oil, Mrs Tribe's vague smile and protruding eyes as she looked on from her high armchair, and sewed some old curtains together for Titania's robes.

It was the kind of household where everyone seemed to do what she fancied at the moment, where total strangers (sometimes renowned writers or painters) would be found wandering through the passages looking for one of the girls who had asked them to come and forgotten to receive them; where nobody was surprised at any remark or any opinion, and where a tea party might turn into a dance, a private view into a charade, or a charade into a philosophical discussion (going on to three in the morning) on the nature of God, or the need of a new art of the theatre.

I remember one evening when we had "dropped in" for supper (Chester was speaking somewhere in the west) we found the whole family engaged designing a pantomime Puss-in-Boots, which they agreed should be done seriously. For the Tribes were extremely serious about "art". When the question, for instance, of whether the cat, played by a friend, a real actress called May Bond, should dress up like a cat, and use a cat voice, or should simply wear a striped cloak (made out of an old quilt) and a cap with ears, and a tail, and otherwise perform in a dignified manner, occupied at least two hours, and long telephone calls to two celebrated actors. In the end it was decided that the cat should be dressed like a cat, and wear a cat's head, but talk in a dignified manner with a human voice. During most of this time I was made to understudy the part of the cat, in Tom's riding boots, which we fetched for the purpose, and sometimes wearing a cardboard mask (which was actually a lion – Totty Tribe painted it grey) and sometimes a cap, while Julie Tribe, as stage manager, prompted me, and Tom as the Marquis of Carabas described his misfortunes. And before we knew, it was past one o'clock.

I suppose the preparation of Puss-in-Boots (it never got beyond a sketch of a first act) took up twenty evenings altogether in the winter of 1912, but in recollection it seems to have been the most important event of the year. It was a special experience (like the memory of a first holiday abroad) which was like nothing else in my life. And I understood very easily how, walking home through the dark streets, arm-in-arm with Tom, we still felt (even while we were laughing at Julie's "artistic" earnestness and Totty's furious arguments about the proper decoration for the cat's tail) that an evening with the Tribes was something precious and unique. "They're so real," he would say; "they never pretend." And if, thinking the Tribes encouraged the boy in his indifference to school work and his dandyism, I suggested that they were also rather careless in their love affairs, and their money affairs, too, he would say indignantly that even if Totty had been divorced and Pru was living with a married actor, and Mrs Tribe was always borrowing money from the people who came to the house, still what he liked about the Tribes was their "terrific honesty".

69 And however late it was or cold (provided that it was not raining; neither of us could bear to be rained on), when we reached the Embankment we would, as if by a simultaneous impulse, cross the road to walk by the river. Often we would walk up and down for another hour, talking and laughing, and *wondering* at the Tribes and their extraordinary life, wondering how they could grow so excited about whether the cat should speak like a cat or a human creature and whether its tail should be movable or not. And we would lean together over the wall and look at the river with its great snakes of lemon yellow light wriggling slowly under the lamps on the bridge (and snapping off their tails every moment and then growing new ones), and Tom would say that what he liked about the Tribes (both of us were always saying what we liked about the Tribes) was that they did not care a curse about money or politics or getting on in life, or about what people thought of them. And I knew exactly how Tom felt, and why, when we turned from the wall again to go into the house, we hesitated and did not go in after all, but walked along the river again, enjoying something so delightful, something that was not so much the Tribes' quaint obsessions with their various "arts", as the mysterious vivacity in our own feelings, which we seemed to catch from them, that we could not bear to go back into an ordinary respectable existence behind our nicely painted door.

And this private enjoyment of ours, each visit to the Tribes and their "artistic" circle, was between ourselves. It was like a conspiracy. I remember that it was on one of these evenings when we came home late and had just crossed the road to look at the river, when we saw by a light in my bedroom facing the river that Chester had come a day before he was expected, and Tom asked me at once not to say where we had been.

"But why? He knows that the Tribes are friends of yours and that I sometimes go there, too."

"Yes, but he might want to come, and you know that he doesn't really like the Tribes."

"He would be very nice to them."

"But that's just why I'd hate him to come. I do so hate to see him putting it on."

"I don't think you ought to say he puts it on – he's naturally enthusiastic. It's his great gift – it makes him such a good speaker."

"Well, turn it on. Yes, that's really the trouble."

"But are you sure we don't imagine that, because it's what people say about him? Are you sure we're being fair? And you know he *believes* in being friendly wherever he can – that's his religious side."

"Oh yes, I know he's got terrific standards."

It may seem rather extraordinary that I should discuss

Chester with Tom in this manner. But it came about quite naturally, because the papers were always discussing him. It was simply the consequence of his being a public figure.

70 Luckily on this occasion I did not promise secrecy, for as soon as I came upstairs (I remember the whole incident for this reason) Chester said, "Where have you been? I suppose with those extraordinary people in Tippet Street." And then at once (showing no further interest in the Tribes) he began to tell me about the crisis (apparently he had been annoyed only because I had not been at home to hear it at once) that had brought him back to town – that is, the rumour of a secret understanding between certain Cabinet Ministers and the Committee of Imperial Defence to propose a special (and much increased) army vote. For, of course, there were little groups within the Cabinet, with different ideas, and they naturally worked against each other. That is, they "sounded" each other and tried to get support for their own policy before they took a definite line. Chester used to be annoyed with me when I talked about secret diplomacy in the Cabinet, but, in fact, he was always sounding some colleague, and now he was convinced that some of them were making a plot to take a strong line on armaments, which would force the peace group (himself and Morley and John Burns and perhaps one or two more) into resignation.

And his old suspicion made him so excited and angry that he could not sleep. He kept walking round the room and saying, "You can't trust any of 'em except Grey – and I'm not sure of Grey either. He doesn't actually lend himself to their intrigues, but he has his own schemes. He doesn't tell you what he's really up to."

All this time, in fact, while there was talk of war, and the

Cabinet was divided about our policy, Chester was in a very nervous state. So I was especially anxious not to have any concealments from him when Tom at Easter asked me to keep a secret which he could only tell me under such a promise.

"But, Tom," I said, "I don't like secrets – they complicate things so much, and they always come out in the end."

"I can't tell you unless you promise. I mean I couldn't. And you mustn't give the least hint. And I'll know if you do give the least hint. I can tell just by the way Papa looks at me and says, 'Hallo, Tom; what a very nice tie,' meaning that he hates my ties, and that he is reading my soul but doesn't think it expedient to refer to it."

"Oh, Tom, that's not fair. It's just something you imagine about your father."

"Perhaps I do," Tom said, still looking unusually serious. "But *if* I imagine it then I imagine it and I can't help it. Are you going to promise? I think you had better. This is what Papa calls a turning point."

I hesitated, for I hoped that the boy would tell me without a promise. He usually did so. His natural high spirits and affectionateness made it very difficult for him to keep secrets from anybody. But when, after a week, I found that he was still preoccupied, and even irritable with me, I saw that unless I promised I should not be told, and I was afraid to take the responsibility of ignorance. For it seemed to me that in our special relations (Chester being more cut off than a father should be) I ought to be very careful not to lose Tom's confidence. So I made the promise, and he told me at once, with great relief, that he was engaged to Julie Tribe and had decided to leave school as soon as possible, because it was doing him no good, and go on the stage.

Julie, it seemed, had a small legacy, due on her eighteenth birthday, and had already arranged to invest it in setting up a theatrical company, with a certain producer called Gavin Marker, in order to bring out the plays of a Swedish writer called Strindberg.

Strindberg, Tom said, had just died and it was an absolute scandal that several works of the great artist had never been performed in England.

And now I was glad that I had managed to buy Tom's secret, for I was able to make a bargain with him that if he would finish his time at school I would support him when he told Chester of the engagement.

I pointed out how important it was for a serious actor to have a good education, and here, luckily, Julie herself was on my side. So in the end it was agreed that he should go back to school for one more term.

71 But I found, to my cost, it was very dangerous to keep secrets from Chester. He had too many spies. I don't mean that he actually encouraged people to spy for him (he had not chosen Bootham as a spy; he had only come to find his information useful), but that there was always a large number of people ready and even eager to give him information. Like other public men, in fact, he had an enormous circle of acquaintances everywhere, who were always ready to tell him things, either in what they thought the public interest, or to seem important, or often, I think, just for something to say to the great man which would be sure to interest him.

So somebody or other told him, about a week later, that while he had been away Tom and I had spent several evenings at the Tribes'. And he said to me one evening, apropos of nothing, "Does Tom see a lot of that artistic family?"

"The Tribes?"

"Yes, that woman who goes about in old curtains and the fat girls who powder their faces in such a ghastly manner."

"I think he does keep up with them. They've always rather pursued him."

"I should think they were the worst possible friends for Tom with his taste for trifling."

"They are what you might call a little bohemian, but they are not really bad girls."

"I suppose he's there tonight – I wish you'd go and see. You know them well enough, don't you?"

"Oh, but he went to supper with Aunt Latter and Jim."

"So he did."

I knew very well that Tom often used a visit to Aunt Latter as an excuse to escape for the evening, which he would then spend at the Tribes'. But I daren't say so or I should have had to pursue him there and give a report.

And Chester was obviously in a mood to inquire further, when I happened to remember that he had been lunching with Wilfred, and I asked him if he had got any "tips". And Chester said, yes, to sell some rubber shares, and he had made a big profit. So I was able to congratulate him and to suggest that he should buy himself a new car, more consonant with his dignity (we had had a car for some time, but it was small and already old-fashioned), and he laughed at my "extravagance" (but he liked to think that I was extravagant – it was a quality he enjoyed in a woman, and he enjoyed, too, feeling that now he could afford me), and ended in pulling me down on his knee and telling me that he could see through me with half an eye and what I was really hinting at was a tiara. This, of course, was nonsense – it was Chester who was thinking of jewels. Quite lately (after another good tip of Wilfred's) he had given me a necklace and earrings.

This was why the *Tarbiton Gazette*, in its spite, described me at the opera as wearing the "famous Nimmo diamonds and a frock of the most daring Parisian cut". The famous diamonds dated only from my last birthday, and Chester himself had chosen the frock – it was he who liked me in a "daring cut" – because he wanted me to be admired.

I was sometimes embarrassed by the frocks he chose and especially by his expecting me to wear all my jewels on occasions which were not suitable, but I could not refuse so generous a man. He delighted to give presents, and he loved to know that they gave me pleasure.

And I resented very much that our private affairs should be complicated with party politics – family life has its own politics which are troublesome enough. I hated the feeling of deceit (and danger, too) when I diverted Chester's mind from the Tribes by talking about investments. I know the most devoted couples do have to study each other's moods and cajole each other, but it is always an uneasy proceeding. One feels treacherous and dreads detection and some cynical retort.

Yet I had, of course, to warn Tom that I had lied to Chester about his evening visits, in case he might give us both away. One lie needs another. And this meant, of course, that on the next day the boy said in Chester's hearing that he must call on Aunt Latter, and then did not spend even a minute there but went straight to the Tribes'. And when I pointed out how dangerous this was, he said that Aunt Latter would be delighted to help him because she was furious with Chester. In fact, from this moment I was drawn into such a mass of lies and tricks that I never had a minute's peace.

72 For within this month (Tom was back at school and I was hoping that he would forget Julie Tribe in football) Mrs Tribe came to see me and asked me if I had heard of this ridiculous affair with Julie. I confessed that I had, but said that I was bound to keep the secret. "Poor little Julie!" Mrs Tribe said. "She never had any sense. I'm surprised at Tom."

"Julie always seemed to me a fairly responsible person."

"Oh dear!" And she smiled at me her gentle affectionate smile. "A perfect child. Your Tom is quite a man of the world beside her."

"But, Mrs Tribe, Tom is only a schoolboy – Julie has been acting for years. She can't be quite so innocent."

"A complete baby," Mrs Tribe went on in her soft voice, and smiled all the time. She never listened to anybody. I dare say she had learned obstinacy among the Tribe daughters, who argued all day. "A perfect baby; and Tom has really behaved very strangely."

In short, Tom had "compromised" Julie, and also borrowed fifty pounds from her. And Julie was now threatened with a summons. "What I'm so afraid of," the voice said, "is that if there is a court case something may come out in the papers. And they do so love to exaggerate. I believe they would invent scandals if they could not find any."

Now I'm not going to say that Mrs Tribe (this is not her real name, of course) was blackmailing me, even though Tom strongly denied that he owed Julie a penny, except for one set of ballet tickets which he had forgotten and which had cost only five pounds. Mrs Tribe may have been deceived by Julie. And what is blackmail? Where does a fair warning stop and blackmail begin?

But as it was, I was glad to get off with twenty pounds

and a promise of the rest if Tom admitted the debt, because I was terrified, just then, at the very idea of anything coming out in the papers about a Nimmo.

For it was in that week that the famous Contract Case had burst upon us, like a thunderbolt out of a clear sky, or, one might say, out of the drawing-room ceiling.

73 The Contract Case is often mixed up with the Marconi Case, but it was three months earlier and quite separate. They have only one point in common. But though I don't want to dig up ancient history, I should like to mention this point, because no one else has done so.

The whole point of the Marconi Case was that three Ministers did not tell about their Marconi shares until there was so much talk about corruption that they had to explain. And people thought they had waited so long because they had something to hide.

But I am sure that they hesitated to tell (though they had done nothing wrong) because of their feeling that, though they were innocent, they would get no justice, in fact, that they might be utterly ruined by some perfectly senseless explosion of spite.

For there is a special kind of jealousy and spite which gathers round any important man, not for anything he has done, but simply because his name is often in the papers. It is because of this spitefulness that even nice people repeat such horrible stories about royalties and statesmen – stories that come from goodness knows where. They seem to steam up out of some crack in humanity like poisonous gases out of a peaceful-looking volcano.

It was this spite which so nearly wrecked Chester's career and started all the stories that have been told ever since and are quite untrue; for instance, the statement, which I read only last week, that he had foreseen the "exposure" and made arrangements to "cover up" his dealings.

He had nothing to cover up, and as for foreseeing the crisis, he had no idea of what was in the wind, when some Conservative backbencher (I can't even remember his name) put down a question about shareholders in a company called Banks Rams, asking who they were, what their holdings were now, and what they had been three months before.

Banks Rams was a private company (which is why Chester had not been obliged to resign his directorship) making certain electrical equipment for Western Development which had just received a contract for wireless equipment. Wireless telegraphy was then very much in the news because Marconi had been sending messages half round the world and everyone was talking about it. Various companies had tendered for the contract, and the suggestion was that Chester, as a partner in Battwell Engineering (I'm afraid this seems a little complicated, but all business affairs are complicated – they get mixed up in each other like family relations), knew that if Western Development – Wilfred's company – got the contract, Banks Rams, which sold things to Western Development, and Battwell Engineering, which sold things to Banks Rams, would also make a lot of money.

In fact, Chester was actually offered four times the old valuation for his Banks Rams, within a month after the announcement of the contract came out.

Now it was quite true that Chester had bought more shares in Banks Rams, but it was not true, of course, that he had had any private information about the contract, or used influence to get it. He had simply guessed that if Western Development won the contract Banks shares would go up as well. It was, as Aunt Latter and Jim said (but Chester himself did not agree, he did not approve of speculation), a fair gamble.

Chester, in fact, made good investments, because he had the imagination to see what might be good, and not because he had special information.

Luckily Cousin Wilfred, who was a director of Banks Rams, had warning from some friend of his that one of the Conservative papers was going to make a fuss about the share dealings. And he rushed up to town by the night train to warn Chester. He did not risk a wire. Chester then sold out all his new holdings, of course through his agents, and was able to make a statement in the House, actually on the same day when the question was asked, saying that he had bought no new shares in Western Development for a year past, and his holding of other shares connected with the electrical industry was actually smaller than in any previous year. He said also that in view of the Government interest in wireless development he saw that it might be expedient that a Minister, even in a Department having nothing to do with wireless contracts, should break off his connection with any company making electrical equipment. He therefore proposed to give up his partnership of nearly eleven years' standing with Battwell Engineering. This statement was received with applause, and it was generally held that Chester had cleared himself.

Now you may say that this explanation was not quite candid, and that Chester escaped, thanks to Wilfred's warning and his own power of appealing to the House. But this suggestion makes me angry. Because the truth was (and is) that Chester *did not have information*. He did not do anything that any clever businessman would not have done, and won great praise.

But owing to the very special conditions of politics, and the way people treat politicians, looking for a chance to find the smallest fault with them, and quite ready to invent faults that don't exist, it would have been *quite misleading* for Chester to have told the whole story of Banks Rams. It might have produced a *great injustice*, that is, the ruin of Chester's career. I know it is a very difficult question, what you can tell the public – it depends on the public mind at the time (and I often think, after my experience as a Minister's wife, that ten per cent of the public mind is just plainly and simply lunatic and, of course, being lunatic, makes nearly all the noise and *seems* to have all the influence); but anyone knows that the noblest men have thought it right to be careful of how much they tell. Nobody, for instance, would say to a country at a critical moment, "You have no army and no proper defences," because it might stop it trying to defend itself. It's no good, in fact, pretending that there is any easy way to solve political questions, because they are all so mixed up with feelings and prejudices that people have to be persuaded and induced to do and think rightly (unless you just shoot them, which is impossible in a democracy).

And Chester was quite right, therefore, to arrange his statement so that people were persuaded to believe that he was really innocent, because he *was innocent*. And it was true to say that he had no warning which enabled him to "cover up", because he had nothing to "cover up" in the sense in which his enemies used the word.

You must forgive me if I enlarge on this ancient history (but the contract scandal *is*, after all, history, and nearly always falsely stated), because I have found that even the truth won't convince people. Only last week, when I was on the subject to a clever young woman from Oxford (she had called to get some facts about this very Government), I saw a half-smile on her face. She thought I was deceiving myself (and probably she had heard somewhere that I, as Chester's "Delilah", had a personal interest in the argument) and that Chester was really "crooked" (in the horrible modern phrase) and "got away with it" by "outsmarting" his critics.

I was so angry with her that I would have accused her of being shallow and cheap, if I had not realized that in other respects she was a very warm-hearted and honest creature, and only silly (like so many others – clever or not) about "politicians"; as if they were naturally wicked because they have to "manage" people. But I'd like to know what would happen if nobody tried to manage people, if mothers always told the facts to children (saying to the stupid ones that they were stupid) and never took any consideration for their nerves and their fits of temper and frights and silliness.

And what I am trying to do in this book is not to make out that Chester was a saint (which would be stupid, after all the books and articles about him) but to show that he was, in spite of the books, a "good man" – I mean (and it is saying more than could be said of most people) as good as he could be in his special circumstances, and better than many were in much easier ones.

I really think that politicians (I mean good honest ones who have good principles) can be more admirable than saints, because they do far more difficult work and are not allowed just to "save their souls".

But I am being carried away from my point (because of this clever girl who may actually write history someday and because people who never took the least responsibility in politics except to vote once or twice in elections when it did not interfere with their golf or a concert, talk about Chester as if he were the prince of darkness), which is the contract scandal and how it affected Chester's life.

For though, as I say, he was able to give a complete explanation and establish the truth (by resigning his directorship, which cost him over a thousand pounds a year), yet a great many people went on being suspicious because, of course, they don't really understand anything properly.

And though the Prime Minister accepted Chester's explanation, he was violently attacked. Indeed, I can't describe the violence and bitterness of these attacks. Chester was abused as if he were the lowest kind of criminal. Many of the letters, especially some of the anonymous ones, were obscene; one would think they had been written by madmen, and I quite believed Aunt Latter, when she said that half the population of the world was more than half mad, and the only thing that saved us from everlasting war and misery was that it was mad in different ways. The mad dogs kept biting each other.

Chester himself, though he carried himself bravely in public, was actually so upset that we were afraid he would have a breakdown. He could not eat or sleep, and would walk about half the night, going over the affair with me and explaining over and over again that investment was not speculation; that even if the shares had gone down he had meant to keep them. And he was very bitter against the extremists in his own party who were trying to ruin him and drive him out of public life.

Already he had been asked to resign from the Bethel Committee at Tarbiton (which raised funds for lay preachers), and some of the worst letters had come from chapel members.

74 Mr Goold had for a long time been writing to Chester, disapproving of almost everything he did. He accused him of deserting his principles (especially in supporting navy estimates) and one afternoon, just after Chester's explanation, he suddenly arrived in town and startled me very much by telephoning to ask me for a private interview.

Mr Goold was now very prosperous and had changed a great deal in the last few years. He was much fatter and whiter, and he dressed always in very good broadcloth. If you had cut off his head the rest of him would have looked exactly like a small tradesman who has become rich and fat and pompous and self-satisfied. But his head seemed to belong to a different man. His face was quite thin, and there was something mad about his eyes and hair. The hair always looked as if it needed brushing; it stood in unexpected tufts, like a field of corn that has been laid by a storm – the same storm perhaps which gave his eyes that queer expression as if he had had a terrible fright.

I think perhaps Mr Goold did have a fright, a kind of everlasting fright at his own success, and its consequences. I think he was a man who never understood (or was afraid to let himself understand) how "things happened" to him. For instance, as a young evangelist he had always been very fierce against the vanities of the world, the luxuries of mammon, etc, but now (having left the old family house next to the original shop, of which he had been so proud) he was living in a tall hideous new Gothic villa on the Chorlock road, which, though it was merely a large villa, was ostentatiously luxurious, brilliant with paint and window boxes, with a double drawing room, new furniture from Maples, maids in uniform, a vinery and a peach house in the garden. And Daisy could be seen any day driving to the shops in a barouche and pair, dressed in the latest from Paris (the daughter, now twelve, was never seen except in silk frills) and flashing with diamonds.

And the villa, the carriage and the diamonds had all "come about". Goold would say that the house was "more convenient," the carriage was "an economy" with all the driving he had to do, and Daisy herself had (I really believe) no idea of her part in obtaining them. When I went to see her (she always went shopping with me when she came to town, and lived in my pocket when I went to Tarbiton) she was still full of laughter and terror. She trembled at Goold's glance and giggled behind his back. And she would say to me, "Oh Lordy, he never do anything I ask him."

However, I had watched Daisy obtain the carriage when they were still living in their old house at Tarbiton. She began by saying (in my presence, to give her courage) that it was a pity they only had "that old trap", which spoiled her clothes in the rain, and rattled her teeth out. Goold answered that the trap had been good enough for his mother, and Daisy had said, "Oh yes, no one didn't want any different, only it was a pity."

And then she began to get soaked through in her best frocks (and she even managed to tear them), and the trap to suffer extraordinary accidents. It ran into ditches, and collided with carts. Whenever Daisy took it out there was sure to be a calamity, and all her explanation was that "it was that old trap that was so crazy you couldn't drive un straight".

And I am sure that Daisy really believed this. She had taken a dislike to the trap and a longing for a carriage; and when Daisy wanted anything (like a child wanting a piece of chocolate) it occupied her whole mind and imagination. For she had no other distraction. She never read a book, or thought about anything; she had no interest in any art or game; she had none of the work which fills up the lives of cottagers – scrubbing and washing and gossiping in the market. She had nothing on earth to do but brood on the inadequacy of the trap and yearn for a carriage. So she would drive it with such despairing expectation of misfortune that it naturally turned corners too sharply, and ran up on the bank, or backed into gateposts. And in the end Goold bought a carriage. But not for Daisy. His reason was (and I'm sure he believed it) that the trap was worn out and the carriage "offered itself" as a bargain.

And as for Daisy, on my next visit to Tarbiton, when we went for a drive in this famous barouche, she assured me that it was "a real bit of luck".

75 Daisy had her usual stories about her master, and we had laughed so much together that people on the road looked at us with surprise or disapproval. Daisy had a story about a twin-bedded room at a hotel when Goold had been surprised one morning by the chambermaid, in her bed ("these latter years Ted have took a fancy to it in the morning just when I get my best sleep; and, oh Lordy, how cross he do get if I drop off in the middle – he's ready to bite me"), and had tried to escape, but, unluckily, when he jumped out of bed, had caught his nightshirt in the bed table and split it in two – "as you mid say he was as naked as Adam, and – oh dear – you know that he'd been caught a bit too soon and so – you see – oh Lordy – and the girl ready to drop the tray – " Daisy was never able to finish this story. It reduced her to hysterics. But on this same drive, the discovery that we might be a few minutes late for tea put her into such a fluster that she actually moaned, complaining against the horses ("but then

Ted won't think of a moty car") and the road ("Tarbiton do be nothing but up and down") and the coachman ("he never will mind what I say"), a fluster which was justified when we arrived and found Goold strutting about the front garden of the new villa, with his watch in his hand, and his face purple with outraged dignity.

"Late again – that's every day this week."

And Daisy, pouting, with her little eyes wide open, and her little red forehead wrinkled to her hair, "Oh, Ted, 'twas the horses."

"It's always the same story."

"But 'tis true, Ted – they'm just slugs on these hills."

He pushed her into the house, and I heard him abusing her all the way upstairs, and when she came down at last to give me tea she was red-eyed and red-nosed. I even suspected, by a large red patch on one cheek, that she had had it slapped, but I may have been wrong. For if it had been so I think Daisy would have told me. She told the whole world about all her affairs and how fearful she was of her Ted. And yet at that very time the villa was being enlarged by a wing (the villa had had additions every year, beginning with a new kitchen, because the old one had failed to give Goold even his breakfast), and before the year was out Daisy had her car. So that Goold was perhaps justified in losing his temper with the woman, and even slapping her now and then on that round rosy face, whose simplicity (a perfectly genuine simplicity) appeared like the mask of so deceitful and mysterious a power.

76 Now because Goold disliked me so much and had so much influence in Tarbiton, I had always, for Chester's sake (and my own peace), tried to be specially nice to him. So, although I had seats for a very good concert that

afternoon, which I had been looking forward to, I answered that I should be very glad to see him; I had been wanting to see him for a very long time.

I was perhaps a little too effusive, for when the man arrived he became so affectionate that I was embarrassed. As I say, there was a kind of madness in Mr Goold, which made all relations with him nervous and a little hysterical. For instance, at the very moment while he was holding my hand, and assuring me that no one appreciated more highly what I had done for Chester, he noticed a little powder rouge on my cheek (I looked afterwards in the glass and saw that I had been rather careless with the powder) and faltered, and made a face as if he had tasted a sour gooseberry. But then at once, recollected himself, and took another grip of my hand, and said most earnestly (but rather angrily) that he knew what I meant to Chester, and how great my influence could be in every direction. And he said that he had become glad of Chester's marriage because on getting to know me better he had seen how much Chester needed a beautiful and accomplished wife to help him in his career.

What the man meant was that I was destroying Chester by my pleasure-seeking way of life. But he had never before been so polite in saying so – I felt confused by his earnestness, his anxiety to win me over. And pressing my hand still in an affectionate manner, he said, "You and I, Nina, know how little it profits a man to gain the world if he loses his own soul." I could not bear to hurt the poor man's feelings, and so I answered by a question (not to contradict him – this is a good way, as Chester had shown me, to argue with "difficult" people), if he really thought that Chester had lost his soul.

Then Mr Goold looked furious, and almost as if he were

going to cry, and said, "Do you not see how he has changed in these last years?" And when I asked if he didn't think everybody kept changing a little, and especially when they changed their town and work, he said, yes, "it is London that has destroyed him, London society".

Now we did not move in "society," we only touched it on the outside. There were, of course, a lot of society people who had taken us up (Lady Warwick was quite a friend, and had actually quite radical ideas), but they had not taken me in, and never would, because we were not relations except through Cousin Porty, who was not himself a society man. He was far too lazy to be bothered with it. Indeed, I had often thought it was a blessing that we were outside society, because being in society means that you have to be "social" and tremendously friendly with people, even if they are bores; and goodness knows we had enough bores already in our political assortment.

But I knew I could not explain this to Goold (who thought that all lords were in society), and so I asked him if he thought it wrong for us to entertain. But he only stared at me with his distracted eyes and said that you could not touch pitch without being defiled.

And I felt sorry for the poor man, because how could he know what he did not know, and, of course, with his education he knew almost nothing that wasn't at least slightly nonsense somewhere. So I said that Chester had been very distressed by the attacks upon him; and he answered that he might well be so, for the Radical Council threatened to withdraw its support and look for another candidate, "who will truly represent our Christian people, and lift his voice against the bloody-minded men who seek war in Europe".

77 This did alarm me very much and I telephoned to Chester before he came home to warn him that Goold was waiting for him and of what he had said. But Chester answered calmly enough that he was expecting a visit and that Ted had no idea of political realities.

I had been very anxious about Chester. Although he was such a strong energetic man, he could be fearfully tired, and when he was depressed he would collapse like a child who has had too much excitement at a party and does not know what to do with itself. And when he came home that evening from the office he was in his gloomiest state, ate nothing and groaned aloud when I reminded him that Goold was coming back to see him.

So I was surprised and relieved that night when he came in at last with a very lively air (he walked across the room on tiptoe, which was always a sign of excited reflection) and said suddenly, "All the same, Ted is a good friend."

"I hope he was more reasonable with you than he was with me."

"Feeling against war is a tremendous thing – in the country generally. Anyone who could mobilize it – " He stopped to pull off his shirt.

"Isn't that just what you thought so dangerous?"

"So is war. And, after all, if we call ourselves Christians – " He stopped again and then said very seriously that what people were always forgetting was the immense *truth* of the Christian idea – and what he meant by truth was the *practical truth*, something that *worked*. No one would care to say that the Christian martyrs had wasted their lives.

He thought again for a moment and then exclaimed in a different voice (and looking at me as a husband looks when he is opening a practical discussion), "He wants me to resign on the navy estimates." And then laughing at my expression, "Don't be so frightened! He promises that I'd come back as Prime Minister within the year."

"But suppose there is a war and we lost it?"

"Then according to Ted I should come back as first President of the British Republic."

I was taken by surprise, and also I did not know what to say. When Chester was in this "stirred-up mood" he was so full of whirling ideas that it was very difficult to say the right thing. For the ideas and feelings were all different and you never knew from moment to moment which was in command.

And now before I could find the right remark, Chester looked severely at me and said, "You think that's wild nonsense, but Ted's not so stupid. If we lost the war, there would be every likelihood of a republic, and if the PM and, say, Lloyd George, as ex-war Ministers, were out of the running, I should stand a very reasonable chance of the leadership. Who else can you think of?"

I said hastily that it was obvious that he would be the only choice.

But he was not quite appeased and said abruptly, "But putting these *fantasies* aside" (meaning that, unlike Ted Goold, I had no faith in his future), "the immediate job is Tarbiton. And I'm going down at once – tonight, if I can catch the train; if you could manage to pack my bag?"

This was the first I heard of Chester's "move to the left" of 1913 and the "Machiavellian tactics" which made him a "byword for hypocrisy and chicane".

I am quoting from the review, published last week, of *Memoirs of a Cabinet Minister*, where one of Chester's letters is printed, in which he writes that he was "inclined to try a pacifist line", because, though it was obviously a "bit of a toss-up" whether war could be avoided, there was no doubt that very influential and well-organized sections of the constituencies were all against war preparations of any kind.

This, the reviewer thought, was a quite disgraceful revelation. But I can't help feeling that he is being unfair, or perhaps he simply doesn't understand the situation. I spent twenty years in politics (without any prejudice in their favour), and I still think that there is less "hypocrisy" and "Machiavellianism" among politicians than ordinary people.

Politics, after all, is a kind of war (and in many places they still shoot or even torture the defeated), and people who are fighting for their lives (at least their political lives) have quite a different view of things from those who only work and eat for them.

No one thinks the worse of soldiers for inventing stratagems to save their own lives or to kill the enemy; it was no worse for our visitors at the Parade to discuss (as they did even too often) how to "dish" the Tories, "dodge" some awkward attack, or "capture" some section of voters with a promise that "won't commit us to anything definite", suggestions which came often from "good" people, who certainly never told a deliberate lie in their lives.

I think hypocrisy is a very rare vice. Tartufe and Pecksniff always seemed to me very hollow characters – quite untrue to life. People don't need to be hypocrites. They can so easily "make" themselves believe anything they fancy.

78 When Jim was seventeen he came to me one afternoon and proposed a sail in the Major's yawl – the Major was away, but (so Jim said) we could always borrow the yawl.

It was March, very stormy and cold, and even the fishermen had kept their boats in harbour. They had warned Jim already that morning that it was blowing up for a gale and that it was madness to take a boat into the open sea.

But this warning, for Jim, amounted to a "dare" and he was always ready to kill himself for a whim of pride or glory (or, as Aunt said, cussedness), and, besides, it was the last day of his holidays, and his last chance of a sail.

The very idea of a sail in such weather, not to speak of beating out into the Atlantic, was horrible to me. But Jim pointed out that he could not manage the boat alone – he must have someone to handle the fore sheets while he steered the "clumsy old scow". And I was not brave enough to refuse. I murmured only that it seemed rather rough out at sea and that the Major had forbidden us to take the yawl out in bad weather. To which Jim answered only that the poor old Major was losing his nerve and if I was afraid of getting wet he would ask Cousin Monk, a boy I particularly detested. And I declared at once that I was longing to go.

As soon as we were beyond the heads we found that the fishermen and the Major had been quite right. The wind was coming in gusts that nearly laid us on our beam and the seas were breaking right along the deck.

And when we turned to get back to the mouth of the estuary we both saw at once (we were drifting so fast) that we had very little chance of making it. And I cried out (I was quite terrified), "We'll never get back."

Jim answered at once, "Get back where? Did you think we were going back to the Longwater?"

"But where else can we go?"

"What I thought was – with this lovely blow – we could do our Callacombe trip."

Callacombe was a small fishing harbour about ten miles along the coast, and it was true that we had proposed someday to sail there – but in good settled weather. Callacombe was among dangerous rocks and tides – a bad harbour with a shingle bar and a very narrow entrance.

I said at once that we could never make Callacombe in such a storm; we should be smashed to pieces on the bar if we ever got so far.

But Jim, already steering down wind, answered coolly, "A storm? What storm? What's wrong with you? This is just the wind for Callacombe."

I saw that he had turned from the Longwater simply to avoid a possible failure in my eyes and decided that the weather was ideal for the Callacombe run, to carry off the affair in style.

And already, of course (that is, in two minutes after Jim turned down wind), we had no choice but to go on. We had to run before the wind and hoped to keep in front of the seas which were now breaking or rather bursting (as big seas do when the wind is changing and getting stronger) as high as our mast, or at least our mizzen.

As I say, I don't like the sea. The kind of sailing I like is on a summer day with a nice breeze, not too strong, in the Longwater, with a comfortable seat in the stern and the prospect of a good tea at the proper time. It can be imagined what I felt that night in a real storm (and nothing is more terrifying) in a small boat. It was now pitch dark; the wind was making a noise in our shrouds like terrified cats; great blasts of sleet were shooting across and rattling in the sails like gunfire; and behind all that there was the extraordinary *row* (they call it a roar, but it is not a bit like roaring) that a storm makes, a mixture of yowling and whistling and crashing (like a mob breaking windows) and hissing and shouting, that makes your head feel as if it were being crushed in a screw; and the boat was leaping and whirling about, so that, even holding on with all one's might, one was nearly being thrown off every moment.

I did get thrown down several times in the cockpit (neither of us dared to step on the deck), and, as it was full of water (it was supposed to be self-emptying, but it kept filling up too quickly ever to be less than brimful), each time I was nearly drowned actually in the boat. Once at least Jim pulled me up by the hair and shouted something about my being more trouble than I was worth; but I was too knocked about to care. I was just a piece of wretchedness.

But suffering as I was, I still managed to carry out Jim's orders when sometimes (needing two hands at the tiller) he made mouths at me and jerked his head, meaning "cast off" or "belay".

After hours of this agony (or perhaps an hour) the lighthouse on Callacombe head came into view, and when we were on top of a high wave we could see the village lights below.

Then Jim (who was steering marvellously) edged toward them on the backs of the waves until the harbour was right in front and we could run straight at it.

We had only two sails set, the foresail and spanker (a very small one), but we were rushing along like an express train, and every second sea (the ones that did not break over us) got under our stern and lifted us and hurled us forward like a surfboard.

We could see already by the lights on the jetties that the tide was not very deep on the bar – the waves were breaking along its whole length and sending up great spurts and fountains twenty feet high. In a minute we were right upon them. And I thought, "So I really am going to be drowned! What a fool I was to come! Jim has killed me at last!"

And, in fact, we ought to have been drowned – it was only a million in one chance that ran us into a patch of oil from a wrecked motorboat just at the bar, so that, though we actually struck upon it (and opened all our seams – the yawl sank at her moorings that night and Aunt Latter had to pay the Major nearly a hundred pounds for the damage), the following seas did not break down on us and smash us – they just lifted us in two more bumps, over the bar and into the harbour.

I was then so suddenly and completely exhausted (at fourteen I was growing much too fast) that I had to be carried into the inn, where we were both given hot brandy and the landlord sent a message to the coastguard. Apparently a general alarm had gone out to all the coastguard stations and police.

And while I was sitting in front of the bar-room fire, wrapped in warm blankets, and sipping the brandy (I still remember how it wrinkled my nose), and feeling in every bit of me the indescribable bliss of being still alive, and not only alive but alive without absolute disgrace (since I had not completely lost my head or quite failed as "crew"), I perfectly understood (just as I could feel the solid armchair beneath my comfort) that Jim's pretence of having planned the whole journey had "kept me up" (partly in indignation) and perhaps saved us from being swamped in the first five minutes.

By pretending he had made an enterprise out of the trip, for even if he was pretending (as I knew all the time) he was making a real difference by suggestion that we could *make* the whole affair rather glorious instead of a stupid escapade and a miserable struggle not to be drowned.

I can't say I grasped this, but I was full of admiration and something like a passionate devotion for Jim, when all at once I heard him laughing and saying in a voice and manner I had not noticed before (but I realized that I was overhearing a new Jim – Jim as he was among men), that if it hadn't been for that spot of oil we should have been done for; and, anyhow, it had been a toucher whether we came through at all. "I didn't think we had a hope in hell when I found that we couldn't get back to the Longwater."

In fact, Jim, laughing all the time, gave up the whole idea of a planned expedition and described how frightened he had been and what "God's own luck" we had had "to come through".

I felt very much "let down" by this candour, especially when he said that he had been expecting "the kid to collapse any old minute" but that she had "probably been too scared".

It was only on the next day I felt the comfort of not having to support the enormous lie that we had always meant to go to Callacombe.

79 No one would dream of calling Jim a hypocrite for pretending to himself and me, in the middle of a violent storm, that we were doing something reasonable and possible. And no one has any right to call Chester, who had ten times more imagination than Jim, a hypocrite for pretending in the middle of a political storm (which went on all his life; he was never "in harbour" – there is no such thing in politics) that he had always meant this or that when, in fact, he had only taken note of it as a "way out".

The truth is that a man like Chester, just because he had such a lot of imagination, such power of putting himself in other people's places and minds, was *nearly always sincere*.

And, unlike Jim, who had no idea of "taking up a position" (Jim may be thought very Tory, but he was really not political at all – he simply followed his convictions and instincts), Chester needed always to believe what he took up, he *needed to be sincere*, for if he had any doubts he could not "put himself over" with effect. Sincerity (as he well knew) was the secret of his power as a speaker; all those sudden "virtuoso" changes of voice, and similes and inspired gestures were the direct result (as, I suppose, in most great preachers and saints) of a "burning" conviction.

And it was quite easy for him to get sincerity at Tarbiton. For instance, as he described it to me, just before the chapel meeting where he made the decisive speech, a small group of local "saints" had met him at tea and asked him to explain his position toward armaments. Of course, in that church people are very outspoken; quite simple members of the congregation ask the most awkward questions, even with the minister, the sort of questions people in our church rather hesitate to ask even of the youngest curate. So these people asked Chester quite flatly how he reconciled it with his conscience to vote for armies and navies; and when he gave the usual explanation, which had sounded, as he said, quite reasonable in London, they said bluntly that they didn't see how anyone could repeat the sixth commandment, or believe in Jesus when he spoke of forgiving enemies, and then vote for armaments.

All this, of course, had a great effect on Chester (you must not forget that he was in a very nervous unsettled state, for, of course, his position in the Cabinet *was* very shaky, and, in fact, the papers were already writing about a "reshuffle" and assuming that Chester would be "dropped"), so that he was very open to impressions.

Then they prayed together and, as Chester said, "It was

deeply moving – a revelation. I owe an eternal debt of gratitude to Ted for making me understand the force and truth of local feeling – a truly Christian feeling."

And after that prayer meeting he had no difficulty in showing a "burning conviction" in his address. In fact (and this is proof of his sincerity), he went a good deal further than he had intended, so that he was quite perturbed by the excitement afterwards, the fuss in the papers, the questions in the House, the demands to know if he spoke for the Government and the charge (which, as we know now, was justified) that his "peace line" would encourage the German warmakers.

But Chester could not know that – everything was too confused. And meanwhile he was "renewed in spirit".

Of course, the renewed man was still Chester and therefore "political"; and when the address came out and made such an immense to-do he was naturally interested in its political possibilities. But this is only to say that to a man like Chester, whose politics were mixed up with religion and whose religion was always getting into his politics, this was the situation which he was accustomed to "handle". It did not prevent his religion from being "true" that he knew how to "use" it.

80 And it was now, at the worst time (as it always seems to happen), that my lies and "disloyalty" to Chester came out, not, as I feared, from Mrs Tribe, but a quite unexpected source. Aunt Latter, ever since the famous defeat of the old guard, had made herself something of a nuisance to Chester. For though she considered herself his friend and came often to the house, she always found fault with his ideas and speeches, and she loved to drop "unfortunate remarks" such as "You'd better keep up with

Mrs So-and-so – she has a big pull with such and such a Minister."

Chester hated talk of "pulls" and "influence" (at least in public), though in fact half our entertaining had no other object and I was instructed to have bridge partners always ready for a certain lady who was said to have influence with the Prime Minister (and the players had to let her win). And though I suppose even Prime Ministers must get information from someone about people to whom they are giving jobs (no one likes to take a cook without a personal interview with her last mistress), yet there is something in the idea of "influence" which upsets quite reasonable people. And, of course, some of our "locals" were scandalized at the very hint of Chester's "pulling strings".

Aunt's excuse to me, when I remonstrated, was that she couldn't stand Chester's "damned hypocrisy" or she would say that she had not noticed visitors. But really she was driven by that demon which made her angry with everyone she helped; the more she had done for them, the more she seemed to hate them.

The truth was, I think, that she was an unhappy woman, who, perhaps from pride, repelled even gratitude. Certainly with all her work for others she had very little thanks and almost no affection. And for years she had been growing more unhappy. She had had to let Palm Cottage after paying Jim's gambling debts, and spent her time with relations, with all of whom she had quarrelled, or at the little flat round the corner, where she was apt to drink too much and get into a very untidy state.

In fact, the doctors had warned us about a year before this time that it was not safe for her to be alone. And we were consulting the family about a companion for her (whom she would certainly have refused), when she suddenly gave up whisky, cleaned up the flat and bought herself some new smart and rather gaudy clothes (her taste was old-fashioned, so that she succeeded in dressing in Daisy's "bad" taste, simply by having her dresses made in the "good" taste of ten years earlier) and began to appear at parties. And all at once it was discovered that she was a remarkable woman. People began to remember stories about her and to repeat her eccentric speeches as if they were epigrams. They also reminded each other that she had "made" Chester. But they liked her all the more just then because she had quarrelled with Chester and said such rude things about him, such as "You can always trust Chester – he never fails himself." Or "Chester has a very good conscience – it has to be good to stand Chester."

And she said these things with such delight and appreciation that everyone appreciated them, too, and went away feeling roused up and encouraged. It was wonderful, they said, to see how that battered old woman enjoyed life. And no one wondered more than Chester and myself.

But the reason was discovered when a little book came out by a journalist who had travelled in Africa and visited Dutchinluga. And he had described Jim (under initials) and his work for the Lugas as "typical of the finest type of British administration among primitive peoples". The little book was very well reviewed, especially among the radical papers, which were all for defending people like the Lugas from "exploitation". And it was pretty soon known, too, that Aunt Latter had met the journalist at home and given him information about Jim, which encouraged him to visit Dutchinluga and "write up" Jim's work. In fact, the book had been Aunt's plan and her success.

When Jim came home on his next leave he was quite a hero among the drawing rooms, and both he and Aunt

Latter, in their different ways, thoroughly enjoyed it. So did I. Nothing more delightful had happened to me than to see Jim at over forty getting some recognition for all his years of really hard work and true devotion. I was only irritated (suspecting a mean jealousy) when Chester said that Aunt's enterprise had its bad side – men in Government jobs were expected to avoid publicity.

"But why," I asked, "should everyone be praised except the men who do the real hard work?"

"There are reasons," and he explained that if Government officials became "popular" figures they might get too much power over "the people's elected representatives", and so on. But I did not attend to him and thought that Jim was a far finer man and did far better work than most of the "people's representatives".

Jim's conduct under this sudden and unexpected glory only strengthened me in this opinion. He was perfectly modest and simple in front of the most extravagant flattery. He would say, "Well, I went to Nigeria because I wanted a job, and it's been a good job." But this, of course, only increased the admiration of the ladies. I found him one day in a famous drawing room quite surrounded by lovely girls who were asking how he could bear the climate and the insects and the solitude, a position in which most men look foolish. But Jim's old-fashioned manners stood the test.

He answered their questions as if he had been going through an examination ("the climate is not so bad if you don't drink too much"). They found him rather dull but completely satisfactory. And when he left Paddington for the African boat there was quite a deputation to see him off.

And then, less than a month later, when he should have arrived at Dutchinluga (in the mountains), we heard that the Luga district was to be merged in another and Jim was to look after them both and also shift his headquarters to a village in the plains, very hot and damp, and fifty miles from his beloved Lugas.

Jim did not express surprise at this unexpected blow. He wrote only, "It's the boys in Aiké Square (which was the Nigerian Downing Street or Washington). They want to kill me off for being a bit independent. And they want to kill the Lugas off when they're finished with me. They killed old Brown in just the same way; sent him to a fever hole and buried him in six months."

But for Aunt Latter the news was like a thunderclap, and she was round at the Parade within half an hour to see Chester and make him understand the monstrous wickedness and injustice of the Nigerian Government.

Again I was surprised by the way these two, who really detested each other, came together. When I looked in from shopping I found them, to my astonishment, almost in one chair (Chester was sitting on the arm of it) and complimenting each other like two impresarios or ambassadors after a war. "But, my dear Aunt Latter," Chester said (and he had never called her Aunt Latter before), "of course I shall do what I can for Jim – I'm sure there has been some mistake. I am very glad you came to me." And then Aunt Latter began to say how brilliantly Chester had "turned the tables on the old Liberals by his peace campaign".

"Ah, that contract affair – it was a pity I could not consult you, but you were so ill at the time (Aunt Latter had been drunk most of the time). It is good to see you looking so well again – quite your old self."

For the truth was that Chester was very glad to be friends with Aunt Latter again. Since the scandal we needed all our friends, especially the hostile ones. They talked for half the afternoon. And either because they were really sympathetic, or wanted to give each other hostages, Chester told Aunt about some of the latest intrigues in the party and Aunt told Chester about Tom's new passion for the modern stage. So it came out that Tom had been visiting the Tribes almost every day and that he was in the habit of going on there from Aunt's flat; and how, too, both Jim and she agreed that the Tribes were a very bad influence on Tom, and encouraged him in his bad taste (Jim, even more than Chester, had always detested Tom's tight-waisted suits and velour hats), as well as his weakness for acting.

81 But what upset Chester, of course, was the discovery that I had hidden Tom's visits. With his extraordinary memory he at once recalled my remark that Tom could not be at the Tribes' because he was with Aunt Latter, and set his spies to work. I believe the man he saw (it shows how his information came to him) was an MP who owned newspapers and knew an editor who knew the journalist who had married Totty Tribe. In any case, he had the full story within twenty-four hours; and when I was half asleep after lunch in my own room, and without my frock, he came in and asked if I had remembered to ask certain people to dinner. Then suddenly, not looking at me, he said, "You don't think there's anything between Tom and that Tribe girl?"

"I wonder?" (What else could I say?)

And he started across the room, glancing at me with an expression which seemed to mean, You are looking very nice in that negligee, and said, "You don't know of any entanglement?"

"No." And to change the direction of his ideas, I put up

my arms and said, "Sit down for a moment and talk to me."

Whereupon he stopped short, not exactly glancing at me, but looking judicial, and said, "Are you sure?"

And at once I saw that he had found out something. So I said at once (looking and feeling very foolish as I took down my arms), "Tom did say something to me, but it was to be a secret."

"Otherwise, you have been conspiring with Tom to bamboozle me."

"But, Chester, I had to promise."

"You needn't have told quite so many lies." And he became suddenly very angry and asked me if I realized what it meant to him to find that I was as bad as the rest, or even worse, because I had no excuse for treachery. He said that he had tried to be a good husband to me; God knows he had given me every freedom, and I had used it only to deceive him and to make a fool of him. He was apparently the only man in London who did not know that his son was running about the restaurants with actresses. "I dare say," he said, "you have ruined the boy – as well as teaching him to lie. I have experienced a fine variety of treacheries in the last month – but I didn't guess for a moment that the worst of them was going on in my own house." And he sank down on the sofa and put his hand over his face and gave a sigh that was very nearly (but thank goodness not quite) a sob. And I thought, "Really he is 'putting it on' a little too much."

Both Tom and I had noticed that since the "scandal" Chester had become a little more dramatic, more excitable; even in private life he seemed sometimes to be "acting himself". And we had agreed that it was hard for a man who spent so much time in the limelight to be ordinary and that it was very unsafe (as well as unfair) to suspect him of "performing", because he "put on an act" even at breakfast. He was nearly always true to what he felt at the moment.

So I "played up" to him and knelt down on the sofa beside him and implored him to forgive me and not to upset himself too much. A big debate was expected at the House that evening and he ought to keep himself fresh for it.

But he pushed me away (though quite gently – he was very dignified) and got up and said that, of course, he forgave me, but I did not seem to understand what a blow it was to him to find that he could not trust me even in such a vital matter as Tom's life.

I apologized again, and he forgave me again, and I thought that the matter was over. Two scenes were generally enough even in bad cases, and, besides, I knew Chester's maxim in all relations, social as well as political, of "beginning here". I had heard him say, half in joke, that the rule is precisely that of the Stock Exchange, "cut your losses" and "nothing is worth more than today's price"; that is, he was always ready to forgive anyone who was still useful to him.

But I was quite wrong. I had not allowed for the change due to the scandal (which made him feel still more insecure and suspicious, still more anxious for loyal support), the religious renewal, and something desperate and impatient which Tom and I had noticed as "putting on an act". And I had forgotten again that under all his performances and maxims Chester's love for me was real. It was a true thing that he could not help. So my "deceit" had made a deep wound – he never forgot it. And the discovery had come at the worst possible time for Tom and myself.

82 The usual story is that Chester destroyed the only serious interest Tom ever had by stopping his going on the stage. But who could have told that it was going to be a "serious interest"? The boy was only eighteen. And he did not do it without consideration. He actually attended, with me, a rehearsal of a Strindberg, and I was almost as much shocked as he was. It is a play about a countess who "gives herself" to a groom and then commits suicide. As Chester said as we came out, nothing could persuade him that Strindberg was "good for anything", especially in such terrible times when civilization was being undermined from all sides.

But Chester even then was not unreasonable. As soon as Tom came home that night he said how interesting he had found the performance, "though I admit I did not quite see why Strindberg is so important".

"He is so true," Tom said. "He's not afraid of anything."

Chester, who was walking about the room, seemed to ponder on this, and then remarked that you could say that of Crippen (who was a famous murderer at that time); but then at once before Tom could be offended he said quickly in a very sympathetic voice, "But, of course, I am a mere philistine – I need instruction. Tell me why Strindberg is great."

Tom began a long speech about realism and honesty and getting down to earth and technique and originality – all the things which were gospel at the Tribes'. And Chester listened attentively. His expression seemed to say, "No doubt we will soon come to the point."

Chester was now, at fifty-three, quite grey, and his face, though fresh and clear in complexion, deeply lined. Looking at him, one could not forget that he was a man who had fought desperate battles for what he believed to be right, and was used to big responsibilities.

It is very hard for anyone to talk convincingly about high art to a soldier fighting for his life and other people's lives, and, of course, that was how Chester saw himself and how he appeared at that moment. Tom soon began to falter and lose his way. Besides, to tell the truth, he was so completely Tribalized (as Aunt Latter put it) that he had never questioned all the nonsense the Tribes talked about art – he had hardly thought of it until he tried to put it together and make sense of it.

But the boy's confusion seemed only to make Chester more sympathetic. How gentle, how affectionate his air, how thoughtfully he murmured at intervals, "I see"; somehow, in the very patient kindness of his tone, making the explanations seem inexplicable and ridiculous, as, of course, they were.

At last Tom, quite lost in his own mysterious argument, turned red, broke off abruptly and said, "But it's really his art that's so wonderful – and you don't believe that art matters."

Chester jumped up in indignation and said that, on the contrary, he set the highest value on art – real art. Nothing had so much value in education – to elevate the mind and refine the senses. And no doubt Strindberg did so – no doubt he was among the great benefactors of humanity. He (Chester) was not criticizing – he only wanted to learn.

And then suddenly, with a complete change of tone and look (as if afraid that he had been tactless), he cried, "But come, this is no time for such dry subjects. What about a little something before we go to bed – a little punch or some of your mother's famous mulled claret?"

Nothing more was said about Strindberg. Chester knew exactly where to stop. Tom did not have a chance of resenting "interference", and though he was angry with

Chester he was also ashamed of his irritation. I was not surprised to hear, some weeks later, that he had thrown up his part on the excuse that he wasn't good enough.

And it was not only Chester who was pleased; I must confess that I, too, felt a great relief. I thought it a pity if just then, at such a critical time for Chester, and the country, too, Tom should give up the university to devote himself to a decadent creature like Strindberg.

You may say (and young people point it out to me now) that civilization is always in danger – there has always been a crisis – parents and bishops and politicians are always discovering that art and literature are threatened with decadence. But, after all, there *is* such a thing as decadence and it does happen to nations and arts and so it must begin sometime and somewhere. It is true that Chester was in a religious state of mind when we saw Strindberg and that I was feeling guilty and remorseful, but I still think it may be a decadent play (I mean that in another hundred years historians may say that things began to take the wrong direction with writers like Strindberg) and so it is not fair to blame Chester for thinking so and letting it appear.

As for the other charge that Chester broke off Tom's engagement, it is quite false. We had arranged, indeed, to go and see Tom about it at Eastborough (Chester had said one thing at a time and deliberately waited till the Strindberg danger was over before approaching the second problem – he wished only to postpone an announcement), when the news leaked out. One afternoon there were paragraphs in two evening papers about Tom, one saying that that Mr Thomas Nimmo, son of the Minister of Mines, was engaged to Miss Julie Tribe, and proposed to take up a dramatic career; the other in a more popular paper (with an immense circulation), that "Tom Nimmo, aged seventeen, son of Chester of that ilk, whose eloquent vindication of his investments so successfully persuaded his party that he didn't mean to do it, in the contract scandal, wants to go on the stage, but Papa says no. He thinks that 'playing many parts' involves too much artfulness."

The result was a mass of inquiries and letters, more paragraphs in the papers all over the country (the story went right round the world and both Tom and Julie had letters over a year later from places as far away as Hong Kong and Nebraska) – a tremendous fuss.

Tom had been amused before when Chester and I discussed what to tell the reporters, but now, for the first time, he experienced that feeling of insecurity which comes from discovering that once a piece of "news" goes out about you (and it may affect your whole life) you can never catch up with it. It may be quite false, but still it will be repeated and believed.

Tom, when he realized this, was very "rattled" and telephoned Chester to assure him that it was not his fault that the papers had got hold of the story. He was chiefly worried by the idea that it would do Chester harm at a time when what Tom called the "ghouls" were all trying to dig up something against him.

And they agreed between them that Tom should deny everything; as Chester said, nothing was official or settled, and in any case one was always allowed to deny things to the press. Ministers did so every day.

But, of course, the Tribes thought that they were being jilted (they were very suspicious of "these politicians"); Mrs Tribe threatened an action unless the engagement was confirmed; and Julie, who would not hear of an action, yet did not see why Tom should have told "all those lies".

And from this time the affair between them went badly. They could not go anywhere together in Tom's holidays without stares and often photographers; and while Tom hated all this publicity, Julie rather enjoyed it. She said it could be useful, and gave interviews. And though she refused to talk about the engagement (she was a very nice honest girl in spite of her rather dominating temper), she talked a great deal about the neglect of Strindberg and her plans for a Strindberg season.

In fact it was the publicity which came to Julie Tribe at this time which set her on the path to her present glories – it brought her the offer of her first West End part (the housemaid in a Pinero farce). It also brought her a good deal of attention from men much more experienced than Tom, who was naturally very jealous and bitter. So that he was always slipping up to town (against the rules) to see what Julie was doing, and it was not surprising that he failed in his school examinations and finally, having missed the last train to Eastborough, was caught trying to climb into his House and expelled.

And when we appealed to the headmaster to let him finish the term (there was only a fortnight left) so that we could take him away quietly without the black mark of expulsion (and we marshalled three governors – one of them a duke – to support us), he gave us to know that for a boy in Tom's position, a prefect, no forgiveness was possible. But I was pretty sure that the real reason was because poor Tom was Chester's son, and the master daren't let him off in case it was said that he had favoured him.

It was only by an appeal to certain "friends at court" that we got him into Oxford. And if you say that this was using influence, I must point out that it was only fair that Tom should have some advantage from Chester's position, since up to now it had been a handicap. And it still was a handicap, for at Oxford he was at once surrounded by a special atmosphere of friends and enemies. He was popular as a martyr (because everyone believed that Chester had stopped him from marrying Julie and acting in the "immortal" Strindberg) among the clever and artistic set, and detested by the old-fashioned and county set. And both sides, of course, never forgot that he was a Nimmo.

83 I had always longed for Tom to have plenty of happiness, and now it seemed to me that it was going to be hard for him to achieve even a little. He understood this very well (he understood everything I felt) and it brought us still closer together.

But quite apart from my devotion to Tom and his to me, for we had always enjoyed each other's company and loved to go about together to plays and concerts, we were in a specially close relation as Nimmos. We understood what it was to be in Chester's family; it was quite noticeable how the atmosphere changed for us when even close friends of Tom went out of a room and left us together. It was not as though (as in most families) the air had become less intense (and also less interesting), but quite the contrary, as if a pressure had returned upon us – as if we noticed again the preoccupation and anxiety that strangers had relieved. In fact, we were always aware of a situation, asking each other "How are things?" meaning not only the political situation as it affected Chester (which was still very anxious – he was always being attacked) but the family situation: what Bootham was telling Goold, what Goold thought about Tom's future. But though, when we were alone together, we felt these anxious preoccupations more, yet they made us want to be together, and also, I think, to seek distractions and pleasure for each other.

Chester was too busy to pay many visits to Oxford, but I went often, for Tom was always asking me to come. He would meet me at the station with a smart hansom and whirl me away to my hotel, like a young lover cutting a dash before his darling. He would have flowers and chocolates in my room (knowing my passion for both) and provide me also with his own special brand of expensive cigarettes. He wanted even to take me to balls, but I refused to make myself ridiculous at nearly forty years of age by dancing all night with boys of twenty.

And as for the idea that I "broke out" with Tom, and that we indulged ourselves in all the gaieties, it is absurd, and perhaps it comes from a wrong idea of what life was like in those days. It is true that there were plenty of parties, but I doubt if people nowadays would think them at all gay. There were too many rules and formalities. Tom would complain when he went to a ball that he had to dance so many "duty dances" with plain stupid girls who danced so badly that he would much rather have been in bed. And he had to pay so many formal calls, and send out so many flowers to hostesses, that he would prefer not to have any parties at all. But, in fact, he never refused a party or a ball, and he was extremely particular about the shape of the tall hat in which he paid his calls.

For if the parties were sometimes dull and social duties often a bore, there was somehow a great pleasure in feeling that the "social machinery" was at work and that we were playing our part in it. And as for my encouraging Tom to be a rebel (or thinking of the Tribes with their "freedom for art" as rebels), art was quite an important part of the machinery. How often was I expected to waste an afternoon at an exhibition of pictures because they were by some young artist who "ought to be encouraged", or to buy tickets for amateur theatricals in which some friend or supporter was acting as footman or maid!

It was, in fact, as a social duty that I went to some undergraduate's rooms, to see a college society called the Burlesques playing what they called some "turns", and I did not know even that Tom was taking part. There were some songs and then a little play called *The Prog and the Lady*.

Tom dressed as a pierrot, but wearing a gown and mortarboard, pretended to be a proctor (who is a kind of university policeman) catching an undergraduate with a young woman (she turned out to be the fat-faced girl May who had played the cat in the Tribes' pantomime) and taking the young woman away from him.

There was an audience of mothers and sisters which was most enthusiastic (but really the songs were not very funny), and afterwards a champagne supper, when the actors were congratulated by everybody. It was all very proper in Eights Week, like dances and concerts and picnics. No one dreamed of anything subversive in Tom's "taking off" a proctor.

In those days there was beneath everything a sense (in spite of the "wicked" Liberal Government) of security and peace. I don't mean that no one expected the war – everyone said that war was likely. That confidence, in fact, which we all shared was something very mysterious; it was, I suppose, simply a feeling that life would always be worth living, and the peace which seemed to rest on the fields and the lovely town, and to sound from the water plopping under the punts, and to shine placidly on all the different rivers when you looked from bridges, was not really there at all, but in people's minds and souls. And so our calmest gaiety, simply walking in a college garden to look at the flowers and show off our frocks, or dawdling to the barges along avenues of big trees, was still a very deep kind of pleasure. And the barges (they are houseboats built like ships and all different, with figureheads and coats of arms), with their new paint and their flags flying, and their roofs crowded with mothers and sisters in summer frocks, so that they were like old-fashioned bridesmaids' bouquets of small tight blooms, mignonette, asters, violets, pinks, seemed like a fleet in line ahead moving forward (as the river flowed past) in a stately manner at about one mile an hour toward some imperial water festival.

Yet on the barges it was hot, and there was nothing to do in a whole hour between the races (which passed in a few minutes). We sat under our parasols and chatted and criticized each other's frocks, or studied each other's sons and daughters. There was a twittering sound of voices all round, sounding, as they always seem to sound over water, very light and as it were full of air, a feeling of large stretches of sky and time surrounding us; and I dare say that many people nowadays would have been exceedingly bored. But as I sat on my hard bench, with one leg going to sleep, and listened to Tom talking about the last comedy we had seen together (he often ran up to town for a matinee with me and he was very critical – he would discuss the weakness of Pinero or Barrie for months afterwards), I felt an immense calm gaiety, as if, so to speak, I had just inherited such an immense wealth of delights that I did not need to be extravagant; I could afford simply to feel the comfort of being so rich without the trouble of spending.

And, in fact, all about me there was the same peaceful rich happiness. The girls leaning over the rail and looking thoughtfully at the river where the sun made slow dignified

minuets among small lazy bumps of water were so full of
the knowledge that this was a special occasion that it
seemed to come out even in the set of their shoulders and
the shadow of their eyelashes fixed attentively on their pink
cheeks.

And this seemed to me, in some extraordinary way, the
only real world. I knew, of course, how important Chester's
work was, among all our anxieties and confusions in
London; and that this was a week of holiday (or rather two
days – I could only spare two days), but I did not feel as if
I had escaped out of a real world into playtime, but as if
that life in London were play (a very difficult exhausting
game, but still a game) and this place, full of young people
enjoying themselves, and flirting in the rather serious
manner of sisters under their brothers' and mothers' eyes,
and discussing races and careers, examinations and balls,
had the only solid truth and importance. And I suppose
happiness is a very real thing. It is what we live for. So that
Tom's happiness, as he entertained his ugly clever girl, and
made love to me (even though he laughed at me a little),
had the quality which belongs to things that one would not
dare to spoil.

Again, when Tom and his friends and the girl May were
invited to perform at a big charity fete, and real
professionals, as he pointed out, were also to make an
appearance, I was delighted for him because he was so
delighted. I still remember the night when the news came
and he brought me the letter in his hand. "Here's a surprise
– but do you think it's a joke?"

"No, I'm sure it's not a joke. You don't realize how good
you were in the Burlesques."

"Do you really think I ought to accept? Could the papers
make anything out of it?"

"I don't see how."

"The *Tarbiton Gazette* tried to make politics out of my grey bowler."

"The great thing is that it's for charity – it might even please your papa."

"It really would be rather a lark and I'd like to meet some of the Stars. So long as Papa doesn't want to see us perform."

"I'm afraid we can't guard against that unless we don't tell him at all, and that would be risky."

And Tom agreed that Chester would have to be told. "Of course, I oughtn't to mind if he does come – he's been so good about everything."

"I'll stop him if I can."

"You know what it is when he congratulates you and you know he rather despises the whole thing."

Actually the Burlesques were such a success at the fete that they had more invitations and were asked to go on tour. This did alarm me a little, because I still wanted Tom to take his degree and go into some serious profession like diplomacy or (as Chester preferred) the law.

But Tom was so delighted at the idea and so sure that it would not interfere with his work that I hid my doubts. And as for Chester, though we crossed our fingers every day, there were no "repercussions," as Chester called them. When he asked what Tom's recitation (we had used this word to him because he was accustomed to the idea of "recitations" even at religious gatherings) consisted of, I said that it was only a skit (which was the smallest word I could think of) and Tom set no store by it.

Chester took this very well and said only that he supposed he ought to "fit it in somewhere".

"There's no need at all for you to see it – Tom knows

how busy you are. In fact, I rather think he'd prefer you *not* to see it – it's such a trifle."

"But he mustn't take up this attitude that I'm unsympathetic – that's not fair."

"It's not that at all." And I said that it was because Tom admired him so much that he sometimes felt rather overwhelmed by him. Chester listened to this attentively, and I could see that he was pleased. But he said again that Tom must not think that he was unsympathetic to the arts, of any kind. He had the highest respect for artists.

84 But luckily Chester was so busy that he had not time even to ask when the Burlesques were performing. He had so many invitations to speak that he could not accept a quarter of them.

Nothing disgusted Chester so much as the charge (I showed that it was much too simple to be true) that he "took up" pacifism only because of the contract scandal, in order to re-establish his position in the party. But it really did turn out luckily for him. The tour in the west, early in 1914, had the most wonderful results. Letters of quite a new kind began to flood in; and although Chester's enemies never forgot the "scandal", he made thousands of new friends, especially among the poorer religious people. Indeed Wilfred and Aunt Latter agreed that by what they called his clever move to the Left he had made that scandal into an actual advantage, because he was able to represent the attacks made upon him as wicked attempts by the Conservatives, and the war-makers, and the Right Wing of his own party, to discredit him; which was true, of course, because they did want to discredit him.

And since the whole nation was now very much alarmed by Germany's war preparations, there was a great increase in pacifism. Everybody who was afraid of a war was trying to stop it, either by making preparations to fight in order to frighten Germany or by opposing preparations to fight in order not to annoy Germany. Chester became suddenly one of the most powerful men in the House, and it has been said since that, at the time of the famous secret meeting, he could have brought down the Government and come in as Prime Minister. And this, too, is held against him as a deliberate attempt to play "politics", when the nation was in danger.

But there was no deliberation about that meeting – only I know the indecisions and agonies of that time.

It started, like nearly all such affairs, from different circumstances which suddenly, a long time after, joined together to make a strong effect. One day when we were at Bristol three local MPs asked Chester to preside at a meeting of Western Radicals who were opposed to war preparations. Chester was promised that at least a hundred quite important people would attend to fight "the wicked plan for sending a British army to fight in France". And they told him that he was the only man of the front bench who still held the confidence of Christian people. "In the matter of a real peace policy your voice would have the most decisive effect. You are the man of the hour if only you will act – the whole country is waiting for a lead."

Chester refused this invitation on the grounds that, as a Minister, he could not openly attack the Government (up till then his speeches, however violent, had simply been aimed at the "jingoes" or the "war-makers" – he had most cleverly avoided any direct attack on the Cabinet).

And now he was most indignant at the very suggestion and kept on speaking of it even at night. "What do they take me for?" he exclaimed, at a most unexpected moment when he seemed intent on anything but politics. (But I had noticed long since how politics goes on spreading through one's whole life. It is like "drains" – you may be in the garden but they seem to hang on the air, to get even into the flowers. You smell a rose and it reminds you of the plumber.) And I had to think for a moment before I answered (meaning to please him), "They depend on you for a bold lead."

"My dear girl, the PM would have to turn me out of the Government."

"Would he dare? You have so much support. It would split the Cabinet."

"That's an old story. The papers are always expecting Ministers to resign – on principle. But when it comes to the point you find they have some other principle which is all against resignation." And then he said in a reproachful tone (for apparently he had expected me to do two things at once, like himself), "You don't take much interest in me nowadays."

And I hastened to do what was necessary. For as Chester grew older, somehow our routine had become more complicated. I mention it because of later developments, and because (what people don't always understand) it was important to Chester in a way which affected his mind and nerves very deeply.

I don't mean that this relation was still the very "moving" thing, the "revelation", that it had been for Chester (it changed all the time like our other relations) but it was much more kind. We both knew that it was the only way in which he escaped completely from tension and was really himself, quite careless of what anyone thought of him (because there was none to think badly except myself, and he knew that I was sympathetic, and delighted to do anything at all to make him peaceful), and full of tenderness and gratitude, which are feelings that make everyone feel better. But (to show how excited he was in this month) on that evening, instead of going contentedly to sleep in my arms, as usual, he woke me up twenty minutes later with the exclamation, "Splitting the Cabinet! Cabinets are a lot tougher than they think, a whole lot!" And I realized his mind was still full of the idea that he might take the lead for the pacifists.

I say that as Chester grew older and more harassed, he needed me more. And for some time now he had got into the way of looking for me at very unexpected times (breaking off in the middle of work to see what I was "up to" and to tell me some piece of news or complain of some "treachery"), and this made it difficult for me to arrange my own affairs. For instance, in this weekend Tom's concert party had arrived at a place called Ronnsea, not twenty miles away, and Tom had written to say that since I was so near he hoped I could slip away to see the "show".

I could not think it was possible – I made various plans, but all of them seemed too dangerous – Chester would discover something. And I should not have taken the risk if he had not been invited, suddenly, to speak to a meeting of local agents. This gave me four clear hours and I could not resist so rare a chance. I took the first train to Ronnsea, meaning to be back before dinner.

85 I had been to see the concert party before, on tour, and it had always been quite delightful. They were all so young, so friendly to each other and to me, and so full of joy and excitement at their success. For they had been very successful everywhere, and I don't think there was any doubt that Tom, and possibly May Bond, had a real genius for this kind of entertainment. Both of them were natural mimics, and Tom had a gift for inventing these "turns", which are still remembered by some very good critics.

And what was so amusing and attractive about the party was that they were continually improvising among themselves – they were full of invention, so that they made each other laugh as well as me. And I don't know how it was, but all this laughter went to my head so that when they begged me to stay for the performance I gave way. I could not bear to leave them; I felt as one does at a very good party, that one never wants it to stop. So I sent a wire, "Delayed. Don't wait dinner."

But Chester (as I might have expected) had already traced me. He had telephoned to the hotel *before* the meeting, simply (as he put it) to hear my voice, and, finding that I had gone to the station, had set Bootham to work, who had telephoned in all directions, including Ronnsea, and discovered the concert party of which he had, of course, been suspicious.

So just when the performance was beginning, to a small but quite enthusiastic audience, there was a great noise outside, a policeman put in his head from the side of the little stage and said something. May, who was in the middle of her act, broke off; the curtain came down, and Chester was seen walking up among the chairs, accompanied by three local officials and followed by an enormous crowd which filled all the rest of the seats, and also the aisles along the sides of the hall.

Chester appeared in the highest spirits, smiling about him and beaming and waving his hand; he kissed me most affectionately, and sat down beside me. But then, just for a moment (while people round, who had got up to see what all the fuss was about, were taking their seats again), he looked quite angrily at me and said, "Why didn't you tell me you were coming?"

"I thought I could get back in time."

"If you see Tom act, I ought to see him too. You give people a completely false impression by coming alone. They'll think I'm prejudiced against Tom and concert parties."

"Nobody knew I was here."

"*I* didn't know where you were and we have to go back to town at once. There's a wire from the office. Bootham was at his wit's end."

And I had to see that my conduct was selfish and irresponsible. Here Chester was in the middle of a crisis which concerned not only his own future but possibly that of the nation and the whole world, and I had run off to amuse myself at a seaside concert party.

I could not even be furious with him for coming to spoil Tom's evening.

And he behaved very well. As soon as the curtain went up and May reappeared, he began to smile, and not only that – he was really attentive, he laughed in the right places, and clapped loudly (a very loud clap, with his hands held very high so that everyone could see his enthusiasm), and the people standing in the aisles (mostly holiday people) stared at him much more than the stage, and looked at first very serious and rather surprised, as if they had not expected the Prophet of Peace (as he was sometimes called) to look so genial and rosy, and to laugh so lustily at a girl in short skirts singing slightly risky songs about landladies; but afterwards they began to laugh when he laughed, and clap with him; and there was that feeling in the air which makes one's nerves tingle, and one says to oneself, "This is an evening I shall never forget, but whether it is more delightful or more horrible I can't tell till I recover from it."

It was obvious that the performers, too, were in a state of nervous tension. May, who needed excitement to be at her best (and liked a little whisky before her songs), was brilliant. Her little eyes simply sparkled with wicked joy, and even her voice seemed more impudent. And Tom, too, when he first came on, seemed unusually good, especially in the monologue written by himself (and, as I think, much better than some of his later really famous acts), when he appeared wearing a German helmet over his pierrot suit and a Kaiser moustache stuck on his upper lip, and made a long speech congratulating Unser Gott on his promotion to Field Marshal.

I had seen this act, which was, I thought, much the best in the whole performance, at least a dozen times, and Tom had improved it till it was a wonderful piece of satire. But this evening, after a good beginning (when Chester called out quite loudly, "Bravo, Tom"), he became at once too stiff and too farcical. At every cheer from the audience, who had realized the situation and were delighted to see Chester's affectionate pleasure in the boy's success, and especially at each of Chester's claps and bravos, he became a little more exaggerated. And though at the end there were tremendous shouts of encore, he would not repeat the act.

Indeed, when he came on again and again to answer the cheers and claps, I could see that he was quite aware of his failure, and that it was an agony to him to go on answering the applause. I was terrified that he would say or do something to show how uncomfortable he was; but he went on smiling (though with rather a ghastly smile) and bowing (though rather stiffly) to the last.

Meanwhile an immense crowd had gathered outside, and

when we came out there were shouts of "Speech!" and "Good old Nimmo!" and "No more war!" And in the end Chester climbed into the back seat of a car (it was a friend's car which had brought him to the place) and made a speech.

I had slipped away to say goodnight to Tom, but suddenly I found myself in the middle of the whole party, close to the door of the hall. They were making a great noise, excited by their success and a record house, and the box-office girl was handing out drinks through her porthole.

Tom, who had put on an overcoat over the pierrot dress, took my arm and said, laughing, "Now for the other show."

"What other show?"

"Papa's – I hope he'll be better than I was."

"But you were very good."

"You know I was rotten." And I noticed that the boy was flushed and smelled of whisky, but at the same moment he said, "I'm not really tight – where shall we go?"

"Perhaps you'd better go and change."

"No, I want to hear this speech. I like Papa's speeches. He's a real artist."

And he really did want to hear Chester speak. He hurried me round the crowd, which was too thick to get through, and brought me to a doorway across the street and up some steps. "There," he said, "right in the dress circle."

And, in fact, we had a very good view over the heads of the crowd. Somebody had taken a naphtha lamp from a stall in the fairground and was holding it up like a torch beside the car, so that Chester could be seen brightly illuminated (though the light flickered a good deal) as he spoke.

I was afraid that the noise of the town and the fair close by, and the sea beyond that, where quite big waves were breaking, would drown Chester's voice, but as usual he seemed to get a bigger voice when he wanted it, and we heard nearly every word. The speech was the one which he always used in smaller towns, for freedom of conscience, and against conscription and increased armaments. And he defended the pacifists, saying that it was they who were truly men of courage.

This may be rather a stale paradox nowadays, but as Chester developed it it was very exciting. Besides, his idea was that pacifists should resist evil, but without arms. They should go to meet the enemy and simply stand in their way and let themselves be martyred, as a witness against the war-makers and blood guilty.

And as with that splendid voice of his he spoke of the grandeur of the Christian's duty, to give his life for the love of his fellows, the noblest religion the world had ever conceived, the religion of abnegation and sacrifice, and then of the fearful danger which hung over Europe and which had risen directly from selfishness and greed and vainglory, I felt that, however "political" Chester might have been in coming to Ronnsea that evening, his words were splendid, and made everything that I had been saying and doing for the last week, and especially everything I had thought about the war, seem inexpressibly mean and blind. I even forgot Tom, who was hanging over my arm, until at the end of the speech, when the crowd was cheering and mobbing the car and the police were trying to hold them back, I heard his voice saying, "He's done it again."

"Yes, he's always at his best extempore."

"It's a good deal in the voice, the way he manages his pauses."

"I couldn't stop him from coming."

"Oh no – he was quite right to come; it was a first-class chance for a popular speech."

"And he meant every word."

"Oh, he's sincere enough" (Tom and I would always remind each other at such times when we felt the pressure severely that Chester, though he had to "play politics", was really a sincere good man). "Oh yes," Tom sighed, "and what he said was pretty important – it got me. I was almost in tears."

I said hastily that he had been very good, too, but he laughed at me and said, "Thanks"; then suddenly he frowned and said, "I felt like a clown – but I suppose that's what I've got to expect."

And as he said this and pressed my arm, I felt all at once such anxiety and sympathy that I forgot my excitement (Chester's voice was still, as it were, singing in my nerves) and said, "But you mustn't feel like that. You must have your own life."

"Have you had a life of your own?"

"It's different for a woman."

"I don't see why."

"Besides, I'm not clever at anything."

Tom did not answer, and as we were walking back toward the hall, in the dark, picking our way through the groups of people who were still talking excitedly among themselves and waving hats and giving shouts, he said suddenly, "May wants to form a company and take the Burlesques to London. She's had a good offer from her agent."

"I'm sure she deserves it."

"What would you think if I chucked Oxford and went along with her?"

This gave me a great shock – and I realized that it would be even worse for Chester. I very nearly cried out that surely he would not leave Oxford for such a trivial cause.

But I had discovered already (I suppose every mother finds the same thing) that the really important crises in family life are apt to turn up at the most awkward moments and in the most casual way. You have to be ready for them in your bath or in bed or half asleep at a committee.

And I could feel that Tom was in a desperate mood not only by his remarks before but the way he spoke now, as if ready to laugh at an absurd suggestion. So I checked myself and said that it was a very interesting idea – May was a very enterprising young woman.

"You think I'd be quite mad to go?"

"Of course not – at least if you're sure it's what you want to do – what would satisfy you." This made Tom very angry and he burst out, "I knew you would say that. How on earth can I tell what would satisfy me till I've tried? This is just a chance to try. But, of course, it's impossible – even you're horrified at the idea of me being a comic."

And seeing him so excited, I had to assure him that he was quite wrong. Comedy was a great art. "Look at Molière and Shakespeare, and even Dan Leno."

And I really meant it – for the boy's distress and uncertainty had, so to speak (like Chester's sudden appeals to conscience), taken me out of my "small views" and I saw that "comics" really were artists and that it would be wrong as well as stupid to discourage Tom from being one. So I urged him to think seriously about May's offer – it might be a good opening.

He did not answer me directly, and after a moment he said in an angry tone as if defying some critic, "People have to laugh, haven't they?"

273

Then suddenly he turned into the hall, and I didn't see him again that evening till he came to say goodbye to me and to congratulate Chester on his "marvellous speech". So I wrote to him at once telling him that perhaps the Burlesques would be the best way to an independent life, and if he chose it I should support his choice in every possible way.

But he threw up his part in the Burlesques actually in the middle of the tour and gradually gave up the whole idea of being an actor. Instead he suddenly decided to leave Oxford (he had failed in some examination) and go to an art school. And he was not very good at art. I don't think he found it exciting enough, and often when he was supposed to be studying he was with friends in some bar, discussing the international situation (which seemed very bad) or going on visits to big houses in the country. For now there was an even bigger Crown Prince's party, and much more important, big businessmen and MPs who were delighted to entertain Tom because he was really very charming and amusing and also, as Chester's son, he was "somebody".

It is said that Tom was an example of the boy who went wrong and took to drink because he was an "artist" in a "religious" atmosphere, where no one had any sympathy for his tastes. This is quite nonsense. Tom had every kind of sympathy, we were very anxious for him to go on with his art. It was he who could not take it seriously. Perhaps he was not narrow-minded enough, not enough of an egotist. An artist has to be very egotistical, or rather mad, to go on dancing or scribbling or painting pictures, when the world is full of such misery and danger. You may say that in the end the artists change the world, but, if so, they do it very slowly, and who can tell that they do it for the best. Tom was too nice and too well behaved to be an artist. And as for drink, he never did "take" to drink. He was, it is true, arrested for being drunk and disorderly (and, of course, the papers were full of it – this started the legend of his being a drunkard) at the time of the secret meeting; but he never was a drunkard, and even in drink always polite and amenable. What happened on that night was that he was very excited about the political situation (as well he might be) and so drank more than he noticed, and afterwards when the party was turned into the street he was involved in a political argument. Somebody in the bar, a stranger who did not know Tom, was making the usual charge against Chester that his peace campaign was a "stunt" to restore his popularity, and Tom called him a liar and tried to knock him down.

86 And it's not surprising that poor Tom could not settle to his art studies (which are quite hard dull work) at this time when our lives were a continuous series of thrilling events, and people were saying every day that the Cabinet was split in two, and that either Lloyd George, or Churchill, or Chester was going to be the new Prime Minister.

And if you think that it's absurd to say Chester could have been Prime Minister, you simply don't understand how people do become Prime Minister, and how ordinary they seem before something happens to make them so.

The peace meeting, for instance, was just such an accident. Chester had no intention of attending it, even when he was promised the support of a hundred members. And when I pointed out that it was to be secret (this was the new plan) he answered, "How could it be private if a hundred members are coming? It would be in the papers the same evening."

Every kind of pressure was put upon Chester to attend this meeting, and, of course, as everyone knows, he did go. But the reason was that at the last moment someone unknown telephoned to him that another Minister was to be present (I daren't give the name) and, as he said to me, to have such a man, so utterly unscrupulous and ambitious, as leader in so dangerous a movement might produce the greatest disaster. Perhaps it is lucky for the country that he managed to arrive first, and was at once accepted (being, after all, the only Minister present) as leader. There were nearly eighty members (not one hundred and fifty as the books say) who (partly because it was a private meeting) talked in the wildest way and completely lost their heads, and passed a resolution to fight against the estimates. As Chester said, the truth was that most of the backbench radicals were bitterly disappointed with the Government, as backbenchers always are after the first few months, and the only thing that prevents them from tearing down every Government is that they hate each other even more, and so they can't work together. But now when they were together on the only principle they could agree on, they became like a revolution, and shouted for Chester to speak; and since it was a private meeting, and he was very excited by the enthusiasm, he spoke just what he thought about the preparations for war. Then, of course, the speech leaked out. Nearly everybody who heard it wanted it to leak out, because the meeting was full of people who felt that the Government did not think them important enough to be afraid of.

The result was the "famous" crisis of July (but who remembers it now?) when it seemed for at least a week that the Government might split and Chester come in as Prime Minister of a new Peace Cabinet. For his pledge, that he would never sit in a War Cabinet, had unexpected support both in the Cabinet and the country.

But, of course, while certain other Ministers were trying to find out which way the "cat would jump", and some others were looking for a "formula", which would allow of a "compromise solution", war started.

87 Mr Round, late editor of the *Courier*, wrote the other day of Chester, "We need not waste pity on the fate of Lord Nimmo. I say with all due respect for the meaning of my words that this man, so early corrupted – this evil man – was one of the chief architects of our destruction. Not content with selling his personal honour for power and cash, he left nothing undone to destroy the very soul of our great cause. And we see the consequences today in the final divorce of politics and morality – the universal collapse of Christian values – materialism rampant and unashamed – the naked pursuit of gain by all conditions of men – the philosophy of grab which dominates all programmes."

Thousands of people agree with every word of this, and there was a time during the war when I myself believed it and came to hate Chester even more than old evangelicals like poor Mr Round.

I said once that I had always been afraid of hating Chester, because for me it would have been so easy. It is torture to feel that someone is really evil and is "getting away with it" – it is so frightening. It makes one feel so insecure – as if there were no real goodness in the world – as if any happiness one seems to possess is just an accident – like the child's who was not crushed with its brothers and sisters when a house collapsed in Tarbiton, because it happened to be playing under the kitchen table.

But what I'm trying to show is that no one has a *right* to hate Chester. After all, people who say they don't want much from life – only ordinary peace and quiet – are really asking (as Aunt pointed out to me so often) a great deal. For the ordinary thing is more like a violent argument about the right road in a runaway coach (like our local coaches) galloping downhill in a fog. If no one drives (and *chooses* a road) everything and everyone, including the horses, will crash.

Perhaps Chester did "get away" with lies and tricks and did help to "destroy our great cause". But all leaders (who really drive and steer), especially reform leaders, do destruction to a cause. Because they set out to make new worlds and new worlds can never be so good (or so new) as people expect. So the dissatisfied ones (and they are always the "spearhead" of reform because nothing on earth could possibly satisfy them – they are born with a hole inside) get furious and start a new party.

So that if I seem to admit some of the charges against Chester, it's because there's no other way to show how a man of his special kind (with political "genius") does get so hated.

And first, about the "great betrayal" as the Round party call it, when Chester was "traitor to his pledged word".

At the beginning of the war I was staying with the Goolds, who had just bought Chorlock Manor and were building new garages for their two Rolls and reconstructing almost the whole inside of the house. Daisy had asked me down for a week in order to advise, or rather to admire, for, as I say, Daisy never took advice about anything. And on the day after the Cabinet decided to declare war Goold came to me with London papers in his hand and asked me why Chester was not among the anti-war Ministers who had resigned. I said that it must be a mistake of the reporters, who had left him out. It did not occur to me for one moment that Chester would not resign. He had pledged himself never to enter a War Cabinet and I thought that this was very good "policy" – it would pay him to resign. For I did not forget Chester's own remark that the last War Government, the Conservative, had ruined itself by going to war and apparently for ever. No one dreamed that it would ever come back.

And Goold startled me into being very emphatic. He shouted that if Chester "ratted" now he was finished – he would be turned out of his seat; he, Goold, would see to that. But every decent man in the place would back him – the whole country would rise against such a turncoat and Judas.

The old man's excitement was frightening. He had been ill for months with blood pressure, and all my assurances that Chester would never dream of "ratting" – that I was astonished that anyone should even imagine such a possibility – did not reassure him. But it soon appeared that all the radicals in Tarbiton were in "a state". The telephone was already ringing with inquiries about Chester's position, and it rang all day. I had to answer for Chester to the agent, half the committee, and both the local newspapers.

The truth was that all these people were horrified by the very idea of another war. I dare say a majority of the whole country was against war. And certainly all the chapels were shocked at the very thought of sending out their sons to do murder (as they thought of it) on other people's sons. Also they argued that if we did not make our Christian protest and actually engaged in mass murder, then there would be nothing to stop the war spreading all over the world and it would cease to be Christian at all. Civilization itself would disappear.

Nowadays all these arguments seem rather silly. People are used to wars and pacifism is regarded as foolish or cowardly. But then, there had been no big war for nearly fifty years and even that war had seemed unnecessary and due only to Napoleon's ambition.

That was why Chester's agent was amazed at his delay in carrying out his pledge and why both he and I kept telephoning to him in town. I really thought there was some mistake. But the only answer we could get was that Chester was away in the country. I had already arranged to go home by the next train and I was determined (like a good "political" wife) to find Chester at once and tell him about all the excitement in Tarbiton. But the moment I entered the house, Chester came from the study and both the children from other rooms to meet me on the landing. They had been waiting for me. And Chester's voice, when he said that he had seen my statement in the *Courier*, seemed like an accusation.

I had not seen the statement myself. It was simply a paragraph written by Round from what I had told him on the telephone that I "had no reason to suppose that Mr Nimmo had changed his views about resigning from a War Cabinet".

I explained that Mr Round had asked for a statement and described the excitement at Tarbiton. "You've no idea of what they're saying about you. Some of them want a mass meeting to force you out of the seat."

"Perhaps we'd better go into the study," Chester said, and he closed the door behind us. Bootham got up, but was told, in the same grave manner, to stay.

All this ceremony surprised me very much. But I saw now that something was *very* wrong – I was facing a kind of family tribunal. Sally, from her place on the sofa, was looking at me with that serious and alarmed expression which one sees on children's faces when a parent is being accused.

Chester took his stand by the window (a favourite place – all faces but his were in the full light) and murmured, "Excitement in Tarbiton – Tarbiton is a little out of things perhaps."

I pointed out that they were waiting for his statement. "Mr Goold says you are missing the biggest opportunity of your whole life; you might have come out as the leader of the nation. Mr Tack says you have lost thousands of votes already. Mr Brown has resigned from your committee."

88 Chester had been looking out of the window. Now he suddenly whirled round and interrupted me. "A leader? But where to? – that's the question." He bent toward me, so that I expected him to point his finger at me in a way he used at meetings; but instead (probably catching my look and seeing that I would think this gesture a little too dramatic for the family) only lifted his chin and said again more loudly, "Where to? That's just what we've been talking about – Tom and I."

Tom was moving about the room in his usual rather restless way, smoking a cigarette and throwing the ash on the carpet. But I thought he had an unusually cheerful air (he was in a very shabby old suit and I found out afterwards that, without telling anyone, he had spent the morning in a queue outside the War Office trying to enlist and had been assured that he would be accepted tomorrow), and now he smiled at Chester and said, "Don't bring me in, Papa. I don't see why you shouldn't do what you like."

"It's not what I like but what is right."

And Bootham said in his solemn way, "If you'll excuse

me, sir, it is a question of moral leadership. People are looking to you for a sign."

I said nothing to Bootham – I detested him too much; but he looked gravely at me as if to say, "Pause before you speak," and said that the Prime Minister had offered Mr Nimmo the Ministry of Production – a key post.

"And a free hand," Chester murmured.

Then, as if to prevent my answering, he sat down beside Sally and put his arm round her shoulders. "And what does my little girl say?"

Sally flushed to the eyes and looked still more startled. But after a moment she answered, "I told you, Papa – of course you ought to stay and fight the Germans."

I knew that his asking Sally's advice had no significance. For a long time (and Sally was only fourteen that May) Chester had begun to ask or pretend to ask her advice, on the same principle which he had practiced with Tom of treating him as a responsible person. And the policy had been very successful with the practical and affectionate Sally. She was already very capable and she adored Chester.

But I was surprised. I thought, "He's putting on one of his special performances. Why?"

I saw, of course, that Chester was very much tempted to take this "key post" with a "free hand", but I did not believe it possible that he could "rat" on all his pledges especially when the four other anti-war Ministers had already resigned. And I said that perhaps Sally did not realize the feeling in Tarbiton (meaning that Chester did not realize it) or the general position.

Chester jumped up quickly and looked at me as at an enemy. "What is the position? A terrible one – and one that no one could have foretold. And my position? The PM says

the country needs me – that I am indispensable. As
Bootham says, it may be my duty – a moral duty – to
change my mind and face the consequences, however
irresponsible publicists like Round may make somewhat
treacherous haste to compromise a situation already
dangerous enough."

And he went to the door. When, seeing that he was
furious with my "treachery", I began to say that I had only
told Round what he had said himself a week before, he
stopped in the door itself and said impatiently, "What
Round does not realize is that this is going to be a new kind
of war – and it's going on for a long time. All this fuss will
be forgotten in six months."

Then he went out and I did not see him again (he avoided
me – a sign of his extreme indignation) before he went away
that afternoon for the celebrated conference at the Sussex
house of Lord G, the newspaper man, where they worked
out his statement for the papers. So that the first I knew of
his "ratting" was the statement itself, where he "confessed
to being deeply misled" and to never having believed it
possible for any civilized people to be guilty of so dastardly
a crime (the invasion of Belgium) against the very basis of
civilized religious liberty, which was the sanctity of the
pledged word. And so, with a reluctance which those who
knew him and his record could understand, he had been
compelled, as an act of conscience, to support the cause of
truth, which was also that of peace and freedom, against
aggression which he could only describe as devilish.

I can still remember my astonishment at reading this
letter. For here was Chester "ratting", and not only did he
make it appear quite an honest thing, but even rather noble,
in owning his mistake. I was quite moved by his words –
they made me feel (like thousands of his supporters who

had been raging against him) short-sighted and narrow-minded, lacking in "vision".

And I told myself that Chester had really been surprised by the sudden attack on Belgium, that he had been indispensable in the War Cabinet, that it had been his duty, just as he had said, to ignore a pledge given under other circumstances; in fact, that in real life one cannot always keep pledges.

And this is quite true. No one on earth can prove that Chester was not doing a rather noble act (risking his very honour) when he "ratted" on his pledges. Quite possibly (if he had time, in the middle of such important and urgent "public responsibilities", to consider the point at all) he believed it himself, even at the time. He certainly came to believe it afterwards.

True, I was left with a very uneasy feeling (and I remember it as part explanation of my "irresponsible and hysterical" conduct afterwards), but this was not because of the "ratting" – it started from something quite different, his tone and look when he had said to me, "All this fuss will be forgotten." I could not help seeing, behind those words, the calculator at work; they seemed to say, "I can break my word with impunity, because, in the rush of new and important events, people will forget about the whole matter." I don't say that I gave any thought to this worry at the time – I was far too anxious about Tom and far too busy to ask why it stuck in my feelings and gave me such discomfort.

And I need not say that Chester was perfectly right in his "calculations". Much less than six months later, in six weeks (but in those weeks the Germans had come within a few miles of Paris), even I was astonished to hear that Round had been writing in the *Courier* about the "Great

Betrayal" and that Goold had had Chester turned out of some religious committee. I asked myself how people could be so small-minded. The whole affair of the pledge seemed as ancient a piece of history as the attacks on Peel for abolishing the corn tax.

89 Those weeks had seemed like an age; it is quite wrong to say that quiet lives seem long – it is excitement and nervousness, and a great many things happening at once that make time seem long. Chester was working night and day; often he did not take his clothes off but dozed on a couch. Tom was training in a camp of mud. The first Zeppelin had dropped its bombs, and I was trying to combine war work (as Mrs Nimmo, wife of one of the war chiefs, I had to be chairman of half a dozen committees and visit hospitals every day) with a new pressure of housekeeping. For since it was wartime, the people who swarmed into the house from dawn (when soldiers on leave would be found sitting on the doorstep with some special news or complaint – or because they had no money) to dark (when Chester's colleagues would arrive in taxis with secretaries) all expected meals at any hour. And the people, too, were different. Tom's friends from camp, millionaires taking up Chester's contracts for various raw materials, generals trying to get support for their own plans of campaign – just because they did not mix well, behaved as if the place was a kind of hotel. And though this free hospitality was Chester's own policy (he said that he got his most important information from young cadet officers just out of the trenches, and even Tommies), he himself was guarded so carefully in his study on the top floor that I was not allowed to admit that he was at home except to the "special list," people like Lord G, the newspaper man, or chief Ministers. Yet he was annoyed if he missed anyone from France.

No one could complain of this. A man so burdened as a War Minister has to be surrounded by a wall of routine – he is like an institution which would not work at all unless it was organized. But it meant that visitors had often to be kept amused for hours, and our expenses, especially for liquor, shot up to amazing heights. It was a mercy that Chester's shares had begun, in the second year of war, to go up with them. As I discovered, a great man, or at least a statesman in power, had to be rich; and though the Government gives a Prime Minister all that is necessary in housing and servants, we had nothing from it except the bare pay and a policeman to keep anarchists or Irishmen from murdering us in our beds.

One day a bomb *was* thrown through the dining-room window, but it did not go off. And we scarcely noticed the danger from such things (every one of the Ministers had been threatened) in the agony of the Somme battles which had just begun. Tom was already an officer (the chance of an officer being killed was three times that of a Tommy), and one wondered that one could eat or sleep, much less gossip with callers and buy hats.

But what we had all discovered in this new world was how much ordinary life had to go on in an ordinary way, in spite of the misery all about and the heroism which went on, too, all the time. It was like being in a boat that needs the same handling whether it is passing over five feet of water in a peaceful estuary or over five miles in the middle of the Atlantic.

90 It was in the second year of the war that Round got up his charge that Chester had deliberately murdered a young man called Brome.

This was a case where a young man started a strike and then had his exemption taken away and was put into the army and sent to the front, where he died almost at once of heart failure. Apparently he had had a bad heart and was not fit for service.

The truth is that Brome was giving a lot of trouble (just when Mr Lloyd George was beginning his great "drive" for munitions – every strike meant that more of our soldiers were killed at the front), and that Chester never heard of the bad heart till the man was dead. The medical report was held up among a mass of papers which were not urgent.

It was the secretaries who decided what was urgent and what was not. And there were cases much worse than Brome's that never came out. A busy Minister has to be "callous", he hasn't time to look into each case; he is an institution that does not even know separate persons but only "classes" or "types".

All Chester's friends begged him not to worry his head about the "unfortunate Brome case", and I dare say that if he had allowed himself even to think of it except as a "case" and a nuisance to *him* (like many more similar misfortunes) he would have lost his nerve and become useless for the work of the institution.

I was very indignant with Round for these unfair attacks. But it was only about a month after Chester's explanation in the Brome case that we had an important dinner. I was dressing – or, rather, changing my frock (however, it was rather a nice frock; although at this stage of the war we did not "dress", Chester had ordered me to look my best), when I heard some shouting in the street outside, or, rather I was half aware of it as well as many other things. A woman is used to feeling in half a dozen places at once, and while I was powdering with great care (Chester hated a sign of powder) I was still in a quiet panic about Tom, still worrying about Jim, who had not written for two months, still praying that the dinner would be eatable (we were beginning to have "servant trouble"), and still raging against the shop that had not sent my new shoes. I did not take notice of the shouting till I got up to have my frock put on; and then, while the maid was holding it up for me to dip my head into it, I looked under the blind, only to make sure that "our" policeman was keeping a path open to the front door.

The crowd, however, was not big enough to be troublesome – there were only a few casuals there (not the mass of "professional" starers that would come if there had been anything in the papers about the dinner), and what was happening was that "our" policeman was pushing an old gentleman along the pavement away from the door, while a rather common-looking woman and a very tall man in a very shabby hat seemed to be remonstrating with him. It was the old man who was shouting – his tall hat had fallen off. But at this moment the woman picked it up and dusted it on her sleeve and tried to put it back on his head. Suddenly I recognized Daisy and realized that the old man was Goold and the tall one Round.

I was so startled (thinking that there might be an "incident" which would get into the papers and upset Chester) that I hurried on the frock and ran down at once. But Mr Goold was in such a state that he would not listen, and Daisy was still trying to make him put his hat on.

And when I told the policeman that these were friends and asked Mr Round to come in, he answered in a loud voice that it was impossible. "It is too late, Mrs Nimmo; we have been refused an appointment on three several occasions and now we are turned away by a flunkey."

"But, Mr Round, the man did not understand."

Round then said even louder (he was speaking to the crowd quite as much as me), "And perhaps you don't know that on account of Mr Nimmo's dastardly letter to the *Lilmouth Standard* Mr Goold has been forced to withdraw his name for the county-council election."

"But what is all this about, Mr Round ?"

"Oh dee-ur!" Daisy was saying; she never paid attention to anyone else's conversation. "Do make him put on his hat. He's had the snuffles all week, and if it gets to his chest, it'll be a regular flu."

"It means, Mrs Nimmo, that your husband has stabbed an old friend in the back – and probably killed him."

"Ah dee-ur!" Daisy said. "If only that motor would come."

Mr Round, who always pretended to be very cool and always lost his temper, now began to make a speech about traitors to their class and cause – always the most vindictive enemies of those who dare to have an opinion of their own. And, like Daisy, I was immensely relieved when the Goold car arrived at last and he tried to get into it. He was so weak and confused that Mr Round had to stop speaking in order to help us lift him into it and to support him inside. There was one fearful moment when he seemed to sink into himself and I thought he was dying.

But Daisy was wonderfully calm. Seeing my fright, she kissed me and said in her "lullaby" voice, "Poo-ur Nina! What a thing to come on a party night! But there, don't ee mind um – it's just Tarbiton. You run in and get on with your work." In fact, I had been so shocked by Goold's collapse and Round's talk about some letter to the Lilmouth paper that I had forgotten the time. Now while I stood confused and as it were stopped in my mind, I found myself in the middle of a crowd which was staring at my frock and myself in that greedy manner which makes one feel equally disgusted with it and (what is strange) oneself. I felt disgust like a sickness as I picked up my skirt and went hurriedly up the steps.

91 Helpless anger is frightening, because, I suppose, it makes one remember the injustice going on everywhere all the time which at any moment may flood over oneself and drown one in poison. I could not forget old Goold's cries, his purple face and trembling feeble legs (it was only because he was old and ill that Daisy and I could treat him like that), while we bundled him into the car to keep him quiet. As I went into the drawing room, I was shaking in my knees as after a narrow escape from some unforgettable horror.

There I was startled to see Chester, in his velvet jacket, back to the fire, with Bootham, carrying some papers (probably of no importance – he loved to carry papers), and Sally on each side of him, like supporters.

Sally had lately been excused from school to do "war work", and in fact she was already taller than I. All three could look down on me, and did so now: Sally with her air of grave but understanding reproach; Bootham with his sheeplike stare which seemed foolish or arrogant according to your mood; and Chester with that ironical expression which he had begun to use since my "treachery" over the resignation crisis, and which meant, "And what is our little lady's newest prank?"

I had been careful never to hint, even faintly, any criticism of Chester since that "treachery". For though he had such a poor opinion of my judgment, he had always resented the least failure on my part to agree with him.

And to do Sally justice, she often undertook to tell Chester things that he might not like, as when we found that his chauffeur was selling information to the papers.

I did not resent this arrangement, because I felt that it was due to his love for me (or at least our special relation), and indeed he would often punish me for any fancied lack of enthusiasm for his political acts in a way which had to do only with our "intimate relations". I cannot explain these subtleties, but any wife knows how an angry and touchy man, while seeming to be affectionate, can make her feel that she has sunk herself to nothing better than a convenience.

But now, perhaps because I was so shaken, and certainly because of the way the three looked at me, I forgot all my prudence and asked Chester if he had heard Round speak. "Did you really write to the Lilmouth paper about Goold's record?"

"You know very well that Ted made a fortune out of the last war."

"But all that is so long ago – you didn't bring it up against him now?"

"I said that it was not for men who had profited by war to take up this lofty attitude toward old comrades with a different idea of their duty. My dear Nina, I'm sorry for Ted, but he has brought it on himself. He's become a real danger. He was out to split the party in the division."

"He's been saying the wickedest things about Papa," Sally said, "and then to choose tonight for making a scene – that's really too mean." And she came toward me to arrange my necklace, making with her lips and eyes a sign which meant, "Don't upset him now whatever you do."

In fact, I had remembered already that I could not have chosen a worse time for my outburst – Chester had been in

291

a highly nervous state for a week past. It was the time when Lloyd George was forming his opposition in the Cabinet (but still some time before the public knew of the crisis), and Chester, like several other leading Ministers, had to decide whether to follow him or Mr Asquith. It was not at all certain that Lloyd George would succeed, and if he did not he and his supporters would have to resign.

As Chester said, not only his own future was at stake but the whole conduct of the war. And the party tonight (Lord G, the newspaper man, and three Ministers were coming) was highly critical.

So I said no more; and the arrival of the first guests a moment later sent Sally and Bootham away and caused Chester suddenly to treat me with charming politeness. But I thought, "Even if I am to be punished, I could not help speaking. He did not see that old man collapsing on the pavement."

And as I sat at table and listened to the old lawyer on my right, who always considered it necessary to flirt with me, all sorts of things rushed together in my mind. I realized why Chester, some weeks ago, had wanted an old bundle of letters. I saw that Chester had planned the attack on Goold by bringing up a scandal seventeen years old, about some tinned meat sent out to the troops which was said to have poisoned some of them – a terrible case, but so long ago; and Goold had not known that the tins were bad.

I was astonished, not so much that Chester should do a cruel thing as that he should *allow it to be known.*

What is incredible in a person you respect is not that they should do something evil (which might be an impulse) but that they should plan it coldly and brazenly. That seems like an unnatural thing, as if the walls of some peaceful room should dissolve away and show a landscape of fire and ash.

My eyes were drawn continually to Chester between the candles, as, flushed with excitement and exertion, he kept bending to one side and the other (he liked to talk to both sides of the table) and making those graphic gestures with which he illustrated a story or imitated some victim. It was as though I had never seen before *this* man (to whom I had been married for twenty years) who had suddenly revealed himself capable of a cruel and spiteful plot against an old friend.

I said to myself that he had only defended himself; that in the whirl of his life he had not time to be particular in the choice of weapons. He had taken the quickest and most certain way to break an enemy and destroy his influence. I told myself that he was not really a cruel man – he was only a very busy and anxious one who had to make decisions quickly and carry them out firmly. But I remembered, too, one of Aunt Latter's angry remarks, that I was a woman who excused everyone and everything because I did not want the trouble of condemning; and this, too, made me uneasy and depressed.

92 The party was a great success. We did not see the men again after dinner, and they agreed together on some very important moves in the plan to break up the Asquith Government. Chester, coming to bed at past two o'clock, was quite feverish with excitement and happiness. That is to say, he affected a casual and rather joking tone; and though, as usual at night, he was quite drawn with weariness and his eyes had that brightness which goes with extreme exhaustion (and a good deal of champagne, brandy, whisky, etc; Chester was not a drinker even now, but took what others took, and nowadays we never stinted drinks), he hopped briskly round the room and kept striking energetic attitudes. "Well, my dear, do you realize that your little dinner will be in history? We shall have a new Government within a week – and a real War Cabinet."

I saw that he wanted to be complimented. For a long time Sally and Bootham were used to flatter him in a way so gross that even he would laugh or protest. But he enjoyed it, too (who does not, especially when he is so much hated and abused?), and I should have praised him now if I had not been full of that uneasiness. I could not forget the old man's look as Daisy had pushed him up the step of the car with her knee and the noise he was making – like an animal in pain. I thought how fearful it was to be old and despised.

I said to Chester how clever he had been in handling Lord G, a very vain and difficult man, "telling him that he was the real ruler of the country".

"I didn't go so far as that – the man is not a fool," for Chester, since that "treachery", was always critical even of my praise.

"No," I said, "but that was so clever – the way you suggested it by asking his advice about everything."

He looked at me with the ironical smile, meaning, "She does her best"; and then, as if to show me that he was more generous, he began to compliment me. "At any rate you had a triumph – you looked magnificent."

"I could not recognize that Sheffield man without my spectacles."

Chester looked at me again, smiling, but he was irritated and said sharply, "What is wrong with you? You have been glaring at me all evening."

"Nothing."

"Is Jim in difficulties?"

"The last news was a little better."

"As for Ted Goold, I think I have been very patient. And

look here, I'll get him a knighthood – I meant that all along."

I did not want to speak of Goold – I was afraid. But this remark about the knighthood moved some obscure resentment and I said that the poor man seemed to feel that he had been very badly treated.

Chester suddenly became still more angry and asked me what I had expected him to do. "What can one do with people like Goold and Round – cranks and grievance mongers? Round has always thought that he was born to be Prime Minister, and you know that he is really a fool; if he wasn't a fool he would not think so much of himself."

"You used to say that the best way was to ignore such people."

"That was when I was a fool, too – a provincial swellhead who thought my wonderful merit alone would shine down all the powers of darkness. But now I know better. Round and his kind are a deadly peril to the country. There is nothing so powerful among fools as a fool who thinks he knows. He talks the stuff they understand and gives them a conceit of it." He spoke furiously in a tone of complaint, and when he stopped looked at me frowning for a long time as if to say, "What can one do with *you* – with such an obstinate idiot?"

I said nothing more – and this, too, was a crime. I should have assured him that he was right. But though I did agree with him (no one who had to live under police protection as we did could have failed to agree with Aunt about "the mad dogs") I could not say so.

For in our relation, which seemed to me so "organized" and rational, there was on my side, too, especially since the beginning of the war, something incomprehensible – as if I, too, had "nerves" which pursued a mysterious policy of their own.

When Chester now climbed silently into bed and took me in his arms, I said to myself, "Yes, punish me," but not because I felt guilty. And I thought, "I am not hating him – that wouldn't be fair." But it seemed to me that in some nerve which had been shaken that evening on the pavement there was something that wanted to hate.

93 Chester had asked me if I were worrying about Jim, because he knew that both Aunt and I had been cabling to Africa for news of him.

Jim had been ill almost continuously in his "punishment station", and we knew two former officials had died there. Yet we knew, too, that Jim would rather die than call in the doctors and allow them to send him home. To his mind that would be admitting a Government victory and leaving the Lugas to their fate, at a time when they were in the greatest danger of losing their independence (hundreds of years old) as a tribe, being joined in with a foreign race (Mohammedans living in the plains) under a chief whom they hated and then having an immense new trade road driven right through their farms.

The road alone, as Jim said, would utterly destroy their civilization by bringing in a crowd of petty traders and swindlers "on the make".

But we agreed that it would be madness not to tell him that he could not fight the whole Government. I wrote cautiously that the war was so terrible that people tended to forget everything else. Aunt sent him a case of whisky. I had never seen her so enraged against Jim. She swore that she would do no more for "that mule", and she was highly irritated against me when I said that I at least could not stand on one side while Jim was murdered.

"And what can *you* do? You always think there is a way out of everything."

"Why couldn't we have a question asked of the Colonial Secretary? After all, it is a perfect scandal the way they are treating the Lugas."

"And don't you think, my dear idiot, that I hadn't thought of that? But what good would it do in the middle of all this hullabaloo? No, they picked their time well. Jim must just get out of Africa. They'll be glad to let him go, and give him a pension, and then he can bang at them to his heart's content."

Aunt was now at Buckfield (rather to our surprise, she had been frightened from London by the bombs), and she was eager for Jim to retire. She had persuaded Bob to accept him as a possible agent and was even furnishing rooms for her darling. And if anyone reminded her of her old view that places like Buckfield were burdens to their unfortunate owners and ought to be got rid of, she would grow very angry and say she had been misunderstood, and prove by figures that Buckfield could be made to pay very well as a farm under proper management. In fact, since her return to the house, she had fallen in love with it (I suppose she had been happy there as a child) and could not bear the idea of its going out of the family. Her whole mind was filled with this new plan (she actually sold Palm Cottage that year to pay for modern fittings in the Buckfield cow houses) and so she was enraged with Jim chiefly for not leaving the service.

But she did, in fact, find an MP who wanted to set up a reputation for something and had pitched on African affairs. And some weeks later (it was just after the new Government came in and the new Ministers were being asked a lot of questions) this man did ask about the proposed opening of Lugaland and the danger of war with the Lugas, and if the district officer had been removed on account of his warnings on that head.

The Minister answered politely that there was no danger of Luga war and that Captain Latter, whose services were highly valued, had been moved only on account of the rearrangement of boundaries which made it expedient that the district officer's headquarters should be in a more central position. He might add that "the change had greatly enlarged the area under Captain Latter's direct responsibility".

This answer, Aunt said, was just what she expected, and proved that Jim ought to come home to Buckfield.

Aunt took her usual cynical pose, which was necessary perhaps to save her from too violent bitterness, but I had no practice in cynicism. At first I could not believe that the Minister knew the facts, but when I was assured from all sides that Jim's case was only too well known in the Office I became (as they say) rather mad.

It may seem odd after the Brome case and that of Goold and Round (and many more not so close to me) that I was so astonished and shocked by the quite ordinary and routine attitude toward Jim. But I think I was terrified as well as enraged. I saw, for the first time, that the Government "thing" could kill Jim and not care one farthing.

What, after all, can be so loathsome, so terrifying as a Government which does a cruel injustice and, knowingly, goes on doing it, and pretends all the time that there is no injustice or that it can't be helped. It seemed to me, all at once, that the Government was like a beast – a creature neither human nor mechanical, a thing both immensely stupid and enormously cunning, which is laughing at you but also planning some mean revenge.

For the first time I understood why a certain man (a policeman who had been dismissed) kept on throwing stones through Government windows and being sent to jail, and why people wrote letters to Chester (especially since he had become one of the Big Three) threatening to shoot him or burn our house down. One of those furious people, whose letters had bored us so much, was sent to an asylum and we had said, "Of course, he was mad all the time." But now I saw that it was more likely he was driven mad by the meanness and indifference of the *thing* that had ruined him.

I was certainly a little mad all those weeks when I was helping to plan attacks on the Nigerian Government to bring the Luga case before the public.

This was not difficult. Since the change of Government, when Mr Lloyd George turned Mr Asquith out, a good many people who had supported Mr Asquith were very glad of any excuse to attack the new Government, and now we were surprised to find how keen they were to take up our case, even before they knew anything about it. There was quite soon a Luga party, and when Jim came home on sick leave in 1917 no less than seventeen MPs (not to speak of societies like the Clarkson Association for the protection of the African native) were ready to sign an appeal for a Government inquiry. They also arranged a dinner of welcome for Jim at the House of Commons.

Somebody then organized a public meeting; and though the idea at first seemed a little alarming, I found that it could not be stopped. So I went to meet Jim at Southampton in order to warn him against rash statements to the reporters. His role, as Aunt and I agreed, was to be the "unpolitical" officer dragged into publicity by indiscreet enthusiasts.

The reporters, however, did not pay any attention to him,

and Jim himself, before I could catch him, had wired to the MPs a rather abrupt refusal of the dinner (he objected to me that the hosts were a lot of "cranks and pacifists") and agreed to the meeting only if I could guarantee that it would not "go on the little-England tack".

I gave the guarantee, and, in fact, to our surprise, we found that this meeting (in "support of a true policy of trusteeship toward the native of West Africa") was going to be a huge success. The platform would be crowded with distinguished persons including half a dozen ex-Ministers.

94 All this time we had been very careful not to bring Chester into our schemes. We knew that he could not be expected openly to support Jim against any department of his own Government. And when the meeting was proposed, I assured Chester that I would not appear on the platform or sign any vote of censure. The name of Nimmo would not be involved.

"Just as you like," Chester said. "But what good do you think all this agitation is going to do anybody?"

"At least it will let people know what Jim stands for."

"Well, what does he stand for?"

I was astonished at such a question and said that Chester knew very well what Jim stood for – native rights.

"I wonder if he is a good judge of what will help the natives? I know he's done some good work, but hasn't he been rather out of the stream all these years – things have moved since he went to Africa and they're moving even faster now."

"But why should Jim be ruined just because a lot of things are happening?"

"We can't stop history in full course. And history is going all against the primitive – it always did. Jim should face the situation as it is."

"Do you mean that he should let the Lugas be sacrificed because the local government thinks they are too small to matter and no one here will bother about them?"

Chester, seeing that I was growing excited, said no more, and I told myself that it was abominable to accuse Jim of being "out of the stream" simply because he had spent all these years in Africa – especially when the Government had profited by his exile.

I had arranged to meet Jim that same afternoon outside his club in St James's, to tell him where we had managed to find a hall for the meeting (I did not telephone these details from the house in case of eavesdroppers), and I happened to be a little late. And not wearing my spectacles in the street, I did not recognize the waiting figure till it turned and came toward me with Jim's characteristic walk – a kind of lounging stride of the old steeplechaser. It was only the second time I had seen Jim since his landing, and the first in his town clothes; and as he came toward me I was startled by his appearance. He was wearing a blue suit I had seen often before, but this suit, cut in the style of 1910, with its pipe-stem trousers which made Jim's feet (really small well-shaped feet of which he was rather proud) seem absurdly long and flat, and the high bowler that went with it, had suddenly become a little ridiculous. I knew, of course, that Jim, like many who have once been dandies, was strongly attached to his old clothes, but now I was reminded unexpectedly of that conversation with Chester – not so much of his words as his meaning.

And when I came close and met Jim's faded eyes, looking at me out of his long yellow face with the solemn and indignant expression which was now habitual to him (he was thinking of the way he had been treated and the way the Lugas were being treated), I could have burst into tears.

For it seemed to me that not only the Government "plot" was trying to ruin Jim but something even more cruel and powerful – something like that "stream of events" which Chester counted on so openly to make Goold and Round futile and ridiculous. And this seemed to me so cruel and utterly wicked that I could not bear it, and I determined that Jim should not be beaten.

But the result was that we had a sharp quarrel. For knowing that he was to meet some of the Luga Committee, I suggested that at least he should buy a new hat, and he answered that he was damned if he would be seen in one of the things they were wearing now – "and made of rotten stuff too".

"But, Jim, you don't want to look like a dugout."

He stopped and stared at me, not so much angrily as in patient resignation, and asked at last, "An't the old boy smart enough for Mrs Nimmo?"

"You know I'm only thinking of the committee."

"What's my poor old hat got to do with the committee?"

"It's rather nonsense, but you know that appearances do matter even in these things."

"They've had my report."

"It's a wonderful report, but we can't absolutely rely on their reading it."

"Then why should I bother about your committee?"

"But, Jim, it's a very strong committee – all quite important people. That's just why they mightn't have time to read our report and why it's so important for you to make a good impression. If you insist on looking odd they're quite likely to think you are only being crotchety about the Lugas, too."

Jim, angry at the very idea that he was prejudiced about the Lugas, turned dark and said, "I tell you what, Rabbit: your committee sound like a lot of tarts."

"Are you calling me that?"

"Damn it if you don't talk like one; and if your committee is going to judge my case by my hat, it had better go into the same business, too, and good luck to it. Everybody will be delighted and I shall save a lot of time."

And in a moment we were furious with each other. For though I was afraid to hate Chester, I could always hate Jim. I said that in all my life he had never done the least thing I asked; he was the most selfish man I had ever known and I would do no more for him. And he answered that I had become as tricky as old man Chester. He was not going to lend himself to any of my women's work – it was too dirty for him.

95 All this time there was between Chester and myself a "situation". I mean, an unusual tension. There is, I suppose, always a "situation" between husband and wife (unless I have been "corrupted" by living so long in a political atmosphere; I should suppose there is a situation between everybody) and "relations" which need the equivalent of "understandings" and "spheres of influence". In fact, it is a situation which changes three times a day at least. But with old married people who have a good "understanding". the spheres of influence are so well marked out that they can be very free with each other and argue quite indignantly and have "grave crises" without the least danger of an "incident". They are really quite comfortable with each other all the time, and their "situation" can only "deteriorate" if they show themselves "ill-disposed" or, of course, form a new "alignment". And what I meant in those days when I told myself that there was a "situation" between us was that we had stopped being comfortable with each other. In fact, our relations had been critical for many months and as a consequence we were both extremely wary and polite. I was tremendously loyal (in public), and when I represented Chester (at the less important functions) I always tried to say something which would make him seem "human", that is, like an ordinary husband. For instance, at a "Mothers" Red Cross meeting I would say that he was so busy that he had forgotten to change his winter underclothing and every wife would understand how that threw out one's laundry arrangements.

Chester himself, when he wrote out my first speech for me, had suggested such "homely touches" – he said that they were expected and always went down well. But, in fact, we both understood how important it was to make Chester seem "human" (our letter bag proved it to us every day apart from the denunciations of people like Round) when he had continually to refuse all kinds of petitions, by widows of men killed in accidents and poor tradesmen ruined by some new order.

Chester on his side spoke everywhere of the "devoted help and sympathy of my wife without which I don't know how I should go on in these dark days".

Lately he had been even more gallant (in public) – a sign (like those statements always put out by two powers which are secretly mobilizing, that relations between them had never been better) that we were on very bad terms.

Now, too, Chester made no attempt at an explanation. It seemed that he did not even wish to do so. In private, since that evening when I had protested against the sending away of Goold, he had treated me almost as part of his staff – with special duties, confidential and exclusive, but not different in kind from those of Bootham and the detective, who also had the entry into the back premises of the institution. In the most intimate relations he seemed to say, "I am the Minister, weighed down with terrible responsibility; you should be glad to serve me." And I thought, even, that he adopted this attitude (so new and unnatural) out of a wish to punish or improve me, to "teach me"; and this at a time when the relations themselves (either because Chester was aging so fast or was more strained – or simply more anxious for stimulus) were growing always more complicated and demanding.

It was on one of the nights just after my quarrel with Jim, that suddenly (and unexpectedly to myself) I hesitated to do something he suggested (not, of course, by word – but as always by indication) and said, "But, Chester, is it right?"

At once he recoiled and I felt that he was more than furious – he was deeply wounded as by a humiliation. And I said hastily, "I meant, would it be good for you? You were so tired tonight."

"What do you mean right?" he said, getting up from the sofa where we were sitting. I answered that I was not protesting. "And I know it was me who began."

He had retreated to the dark back part of the room, out of my sight, and I did not like to look at him. I could feel again his enormous resentment, as at a crime, when he said at last, "Don't speak of that night now; you loved me then and you can't take it away from me."

I tried to say (for I was frightened by the violent effect of my careless speech) that I still loved him, but I found it impossible to tell the double lie. The nerve which wanted to hate absolutely held down my tongue. And suddenly Chester began to speak with his old eloquence, but a quite new bitterness. He said that he had seen for a long time that I had changed toward him, but he had put it down to the effects of London life and "fashionable friends". But now he was lost and bewildered. What had happened to me – to "our happiness, our mutual trust"? There had been a time when he had depended on "the natural truthfulness" of my soul, as "on the solid earth". Whatever happened to him, he had had that precious assurance ("Now he's quoting from some speech," I thought. "He's listening to himself all the time and thinking how wonderful he is") to give him courage and faith. Wherever he went ("one of his famous repetitions") he had that strength beneath his – (he had been going to say feet, but seeing that this would not be a pretty image he changed it almost without taking breath) – his hopes – it had been, if he might say so, like a wing to bear him up through the storms of his life – and as I knew, he had suffered the worst of storms. And he had valued it. "Believe me, Nina, I know what I owe to that loyal soul of yours, no man better, that candour of the spirit. I thanked God for it every day of my life. I cherished it as the most precious of His blessings. Then why – how has it gone from me? What has brought about this change? Why have you turned against me when I need you more than ever I did?"

I was saying to myself, "Yes, I am disloyal – I don't respect you any more. I see you in your true colours. It is you who have changed into a cunning and cruel man. And I'll tell you so." But when he stopped I could not speak.

There was a long silence, the kind which would have been described in a "library novel" as the terrible pause when one sees one's car rushing into a collision and realizes "in a flash" that it is bound to happen – nothing can stop it. But, in fact, I felt nothing at all – I was too tired and absent-minded. And then like old married people who, as if instinctively, turn aside from a serious quarrel, knowing how little good it can do and how easy it is to avoid it simply by going on with a routine (while free to think bitterness), we both hastened to give way. Indeed, we were so anxious to prevent the other from saying anything irremediable, and therefore more troublesome, that we spoke together. Chester began to say, of course, he might be mistaken, and I said that I certainly had not meant to hurt him and if I had done so I was sorry for it.

And he pretended to be satisfied. We acted a reconciliation; and to my surprise he made me understand that it would be expedient for me as proof of good faith to do all that he had wished as if I enjoyed it.

Chester had long given up his "religious approach," but the religious atmosphere still hung about all his doings. I won't say that on these occasions he felt himself divinely appointed (that would be cheap and not quite true), but only that he felt himself still one of God's "ministry". I thought to myself, "He ought to be in his frock coat sealing an order in council."

It seemed that the important thing was not what was done but why, and that it was not what I felt that mattered so much as what Chester meant me to feel.

I had always, from my first experience, thought of those French novels in which wives make such a fuss about their marital duty with unloved husbands – that they were very "made up for the market". It had seemed to me that not loving a husband made the thing of less importance – a duty which was short and trifling beside the pain of seeing him eat (and Chester was very greedy), or hearing him clean his teeth (he was a most violent spitter), or gargling or taking medicine, or making conversation with him on matters in which one had less than no interest. But now, for some reason, I felt outraged. As I lay awake afterwards, my heart was beating so fast (he had made it beat for another reason and that was horrible to me) that I was afraid he would feel it and discover that I was full of rage and contempt.

96 On the very morning of the Luga protest meeting, the agent who had lent us the hall cancelled the agreement on the excuse that the War Office wanted the place for training. It was too late even to countermand the advertisements in the morning papers. The committee was in despair.

We had already had mysterious difficulties in getting a hall; we had explained them by saying that many managers did not like supporting any criticism of Government in wartime. And, of course, halls were scarce because every kind of "show" was booming.

But now, just when I was getting into a cab to go to the agent (he was also a theatrical agent) and make a last *personal* appeal to him, I had a telephone call from a friend (so he said, but he would not give his name), who said that the agent had been "got at" by a certain General M of the War Office who was a close friend of Chester's and that Chester had sent him to frighten the man.

I can't describe the effect of this revelation. I said once that Chester and Goold and all the "revolutionary radicals" had surprised me by their continual fear of plots – they saw them everywhere. They lived in terror of the "stab in the back".

But now I had the feeling myself – they say the most terrible effect of an earthquake is the sense of *immediate* distrust and fear which it brings upon people. The walls of their own homes which had been their most certain protection – as familiar as their husbands and children – suddenly become a threat, a deceitful screen behind which fresh disasters (floods and looters) may be creeping up; the whole *solid* world becomes treacherous and deceitful. And that is why people in earthquakes go mad. Certainly I was thrown into a kind of frenzy. I told my cab to go to

Whitehall, to Chester's office, and asked to see him at once.

As usual in the morning, his waiting room was full, and apparently he was having a conference of some kind in the office. But the official Private Secretary, Dole, who was rather a friend of mine (he had been at Eton and knew a Cousin Woodville there), arranged to go out of his own office so that Chester could see me in private.

Chester, as he came in, assumed, and let me see him assume, a pleasant expression. This was meant to show me that I had no business to come to the office without warning or appointment.

"Well, my dear," he said, "what a pleasant surprise – and what a charming turnout." He looked me up and down – I had rather dressed myself up for the theatre agent and forgotten to change into something more suitable to Whitehall. "You are a vision of spring."

I said that I was sorry to interrupt his work, but the matter was urgent – it was about the meeting.

"What meeting is this?"

"Did you know they were going to stop it?"

"Ah, you mean the Luga meeting. Well?"

But I was suddenly afraid that he was going to tell me some lie, and so I said quickly that I had been told about "some general who had interfered, but the story was that it was not really the War Office that had set him on".

Chester then gave me a hard look and said, "You realize that this agitation is being turned into an attack on the Government."

"But did you know that the War Office was going to take over the hall?" And I pointed out that it was too late to stop people coming to the meeting. They would be furious and nothing could be done because the committee had spent all its money on advertisements and propaganda. "If anyone wanted to ruin the whole thing, it was a very clever way to do it."

Chester said nothing to this. And his silence, his bored indignant air, made me sure (I had evidence afterward that was quite certain) that he had either planned just such a trick or at least agreed to it. And I grew still more reckless and said, "Clever but not quite fair."

"I noticed, by the way, that Round has joined your committee."

"I didn't ask him – it was the chairman. And you know Mr Round always was for protecting the natives. He's only being loyal to his principles."

"You call it loyalty to take every means of undermining public confidence in a national crisis?"

"I know he is rather extreme, but then he really does think that he has no right to go back on his principles."

This was very nearly saying that Chester himself had gone back on his principles and had no right to accuse people of disloyalty. I felt myself turn red. But he made no answer and did not seem to have heard me. His expression was full of bored contempt. I had never felt before how much he hated and despised me.

"And now," he said (the "now" was as much as to say, "If we have done with this nonsense"), "as there are fifteen rather busy gentlemen waiting in my room to get on with the war – I shall have to excuse myself."

At his touch on the handle of the door, Mr Dole (he must have expected the signal) came in and escorted me to the street. He asked me how I thought Chester was looking (all Chester's private secretaries – three of them, in turn – had the same way of making this inquiry – like a gardener who asks what you think of his border), and we agreed that he was bearing up well considering the immense strain of his responsibilities and that, in any case, he would have to go on bearing "because he was indispensable".

Then I was put in the official car for home. But I stayed only to pack. I had decided already to go at once to Buckfield. My excuse was my weekly visit to Aunt Latter, which, in any case, would have been due in two days. But my real motive was to escape from this quarrel, at least for a day or two.

97 Chester believed that when I went off to Buckfield that Thursday I meant to leave him for good. And perhaps he was right. But if so, I did not admit it to myself. I was simply running away from an impossible situation. I told myself I could not go on with it. I wanted to forget Chester. When Aunt asked me how my "great man" was and if he had been "up to anything more than usually slippery", I said, as usual, that it was not fair to call Chester slippery. And I did not tell her about his trick to ruin our committee because I did not want to hear her abuse him. I should have felt ashamed either in defending him or criticizing him. Besides, Aunt Latter had asked out of routine; what she really wanted to talk about was her plan for Buckfield which had gone into a new chapter. She had heard that Chester was looking for a country house (in fact, we had been looking for the last two years – the idea was to give Chester some peace at weekends) and had resolved that he should buy Buckfield. "They are bound to give him a peerage some day and it would be very suitable for Tom to be Lord Buckfield. That boy loves a character part and he has never known what to do with himself. The war was a godsend to him, but, even with our generals, it can't go on forever."

Aunt was now full of good arguments for the darling

project. She pointed out how reliable Jim had become since he had given up horses and taken to Lugas, how he had gradually paid off his debts and even saved a little toward publishing his book on Lugaland. He was devoted to Tom and had always loved Buckfield as much as Bob detested it.

I did not trouble to point out that Chester's chief requirement, in a country seat, was that it should be near London. The plan seemed too much the wishful dream of Aunt's old age to be alarming. The last thing I wanted was for Buckfield to fall into Chester's hands and become a political headquarters.

Like Jim, whom I had first met there, I had always been devoted to the house, for though it was Tudor, with a lot of dark little low rooms, and cold stone floors, it was not furnished in period, and Bob had spread carpets on the floors. There were no great clumsy lumps of oak badly carved with hatchets, or refectory tables to remind one of monks and their dreary routine. The oldest chairs were some of Charles II, quite fragile, and there was plenty of walnut. And there was no uniformity anywhere. Some of my favourite things were Victorian – armchairs in red velvet, and immense mahogany wardrobes. It was a used house. And its shabbiness was an ancient shabbiness which for some reason is always peaceful to contemplate, like history. The hole in the hall carpet (a tragedy at the time) had been scratched by the setter whose portrait was in the picture of our great-grandfather, going out to shoot, a red-faced man who, they said, had talked such broad Devon that when he spoke in the Commons no one could understand him. The notches which disfigured the drawing-room door were the heights of his children and grandchildren and great-grandchildren. Bob and Jim were marked there, and there was a nick which was supposed to record my height at four years old when I had first come back from India.

The ruined wall at the end of the stables was a relic of a fire when the Luddites had set fire to a threshing machine in the stackyard, and burned down the old barn, in the year after Waterloo. The holes in the stable weathercock were the record of a shooting match between Jim and Bob, many years ago. And these scars were part of that special air which belonged to the place and which made the wounded who came there for convalescence (Buckfield was too remote and inconvenient for a hospital) say that it was the most delightful house of all they had known. Yet it had no "modern comforts", no central heating, no shower baths, no hard courts, and it was far from theatres and cinemas. Above all, as Aunt Latter complained, it was relaxing.

But I thought that the relaxation of Buckfield was not so much in the climate as the "atmosphere" of the place itself. It was quite true that after only one night at Buckfield I felt relaxed, but it was not so much in my flesh (though I slept there so deeply that it was like passing out of the world altogether for hours on end) as in my whole self. Something tense in me seemed to dissolve away in that sleep, so that my mind, when I waked up, was not, as in London, at once concentrated to meet some "crisis"; it seemed to have spread itself abroad all through the house and yards, even the gardens and fields, the lake (full of weeds and mud) and the local sky. For one thought of Buckfield as having its own sky, enclosed in an irregular wall of low hills and straggly woods, broken by the tower of the church and the chimney of the old cloth mill and looking, for some reason, like the house, both comfortable and affectionately aloof, with the face of an old nurse.

So that, while I lay there, the clinking of a pail from the

yard, the voice of the old cowman Pratt abusing somebody in the kitchen, the noise of Jim's bath water running, the sound of a plane fading away, all seemed to be going on inside my feeling as if my lazy mind had lapped round them. It was as though my mind, in relaxing, had become much larger and aware of quite a different kind of life, a life, too, in which it was much more delightful and much "easier" to live. This, I say, was my feeling, though I knew quite well that old Pratt got up at six to milk, and that Bob worked twelve hours a day to keep the place "going", which, in fact, with all Bob's sacrifice and contrivance, was getting steadily shabbier and more ruinous. As Aunt Latter said (and told Bob every day), he was a bad manager, and while other places round were doing very well with their farms, Bob always had a deficit.

But if Bob was losing money, in spite of his hard work, and though he was always deep in local worries about labour and cottages and repairs and hunt subscriptions (Bob detested hunting, but he supported the hunt which had been founded by a Latter), he was himself part, and a very important part, of the Buckfield "atmosphere". For he, too, merely by the way he walked, slowly and unevenly, with his head on one side and his stick dragging behind him between his hands or carried across, gave one a feeling that at Buckfield there was always time to think. In fact, Bob, though he was busy from dawn to dark, always had time to talk to anyone, usually about serious subjects like the war or the prices and in a way that would have seemed unusual in town; that is, a "large" way. For instance, he had a theory that the causes of the war could be detected in German art, and listening to him one's mind seemed to spread over history just as it was apt to relax over the countryside. Of course, country people do tend to take "large" views (Goold's views which Chester despised so much were "large" in the same way; he thought the cause of the war was in "sin"), but Bob really did know about art, and he could be very interesting about national art as a revelation of national character.

98 My usual stay at Buckfield when I came to see Aunt Latter was two days, and, as I say, I never admitted to myself that I had meant it to be longer; but after two days I wired to Chester that Aunt Latter was worse and I could not leave at once. And after a fortnight I was still there on the excuse of the arrival of two convalescent officers who needed some attention.

I did not explain that one of these officers was Jim, who had actually been in a military hospital for his persistent fever. But I had the good excuse that he was really ill and spent most of his time in his room, with a huge fire, writing an immense report on the Lugas which he meant to offer to the Colonial Office with a threat to publish it if they did not give it proper attention. "That will bring those bastards in Aiké Square to their senses," he said. "They hate nothing like somebody going to the Head Man."

Though, as I say, I had no idea of leaving Chester, I had no idea of going back to him either, and had just sent another excuse (that I was helping at the local Red Cross Fete), when one morning Chester's doctor arrived for lunch. Chester, he said, had asked him to look in and to bring back a report on my health.

The house party – that is, Bob, Aunt Latter, three subalterns recovering from gas (Jim stayed in his room) – were very pleased by this visit from the great Sir Connell T, who had once operated on an emperor and had innumerable stories about the great people he had attended.

In all these stories it appeared that he had made these celebrated persons look very small. He was a big red-faced man who seemed as if he should be selling meat, and when he told how he had snubbed the King of This and put the Grand Duchess of That in her place he seemed to get bigger and redder. He would draw in his immense chin, and push out his great chest and belly whenever he came to the point, which was always his crushing retort.

Aunt Latter was delighted with T, because he satisfied two of her ruling passions at once: a love for people who "did things", who had power and weren't afraid to use it, and a general contempt for human nature. But I detested the man (he had always been rude to me at the Parade), and when after lunch he proposed to examine me I said that it was not necessary – there was nothing wrong.

"Your husband asked me to run you over when I was passing and I can't come again. I should not have considered it today if it had not been a special request from Nimmo himself. In wartime I took that for a command."

"But I am perfectly well, Sir Connell."

"Then perhaps you would like to show me your celebrated – what is it, Sir Robert, that people come here for?"

"Possibly the maze – it is the oldest authentic maze and I should be delighted to show it, but it isn't, I'm afraid, in the best of order."

And Bob after lunch set out to show him the maze. But first of all he demanded my presence (and Aunt Latter ordered me to go) and then he dismissed Bob.

"All right, Latter, Mrs Nimmo will show me your garden. I want a few words with her by ourselves."

Bob, slightly surprised, apologized and disappeared (nobody could disappear with such suddenness as Bob when he knew he was not wanted), and Sir Connell said to me at once, "Why try to dodge me, Mrs Nimmo? That won't do any good to anybody, will it?" I asked him what he wanted. "I have come to suggest that, if you thought of returning to town, I could drive you up with me." I said I had not thought of returning. "Don't you think it is time?"

"Nothing has been said about cutting my holiday short."

"Come, come, Mrs Nimmo, we aren't playing at cat's cradle. You think you have a grievance against your husband, and he, I may say, has the sharpest sense of grievance against you. I can't believe that the guilt is all on one side."

I said that I did not think so either, but that all these things were rather private and I did not know that I wanted to talk about them.

However, at this snub (which I made as polite as I could) T swelled up like a huge toad and his cheeks became quite magenta. Then, in a kind of growling voice, he said that since I had used the word private he would venture to go further and say that as a married woman of twenty years' standing I ought to understand that a sudden cessation of accustomed habit could be extremely injurious to a man of Chester's age and high nervous tension. That, in fact, he had been treating Chester already for persistent insomnia, but the condition, not to his surprise, had refused to yield to treatment. "I am not alone in my opinion, Mrs Nimmo, that your husband is headed for a general breakdown – in which case I shall be obliged to hold you largely responsible, before him and before the nation."

I did not believe this. I knew Chester's nerves, how resilient they were and how responsive to his mood. I said only, "Did he send you to tell me this?"

He did not answer this, which made me certain that

Chester at least knew of this argument. He assumed, instead, a disgusted air (an air I had seen before in a great specialist when asked an "insubordinate" question by a patient), and said, "I don't know, Mrs Nimmo, what your intentions are, but if you are relying on the fact that a man in Nimmo's position must avoid at all costs the publicity of a legal action, you ought to remember that there are other means in this case by which he can be vindicated."

And when I said that I did not understand what he meant, he answered that, according to his information, the "man in the case" was in the government service and was therefore "subject to discipline".

What astonished me in this was not Chester's suspicion that I had been misconducting myself with Jim but the threat. I could not believe that he was capable of such a despicable act. "And how stupid, too," I thought. "If it is really true, and if he did force me to go back to him, he would know that I was hating and despising him every minute of the day and night. What good would it do him to get me back on those terms? I should have every reason to run away again."

I was so angry that for a moment I could say nothing to T., who remarked then, "And I'm told that your friend is not in a position to take any chances."

I asked him if he wasn't ashamed, or at least afraid, to say such things without proof. But he was one of those very self-satisfied arrogant men who are proud of being brutal, and answered in the tone of a policeman speaking to a streetwalker, "Come, Mrs Nimmo, we weren't born yesterday. Your married reputation is not quite good enough for that tone of voice."

I walked away from him into the house. But he actually followed me down the path, and said in a loud voice, "And as for being ashamed, I could say a lot more about a woman who deserts a man in Nimmo's position, a man who is giving his life to his country in the truest sense of the word."

But he was fat and short-winded. I escaped after that, and I was glad to escape, because he had managed to throw me into such a state of rage and confusion that I did not know how to defend myself.

When I reached my room I decided that I could not go near Chester again. I locked my door and packed. An hour later I was still trembling with hatred of Chester and his doctor friend. But when I had finished packing and sat down to think where I should go, it struck me that I was not trembling only for anger but because I was afraid.

I had often been afraid before; I had been twice terribly afraid for my life in a small boat during storms, but I never before had a fear like this. For I understood now what the man had meant about Jim and my bad reputation. No doubt it had been common talk for years (and I would be the last person to hear of it) that I had been married in a hurry, that Jim had always been my lover. And what did discipline mean? That Jim would go back to his punishment station? I knew of a captain in the navy who had been sent off to the Far East to keep him away from a certain general's wife. The story was a commonplace in town.

Even to think of such things was a humiliation – to let them frighten one was loathsome. But I did not leave my room. I sent down an excuse before lunch; and I was still undecided, or rather I knew that I could not decide. I was waiting on events.

Later Sir Connell sent up a message to say that if I had changed my mind there was still room in his car. And then I saw quite plainly that I was beaten. I dared not take risks with the new Chester and his bodyguards.

This policeman-doctor made conversation all the way in the car, not polite conversation meant to ease the situation but talk meant to pass the time for himself and give me a lesson by the way. He told me about a patient of his, a woman, who had lost her only son in an accident and gone mad because she had persuaded the boy to keep out of the army. He told me of a boy who had been wounded three times and asked to go back to the front line. "And his mother wanted him to go – she is proud of him, would have been ashamed of him if he had not. A real *service* family." I had heard such stories a hundred times. Tom had been twice wounded and was in the trenches at that moment. What was strange to me was the way this man told them, as if to say, "This is war, and a good thing, too – it's time you spoiled women learned to toe the line."

And I remember this stupid "instructive" conversation, because when Chester at last came to me I recognized in him the same tone and attitude.

99 He had been busy when I arrived and so I had to wait in our room. It was already past twelve o'clock, but I did not undress. I could not go to bed until I had found out what Chester intended. For I still could not believe he was capable of sending a notorious brute like Sir Connell to offer such a threat. "He has changed a great deal," I thought, "in these last years, especially since he has been what Mr Goold calls a 'power in the land', but he could not sink so low or be so stupid as that."

All this time I heard the murmur of voices from the study on the other side of the landing and now and then a silence when Chester himself seemed to be speaking. I would find myself holding my breath to listen, as if I could find out by some intonation what this "new" Chester was like. Then suddenly there was a loud burst of speech as the visitors came out on the stairs and said goodbye in the tones of men who have been in conflict, hearty and effusive (one of them I knew – it belonged to a renowned "political" general); the cars drove away, the door began to open and as I jumped up, Chester turned to say goodnight to Sally with that special tenderness which he had always used to her. And while I was reflecting that he had admitted this girl of seventeen to his conference, he walked in.

He showed no surprise at seeing me in the room and said only, "So you came back with Connell?"

"He said that I must come back; he seemed to think he had a kind of license from you to bring me back."

"Quite."

"Did you know he was going to threaten me?"

Chester was walking about in the dressing gown he often used when he had to work late – putting it on in place of his frock coat or jacket and his stiff shirt. He was obviously tired and he did not seem even to give me his whole attention. He looked at me now with a frown and said, "Aren't you going to bed? It's past one o'clock."

"Did you really mean that Jim would be punished if I didn't come back this very night?"

"I thought it quite time to stop the affair before it got out of hand."

"You don't think I went to Buckfield to be with Jim?"

"I shouldn't be alone in thinking so – half London is talking about it."

I said, of course, that this was untrue, that I had nothing to hide.

Chester jerked his shoulder irritably and said, "Very well, we needn't discuss all that."

"But you believe I'm telling lies."

"My dear Nina, the incident is closed."

I said that if he thought so badly of me he might as well send out for some street woman. But he answered that, as I must know very well, the very idea was disgusting to him, "even if it were possible for a man in my position to have any dealings with such creatures".

"And so you put me in their place. Aren't you afraid I shall hate you?"

"I don't put you in anyone's place – you are my wife. No one can take your place with me or mine with you. Now for God's sake let us forget all this and be as we were. We start again from here."

I asked how we could start again when he believed and did such things, but he answered impatiently, "Nothing will happen to your Jim. I don't see what he is doing away from his post in wartime, but nothing will happen to him on my account. Does that satisfy you?"

"So the threat was simply a trick to bring me back and now you want to forget it."

"My dear Nina, I'm not asking you to be romantic. Here we are – what are we going to do? That is the only thing that matters now."

But I answered that, of course (I was irritated by his hint that I was being "romantic"), this kind of argument might be true in politics but it did not apply here. The important thing was not some political arrangement but what we felt about each other – and how could he expect me to forget what he had threatened and how he had brought me back?

He cut me short in this speech (before I could go on to say that if he meant by "romance" ordinary respect and kindness, then I supposed I was romantic) by going into his dressing room and closing the door.

I was startled by his anger. But I saw that he *had* played

a trick – a trick that was growing familiar. He had brought
me back by a threat and then said, "Come, let's forget the
past. We'll let bygones be bygones and start again." "No!
No No!" I thought, as I threw my clothes off. "That is the
trick he always plays now. That is what he has done to
Goold and Round and all those people he has swindled –
the 'time trick'."

And this not only seemed to me a despicable trick but it
frightened me, again with the sense of a fearful insecurity;
it made me loathe again the "thing" that was destroying
Jim's life and was proposing to destroy mine.

What surprises me still is that Chester, at this time, did
not make any attempt to hide his strategy. There seemed
nothing left of the old Chester, so sensitive and clever, so
skilful in making me feel the weight of his love, except the
nervous energy with which he pursued his object and his
firm belief that God was on his side.

Meanwhile, he had put me in a very humiliating position.
I dared not go away again, for I could not trust his word
that Jim would not suffer; and I was treated like a criminal.
Sally was the real mistress of the house. She kept the books;
and Bootham and she arranged even the private parties.
What I had not realized was that an institution must go on,
and so all the things that I had done (they had none of them
been very important, but all together they were essential)
had had to be done by someone else. So Bootham was now
arranging for house repairs and keeping the calendar of
private engagements; Sally was doing the housekeeping;
and both together were arranging the official dinners and
receptions. Bootham, indeed, was now the most important
member of the household. He went everywhere with
Chester and gave orders like a major-domo. He even had
his own secretary, for the new typist, a young girl fresh

from school in Tarbiton, worked only for him and adored him almost as much as he adored Chester.

Sally was affectionate to me. She told me very often how glad she was that I had come back, and how Chester had missed me, and how selfish it was of Aunt Latter to keep me so long. "One wonders sometimes if she realizes that there's a war on or what it means for people to be kept from doing their bit. But I'm afraid Aunt is rather self-centred – you spoil her, Mama dear."

All this was said while holding me affectionately by the hand and looking at me with a serious expression which meant, "Are you going to be less selfish? Are you going to realize how much you have been spoiled by everybody, by Tom and by me, by all these foolish old men who haunt the house, by that pernicious Uncle Jim, and, above all, by Papa? Are you going to do your bit?"

Sally treated me kindly but watchfully as a moral invalid; Bootham (at thirty-three he was already plump, with large cheeks which made even his hare's eyes look small) with the dignified air of a man who knows his value and does not fear criticism. Bootham and Sally were not on good terms. When Bootham panicked (for he was still apt to lose his wits in a crisis), Sally, who, at seventeen, saw no reason for alarm in any situation, would say impatiently, "No need to get excited, Boothy. Keep cool. The sky won't fall even if you have lost Papa's umbrella. And I'll bet you a good deal that it's in the coat-hole where it ought to be. You are the world's worst looker." And when the umbrella was found, he would look absurdly sulky; while the girl, who had no tact and, besides, seemed to have little real respect for the oafish creature, would laugh at him and rub his wounds with salt. "I told you so – it's no good looking so cross. Besides, it doesn't suit you."

I think they were at this time very jealous of each other. A quiet struggle for power (one of those struggles which, I suppose, is quite inevitable round any important and powerful person) was going on. Sally, as she grew into a woman (and she was maturing from month to month), bad begun to realize her favoured position and wanted to use it. But although Chester adored Sally and saw so much of her, he did not even pretend to take her advice; while Bootham (though Chester had no opinion of his sense) had, I think, real influence, because so many things that Chester had "no time for" (like minor party affairs, selection of local committees, subscriptions to clubs) all fell into his hands.

But though Sally and Bootham were working against each other, they combined against me. None of those duties which had come to them in my absence was allowed to return to me. And when at last I asked Chester if he really meant Bootham and Sally to choose my guests for dinner, he answered only with a vague stare (which meant, "What new triviality is this"), and the words that, of course, I could entertain anyone I liked, but as Bootham had the latest official lists and had been making all arrangements for some time it would save trouble and confusion if he went on doing so. It was impossible for me to argue the point. It would have led only to humiliation. In Chester's mind I was a small-minded egotist making a fuss about trifles.

100 It was on this day that I decided I had no "right" to bear any more humiliations. But when I asked myself how I was going to escape I could not see any answer. I dared not go to Buckfield or Jim might be made to suffer. I had only a few pounds in the bank and no power to draw cheques on Chester's account.

And now I gave myself up to hatred. I would feel at any moment, "What is this extraordinary thing that has taken possession of me?" and know at once that I had fallen into hatred. Then I would call up Chester's look and voice as I had seen him in the act of saying, "We begin from here," and say, "I have every right to hate him."

Hatred kept me awake at night, and even if I slept I seemed to be occupied with it like an illness which makes one's sleep in a hospital a kind of haunted "possession". Chester had returned to my room on the second day. He came without a word and behaved as if I were not there. His motive, I saw, was to assert a right and make me feel my guilt. I could not even use a sleeping draught, for since the "accident" with the pills, though it had taken place ten years before, Chester had kept such things locked up in his safe and if I wanted one I had to ask him for it.

And this, too, was retribution (it was my own fault that I could not be trusted), so that I might feel that sin brought its own punishment, that God was not mocked.

So that while I lay there and heard the man's irregular rather harsh breathing (he, too, could not sleep) I knew that he was quite pitiless and completely satisfied with himself. "He has become a god," I said to myself. "He would kill me as he nearly killed his oldest friend, poor Goold, because we have not given ourselves over to him, bodies and souls."

Then my hatred seemed to grow suddenly so enormous that I could not bear it. And suddenly, without any thought of what I was doing (perhaps I did not know what I should do next), I jumped out of bed. And, seeing that the window was a little open, I pulled up the bottom sash and began to get out. Now I did know what to do. I could not go back and I was saying, "I'd rather die."

But there was a little ornamental balcony outside with a

low rail which stopped me from throwing myself straight down on the pavement. And at that moment a cab came to the door below and I heard Bootham's voice asking the cabman what the fare was and then Sally calling out, "It's one and six – I've got it." They had been to some meeting. This made me hesitate – it seemed to me an abominable act to throw myself down at Sally's feet. And in the instant Chester was out of bed and had caught me by the arm. He said in a thick furious voice, quite unlike his usual tone, "What are you thinking of? Do you realize – ?" And I suppose he was going to ask me how I dared to kill myself and make more trouble for him.

And for a moment, between my hatred of him and the impossibility of escaping from him, I felt as if my brain had flown to pieces.

But just then Chester's pyjamas (he had taken to them at last when he had begun to visit generals – but he did not manage them very well) began to slip down and he grabbed at them with such an offended look (as if they had tried to "betray" him) that I had a horrible impulse to laugh.

And all at once the whole affair, and even my horror of the man, seemed quite ridiculous – an immense fuss about nothing. I muttered some lie (a very unlikely lie) that I had heard Sally's voice and had meant to call to her. And at the same time, as if to change the subject in the only possible way, I pressed myself against Chester, though only very slightly, in a manner which he could understand if he liked. He was so astonished that he exclaimed again, but in a bewildered tone, "What's all this?" But then at once (the charm of Chester was always his quickness of mind) he did understand, and said, "Very well, but I must get to sleep." And he turned round and went back to bed while I followed like a Trojan captive on a rope, with a feeling of submission

so acute and complete and sudden that it was comical, like
something that happens to a clown at the circus.

Yet I did not feel humiliated – far from it, because it
seemed now to me that I was doing the only reasonable
thing. In fact, I suppose what had happened to me was
simply another . "conversion", like those which had
happened to me in the first years of my married life.
Somehow or other I had discovered that what I had thought
was an "impossible" situation was not only possible – it
was quite absurdly simple.

But the change came so suddenly and so unexpectedly
that I was filled with laughter, even while I "behaved
myself". For it seemed to me so unimportant and I thought,
"Still I am doing my bit."

And in the morning, as I lay awake, while Chester was
fussing in and out of the dressing room and rustling his
newspapers (we took six every morning, which came in
with the tea, and my counterpane was covered with them),
I remembered how "nice" I had been to him though I
detested him so much, and I thought rather cynically, "It
appears that I should have done quite well on the streets."

But just then an unexpected silence made me look across
the foot of the bed and I was surprised for an instant by an
extraordinary shadow on the wall of what looked like a
witch with an immense chin and nose and goggles and her
thin hair blowing up in a draught. I thought, "What a
caricature!" and looked at Chester on the rug in front of the
just-lit fire (even in May we had a fire for him) – Chester in
his baggy pyjamas stooping down and peering through his
big new reading goggles at a newspaper beside a table light,
which was shining through his white hair onto his shiny
skull and throwing deep shadows under his big eyebrows
(so that the eyes were in dark caves) and under his nose

(which certainly stuck out more as his cheeks had grown thin) and his underlip (so that the famous "fighting jaw" seemed to be thrust even further forward) ; and suddenly, in front of my eyes a kind of transformation scene took place.

When as children we had been asked to the Christmas party at Slapton there was always a magic lantern, and one of the favourite tricks of the local operator (he was a solicitor's clerk in Tarbiton, and the party was his great day, too) was to put the new slide in before he took the old one out. This gave us children a strange and delightful sense of being for the moment suspended between two states of excitement and enjoying at once both the satisfaction of the past and the anticipation of the future, already throwing its bright suggestions on the screen.

Now in the same way the Chester I had known for more than twenty years grew suddenly dim and melted into the worried haggard fierce old man, who then stood before me like an apparition. And I almost cried out those words which I had repeated a thousand times in the last five years without knowing what they meant, "*But he has changed.*"

I was looking at a different slide, a different man. And for the first time I understood what Sir Connell had been talking about when he had said that Chester was in a "special position", and that he "was giving his life to the country in a true sense".

And then I was ashamed. So that when Chester, dressed at last, came out of his room to give me some orders for the day to appear at a certain reception with him (I could see he wanted it to be published as soon as possible that the stories about our differences were quite unfounded), I said to him, "Do you forgive me?" and though he answered abruptly, "Yes, yes, that's all over," as if he really could not be bothered with my whims, I felt only the more anxiety to be "good". For I understood how much this new Chester had to be "handled" with sympathy and patience and (something that Sir Connell had tried to teach me) that he deserved it like any other victim of the war – he, too, was a wounded soldier.

101 Tom got his Military Cross in 1918 and this gave great delight to the whole family.

There is no doubt that Tom enjoyed the war – that is, he enjoyed it more than peace. For it gave him plenty to do (and Tom was quite sure that it had to be done) and I suppose that's what most people need to be happy, or at least, not unhappy. So we were greatly relieved when he decided to apply for the regular army; if possible in Jim's old regiment.

I say we were all very proud of Tom's decoration, but Chester was especially so. He received letters from all over the world – two kings and three presidents and all the different parties in the House of Commons congratulated him.

And now all at once Aunt Latter's "wild" scheme for Buckfield became quite an accepted arrangement. Chester himself proposed to buy Buckfield so that Tom could retire at last to that family house. Meanwhile Jim could be the agent and Bob could go to his beloved Italy and finish his book. I was startled by such a plan, but Chester, it appeared, had been brooding on it for some time. For when I said frankly that if we went often to Buckfield we should be seeing a good deal of Jim, he answered (looking at me with his "impressive" air, which meant, "This is a big and bold scheme – a typical Nimmo move, a really imaginative solution to the whole problem"), "Quite – so you would be able to keep an eye on Jim, and Tom would have some settled point in life. After all, it is the family place, and Tom is the heir presumptive."

I see now how Chester had come to his plan. He was saying to himself, "This woman can't be kept from her lover and her continual attempts to get away with him are an everlasting scandal and nuisance. If I am to keep her I must make some arrangement which will allow her to see the man without attracting attention and without upsetting everybody's nerves."

But I could not quite believe that Chester had become so "French", and so I said doubtfully, "There's no agent's house. Jim would live in Buckfield itself."

"Jim and I have got on very well for fifteen years. If that's your only objection, I'll go forward." And he wrote to Bob that very day. Chester never wasted time in carrying out one of his "flashes of genius".

Bob and Aunt were, of course, delighted, and the lawyers were set to work on the titles. Jim wrote a long letter from Africa to say he was glad that Chester had found out at last what a place like Buckfield stood for, and he would be very glad to do what he could to keep the old ruin warm for young Tom; and Tom declared that it would be just right for him to retire to as a bottle-nosed brigadier in about forty years.

102 It may seem surprising that Chester (who had so fiercely attacked the landlords) was ready not only to become one himself but anxious to make Tom a hereditary squire. And I must explain that all of us, Chester and Jim and in fact everyone of our age and standing anywhere, were growing alarmed at the general collapse of moral and social standards. Chester admitted quite freely that the old landed families were a valuable factor of stability and that squires like the squire of Buckfield, with energy and capital, should play an important part in the national life. He himself was ready to show the way. As for Tom, we were both eager to see him "fixed" for life in some reputable position.

For it seemed to us all that the young were running wild and would find settling difficult in the peace (of course, we imagined peace as not greatly different from the times before the war when young people who paid no attention to modes and morals very soon spoiled their lives and often their parents' lives, too).

I need not say that Chester could not express these feelings in public. It was absolutely necessary to keep the young soldiers, and especially the factory girls, fighting and working as hard as possible, and they were already (knowing their power) very touchy and rebellious. In public, therefore, Chester would say that for his part he absolutely repudiated the suggestion made in some prejudiced quarters, hidebound in the bonds of the old world of Victorian patriarchy and hieratic privilege, that the young people of the nation whose heroism had saved the country were not worthy of that full measure of freedom which had come to them in the necessities of war and which they had so nobly earned. Had they not proved themselves in trench and factory?

It was only in private that he told stories about his women secretaries who had illegitimate babies, and about the immorality in the factory camps, and the spread of venereal disease and the looting and cheating that went on everywhere. He was often in quite a fever of gloom about the future of Britain with such citizens. I can remember one evening after it came out that Tom had spent a night with the girl May Bond (one of Chester's "spies" reported the

fact with the quite kind intention of warning us that the girl
had a bad character and slept with all comers), when he
told me that the very framework of Christian Society was
tottering. Nothing could save us but an evangelical revival
– a new Wesley. And he added these surprising words, "It's
not only the young – the masses are out of hand. It's the
case of the Gadarene Swine over again. What we will need
after this war is ten years of the strongest kind of
government. But where is it coming from? Lloyd George? In
my view he would be a disaster – he would split the country.
For good or evil, he has lost the confidence of the solid
classes – the people who are the real backbone of the
Empire and whom we will have to depend on to hold it
together in the reconstruction. As for me, have I the
physical strength?" And then after a moment's deep
reflection he sighed. "Of course, I could not refuse – when
millions have died in the trenches." And when I asked him
if any of the other Ministers had been discussing this
question with him he said, "Only by hints; but, frankly,
everything points to me. Who else is there?"

What was unexpected in our new relation since Chester
had crushed my last rebellion was its extreme frankness. He
had never taken so little trouble to act a part with me; often
he was so indiscreet that I was frightened to find myself in
possession of such secrets. He showed me not only his
enormous ambition and self-confidence, his contempt for
the "masses" and fear of the "mob", his distrust of all his
colleagues, his jealousy of the Prime Minister, his belief that
"freedom" had gone too far and the country needed
"strong government", but his moments of despair. Night
after night during the German "breakthrough" in spring,
1918, I would find, when the "Minister" had taken off his
frock coat, a weary little man at once tired out and restless

in a kind of desperation (as if he were running a race for his life and dared not stop), who made not the least attempt to look like the great Nimmo with his celebrated "debonair vitality" which was one of our "invaluable assets". He would collapse on the couch and groan aloud about his indigestion, about the strikes ("can you believe that men could sink so low?"), about the news, "Do you realize, Nina, that we may lose this war? Do you understand what that would mean for us and the world? It is a thing not to be breathed. If it were admitted now, we *should* lose – for a certainty. When I heard that ill-conditioned skunk in the House tonight trying to undermine confidence – *now* – when our men – when Tom – are fighting for survival, my blood boiled – I felt like murder. Such men are traitors. Perhaps I was too rough with him. It is never wise to lose your temper in the House. But at such a time as this one grows disgusted with these vermin, men who would play politics at the last judgment."

And my duty was, as I rubbed his chest (again his winter cold had hung on into March), to tell him that he should not worry about such creatures, they were too small; and to say that he ought to reserve himself for big decisions which no one else could deal with because no one else had his intuitive genius.

At this time I noticed that Chester much preferred to be admired for his flair or intuition rather than his cleverness. I used words like "inspiration" and "magic touch" – even his "Nimmo luck". This suggested that his success was due to some mysterious power, and he liked to believe in this power, because he knew only too well how easy it was for ordinary human statesmen to be ruined by some accident which no mere cleverness could foresee.

It was those nights which made me understand why

Chester had sent his bodyguard to bring me back and why he had said, "You are my wife. No one can take your place with me and mine with you." He was, in fact, far wiser and deeper in his "political" idea of human ties than I had been in my romantic one. For where I had said, "It is just what they say of so many important public men, that all they want in a woman is a competent mistress and someone to look pretty at the head of their tables," I found myself bound to him in a relation which was still "spiritual". For I knew a Chester unknown and unimagined by anyone else in the world, a man full of whims and nerves and feelings, who needed from me something that I only could give, not because I was a woman but because I was myself, because I knew him through and through, because our ways had grown to fit each other, because he could trust me (even though I was disloyal in not admiring all his "political acts") to be sympathetic in a thousand things which the most adoring stranger, even Sally, would not perceive.

And though it may seem strange (and I cannot say I understand it even now) that a few words of flattery from me – that is from a woman he scorned, so far at least as political sense and moral integrity went – gave him such encouragement, just as mere contact with my body gave him sleep and peace and energy, it was apparently what he had counted on. He knew what he wanted and where to get it (and this period was what did him so much good – he always knew – even when he was not thinking of me at all), that he could have escape and affection. It was not what I said that mattered so much as that I was always there to say it.

A pretty woman knows she's pretty, but she still goes to her glass sometimes only to look at herself, and each time she discovers for the first time how remarkably pretty she is.

And I found, to my surprise, I enjoyed giving Chester this pleasure; I delighted to see his spirits revive, simply from my praise, and to hear him say, "Well, my dear Nina, we all know that you are an accomplished flatterer; but all the same, I think I can say that I do have something – a kind of second sight. My grandmother was Scotch. It's really a political sixth sense. I do, nine times out of ten, find the way out where others are completely stumped. Call it flair if you like, but the proof is in the facts for all to see. If I hadn't acted with decision about raw materials we should have been in queer street; we should have lost the war long ago."

103 Chester was deeply concerned about Tom, because, he said, the "boy has always been too fond of amusing himself – he has never faced life as a challenge and a test", and he would have attacked him over the affair with May Bond ("it is a plain duty – a Jezebel like that is the worst possible influence") if I had not appealed to his "well-known intuitive understanding of the young".

So that he said nothing to Tom directly about May Bond, but spoke of VD, the immorality of the modern young woman (especially comedy actresses – May was in a revue), and the ruin of various young officers who got into their hands. He also quoted some important people as saying that peace would be the true testing time for the country and especially for the new generation, so many of whom had had no opportunity to acquire the habits of steady work at unexciting jobs, modest ambitions, and self-control.

All this seemed to me very true, and yet I trembled when Chester, in that great-man manner which was now second nature to him, solemnly delivered it to Tom. And I was delighted with the way Tom took it, listening with a most respectful expression and agreeing with everything. He had never been so tactful with Chester, so respectful to his lightest word.

In that week we were all, for the first time, together at Buckfield. It was an experiment in family reunion. Jim had just arrived about a month before on sick leave; Tom, convalescent after his arm wound, had still a fortnight before his board. And what was delightful and surprising, it seemed already that Chester's "French" plan was completely successful. Bootham had adapted some old rooms in the wing for offices, and Chester spent his day between work in this remote part of the house and occasional strolls in the garden. I was free to read, to walk with Jim or Bob, to gossip with Aunt – my only duties to answer my letters promptly, dress rather too well (Chester objected to country clothes), and to be in bed early. Tom seemed perfectly content to go riding or fishing with Jim – he was charming to us all. He was not in the least put out when Jim found fault with his casting (they practised for hours on the tennis court) or his horsemanship (saying that his seat was even worse than his hands and he rode like a tailor); in return, he sympathized warmly with Jim's Luga campaign and declared that it would be a crime if such a sporting people should come to be "syphilized," by means of the new motor road.

And yet Jim contrived to quarrel with the boy. I have said that both Chester and Jim were disgusted by the general decline in morals. When Jim came home in 1918 for his second war leave he professed to find (and perhaps he was right) an immense change for the worse. It was embarrassing even to walk in the streets with him, for he would talk loudly about war profiteers, and, of course, almost everybody had got higher pay and more profits in the war.

Only colonial officers had the same pay, or even less. And Jim saw everyone as a "profiteer". He declared that the women had had the time of their lives and the workers had "cashed in" on the troops. But he was especially disgusted with the "young" and even with the way they dressed. He would glare at girls in short skirts (which were not yet higher than mid-calf), and lipstick, which was just becoming obvious, caused him to mutter loudly about "trollops" and even (but not clearly enough for me to hear) "bitches". He objected also to their smoking in public (which I still think unbecoming) and their manly stride. Above all, he was enraged against the young officers. Many of the young officers did, at this time, affect a very free and easy swagger; quite different from the old regular officers, like Jim himself, whose whole art was to be unobtrusive, and who despised the slightest eccentricity of dress or manner as much as a Roman priest would despise a fellow priest who tried to attract attention to himself by richness of dress.

The subalterns of that time had one trick of taking the stiffening out of their uniform hats and wearing the result, a soft and floppy cap, with an immense peak cocked over one eye and the soft part turned backward and hanging out behind, which always infuriated Jim. And it exasperated me to see him infuriated. "What does it matter," I asked him, "if they do want comfortable caps? I think they have earned the right to them."

"You know damn well they don't do it for comfort but swank. Look at that hairy-heeled tout over there; did you ever see such a monkeyfied specimen?"

"He has two ribbons and two wound stripes."

"That doesn't entitle him to disgrace his regiment."

"But, Jim, the poor boy may be killed – probably will be killed the next time he goes out."

"Anybody can get killed – that's part of the job."

"You know you don't mean that, and I hope no mother who has a son at the front will hear you say such a thing."

But, of course, Jim did mean it, and to suggest to a man like Jim that he ought to be careful of saying things which might make him enemies was a certain way of provoking him. He answered me in his rudest tone that he hoped he was permitted to say what was what, even if the war had got too much for some people. And he asked me how long I had been in the army and what I knew about it.

All this was just what I should have expected from Jim, with his downrightness and his narrowness. But I suppose what we hate in people is just their firmness of character which will not give way to us. And for Jim, the fact that many of these young men wore decorations and wound stripes (which impressed Chester and his colleagues so much that quite high Ministers who came to see us had the most apologetic air, even with second lieutenants) was not important. He had been a soldier himself and took bravery for granted. And I, too, detested all the swaggering. It was part of a general "don't care for anybody" feeling which I found very alarming. But I was more frightened that Jim would be rude to some poor boy who was going to be killed next week.

Jim and I, though we quarrelled so much, had long ceased to hurt each other. I think we even enjoyed this quarrelsome relation, which was the closest permitted to us. So I did not need to use tact with him, and I warned him frankly, before Tom came on leave, that Tom sometimes wore his cap at an angle and I would not have him insulted.

"He's very fond of you and you ought to get on with him quite easily."

"You think I'd better not quarrel with my bread and butter?"

"I'm sure he will agree with anything you want to do at Buckfield."

"I may be a has-been, but I've got the idea. Tom is to go to the devil his own way."

104 And as I say, at Buckfield Tom and Jim were on the most affectionate terms. But toward the end of Tom's leave he appeared one day in full uniform (he had to attend a medical board in Taunton), and while he was lounging in the hall waiting for the car Jim and I came in from the garden.

Now I have to admit that in my warning to Jim I had not said (I suppose I was making the "best of it") that Tom's cap was a soft cap, and not only that but one of the most dashing type. Tom had had it made by his own tailor to his own pattern, and he wore it (especially since he had won his cross) resting on one ear, as it was at the moment.

Jim gave this fatal cap one glance, then turned abruptly away and walked to the window. Then with another quick glance at the cap, he went to the fire. Then he fixed his eyes on the roof over the stairs and his mouth as if to whistle. But he did not utter a sound, and the effect was as if he was tasting something very bitter. At last he said in a thoughtful tone, "That's a comic hat, Tom. Where did you pick it up?"

Tom looked up in surprise and said, "It's my usual hat."

"You don't mean to say you go round in a gawblimy hat."

"It's my only one; at least it's comfortable."

"That's what we are told by all the gawblimy touts who think it swank to make a comic cut of the King's uniform. But I didn't think you would fall for it."

"I'm sorry, Uncle." (Tom had turned pink, but he was

smiling a little.) "I suppose I'm only a temporary gentleman."

But the worst of Jim's breeding was that he would hold in his temper until it was too strong for him, and then it would explode with a violence unjustified by the actual occasion. He answered in his rudest tone. "I don't notice it. You haven't even enough manners to get up when a lady comes into the house."

"What lady, Uncle?"

At this I was really afraid that Jim would hit the boy. He turned that greenish yellow which meant that he was in a rage and took a step toward Tom. But I said hastily, "Tom only meant that mothers are in a special department."

"So I notice," and Jim turned his anger on me. "It's because you let him treat you like dirt that he behaves like a pup. But that's no reason why I should hold my horses."

"I'm sorry, Jim, but I don't really need defending from my own children."

And Jim, in one of those cold rages which made him capable of anything, answered, "Whose children?" For one fearful moment I thought he was going to say why he, too, had a right to feel a special concern in Tom. I lost my head and there was a silence which seemed unending. Then I said in what seemed to me a very uncertain voice, "You may think you have Chester on your side, but it isn't so at all." Jim opened his mouth to speak, but only made a small noise, and then went out of the room.

And being frightened and angry, I attacked Tom as well. I told him that he should not try to irritate his uncle, however old-fashioned. For Jim was very fond of him and that was why he worried about his behaviour.

But Tom, though still rather red in the cheeks (like me, he coloured easily), was perfectly good-natured about the whole scene. "Poor Uncle! He's probably had bad news about his Lugas."

"And you know, Tom, really they're all very proud of you. Uncle Bob wants your portrait painted, with the ribbons, for the hall."

"I should feel a bit of an ass at full length in a captain's uniform. I'm not a VC."

"It wouldn't be for you but your children."

This made him laugh. "So you've married me off already and settled me here to keep the maze clipped."

"But, Tom, it was your own idea – that when you retired from the army you'd have Buckfield for a home."

"I don't know if I'm so keen on the regular army – it might be too regular."

"It was your own choice. And what else could you do?"

"Poor Mummy, don't look so worried – I'll be all right. But I think I'm owed a little peace and fun after all this war – if there is any after." And he kissed me so affectionately that I could not go on quarrelling with him. Besides, in my heart I felt that he was, indeed, owed a little fun.

He told us that same day at lunch that "unluckily" he had given a promise to some people in town to see them before he went back to France (in fact, as the postmistress told me, he had wired to these "people" that morning, "SOS Desperate"). And the next morning five "people" (two subalterns and three girls) came for him all the way from London, in an enormous red car with a strap round its bonnet and such a low hood that they had to creep from under it backward, on all fours.

105 I can still remember the sensation caused in Buckfield by this carful of London girls. All were "made up" with painted lips and cheeks, and no one in our parts had ever seen women, except the lowest class of streetwalker, flaunting about with obvious paint on their faces, paint that was meant to be seen.

Of course, the fashion had been coming in for some time, but very discreetly, and only among the new class of girls who haunted the training camps and who were, in fact, most of them amateur prostitutes. And now, apparently in a few months (but they were, as it turned out, the last months of the war, when it suddenly began to seem that we were going to win it), it had spread everywhere through the towns.

The effect was to make it seem as if some plague of corruption had rushed through the nation, and to confirm Chester and Jim in their disgust at "the young".

Even I was shocked and asked Tom, while I was packing for him, what had happened to May Bond and where she had gathered such friends. But Tom, as usual, only laughed at me and called me a comical old thing. I did not see him again before he went back to the front, and when, three months later, the war was over, he only waited to be demobilized to go away with these same friends on what he called a spree.

Those who wonder at the collapse of morals after that war simply forgot what it was like to come suddenly from the desperation of the spring of 1918 into the victory of the autumn. Everyone wanted a holiday to do what they liked – the quiet ones wanted to go home and think and the gay and lively wanted a spree. The soldiers were so wild to get out of the army that some regiments almost demobilized themselves. They were tired of discipline, and it would have been dangerous for the officers to try to keep them in order. But, indeed, most of the officers themselves were disgusted with "red tape" and "regulations". It was the thing, all at once, to make fun of the "Brass Hats and the Frocks" (that is, statesmen in frock coats), and in fact everyone who had been in power during the war, so that all government became a joke.

Even the peace conference was a joke. And those who did not laugh at all the important people in the war simply hated them. It seemed to be true, what Aunt had said (and what I saw myself when Chester became one of the "live wires" in the Cabinet), that the more a government governs, the more it gets hated; and since the war the Government had had to govern nearly everything and everybody – it had gathered immense hatred. It seemed that people had to burst out (like a bottle of home-made ginger beer when it "works", and the cork has been put in too tight) and that the Government was the natural thing (being on top of them) to burst out at.

Chester, of course, found all this "irresponsibility" detestable. He had given up all idea of buying Buckfield when it appeared that Tom had no intention of settling there. He was all the more irritated against the boy when we heard that he had tried (after spending all his gratuity) to raise a loan on his chance of inheriting the place. Tom, of course, was still a possible heir, and when Bob died suddenly that year without a will and Jim inherited, he went down and was received by Aunt (Jim was still in Africa and so she was in charge – already full of her "improvements") in great style. It was on this visit, indeed, that he gave his imitation in the village hall of a nervous general keeping up morale by visiting his "boys" in the front line, and took part in an amateur review which showed the great men at the peace conference shouting abuse and threats at each other.

He was a great success as the local hero. But he

absolutely refused an offer to do the same act on the stage for fear of causing embarrassment to Chester.

Tom may have been "irresponsible" at this time, but he was not a waster. He was simply not ambitious to be a success in Chester's or Jim's "line". He was never bitter or disloyal. He was always proud of Chester. He canvassed for him in the "khaki" election just after the armistice, when Mr Lloyd George proposed to hang the Kaiser, and in the terrible year of 1922, when everything seemed to be falling to pieces (and Tom himself had no job), he drove all the way to Tarbiton to take voters to the poll.

106 This was the election day when Chester was pelted in Tarbiton market place, a day that nearly killed him. And Tom was even more furious than I was when we saw Chester, who was speaking from the back seat of the car, stagger, and realized that he had been hit. Part of the crowd had been noisy, but we had been used to interruption all along – shouts of "Who made the war?" or "Why don't you join up with Russia?" We were quite accustomed after all these years to the fact that Chester had enemies, but that they did not make any difference. In fact, they had been a proof of his popularity. When in 1917 his friend Lord G bought the *Courier* and turned Round out of the editorship (Round could not get another job, and he had four children – he ended on relief) there were very bitter attacks, but also dozens of letters saying that Round was a traitor and praising Chester for his courage in getting rid of him. For every new enemy, it seemed that he made hundreds of new supporters.

He had been warned by his own committee before the "khaki" election that if he went on demanding the trial of the Kaiser and supporting conscription he would lose the confidence of his supporters and the seat; and he had paid no attention at all. He had made his strongest speeches in favour of both (in order to start "a real international law with teeth in it") and he had described his critics as a lot of half-baked impracticable fanatics or foolish old women. And then he had won by three thousand votes, his biggest majority, so that the "experts" looked rather foolish.

This time he did not answer stupid questions at all or only with the contempt they deserved. (To the question "Why not join up with Russia?" he shouted, "That's a good idea. Why not? We shan't miss you.")

You may say (as people say of every important man who has misfortunes) that this was not the Chester of the early days, so quick and suave; but how could he be? He was past sixty years old, and for the last eight he had been worked and worried to the limit of his health. He had had no time to look after himself, body or soul, even to think or read or to ask himself as he had once done so often, "What is happening to my character?" He was like a man who comes out of a desperate battle for his very life and the life of his country, to find himself badgered by a crowd of mean creatures who hate him for the most trivial reasons – such as having to pay more for tobacco. Chester often said to me in those bitter days that a statesman who expected gratitude was a fool, but at least he had not expected to be abused for his part in winning the war.

And now, as I say, somebody threw a rotten orange at him in Tarbiton market place, and before the police could even begin to move a shower of filth came down on us – eggs, tomatoes, banana skins, cabbage stalks, and even dirtier things. I tried to pull Chester down by the coat-tails, and Tom shouted to the chauffeur to drive on; but Chester himself would not sit down or make any effort to escape.

He was furious and disgusted. He stood and shouted that he was not going to be silenced by cowards and blackguards, that he had too high an opinion of the real people of Tarbiton to tell them anything but the truth.

Tom was even more furious than Chester. He kept on jumping up and yelling insults and challenges, like "scum" and "dirty swine". I had never seen him so angry and excited; it was incredible to him that people could dare to insult his great man.

Luckily nothing of Tom's abuse could be heard, for the whole crowd was yelling and booing and fighting among itself. And when at last the car began to move (the police had cleared a few yards in front of it) a young man (he looked like a farmer in for the day; some of the moor farmers were very fanatical) caught hold of the steering wheel. This was too much for Tom, who got out of the car and rushed at him, and when he let go to defend himself the chauffeur put down the pedal and the car made a leap forward; and Chester lost his balance and fell on top of me and Tom was left behind.

But in spite of my worry about Tom, I was very glad to get Chester to the hotel, where we went to change every stitch and take baths.

Chester was not much hurt, except for a bruise on the cheek, but he was so excited that I thought he would be ill. He could not keep still, and he kept exclaiming that the whole thing was incredible. "After twenty years! After all I've done for them!" He could not get over his astonishment at the wickedness of the people. "Those questions – and the hisses at the factory – from men who owe us unemployment insurance. It's incredible! But the attack in the market place was not very clever – to bring in a lot of hooligans from outside. You could see that the real locals were disgusted, and I don't blame them. I should think that Tory brainwave will about double my majority."

And this was a consolation to me as well, and to Tom, when at last he was brought back by the police, with nothing worse than a black eye. He was now inclined to laugh at the whole episode, and gave a very good imitation of his fight with the young farmer, who had apparently got it fixed in his head that Chester was anti-Christ.

I suppose politicians and their families who are surprised when they lose an election are figures of fun, but I cannot describe our astonishment when that evening the results were brought to us in the Mayor's parlour, and we were told that Chester was beaten. I did not feel anything – even consternation. It was as though my brain could not understand anything at all. And Chester obviously could not believe his ears. He turned a very dark colour, almost purple, pulled up his collar (he wore rather high collars still with a very broad wing), cleared his throat, and said that some of the boxes could not have come in. And when he was assured that all the votes had been counted, he demanded a recount. But then his agent pointed out that the Conservative majority was over three hundred, so that a recount could hardly change the result.

Bootham said then that, after all, we had been betrayed by our own side in one of the dirtiest elections ever seen, and this gave us our cue. Sally said in her serious impassioned way that Chester had won a moral victory, and Tom that the whole thing was a ramp.

Chester then recovered himself a little, pulled down his coat in front (a trick of his before beginning a speech) and said, "Yes, that's obvious. It was an open conspiracy, really a disgrace. At any rate, it will make the country wake up. People will see that it's time to stop the rot before it brings the whole idea of democratic government into contempt."

And then we all, including the agent and his committee, assured him that the defeat was a blessing in disguise, because it would give him a rest and enable the party to find him a really safe seat, away from Tarbiton, which had never deserved him.

I think we all felt that he was even more shaken than he appeared, and I know some of us were afraid that he would say something in public to show his feelings. But thank goodness even in this fearful and unexpected disaster Chester did not lose his political sense. When the Mayor came in to condole, he actually achieved a smile, thanked him warmly for his sympathy, and said that the election had been perfectly fair. And afterwards he made a very good little speech from the balcony of the Town Hall, congratulating all sides on a fair fight, and only deploring the split in the Liberal party which brought so much danger to liberty.

But we were all very glad when at last we could get him away to a quiet hotel while our man was bringing the car through the crowds.

And it was only just in time. All at once he became quite collapsed, so that Tom and Sally had almost to carry him into the sitting room, and when Bootham fetched a very stiff brandy he took it without a murmur.

And then noticing me, he pressed my hand and murmured something about a complete rest. I recognized the phrase and saw that his idea was to take a holiday on doctor's orders. For statesmen out of Parliament this is like actors resting, and I said, yes, indeed we would have a real holiday at last. I really did feel that he needed a long holiday. But I had no idea how ill he was till the next morning, at six o'clock (and we had not got to bed till four), when I came awake suddenly in a fright and found him walking about the room and talking to himself.

107 The dawn was just beginning, and the room was filled with a greenish light which made all the furniture look cold and queer, as furniture does look at times when it is not usually noticed. And Chester seemed so ghostly and wild that I thought for a moment it was simply an effect of light, like that which made the furniture so green.

"Chester dear," I said, "you'll catch cold, and you know you can't afford to catch cold this week, with the big speech on Wednesday." But he stared at me and said, "Speeches won't do any good."

"But, Chester, I thought the idea was that you would make the speech before we take our holiday so that you can take things up again at the next by-election."

"Yes, no doubt I could go back to the House, but would it do any good?"

"They need you."

"It seems to me that the country is rotted all through. It was just what we were told, that war would destroy us body and soul, whether we won or not."

"You are too tired, Chester. Have you slept at all? Did you take your powder?"

"No, I don't want powders. If I can't sleep, I can't sleep."

And he looked so shaky, so worn and old, that I was afraid he would make himself ill.

And I got up to persuade him to come back to bed; but he was angry even when I touched him. He looked at me quite furiously, and said, "It's no good playing tricks. I am not a child; I'm not ill. No, there is too much rottenness – here, too."

"What do you mean?"

"We are afraid of the truth – we are not honest with one another."

"What have I done?" (for when Chester said "we" he always meant me).

"You think I am finished. You are trying to keep me quiet. You agree with everything I say, but you don't believe a word of it. You think all this that I am saying is just a joke – the sort of joke Tom has been making about the Government. You think I am talking the usual kind of nonsense that can be expected from a Minister when he is put out of office. For a long time now we have been lying to each other – there is no truth anywhere." And he accused me of hiding things from him, "as usual".

That Chester had heard, through his "information service", Tom's "take-off" of Ministers at the peace conference was not surprising (the turn was so good that Tom was often asked for it), but his bitterness was extraordinary.

"I don't mind what he thinks of me personally," he said. "I only wonder at his shallowness."

"But, Chester, it was only a joke; you know how clever he is at mimicking people."

"It is just what I said. If he thinks the peace of Europe and the difficulties of the settlement a joke, he is shallow; and if he does not, his 'joke', as you call it, is in the worst of taste. I did not think he could fall so low, even among all the rottenness." And then, looking at me again with the same angry disgusted face, "Living openly with that painted prostitute."

"She isn't a prostitute, Chester – she's quite a serious actress."

"I notice *you* have begun to paint."

"But everyone uses lipstick now. If I did not use lipstick I should look ill."

"That's the cry everywhere – it's the rule. Rottenness is the rule. Mothers paint their faces like harlots, and their sons propagate lies to raise a laugh among drunken wasters."

The man spoke in a quiet voice, but I saw that he was fearfully excited, and so I did not answer him, but took his hand as if to appeal for understanding. But I could feel that he was trembling, and I thought, with surprise, "Perhaps he is really done for; perhaps his career is really finished and he has become hopelessly out of touch – a silly old man who can only complain of the times and abuse everybody."

And even while I was thinking it, Chester suddenly took his hand away and said, "You think I am an old fool. You agree with Tom. But he has always belonged to you – you saw to that – you and the Latters. You were determined that I should not contaminate him – he was to be a gentleman. And so he is one – a gentleman and a parasite like the gentleman who came as my guest and took the opportunity to seduce you. Naturally Tom hates me – I'm what he calls an outsider."

I said that no one ought to call Tom a parasite – he was doing his best to find work.

"You mean I have no right to complain – that, of course, is true. I have no rights among the Latters. I understood that from the beginning. I was a convenience who might save that sacred family a scandal and be useful to it if he got on well enough – if he could be taught good form and the game of jobbery; that is to betray his own class and everything it stood for."

This astonished me so much that I could not think of any answer. It was so long since Chester had talked about class, except to abuse the workers for their lack of patriotism and their "treachery" to himself, that we had all thought him cured of that obsession.

"I'm not accusing you," he said. "How could you think differently? You were brought up to the game. You were loyal to your lights. I recognized that very soon in our life together, that I was alone in my own house – that I had been a fool to think that you and your kind could ever be at one with mine. Why" (he gave a short laugh) "the Latters even declared war on my poor Harry Bootham – he was too devoted, too loyal – he must be levered out. I must be kept away from the least of my own people – cut off from all contacts."

And when I reminded him that it had not been me who had turned Goold away, he only went on declaring that he had always been alone – it was the penalty he had paid for trying to do some good in the world; to be deserted and vilified by the poor and jeered at by the rich – at the instigation of his own so-called family.

"But, Chester, you must know that Tom is devoted to you – it is the pride of his life to be your son."

"He's not my son – I have no children. By a truly brilliant contrivance, I was placed in a situation guaranteed to make me the obedient slave of family interest, and highly vulnerable to family resentment. I was to live under the perpetual threat of being exposed in the supremely ridiculous role of the duped husband – the captive cuckold. No, please" (he waved his hands to stop my protest), "let's be honest for once and have done with this life of deceits. I know too well that you prefer the easy way and the comfortable dream, but where has it led us? Our life is eaten hollow with falseness."

And now he was so excited that I dared not argue. So I took

his hand and begged him at least to lie down. "You are fear-fully cold. Do get into bed before you catch one of your colds."

"I apologize; all this is in the worst of taste. I am putting you to a great deal of inconvenience."

But it was another hour before he consented to lie down, and then he would not come near me. He insisted on feeling alone.

108 I was shocked by this strange explosion from Chester, and especially the admission, which he had never made before, that Sally, too, might not be his child. I realized that something had broken in him – some barrier or support. But it seemed to me, too, knowing his methods, that he was already making, out of the debris, some new position of defence or attack. And I knew that nothing I could say would change his purpose, whatever it was. For one thing, as I had discovered during many years past, Chester no longer attended to arguments; discussion of any kind with him was a kind of debate. He was not interested in facts, but only wanted to win, so that in this battle words like class, plot, treachery, even truth, and a phrase like "Let's be honest for once and have done with deceits" had nothing to do with the truth – they were simply weapons which he picked out of his store because he thought they would do the most damage to the enemy.

And for another, as I realized that evening, he really was alone. It was impossible any longer to reach him. He had, so to speak, in thirty years of war, made such devastation round himself that to talk to him at all was like calling across a waste full of broken walls and rusty wire and swamps of poisoned water; full of dead bodies, too, like that of poor Brome.

And though he was plainly ill, it was only by bringing in Sally to make a special appeal that he could be persuaded to see a doctor; and he spoke again of plots when the doctor sent him to a nursing home for a month. His blood pressure was dangerously high, and there was even a suspicion that he had had a slight stroke. For a few days his hand was so shaky that he could not write.

And I was very glad when, on his return home, Goold came to stay. The old man had grown very feeble; he could not go upstairs, and we had to put up a bed for him in the "housekeeper's room", but his illness made him all the more ready to be forgiving. The two friends were at once reconciled and carried on long conferences about the political crisis, from which I was very obviously shut out.

But this, too, suited me very well. Chester's new trenches, his new batteries aimed at the Latters, made me feel as if I were under artillery observation, even when he was not shooting at me. I did not like to have my peace feeling spoiled.

And Goold, I thought, was very good for him. He encouraged him with his adoration, and we were all agreed that it would be an excellent thing if Chester took up religion again, because he would certainly need all the chapel vote if he was going to win another election.

109 As for Tom's "shallowness", I said to myself that it was a blessing Tom had the gaiety to make fun when he was still without a job. He had long given up any idea of joining the army. Like many more, after he had had his spree and spent all his gratuity, he could not face army discipline, and yet he did not care, either, for a dull job at a desk So for the last eighteen months he had been living on an allowance (and all I could give him), and loans (Aunt, who was still at Buckfield, gave him money), and hanging about the theatres and bars.

I could not help thinking it a boon when in that same month May Bond gave him a part in a revue (Bond's Bounders), in a scene from some reparations conference (they were having conferences all the time) where two bankers kept crying out for more money and a Prime Minister in a long white beard, with cotton wool in his ears, sang a song called "Don't Wake the Baby".

And I was indignant when Chester, who was only just back from the nursing home, said that he did not want even to hear of this performance – it was too "unworthy".

"How pathetic!" I thought. "He is completely out of touch – he who was so quick to seize on popular feelings. It's extraordinary how he has changed." But as I see now (and no one can understand Tom or Chester who does not understand this), it was me who was most extraordinary in not seeing that Chester had reason to be disappointed in Tom and myself – in not noticing the extraordinary change in my own ideas and in the time.

I remember that in one of Jim's holidays, when I was about twelve, I was allowed for the first time to go cruising with him and my friend Major Freer. I was the deck hand, and I was made to understand that unless I did my duty and obeyed orders I should be sent home by rail. So in our first anchorage, at Milhaven in the mouth of the river, I went up very early to swab down the decks. But Jim was still earlier. He had been bathing and was sitting in a towel on the bitts, shivering and glooming to himself. He was angry with me because the Major had put me in the "lady's cabin", a kind of wooden tomb before the mast, with a narrow door through the partition; and so, as he shared the main cabin with the Major, he had not been able to come to me in the

morning and warm himself with me in bed. He had got up
early instead, to make himself colder and angrier. And I was
angry with him, because I could see he threatened to spoil
my holiday with his sulks, and his misery made me feel
guilty toward him.

So I cried out in a delighted voice, to please myself and
perhaps to annoy Jim, "Oh, how lovely!" For the sun had
just got up about six inches above the top of the sea and at
that angle it always seems much brighter than when it is
right up. And all the other boats all round us with their new
season's paint (it was still only May) were shining like toys
in a shop (but the beauty of it was that they were not toys
but real cruisers which had sailed through the storms and
dark nights) and waving their masts to and fro in the blue
air. Also, of course, I felt, being the only creature in sight
except Jim, a special virtue (all the more so because Jim was
behaving badly) at being up so early to see this beauty and
to do my duty. And in the same cheerful voice (but
throwing in a yoho touch that seemed to me right for the
occasion) I said, "We've held all right, thank the Lord,"
meaning that in spite of the current and the tide our anchor
had not dragged and we were still in the same place –
between a green and white yawl called the *Bessy Bee* and a
white schooner called the *Greyhound*, with two class
cutters just in front.

But a moment later (the morning mist was lifting all the
time) I happened to look up again toward the shore, and I
gave a cry of horror which made Jim spring to his feet with
a most undignified change of expression.

"What's up now?" he asked in a disgusted tone. But I
was too bewildered to answer, for the whole shore of last
evening had disappeared; and when I whirled round to look
past the schooner, the village on the other shore had turned

into a wood with a gasworks in it. And yet all the boats were around me exactly in the same places – it was as though some malicious demon had played a complicated trick or I had gone mad and simply could not understand anything any more.

"It's all different," I stammered at last. "Where are we? What's happened?"

Jim, with a furious glare, stalked past me and almost spat in my face (but no doubt I had been deliberately provoking him with my delight and dutiful sweeping), "You ass! We've only swung with the tide." And even before he had dived down the hatch the whole scene changed again, like a pantomime when the gauze is pulled up, and came out quite solid and ordinary as the Milhaven estuary seen the other way round and about twenty yards downstream. In fact, it looked so solid and ordinary that the whole view had lost its sparkle and I threw down the mop and grew almost as gloomy over the quarrel with Jim as he had been.

I was really I and Tom who had been swung round in the tide of those years after the war and Chester who had stayed, and it was only because nearly everyone had turned round with me that I didn't notice it; and when I did notice the "solid ground" of Chester and his evangelicals I was disgusted by its dullness.

I said that in those years there was a most tremendous outburst of hatred (quite unjust and wild) against the Government, but in fact that was only part of a general explosion which simply blew the whole original world to pieces. It was as if everyone had started again in a moral no man's land. And even if it was not so corrupt as Chester thought for me to paint and rouge (for I did use just a little rouge, too; Tom insisted on it) and show my legs in short skirts (I should have liked to cut my hair, too, if Jim had not absolutely forbidden it), because I was simply following the fashion and had to do so unless I had wanted to look peculiar, it is astonishing to think, now, how suddenly I had become reconciled to the idea that young men like Tom could live openly with girls who claimed to be respectable; that everything could be discussed in the plainest words; that all sorts of vices were not perhaps very wrong but only amusing or even necessary; that both sexes could lie almost naked on every beach; and that there was even something "right" about nakedness; and that all the old moral ideas were petty and ridiculous.

110 In fact, the result of Chester's anger and disgust, the very suggestion that he thought Tom's act frivolous and "unworthy", made me feel that Tom was perhaps doing the "right" thing. I said to myself, "Nearly everyone is making fun of these politicians and their everlasting conferences, and all of them can't be wrong. So long as Tom does not mimic Chester himself – which he would never do – he has every right to make a joke of people who are so ridiculous."

And so when Tom got an engagement, with very good pay, at a certain night club, called Beef on the Tiles (it was supposed to be in the "Parisian" style), and even respectable papers mentioned him as the brilliant Mr Tom Nimmo, I felt I would do anything to see him, so long as Chester did not hear of it.

I had never been to such a place, and perhaps, with all my longing, I should not have dared a visit if one evening, after a very dull evening party, a whole group of people – not by any means all young – had not decided to go on to a night club. Some wanted one club, some another, but half a dozen fixed on Beef on the Tiles (saying it was the most "artistic"); and one of them, who saw me standing by, obviously interested in the discussion, but not knowing me, asked politely, "Are you joining us?" I smiled, and let him put me into a cab. Then I repented, and was terrified. And yet (as I say, all of us were eager for any excitement) I do not believe I could have gone back.

The club in Soho turned out to be underground; it was a long L-shaped room painted terracotta, and full of small tables. The stage was in the middle at the heel of the L. I was glad that our party, four men, all very serious-looking (two of them seemed to be civil servants), and two women, one married and one engaged, both by their dress and manner belonging to what is called good society, took a dark corner; and obviously did not want to be conspicuous. Indeed they all had the air of investigators, or critics, come to see a social phenomenon, but as I looked round I discovered that this was the air of at least half the people at the surrounding tables. There were, in fact, two quite different sets, those who had come obviously to drink and dance (but also looked rather serious – even too serious) and parties like our own who had the judicious air of well-bred people everywhere.

The first performer was a young woman who told stories and sang. I was startled for the first minute by both stories and song, which seemed to me obscene, but none of my neighbours were in the least disturbed and so I felt I was being prudish and old-fashioned; and in two minutes I was quite used to this new idea of what was proper. Then suddenly two other girls came in, wearing policemen's hats, and pretending to clear the way through a crowd. They stood on one side and saluted. And Tom appeared quite suddenly between them. Everyone began to clap.

If I had not known who was coming I should not have

recognized Tom. He was dressed (like the girls) in a pierrot's dress, with a frock coat pulled on over it and an enormous collar round his neck under the frill. His cheeks were painted dead white, his eyes were surrounded with green wrinkles, and he wore a pair of long brown whiskers hooked over his ears. His nose was a great red nose shaped like a moose's.

But even before he began to speak I saw that he was mimicking Chester – his first gesture, raising his hand to stop the applause was purely Chester's – and when he began to speak it was one of Chester's speeches. He spoke of the need for war to defend peace and to support true Christianity. He imitated even Chester's voice, and the peculiar way he had of screwing up his face when he had made a point and was waiting for it to sink in. He even made one of Chester's jokes, and imitated his sudden laugh of enjoyment. But what was terrible to me in all this, everything that Chester did was made to seem cheap and mean. His natural pleasure at making a good joke and raising a laugh suddenly appeared conceited and contemptible.

I cannot describe how I felt in seeing this exhibition. I felt a kind of horror at the cruelty of such an attack on Chester in his failure and illness – I was horribly frightened by something – and yet Tom was so brilliant that I could not take my eyes off him. I did not want to look – it was a kind of agony – but I could not bear to miss a single movement or tone.

And every moment I recognized some trick of Chester's that I had seen a thousand times and not really noticed, reproduced and made significant. When Tom rubbed his hands over each other in the air (a trick of Chester's) the action suddenly appeared loathsome, revealing a kind of horrible self-love; and when approaching a climax, he threw back his head, pointed with his finger, protruded his lips, and mouthed his words, his very mouth, the red twisting lips, seemed so disgusting that one wanted to turn away one's eyes. Yet the voice, the gestures, absolutely fixed one in a kind of trance and one could not keep out the words, one could not prevent them entering in; it was as though they simply took hold of some nerve and danced one's soul upon it like a puppet on a string.

But now something happened so extraordinary that I could not believe it. One of the audience (he had looked very solemn, but now it appeared that he was quite drunk) shouted out something like "Oh, get off it," and threw a piece of bread at Tom, which would have hit him if he had not very quickly bobbed down his head. And some people began to laugh. But in that very second (you could see that for an instant he was astonished and furious, but only an instant) he not only recovered himself but took advantage of the thing and said, "I bow to you, sir" (and he bowed his head again), "as an honoured representative of the great public" (he paused here as if he were going to say public house). "The bread of the people has always come very close to my heart." And he went on to say that this valuable presentation had taken him by surprise – he had given his life to the people, but he had not looked for this magnificent reward. But the audience was already clapping and laughing. One or two (I daresay they were drunk, too) even called out "Hooray!" and "Bravo, Tom!"

But what was terrifying to me was that in that moment when he turned the rudeness into an advantage (and I could *feel* the movement in his mind when he saw his opportunity and jumped at it – exactly like Chester jumping at an opportunity) he seemed not just to be imitating Chester but to *be* Chester. I felt that under the horrible nose and absurd whiskers Chester was acting himself – with all that quickness of imagination and cleverness at grasping and using a situation (people called it artfulness) and even the same joyful excitement in *making a sensation*, in *getting hold of people*, which I knew so well in Chester.

And then, when Tom held up his hand again for silence (with Chester's "religious" air), he seemed to look straight at me (though, in fact, he never saw me – our corner was too dark), leaned forward, put his hands under his coat-tails (another trick of Chester's), and said in a slow, rather treacly voice, "Friends, for I think I can call you my friends, I am but a humble labourer in the vineyard," he made a face at me so ludicrous, so much more "like" Chester's when he was using this tone, than Chester himself; so wild a caricature, such a picture of everything that was loathsome, of the vulgar false cunning hypocritical demagogue, full of spite and trickery and conceit and an indescribable beastliness, a kind of lickerish sensuality; a lustful pleasure in his own nastiness; everything that had been imputed to Chester by his worst enemies (and so cruelly because, of course, there is a trace of all those things in every "popular" speech) that, to my horror, I was suddenly seized with laughter. I heard myself utter a kind of noise, which was neither a laugh nor a cry, a kind of whinny. In fact between horror, and shame at being there at all, and the agony of feeling Tom's words tearing at me, and prodding at me, I lost all control of myself – an easy thing to say, but terrible to feel. I put a handkerchief to my face, and got up, meaning simply to run away, but, of course, the whole party rose with me.

I saw then, even in my confusion and terror, that all of them, except perhaps the man who had brought me, knew who I was. But their faces showed no surprise that I should have behaved so strangely, and their voices were full of solicitude; they even wanted to come away with me.

I could not speak, but I shook my head and made a gesture to show that I wanted to escape by myself; and thank goodness they let me do so. Only the man who had given me a lift at the beginning insisted on taking me home, and he made no comment at all on the evening, except to remark that the night club had been so stuffy that he himself had been glad to escape from it.

111 I had always been very nervous of finding fault with Tom. I knew people (including, of course, Chester) thought that I had spoiled him, but, as I saw it, Tom had had so much against him from birth that he needed encouragement.

But I could not sleep, even with a pill (Chester, since his illness, slept alone, and let me have all the pills I wanted), and the next day I could feel no pleasure in Tom's wonderful success – only horror at the whole performance. I knew I should have to speak to him.

Tom did not live at home now and we rarely saw him there. His excuse was that he had to be near the club and stayed at small hotels in its neighbourhood. And I could not blame him – our house was very depressing. Since the election the very wallpapers seemed dark with failure and defeat. But I knew, of course, that he really spent his nights with May Bond or some girl from the troupe. I could only write to the club hoping that it would find him; and, rather to my surprise, he came at once.

He knew already that I had been to his "show", and he said all the things that actors say when their friends and relations go to see them perform – that it had been the worst night of the week. Why hadn't I told him I was coming? He had not even known that I had been there till the publicity man had phoned him that morning.

I said that I hoped there would be nothing in the papers. And at once Tom became angry, pretending that I looked down on cabaret performances.

"You know very well it's not that," I said, "but because I don't want Chester to know I went to see you mimicking him."

At this Tom (a very rare thing with him) flew into a rage. "Mimicking him? What do you mean? There's not the faintest resemblance. I wouldn't allow it! How could I? You don't really think me capable of such a piece of dirt?"

He was so angry and vehement that I was shaken. He asked how anyone could see any likeness between Chester and that "old ass in brown whiskers". Good God, didn't I know how he admired Papa – the only really great man in the whole bunch.

He said bitterly that he supposed I would call him down if he only walked across the stage in a frock coat. He asked if he was expected to give up the whole act simply because he was Papa's son. He said bitterly, "I thought you'd be pleased to see me making a real start at something. Look at all these officers on the rocks, and I'm earning real money. You've always been at me to get a job, and now I've got one you jump on me."

His indignation was so real that for the moment I was ready to believe I had been too suspicious. I thought that, after all, Tom had mimicked a type often put on the stage. And when the performance itself rushed back on my recollection in all its terrifying detail, I said to myself, "At least Tom does not want to realize what he is doing; the red nose and whiskers are meant to deceive him as well as the audience."

I saw, too (it was so obvious that I might have seen it before), that Tom had to take up this position – he could not admit even to himself that he was imitating Chester or he would have to give up his act. And I remembered that, if he owed a great deal to being Chester's "son", it was also his chief misfortune.

And so I could not argue with him any more; I had to change my ground and say (it was the only way of appealing to him) that perhaps the real trouble (since it misled people) was that he pretended to be a Liberal statesman – couldn't he let the poor Liberals alone?

"It's not a political stunt – I'm not attacking anybody at all."

"But aren't you taking advantage of the rather mean way everyone has turned against the Liberals, just because they were a great Government and won the war and now the peace is not what everyone expected?"

But this made him still more angry and disgusted. He said that I simply refused to understand what he was doing – that he was an artist and his job was to "take off people – anyone you like". All he had to think of was doing it well – as well as he knew how. "I'm not asking you to admire me, but do at least give me credit for doing my best. And you know, some quite good judges do give me credit – they think me rather good."

And seeing that he was thoroughly disappointed in me, I hastened to praise him, saying that I knew he was good. I had seen him and seen how popular his act was.

But he wasn't satisfied. He frowned at me. "No, no, Mum! You don't understand. Most of that crowd didn't know the difference – they'd clap anyone with a red nose. Besides, I was bad that night."

"I thought you were wonderful. It was only – "

"But I *was* bad – shocking bad – completely off. You've

never seen me really *acting*." And he began to explain how on certain days "something clicked" and he really "brought it off, and that's a marvellous feeling. It's like nothing else in the world."

He stopped, looking at me as if wondering if he could trust me. Then he said very gravely, "When I feel like that I know I could be something really big – up with the Robeys and Tiches."

Then suddenly before I could say that I was sure he would succeed he began to laugh at me and said, "But what do you know about that? All the same, when you accuse me of imitating Papa, do you realize that a lot of people about the West End know me better than Papa? One of Respy's" (Respy was the man who managed the Beef) "pals – he's known all over the world – he's put two Prima Donnas on the halls – asked him the other day if Nimmo was my real name. And when Respy told him about Papa, he said he'd never heard of him, but he'd always be interested to meet any relation of Tom Nimmo's."

Tom laughed again, watching me to see how I took this. "Of course, it's a bit comic – these theatrical tycoons live in a world of their own. And perhaps now Papa is out of Parliament and isn't in the papers he's getting a bit overlooked; it's quite wrong really, but there it is."

I thought Tom's look now, with a half smile, was a little calculating (like a small boy's who has just had the idea of running away from his nurse and wonders how fast she can run) and he went on, "The sad thing is, Respy wants me to go shares in a club of our own. It's the biggest kind of chance. I should have all the time I wanted and put on my own acts. But, of course, I should have to find a bit of capital; a couple of hundred would do, but it might be a couple of million if I haven't got it."

And before I could even grasp this new suggestion, he sat down in my chair and put his arm round me. "Come, darling; what's it all about? Were you really shocked? But you know things have changed a bit since the war; people aren't so stuffy."

I said that I was not shocked (for some reason no one can ever admit to being shocked), but I could not bear the idea that he was taking advantage of all the spite against the poor Liberals.

But now something had happened, so that Tom did not mind what I said. He was laughing at me (perhaps you will say that he had finally grown up and found that he did not care whether I approved or no), and said, "At least, you enjoyed my stunt. I'm told you laughed till you had to go out. Why shouldn't you? I was delighted that you did appreciate me – it makes me quite proud."

"I'm not saying it wasn't clever."

"That's something at least. Never mind, Mama, I know you're in a difficult position – and I shan't bother you about the money. It wouldn't be fair. Cheer up, darling; I'll manage. All's well that ends swell."

112 And when he had gone, he left me, as usual, feeling that I *had* been "stuffy", for that was part of the strangeness of that time. To oppose anything whatever on the grounds that it was "immoral" or "inconsiderate" or "disloyal" (I suppose we had all had so much of morality and considerateness and loyalty in the war) not only caused amusement or contempt but made oneself feel small-minded. And, of course, all the people who were small-minded, in any case, made such an outcry about the badness of the young that it really did seem on the small-minded side to go against anyone like Tom.

And that very day I sent him a hundred pounds (in notes, for I dared not put my name to a cheque; Bootham used to go through all the counterfoils sooner or later) and only begged him to add a moustache to his make-up so that he would be more unlike Chester, or at least people would see that he wanted to be as unlike as possible.

But when he started the new club (it was called Respy's Dive, it flourished all that year when clubs were opening everywhere and growing more impudent every night) I soon heard that his imitations were bolder than ever.

I saw very little of Tom in those last months, but there is no doubt that he was immensely happy. Tom enjoyed above all things (like Chester in his different way) the excitement of an audience, and all this time, whenever he came to see me, he had about him that air which one sees only in successful actors and politicians, of having been much applauded and of looking forward to more applause. And I suppose it was true (I have been assured since by very good critics that it was true) that he really was a brilliant mimic and that especially in his acting of the Liberal statesman (no one dared to call him Chester to me) he showed the inspiration of genius. And this did not surprise me. For no one knew Chester better than Tom. He had always admired him and studied him; he knew him instinctively, all through.

I shall never admit that Tom became an evil person. But I do think that he knew, at least subconsciously, that his mimicry was cruel and false; he simply could not resist the temptations of his "art", which was, after all, a real art. And I think, too, that this feeling was one reason why he became so careless and why he slipped away from me in the last months and why, when I did see him, he was always so lively and amusing that it was impossible to have any serious talk with him. I think that he had begun to act a part even with me. So that when I said one day that he was looking very ill and that I hoped he was keeping better hours and not drinking too much, he only pinched my chin and said, "As one of the world's workers to another – life is real and life is earnest."

But the night clubs at this time had become too successful and too daring. All at once the police (under the new Home Secretary, who was very evangelical) began to raid them; and one of the first raided was Respy's Dive.

113 The first thing I knew of the raid was a telephone message from Tom saying that he had been let out on bail, but he wanted two hundred pounds at once for some lawyer (not, I gathered, a very respectable lawyer) and asking me, for God's sake, to get Papa to speak to Hawker.

Hawker was a friend of Chester's, a fellow director in one of the private companies, and at present a Conservative under-secretary.

Tom begged me to go at once; it would be too late in the morning. And, of course, I promised to do what I could.

But I was put in a great difficulty. I was not supposed to see Chester after ten o'clock, when he went to bed. For a long time I had seen very little of him even during the day – he was at work all morning, resting, by doctor's orders, in the afternoons, and most of his meals were taken to him in his study or bedroom.

I could not be sure that he was punishing me. I knew that he was deeply concerned with the political situation – that he was obsessed with what he called the "crisis of freedom" – his belief that the breakup of the Liberal party would be the end of "Christian Freedom" in Britain and even in the world. I could not be surprised that he had little time for any other ideas.

In fact, during the last months since the election and the radical manifesto (got out largely by Chester's group), stating that the party had suffered its defeat because of its desertion of its true principles, a great change had taken place in the household.

The manifesto, whatever its effects afterwards (it caused several more cracks in the party; a party seems like ice – once it starts cracking, everything cracks it, not only hard knocks but the "flowing tide" and its own weight), brought great enthusiasms to the Parade.

Once more the house was full of committee men and lay preachers in creaky boots; and important-looking women, who all (because they did not paint) seemed like ghosts called out of the grave.

All these people looked at me with sorrow or indignation – so obviously that I had thought at first, "They don't like my lipstick." But when I found that poor old Goold would not speak to me (and when he had had to go home again after another attack of blood pressure, he did not even write), and that a certain preacher had been talking, actually in chapel, about the evil influences which had "so long encompassed our beloved leader", I realized that all the old ideas about me had started up again. I was the scarlet woman who had led Chester astray in the first place and taught him to be luxurious and introduced him into "society".

And I wondered if in this new "crisis" Chester, too, had been persuaded that I was a political liability and deliberately kept me away from him.

That was why, even after Tom's appeal, for "God's sake" to speak to Papa at once, I hesitated before going up to Chester's bedroom. And went as quietly as possible in case he should be asleep. But quietly as I stepped, Sally heard me and came out of her room next door (she was a heavy sleeper – I suppose some instinct made her know that I was approaching Chester's fortress) and asked me what I wanted.

She was very polite and obviously embarrassed at having to ask such a question. At that time Sally always blushed when she even spoke to me; she was embarrassed by her feelings about me.

I explained that Tom's club had been raided, and that we had to arrange at once some way of getting him out of the case. She said, "But you know Papa had his powder at ten. If he is waked up now he will be awake all night."

"But Tom can't be left in this frightful position; we only have tonight to get him out of it."

"He must have expected something like this to happen."

"But think of the scandal if his name gets in the papers."

This did move Sally; she saw that Chester might be involved. She said, "Shall I go in and see if Papa is awake?"

And I let her go. She had not before so plainly come between me and Chester (and she was only nineteen that month), but she did it so naturally, so unconsciously, that I could not even feel indignant.

I did not wait for her to call me into the room; I followed her at once, and found Chester just waked, sitting up with an expression so strange that for an instant I even forgot what I had come for. He was leaning on Sally's arm as she lifted him, and his face expressed terror, a wild kind of terror, which was also furious. But the instant Sally spoke to him he recollected himself, assumed that sad calm and patient expression (habitual to him at that time) which Aunt had called his "great and wise man" look, and murmured, to me, "Yes?"

I explained what had happened and what a fearful

scandal it would make, and he answered, "A scandal, yes. But what do you expect me to do about it?"

I reminded him at once that there were several people (I mentioned Hawker, and a high official in the police and an important civil servant) who were friends of his and would certainly get Tom off.

Chester listened with the same wise sad air, and then said, "Even if these people were ready to use their influence, do you think it would be right to ask them?"

"Of course it would; you would do the same for their sons. You did get Mr Q's son into a safe job during the war, and you know how grateful he was."

"A good many things were done during the war which shouldn't have been done."

"You were perfectly right to get that boy out of the war; you knew he wasn't really fit to fight."

"I'm afraid we won't agree on that point."

This meant that he was thinking of his "principles" – ever since the defeat the party had been writing and talking about principles, the manifesto had been full of them; and, of course, I saw that they were important. But I knew, too, how often Chester had found a reason (often quite a good reason) to make an exception in his "general" principle.

And all this time, as Chester gazed at me with his "great and wise man" look, I felt that he was not even thinking about Tom. His look recalled that night four months before when he had said that he had been a fool to think that my people could ever be at one with his, that there was a gulf between him and me.

I thought, "He is miles away from me and Tom; he doesn't even realize what has happened and what it means," and I said to Sally, to get rid of her, "I wonder, would you get my bag from my dressing table. It's got a letter in it from Tom" (though, in fact, the letter was a fortnight old; I had kept it only because it was amusing and affectionate).

Sally understood my motive and hesitated. But Chester said at once, "I'm all right, Sally – you can go now. I'll ring when I want you." Even then she went out slowly and reluctantly; she felt that she was deserting her hero.

I asked Chester at once if he understood that Tom might be put in the dock. Did he really mean to leave him to heaven knows what disgrace and misery?

"Even if Tom was my son, I could do nothing for him now."

"He's very fond of you – he's relying on you. And you used to be fond of him."

"I did my best for him, but you always fought against me."

"You said a little time ago that I was your wife and could never be anything else – and I tried to be a good wife. And now I'm not asking you to do something for me, only for Tom. It's for you, too – you don't want a frightful scandal either. I don't want to be a nuisance – especially just now when you have so many important things to think of."

Perhaps I should not have said this, which meant, in the circumstances, that Chester was so wrapped up in his own affairs that he could not be bothered with anything else. He interrupted me at once (and it seemed to me that for the moment he was moved a little out of his grand attitude – he was almost disgusted) and said that he was quite aware of the possible scandal and the damage it could do. But he had expected some disaster for a long time. And as for my appeal, he could only repeat what he had said already, he could not possibly intervene. He did not expect me to understand his position – I had never made the least attempt to do so – or I would have taken more trouble to avoid alienating his friends and giving a handle to his enemies. Did I realize what I had cost him in the last election? He was not prepared to say that I had lost it for him, but there were good judges who believed it.

He had recovered his temper at once and his air was once more that of the suffering hero who has been betrayed. His voice was gentle and full of resignation, so that his words sounded all the more bitter.

And though I was taken by surprise by this new charge about the last election, I did not even want to defend myself – or feel in the least angry. I suppose that with people who become, like Chester, absorbed into another world, one does not feel ordinary emotions or take what they say as ordinary language. I went out with a sense of confusion as if I had been wrong from the first – an intruder on holy ground. And Sally's face, as she popped out of her room again (she had been waiting behind the door) and gave me a regretful accusing glance, as she hurried back to Chester's side, seemed to say that very thing.

And it was only by pure chance that Tom was rescued. For I had never thought of asking Aunt Latter's help; and as for other members of the family, I had never dreamed of telling them about Tom's life. I had hoped and prayed that they did not know of it. But Aunt Latter, reading her morning newspapers (very little in the papers escaped Aunt Latter; as she got older she read them even more thoroughly), found the report of the raid next morning, and, of course, as it turned out, she knew all about Tom. She telephoned to me at once, and as soon as she knew the situation, though she herself was crippled with her lumbago, and could not come to town, she organized the whole family in defence. Wilfred, Slapton, Jim (she cabled to Jim – he was at Geneva putting the "Luga Case" before the League of Nations), a whole mass of relations whom I had scarcely heard of, including a cousin who was reading philosophy at Heidelberg, all were mobilized.

114 What I had forgotten was that men like Wilfred and Jim, though they loathed Tom and all his ways, perhaps even more than Chester did, had quite different ideas of principle and even law. I don't mean that they hadn't a very strict idea of what was right; but both of them were very critical of laws that interfered with that idea. Wilfred was quite ready to use his influence for Tom, because, as he said, prison would be an absolute disaster for him, while it would not do any harm at all to crooks like the "Respys" who had been there before. And Jim, for his part, had always despised any regulation that tried to stop amusement or sport of any kind, like licensing laws or censorships. So that while Wilfred went to various powerful friends in town, and pulled all sorts of strings, Slapton (who did not need, like Wilfred, to care about his reputation in London with business people if anything should come out) tackled the crooked lawyer. And it was arranged in no time that the "Respys" should take the whole responsibility for the performance and pay the whole fine. They were even prepared to go to prison if we gave them proper compensation. But, of course, when I say the "Respys" paid, I mean we paid, that is, Wilfred, Jim, Aunt Latter, and myself; but chiefly Jim, who was now quite well off.

But Tom had to leave the country – this was one of the conditions laid down by Wilfred and Jim. And they saw that it was carried out, for Wilfred threatened to set the police on him if he did not go. I dare say this was part of

Wilfred's private bargain with the police. If I had known it at the time, I should have quarrelled with them both, but they did not tell me, and they prevented Tom from telling me. They were ruthless with Tom; it is perhaps only a family with such strong family feeling as ours which can be ruthless with a member who has disgraced it. They gave him twenty pounds, and told him to go, and he went to Germany, first to the Heidelberg cousin, but then (as they might have expected) he went back to cabaret, because it was the only thing that he enjoyed doing and knew himself to be good at, and got into very bad company (because in Germany, apparently, the clubs were much "worse" than ours), and began to drug as well as drink.

But even then I am sure Tom would never have gone really "wrong" if it had not been that the Germans could not appreciate his imitations of British Liberal statesmen. In fact, so I was told, he was a failure as a mimic, and had to take small parts in rather disgusting performances, and this made him very wretched. He always wrote quite cheerfully to me, but really I think he could not bear to be a failure and a nobody – he had had such a great success as the Crown Prince – and after only two months, when he was dismissed from some horrible place, he shot himself.

To me, at the time, this was a tragedy which seemed to break my heart; that is, I didn't know how I could go on living; I blamed everyone for it, including, of course, myself. It seemed to me that Tom had been murdered by a conspiracy of stupid and cruel people, the police, the law, the Minister who had set the police raiding, and especially by Chester. I told myself that Chester had never understood or liked the boy; he had been jealous of Tom simply because he was more sensitive, more fine, more subtle, and because he was so good-looking and attractive; and he had always secretly wanted to crush him. At last, out of pure spite, he had taken his opportunity.

Even when I was raving in this way, I think I knew that it was wicked nonsense. I was fighting against a secret wonder if anything or anyone could have saved Tom. For he could never get away from Chester's influence. Somehow Chester had got right inside the boy from his very childhood, so that everything he thought and did was affected. I remembered that the only thing which made Tom really angry was the charge that he was imitating and making fun of Chester, at the very time when the imitation was such a masterpiece that all London (I mean, of course, night-club London) was talking about it, and when Tom knew that it was his masterpiece. The only chance for the boy (when he could really have respected himself) was in a political career, and indeed he had tried it after the war when Chester put him into the radical disarmament committee. But by that time, at least, he had come to hate politics.

And who could blame Chester for all this: for his devotion, his patience, for being rather an overpowering kind of person, and for having, perhaps, a special anxiety to do well by Tom because of Tom's relation to him? The same anxiety toward Sally made the girl adore him, and turned rather a frivolous and lazy child into a very good, serious, and responsible young woman.

But I would not admit anything of this in that fearful week when I went to Berlin with Sally to see Tom buried, and came back to face committee men. I could not bear my own house. I could not bear to hear Chester dictating to Bootham about the importance of unity to all supporters of freedom, and especially I could not bear the people on the stairs who looked at me with surprise and indignation as if they wondered how I dared to show myself among them.

So on the very first evening I sent for the doctor (my own doctor) and made him advise very strongly that I needed a change.

Chester and Sally, everyone, agreed at once that I must have a long and complete holiday, and I was out of London within twenty-four hours.

115 The story is, and I am sure it will be told again, that I ran away to Jim Latter. But for one thing I did not run away – I was driven out (and all Chester's "true" friends were delighted to see me go); and for another, I refused an invitation to Buckfield – I avoided Jim.

Jim, indeed, was angry when I refused his invitation to go either to Buckfield or Palm Cottage, which he had lately bought back at a very high price, as a yachting box. He was angry even though I had the good excuse that at Buckfield I should be alone with him, for in the last few days he had had a final explosion with Aunt (that old busybody, as he called her – I'm afraid, to her face), who complained that her whole "Buckfield policy" was being ruined by Jim's extravagance on "those damned cannibals of his" (his latest plan – bringing over a deputation of native chiefs – had certainly proved very expensive), and walked out in a rage.

The truth was that I did not want to see any of my family. I was too unhappy and too tired. And perhaps I should have gone abroad if my old friend Major Freer had not died just then at a place called Axwell near the mouth of the Longwater. I took a lodging in the village for the funeral, and afterwards, since I had not the energy to go away, I stayed on for a week.

And at the end of the week I found, to my surprise, that I did not want to go. I was at peace; I was enjoying an extraordinary happiness, a special happiness, which had so to speak, gathered round me of itself, out of that familiar air, as if it had been waiting for me to come and crystallize it. And it was like a crystal – transparent peace full of sky and air which was lighted everywhere by an enjoyment which was not at all sleepy. On the contrary, it had a special vibration of pleasure – a quite luxurious delight in its completeness and security.

It seemed to me that I had only just (at the age of forty-five) discovered or rediscovered true happiness and peace. I had "retired from politics"; I had left behind that perpetual grinding anxious effort of "managing" in a complicated household. I was like an old convict escaped at last from an imprisonment which has become so habitual that he has forgotten what it is like to be free. I was learning that immense delight of waking up in the morning to a day at one's own disposal.

I am told that even very happy wives, when they go away for a few days on a visit (or, better, to a hotel by themselves), know a keen pleasure simply in being alone, because love itself is still a bond and a pressure. For me, who had been perhaps even unhappier than I knew, it was like a resurrection.

What a delight to go down the road to the little stony beaches where Jim and I had played in the boats and quarrelled about plans. For the quarrels themselves, now that they were history, had changed into something delightful like a picture of the Battle of Waterloo. The memory of my very pinafores and my hair (in the old photographs), scraped back from my forehead into a comb, so that my forehead, always my worst feature, looked like an idiot's with water on the brain, made me laugh. People who go back to the scenes of childhood are supposed to "live it" all over again, but I certainly did not. For though

I had had so much happiness (except when Jim was on his holidays), it was quite a different kind of happiness from what I had now in laughing at the child I was, and even that child's truly desperate miseries.

I dare say even my happiness was stronger now than then, for I had learned the value of happiness, and I think it was because of this peaceful happiness that when one afternoon Jim stepped out of the Blue Anchor in Axwell High Street and intercepted me on my way to the library my first feeling was one of nervous apprehension.

But he had come, apparently, only to talk about the Lugas. His book had been a failure; no one wanted even to know about the Lugas, and the deputation of chiefs which he had brought over at such enormous expense had fallen into the hands of some African students who had already persuaded them that they were being "exploited". In fact, there was already a Nationalist Luga Committee which was collecting funds actually from the Lugas themselves to fight the "Imperialist Latter Committee" which was "preventing the development of Lugaland" and at the same time "exploiting the Lugas".

All this had thrown Jim into a fever of rage and frustration, and I soon saw that he had made the journey to Axwell only to pour out his troubles to me and to assure me of his determination to "carry the thing through" and "not to let the poor bastards down".

And I knew from the last ten years' experience with Chester what my function was – to make him believe that he was right (but at that time I did believe most strongly that he was right) and to assure him (which I did not quite believe) that he was bound to get "decent opinion on his side" in the end. In this, rather to my surprise (but I had certainly learned a great deal from those evenings during the war when Chester had come home in despair), I was very successful. So that Jim began to write or telephone almost every day. For the Luga affair grew every day more complicated (the chiefs who were living at Jim's expense now refused to go home again – they were enjoying the corrupt civilization of Europe too much), and the swarm of cranks and crooks and idealists and neurotics who surround every nationalist cause got bigger and bigger. And so it was quite natural that Jim should spend more and more time running down to Axwell. He would take me for a sail, to "get some clean air into one's guts", and sometimes he was so loath to go back to that "blasted telephone" that he would stay the night in the lodgings.

Of course, this made talk, and when, to avoid trouble with Chester (whose friends were watching me all the time), I went to take refuge with Aunt at Palm Cottage, he followed me there and stayed in Tarbiton. I suppose it was not surprising that Chester's lawyer came to see me and threatened to cut off my allowance.

But by that time it was already too late. I was too deeply entangled with Jim, and, indeed, to both our consternation (I had thought I was too old), I was once more in that condition which seemed to be inevitable when Jim and I came together.

And since Chester had just been defeated again, in the last great disaster of '24, there was no longer any political reason why I should not be divorced. Indeed, Chester himself (over the heads of his political advisers) proposed it. He wrote reminding me that he had always thought it wrong, in principle, to hold any human soul to a "legal" bond, against spiritual conviction. And he wished me all happiness in my new "responsibilities".

It was a truly great-minded letter and it was passed round

in a cyclostyle copy among Chester's friends and supporters. Chester always said that he did not know how it got out; and perhaps this is true. He was a man who had long ceased to know what did not suit him. But since it had become public (as he explained to me later), he was sure I would agree that it had better have official publication, with proper comment, in his forthcoming memoirs.

116 Chester, who was so cunning in making people "willingly" do what he wanted by creating a situation in which they had no alternative (unless they wanted to *make* themselves miserable instead), who had broken all my rebellions by manoeuvring me into a position where I was glad to be a "good" wife, once said to me in a candid moment that happiness is all a matter of imagination. A fakir on a bed of nails can be as happy as a bride on her wedding day or (a characteristic "Nimmo" touch) a Cabinet Minister at question time who finds that his braces have given way at the back.

But no one likes to be put upon a bed of nails (and I had just escaped from one); I had been alarmed for my newfound peace as soon as Jim had begun to come to Axwell. And just as I had feared (and Chester had warned), the Luga affair went from bad to worse. In June Jim had to confess that he had run out of funds. The committee broke up after a violent meeting at which Jim was voted out of the chair on the ground that he had concealed essential information and failed to disclose financial commitments. It did not matter that he was paying for everything.

In fact, it turned out that he had concealed "financial commitments" from himself. When an auditor was appointed, it was found that he owed thousands, not only for the chiefs' expenses but printing, advertising, lecturers, and mysterious sums for "public relations". It was decided, after a family council, to let Buckfield on a long lease.

Meanwhile the Colonial Office sent the chiefs home at the cost of the Nigerian Government. It was not surprising perhaps that Jim grew difficult. It was his first experience of "real" politics – of the confusion and injustice and spite and trickery which make political life horrible to those who are not brought up to it.

And so far from my pursuing Jim (as Chester believed), what actually produced the catastrophe was my attempt to avoid him by taking refuge at Palm Cottage with Aunt, who perfectly agreed with me that we did not want a scandal. She was in such a state of hatred against Jim that she was delighted to forbid him his own house.

And this was a prohibition which had to be respected. Aunt was now quite mad with drink and fury, and capable of anything. She would scream at the very name of Jim and would wander about half the night muttering, "Busybody – all right – I'm a busybody." And then she would come to my room to wake me and ask me what would have happened to any of us if she had not been a busybody? It was extraordinary how this word enraged her – it literally drove her mad. And the first time she saw Jim approaching the door (she had been waiting for him) she threw up the window and screeched at him, "Busybody. Leave us alone, busybody. Mind your own business, busybody. Ruin yourself your own way, busybody, and let Nina have some peace."

And I had to signal to him not to come in – I was afraid the old woman would have a fit.

But the result was only that I had to slip out to see him, and he was so exasperated against me for my refusing him the house that I could not refuse anything else.

117 No one would take Buckfield even at the lowest rent, and in the end, when we had to sell, it fetched a miserable sum, less than the value of the land. The house was pulled down – most of it went to mend the roads.

And as I had lost my allowance when I was divorced, we were very poor. Aunt Latter, too, was a great expense. She refused any reconciliation, and when Jim came finally to live at Palm Cottage retired to her room (her old room, the best in the house) and lived there by herself, growing madder and more bitter every month. We were in terror she would burn us in our beds, and we had to have a night nurse to watch her.

And she gave us no peace even at night. She would come outside our door to scream "Busybody" and ask how Jim was doing with "his cannibals".

It gave her great satisfaction when the Luga chiefs, as soon as they reached home, issued a statement to the press, declaring that they welcomed the development scheme of the Government and utterly repudiated the devious tactics of the Latter Committee, whose object had now been exposed as an attempt to perpetuate racial distinctions and keep Africans in a state of poverty and dependence.

And that clever young woman from Oxford has assured me that the development policy was really quite an old project of the Government brought in by some new official about 1910 and that Jim had been moved out of Dutchinluga not because he had got into that pamphlet but because the Government was worried about his influence over the Lugas (just what he had been praised for by all the other officials), and they were afraid that the pamphlet might give him some power at home to stop development and to go on being "reactionary" (which is what they had called before "looking after the people" and greatly admired). But I could not tell Jim this story. He would not have believed it, and quite probably it is not true; that is, it is something invented for a book to "make sense" of all those complicated and mysterious developments outside books which Chester called history and, indeed, he made a good deal of it which will never be in books, for even he does not quite know how it was made or why.

In Jim's view he had "bought it" (for Jim history was only books) and he was far too proud to complain. He said only that he might have known the "boys in Aiké Square" would "deal themselves five aces" and it was quite time he got down to something he understood, like growing cabbages. And he actually did go out one morning to dig – the only time in my life that I ever saw him with a garden tool in his hand.

But even on that morning he came into the house every half-hour to find out what I was "playing at". For in those early days of our marriage he would barely let me out of his sight. He cut down my reading (to "save my eyes") and laid down strict rules for my rests, my bedtime, my diet (orange juice had just come in for breeding mothers) and my exercise. Yet he would, if the fancy seized him, take me sailing beyond the heads, in the roughest weather.

And now, too, he no longer put cushions for me in the stern or wrapped me up against the wind, or kept within Staplehead. On the contrary (I suppose because he was always in a certain state of exasperation; even when he was not thinking of the Lugas or his ruined career, he was feeling them in his flesh), he sailed right into the Atlantic, often in the most dangerous seas, so that I had never been so frightened, so cold (and I could never tell if cold makes the fright worse or better, but I think the truth is that first it makes it worse by freezing out all the warm courage, and then better, by making you so numb and wretched that you simply do not care how soon you are drowned); and he would take twelve-mile walks on the moor until I hardly knew where I was putting my feet, and was ready to cry with weariness.

But one day, when I was wondering how I endured such a "life of slavery", it struck me that I was amused at these big words, and that I did not want the life to stop – that I was "in love" with Jim. I put the phrase in quotation marks because it was a state so unlike being "in love" as usually described, so different from any of my old loves or any state at all that I could have imagined. For I saw that so far from being Jim's slave, I belonged to myself more intensely than ever in my life before. And just as in those first days of escape at Axwell, I was enjoying an extraordinary peace. In the worst moments of the day when Jim was at his most pernickety, I still had that deep security and independence.

It was from this secret peace, the independent calm, as out of a private fort, that I found it so easy to submit to his whims, that I could say to myself, "Perhaps Jim has always needed to govern something or somebody and now that he has neither horses nor Lugas he can only rule over me." I must not say that I had found out how to laugh at Jim, but there was laughter in the walls of my fort and in my happiness. And as Jim's baby grew in me so did this love grow, so that I, too, wanted to be with him, and, if he was not with me, to know exactly where he was and what he was doing at any moment.

This, in my private fort, made me laugh at myself. I thought, "Here you are, a gray-haired and rather battered woman of forty-six, madly in love for the first time in your life. For what could be madder than to enjoy being worried, and pestered, wet, cold, frightened and worn out, simply to please a cross man; and (what is worse) to make him believe that you are different from yourself? For, of course, I was really longing, nearly half the time, for my sofa and book if only to be aware of my happiness.

And if Jim was severe in his demands, he was also, for the first time in his life, sometimes complimentary. He would tell me, when I was quite worn out, that I was at least a trier; once he even trusted me with the dangerous idea that I had changed for the better, that I seemed to have learned at last that even a pretty girl can't have it all her own way.

I did not dare to tell him that if this was true he owed a great deal of the new woman to Chester's skilful discipline.

118 I had no sign from Chester from the time I left him till the birth of my son Robert in May. Then, to my surprise, be sent me a note of congratulation and a cup.

He said also that he was writing his memoirs and would be grateful for leave to publish extracts from my early letters. About a month later I had another note asking if he could call to discuss some points in the letters.

I did not care for the suggestion – I did not want to see the man again – but I might, in common politeness, have agreed to a meeting if Jim had not declared flatly that he would not have "that shyster" in the house. He also wanted me to refuse the use of my letters to Chester and to tear up all those that he had written to me, of which I had several hundred, including some (as Aunt had pointed out years before when she had made me keep them) that were of high importance to any historian.

And he was furious when I said that these letters were at the bank and that I was not sure if I had a right to destroy them.

In fact, I suddenly discovered that, as well as a devoted tyrant of a husband, I had a very jealous one. He went into such a rage about the letters ("You've played fast and loose with me for thirty years – God help you if you let me down again") that I was glad to get off by denying Chester the house; that is to say, I wrote those polite excuses (just at the moment it would be difficult to find a time and I was much occupied with the baby) which meant, "You would not be welcome."

I heard no more from Chester after this, but, as I might have known, he was not accepting defeat. He simply changed his tactics.

Daisy Goold had asked me several times to Chorlock Manor, the new house that Goold had built for her when he received his knighthood immediately after the war; but Jim, during our "affair" and when my condition began to be noticeable, had hated me to be seen even by friends (besides, he had always detested the Goolds), so that, though Daisy had visited me to admire Robert and rejoice over my nearness to Chorlock, I had never gone to her.

But now that I was a respectable woman and the baby was weaned, I had no excuse (or wish) to offend my dear Daisy. So when one day she gave me a very urgent invitation, saying that her car would fetch me, I agreed to go, only choosing the afternoon when Jim, who was president of the yacht club, would be attending a conference of yachtsmen in Lilmouth.

Chorlock Manor was an enormous place. And the Goolds kept more state than my cousin at Slapton – there were two footmen as well as the butler at the door when I arrived. But what surprised me very much was to see such a bustle everywhere. The big inner hall was quite crowded, and I saw Goold, in his invalid chair (he had had another stroke and was now quite unable to walk), sitting among the turmoil, with such a stupid bewildered expression on his face (which was now a strange maroon colour) that I felt frightened and wanted to say something consoling to him. But I could not think of anything that would console him, and before I could go forward a carload of new arrivals came trailing between us.

Messengers hurried from door to door in the background and let out a noise of typewriters. I was reminded of many political headquarters. I would have thought I had come back to the house of a leading Minister during a crisis if I had not recognized most of these important-looking visitors as local people: the clerk from the agents, some Girl Guides acting as messengers, and three members of the Radical Ladies Council (who gave me very cold looks) waiting for an interview.

I knew, of course, that there was an almost continuous session of "councils" and "committees" and "conferences" during that summer in the west, and I had seen numerous notices in the papers of a great radical "rally" organized by Henry Bootham, Esq, CBE, President of the Radical Defence Council. But I had not expected such activity at the Manor, nor to see Bootham now come forward with such an air of authority.

I had not seen Bootham for nearly two years; in many years I had not perhaps paid much attention to his appearance. And now I was startled to see how, with his greying hair, his swelling stomach, he fulfilled his dignified part. To look at him now was to think that he must be wise and experienced even though one knew how stupid he really was, and that he had never learned anything but self-confidence, which was due to his never having been trusted to do anything for himself.

Bootham caught sight of me and appeared, though without loss of his statesmanlike manner, slightly astonished (his "important" eyebrows raised themselves a little), and I would perhaps have spoken to him if Daisy, at last, had not dashed forward, actually running, to come between us, and hastily kissed me on both cheeks.

As usual, since what she called her "ladyshipping", Daisy was in uproarious spirits. Having made one rush at me and another at Goold, to shake up his pillows (he tried to say something to her, but at that moment she was talking to me over her shoulder) she carried me off to her "boodwor" (this word, like so many of her words, was a joke, meaning, "An't I a comic and isn't life a comic") and ordered cake and Madeira. She had picked up this antique custom from the other Aunt Mary on some morning visit to Slapton House. But again, she laughed at it and said, "Nothing like doing the polite when it means a nice glass of something for her ladyship." And she threw down two glasses and ate an enormous slice of heavy plum cake.

Daisy herself had grown enormous and her cheeks were of that fiery red that comes often to blonde skin in its forties. She gloried openly in her wealth and extravagance. She was not a remarkably "good" woman – she did not give as much to charity or local causes as my Cousin Slapton with half the means. And though it is not true, as people said, that she was cruel to her old husband, she was certainly not a very attentive nurse. She was much too busy enjoying herself.

And yet somehow Daisy (like one of those institutions to whose faults one has become accustomed but whose active virtues can't be overlooked) had become one of those very popular persons whom everyone is glad to know and even to claim as a friend. She was even distinguished. And now her delight in seeing me (and having me to see her new magnificent house) made us so cheerful that I was still laughing rather wildly at her latest gossip, when her face changed and with a look of extreme innocence which always warned one of some sly move, she said, "But you don't ask me after the old gentleman, his lordship." And for the first time I discovered that Chester had been in the house for the last two days and had asked Daisy to ask me – "because he was fretting about your old letters – and, bless you, you wouldn't believe how they keep the poor man shut away – he can't never see nobody for himself. It's not Christian. And bringing him down here because of a bit of talk – "

Daisy never told a straight story, and was especially crooked when she had any purpose to hide. In this case, as I have found out since, her object was simply to procure for Chester a private interview with me (I suspect he had bribed her with the promise of a promotion in the Radical Ladies League – she has lately been made a District Dame) and to remove from my mind any objection to that scheme.

So I gathered in the next quarter of an hour that there had been trouble in London about some "silly little piece" because "since that Frood put out his dirty books, every silly girl that so much as gets looked at by a man goes off in fits and screams out for the police". And after all, it was hard for the poor old dear after nearly thirty years of marriage – not that he was ever cut out for a bachelor as I knew better than she.

And, in any case, I would know what to do, because there was no real harm in him and I wasn't like poor little Sall or that Harry Bootham, I wouldn't be put about by anything that married women could take for a natural thing and to be pitied, too, in a lord that can't lift a finger but it goes in the paper.

I dare say that I should never have understood the tendency of this rigmarole if I had not heard some gossip already about Chester and some woman in Kensington Gardens who had accused him of an "assault" and had had to be "bought off", a tale which I had treated as one of those slanders that, as I had found, are invented about every distinguished person – the product of some mysterious spite or irresponsibility which describes great actresses as druggers and actors as "perverted" when they are perfectly respectable fathers of their own families.

I did not believe Daisy's hints even now; it was on quite other grounds that I wanted to avoid Chester. But Daisy, perhaps detecting this resolve in my expression, suddenly hoisted herself up and (without a word – she had all the crude simplicity of the moorlander in pursuing her object) walked out of the room. Whereupon Chester – he must have been waiting in ambush – popped in.

119 And I was so startled for a moment to see the change in him that I forgot my nervousness and Jim's suspicious jealousy. Chester had aged very quickly in the war, but now he looked eighty; his head was quite bald on top and his long streaming white hair gave him the look of a revivalist preacher. His long upper lip seemed still longer and his nose was thrust out like a crag. But his energetic "prophetic" head, which seemed to have grown bigger till it was out of all proportion, was stuck upon a body so dried and shrunk that it appeared like a doll's, made of wood and sawdust; there was something angular and jerky in all his gestures which suggested the same idea. He was like a marionette imitating himself.

But he still moved with his celebrated vivacity. He jumped into the room; he darted to seize my hand; he gripped it in his hot little claw while he cried how delighted he was to see me again and looking so well, so beautiful. "You grow younger every year, my dear. What cheeks, what eyes! The west suits you – your native air. Why did we ever leave it?" He stopped, looking at me with his big thin mouth half open, his eyes wide – gazing at me in a kind of astonishment.

And he began, as if unconsciously, to pull me toward him. In that moment I felt a new and deep fear of Chester, which comes to one in realizing that some creature, from sheer egotism or disease or age, has forgotten ordinary restraints and is so far mad.

Indeed, when I tried to pull back, Chester glared suddenly with a quite furious expression and made a gesture with his other hand as if to take hold of my waist. I was exceedingly glad when at that moment the outer door toward the hall was thrown back and first Sally, then Bootham, came in – both a little breathless as if they had been running.

Chester at once dropped my hand and skipped to the other end of the room – the effect was comically like that of a small impudent boy caught in some mischief.

Sally, who was very flushed, fixed her eyes on me with an anxious expression (for Sally I was capable of anything) and kissed me at last with her usual grave forgiving affection. She even remembered to ask after the "baby" – I could not blame her that she did not recall Robert's name. Then, turning to Chester, she said with mild reproach, "You didn't tell me, Papa, that you wanted to discuss the letters today."

Chester had now drawn himself up – he appeared very much the elder statesman, while he advanced slowly toward us. He answered Sally abruptly and rather coldly that he intended to deal with the letters *now* – would she kindly fetch them?

And, turning to Bootham, he said that he would not want him that afternoon – and did not care to waste his time.

I was both indignant and relieved when Bootham answered coolly that he had plenty of time and would like to know Mrs Latter's decision at once, and waited in the room while Sally fetched a file of the letters and a long list of extracts.

It was strange to see how tamely (and gracefully – he was still the politician; he knew how to save his face) Chester submitted to this dictation, saying, "Yes, perhaps that would save Mrs Latter's time."

He sat down then by the table in a statesmanlike attitude – very straight in the back – chin raised and hand stretched toward Sally for the papers – and immediately began a conversation with me which was as private as if we had been alone. For everything had two meanings, one for them and one for me.

As Sally handed over the first typewritten sheet, he turned to me and said, "I'm afraid, Nina, there are a lot of quotations – you were a wonderful hand at description in those days when we were in the van – and sometimes the cart" (laughing and looking round to have the joke appreciated) – "together." Sally gave her little sad smile (she always smiled now as if there was something irreverent in smiling at all – as if we were all at a funeral), and Bootham said, "Those early defeats had great value in giving prominence to the Liberal case." But what Chester was saying to me (not only with his words but a passing glance and the tone in which he said "cart") was, "Do you remember that time at Lilmouth when you were nearly torn to pieces at a meeting because you stood up for me and afterwards we were both taken away in the same ambulance?"

I felt myself growing red, and Sally looked at me curiously, but Chester went on coolly (to make sure of his point), "Here is a bit about that riot at Lilmouth – you quote one of your Aunt's tenants on what he calls the 'wrath of the fool'." And turning over my old letter (I could remember the very ink it was written in; I had just come out of the hospital and found no ink at home but a bottle of violet colour borrowed from the cook), he said, "In those days even ploughboys had a sense of moral issues."

To which Bootham answered solemnly that those times must return or the country would perish. But the remark meant to me (after all the years in which Chester had been trying to make me appreciate moral issues) that I had betrayed moral issues and Chester himself.

This seemed so unfair that I answered him (under cover of a joke) that some of Aunt's tenants had been more moral in politics than in other things.

And perhaps this answer seemed to Chester a reflection on himself (and even his conduct of ten minutes before), because almost at once he made a suggestion so subtle and unexpected that for a minute I did not understand it. The man (apropos of a note about his needing me at Chelsea) said slowly and thoughtfully, with a kind of relish, "Ah, yes, I was planning a reception for that French deputation" (but in fact, the word "need" in most of Chester's letters had an affectionate meaning). "I'd like to use that, Nina; I want to pay a tribute to your powers as an entertainer. You taught me everything I ever knew about the arts of pleasure-giving. Yes, there, I may say, you began my education."

He spoke in so meaningful a voice (with the faintest

emphasis on "arts") that even Bootham looked up. There was a moment's pause.

But Chester went on so smoothly about my abilities as hostess (we both knew that I had not been a good hostess – I was far too absent-minded) that Sally went on making notes and Bootham (who throughout had the air very much of a keeper, at once patient and aware of his self-sacrifice) continued to play with his presentation watch chain.

But now I realized what Chester meant – the phrase "began it" recalled something I had said myself. He was making that old charge (but far more directly – from knowledge which belonged to ourselves), the charge, which his friends had been injecting into him for twenty years, that I had been his ruin, that I had "corrupted" him.

And this seemed to me so mean, so cunning that I felt myself grow hot. For (I thought) even if I gave him certain habits, it was only to make our marriage "work", to make the man happy and to stop him from killing me with his fearful domination. People who live together can't help changing each other – everybody in the world is "corrupting" everyone else. Even if one shut oneself up in a desert island, one bit of one's mind would "corrupt" another bit and try to "convert it" so that they would be able to work together.

And our marriage had "worked" for twenty-five years, and it was only because it had been so successful for him for so long that he had "habits".

He was like an old sailor who grumbles all day about the rheumatism he got by his hard life at sea; though he ran away to sea and never wanted any other life than sea life.

And suddenly I could bear no more. I pretended to remember the time, and got up hastily, saying that I should have to fly, Jim was expecting me; as for the remaining extracts I would agree to them all in advance. I was sure that Chester would know what could be printed.

Chester (he knew quite well why I was running away – he looked, however, a little surprised as if he had not expected me to be offended) then jumped up with something of the effect (as his first biographer described one of his interventions in a debate) of a pantomime imp coming up a trap, and again took my hand.

"And my letters to you," he said. "I'm afraid I shall need a good deal from those too – especially the early ones. The best plan would be for me to come over to Palm Cottage and we'll run over them together in peace and quiet."

He was holding my hand all the time and now he gave it a little pressure (twisting his eyes toward Bootham), which, at that moment, was as much as if he had begged, "Get me away from these jailers."

But I said at once that I should not dream of giving him the trouble – in any case the letters were not in the cottage, but at the bank. I would tell the bank to send them direct to the Manor.

Chester listened to this with his head thrown back and that bland expression which he had so often used when I showed the smallest opposition to his wishes – the screen behind which he prepared his offensives. And he began at once to argue that his letters formed a huge bulk. We should need several hours for their examination. It would be highly inconvenient for me to spend so much time away from home.

But Sally and Bootham at once came to my help. Sally said that, on the contrary, it would be much more convenient to bring the letters to the Manor where extracts could be typed and filed – and Lady Goold would always send a car to fetch me; Bootham declared flatly that Chester could not go at all – it was impossible in his present state of health (Bootham reminded me now of those old family servants, who, just because they are stupid, think they know all about their masters – and because they are conceited, become intolerably "bossy"). In fact, the doctors had already forbidden him to go out.

And again Chester submitted without a struggle – indeed with great dignity. He dropped my hand and said, smiling, "You see how they look after the old man. But I must not complain, must I?" And he made a little speech about Bootham's loyalty ("too rare in these days and all the more precious") and Sally's devotion, which, though it sounded a little strange (it belonged to a fashion already out of date since the war), was very touching even to me, who felt that it was aimed at my disloyalty and lack of devotion.

120 I was moved, as always, by the inflections of that voice, but also, as before, exasperated. And I arranged before I went home that I should not come again to the Manor. Sally would send me the extracts from the letters and I would look over them myself.

This plan suited Sally so well that she embraced me warmly – there was a compact between us to keep Chester safe in the Manor and away from me. And it worked very well. I ordered the letters to be sent and, in due course, received from Sally the list of extracts – not a word from Chester, either of reproach or invitation.

I was the more satisfied with my firmness that Jim proved so unreasonable about my visit to the Manor. He discovered from the paper that Chester had been there for the last week and said (it was true – and I saw how stupid I had been to avoid "unpleasantness") that I had deliberately chosen a day to "slip off" when I knew that he would be out. And he would not believe that I had not known of Chester's presence, nor that Chester had been interested only in my letters. He too, had heard rumours and said, "Everyone knows that the old bastard ought to have been in jail half a dozen times – he isn't safe with anything in skirts."

He brought up all the old accusations, that I was sly, double-faced, etc. And one morning, as I came from my bath, he appeared suddenly before me in the passage (he had been down painting the boat – I was astonished to see him back in the house), took me by the arms and said, "Who was that on the phone?"

I said I did not know – I had not heard the phone. Perhaps Aunt had been phoning. She often called up the librarian about her books.

"All right," Jim said. "I suppose I've got to believe it. But if you did play me up, Nina – you know what would happen – I'd kill you. That's a promise."

I was very glad when the regatta season arrived and gave the man something else to think about than the unlucky visit to the Manor.

This was the first year that Jim had acted as president of the Longwater Club. He was very anxious, therefore, to win the cup and had put it to me some months before that it was a great pity we could not afford a new boat for the dinghy race. I saw at once that he wanted to be encouraged to buy a new boat and so I did encourage him, very strongly, for I thought that he was owed that small pleasure after all his bad luck. Indeed, in the end I ordered the boat, arranging to pay by instalments and, though Jim abused me for the extravagance, I could see that he was very pleased.

And, in fact, he won the first two heats, taking a fellow expert as crew, with great ease. But on the morning of the semi-final he startled me (it was while he was still brooding on the Manor visit) by saying that he would take me as crew. "At least I'll not be wondering what you're up to."

I said that I should be proud to act as crew if he really thought me good enough. But actually I always found racing with Jim a particular agony. I dreaded it more than the dentist. For he was then at his most tense – the slightest mistake or delay on the part of his "hand" would make him so contemptuous of slack, cack-handed people who could not keep their mind on a job, that sparks seemed to fly out of him.

But though, as I say, it was an agony for me to go racing with him, it was also an extraordinary pleasure to see and feel his immense concentration on the set of a sail or the lie of the wind. Above all, that sudden boldness (or perhaps it was gambler's nerve) with which he would suddenly decide to risk everything on a desperate throw, as on that afternoon when we found that the new boat, so stiff and fast in a good wind, could be outsailed in a light one.

Now there is in the Longwater, just above Ferryport, a long creek running south, among steep slopes, which local yachtsmen call the eel-pot, because of its shape and because those who get in can never get out – it is too sheltered from all sides.

But that afternoon, as we turned the buoy for the home run (and the wind was almost dead), Jim noticed a flaw, a mere puff, shaped like a lady's slipper, moving through the ripe corn in a field above this creek. And he knew that from that field (if it did not die altogether in the warm wheat) it could reach the water. So to everyone's amazement he sailed into the eel-pot (someone in the ferry shouted at us as we passed – and everyone in the ferry was roaring with laughter; I saw that we risked being an enormous joke, almost as big a joke as after the Luga affair); and still more to their amazement, he found a wind there that pushed us home by a comfortable three minutes.

And how delighted he was with this victory. Even to be in the same room with him when the members were congratulating him (and not even able to see anything above their heads but the old stocking cap in which he sailed) was to feel that special delight – as if there were a private sun inside him throwing out its secret rays and making that kind of special energy inside one which obliges southern people to dance in the streets.

And it was while I was still enjoying this feeling and the famous victory, having, I suppose, about as much happiness as anyone can possibly have (and much more than any child can have; children have no idea what an extraordinary and precious thing happiness is), that I walked up to the cottage afterwards (I went alone because it was Robert's teatime and Jim had still to stow the gear), and was met by the maid at the front door to say that his lordship had come to stay with Miss Latter and should she put him in the white or the green room.

And when I looked cautiously through the window, there was Chester moving about the drawing room, apparently sorting papers, which he was ranging on the sofa and the tea table. I noticed particularly that he had taken Jim's old racing cups from the mantelpiece, to use as paper weights.

Aunt Latter, too, was there, in her pink flannel dressing gown, with a stick in one hand and her crutch under her right arm, hopping and hobbling round him in the greatest excitement. Aunt was now very bent down – her back was a hoop – so that she thrust out her neck like some bird. With these round shoulders and her thin neck and crippled hops, she was like some old tattered vulture or crow, chattering its beak over a kill.

121 I saw at once the great danger of my even going near Chester alone, and I felt thankful that Jim had won that race and would be kept a little longer at the clubhouse by all the people who wanted to drink with him (at Jim's expense – the winner "stood" drinks) and congratulate him.

I went straight down to the hotel and telephoned from there to Chorlock to ask if they knew where Chester was and if he was well enough to be out by himself.

Daisy, who seemed to be highly amused by the whole affair, said that Chester had got away by the back stairs to a tradesman's van and "they" were in a "fine fuss" because they thought he had run away with the kitchen maid. But she fetched Sally, who begged me to keep the patient very quiet until they could fetch him. They were coming at once and had asked the doctor to call.

And I did not show myself until, half an hour later, the Chorlock car arrived with Sally and Bootham, and I saw them go into the house. But when, very nervously, I joined them in the drawing room and apologized to Chester for my being out when he arrived, he seemed hardly to notice me. He went on talking to Aunt about the need for a clear statement of the Liberal position, and sorting his manuscript, quite as if he were at home.

Everybody, indeed, was behaving as if the situation was quite normal. Sally said, "Here is Mama now. Papa wants to consult you about these dates – " And I said that I knew I had often not dated my letters.

"Some of my notes are not dated either," Chester said.

"How long do you think you will be?" Sally asked. "I promised to telephone to the Manor."

"I shan't be going back today," Chester said coolly.

Sally said that perhaps this would not be very convenient

for me in a small cottage. "If Mama has no room for me," Chester said, "I can stay at the hotel opposite. I must be as near as possible – there are dozens of points we have to consider. You and Harry can go home as soon as you like. There's really nothing you can do for me here."

Aunt, who had somehow lugged down one of her enormous files of cuttings, was interrupting all the time to make Chester look at something she had discovered in *The Times* of 1905.

She was in a great fluster – I had not seen her so animated since the disaster at Buckfield. And now she screamed (she always behaved as if the cottage was still her own property – I daresay she believed it; in any case, such questions had ceased to have any importance for her), "I asked you as my guest. Stay as long as you like." And she turned furiously on me. "Don't talk nonsense, Nina. Of course there's room." And she demanded what I was thinking of. Didn't I see that everything was going to the devil with bells and that anything that would stop the rot – anything with the authority of a book by Chester – was a clear-the-line job? I ought, she said, to be proud to be of use in any possible way – even if I had to sleep on the floor.

She ended, feeling perhaps my lack of approval, by saying that she would see about his room that minute – he should sleep next door to herself – and hopped out, calling "Emmy – Emmy!" for the housemaid.

I said nothing to all this. I had decided already, of course, that Chester should not stay another hour. I made no answer to Aunt, and everyone but she had understood my silence. Chester looked round at me with his most suave expression; Sally and Bootham at once attacked. Bootham said that the doctor could not attend him at this distance, and that all his conferences were arranged at the Manor.

Sally said that there was no one here to take dictation, and no room for his files.

"I don't need the files," Chester said promptly. "I came here precisely to get away from all that sort of thing. Don't you understand that what we want is a new approach? We have been wasting our time for the last month."

Sally said that this was because he had been ill and tired. But Chester now became irritated and excited. I thought that, as in the old days, during a hostile meeting, he encouraged himself to be excited; he began to wave his hands about impatiently. "Yes, wasting time. The fact is, Sally, we've lost our way among all these Cabinet meetings, all these discussions of who put forward what policy and who was responsible for such a decision. Nobody today takes the least interest in such matters, and they are quite right." And when Bootham tried to make some protest, he threw out his palm in his old style when interrupted at a meeting and exclaimed, "No, I know I am right; I have known it for six months – perhaps for years, though I would not acknowledge it even to myself. We have been talking about the old spirit which we must recapture, but we have forgotten what it is; we have lost all knowledge of the spirit and our words are wind. They are worse than wind – they are a smokescreen to hide the vacancy of our hearts, the emptiness of our faith. The cold truth is that we have suffered the fate of every institution, of every party, in losing our way among the dust of our own achievement. We have come down from Pisgah, and forgotten the great vision that led us down. But you won't find that in blue books. It is in the memories of those who fought in that revolution – for it was a revolution – in their memories and letters. Your letters, Nina." And he turned on me. "And your memories, too, if you could spare even an hour."

"But not today, Papa," Sally said. "It's too late, and you know Mama can't put you up. There's no room here and you can't go upstairs."

"I'm afraid it would be rather difficult," I said. "Even upstairs you wouldn't be very comfortable."

Chester began to exclaim again – he would not dream of imposing himself on me. He would go at once, and he began running about to collect his papers.

Of course, we protested, begging him to sit down, to let us pack for him. But he would not stop. There was an absurd and exasperating scene – the little man dashing about the room, panting, blue at the lips, and Sally and Bootham and myself all chasing at his heels, trying to anticipate his next rush, imploring him to be reasonable.

I realized then at once, seeing Sally quite red with agitation (and feeling very anxious myself), how difficult an old man can be – like a wilful and delicate child who does not care what happens to him so long as he gets his own way; an autocrat and spoiled egotist who has to be humoured or cajoled or he may kill himself out of perversity or mere pique.

And it was a moment of terror when he clutched himself by the breast, gave a great groan, and fell gasping on the sofa.

Sally ran to him with a little bottle of medicine out of her bag. Bootham went out to fetch brandy from the dining room. And Chester, murmuring apologies and thanks, gradually breathed more easily. But he still kept his eyes closed. And looking at him I could not decide whether, in this attitude, he looked more childish or more cunning.

Sally, too, was gazing down at him with a little frown and flushed cheeks. I could see that she, too, suspected that this "heart attack" was a performance.

But she begged him not to move, and I realized that in her indignation she was still full of anxiety.

Aunt Latter had now hobbled in with Bootham and the brandy bottle. She began to scream for Emmy and to order us all about. Of course Chester could not be turned out – it was a preposterous wicked suggestion; and why should he not sleep in the back part of the drawing room? We had an excellent camp bed (it was Jim's African bed) which Emmy should set up in a moment.

Sally and I were pushed aside. And suddenly I saw a way out. I said to her, "I hope you will be able to stay, too. I don't know even the proper medicines." And Sally gave me a grateful glance. "I really think it would be better."

"Oh, in every way." Sally blushed a little more deeply but looked me in the eyes. "He really needs watching all the time."

"That's just what I felt and I shouldn't have time."

"Of course not – you have Uncle Jim and Robert to look after."

It was a complete understanding between us and when, a moment later, I heard Jim's step in the hall, I felt the relief of it.

Jim called for me from the front door (he always did so when he came in) and appeared in the drawing room with that expression (rare with him at any time) of thorough content, no doubt anxious to go over the race with me again and tell me what the experts at the club thought of his inspiration.

The change in his expression when he turned into the door and saw Chester lying on the sofa and the housemaid struggling with the bed was as if someone had hit him in the face.

"Chester has had an attack," I said hastily, "and Sally is going to stay with him tonight."

Jim said nothing to this – he was staring with so furious and suspicious a face that I was certain he would burst out with an ultimatum.

But as he looked round at us silently waiting for the explosion and then again at me, the rage went out of his face – to be followed by a most strange and unexpected look such as I had never seen before in Jim – of confusion, even of self-doubt.

One could see almost the exact moment when it had occurred to him that it might be wiser for him, even as a rightful husband under his own roof, to "postpone" (as Chester would have said in a playful mood) "consideration of the measure before the house".

And after a moment he said to the maid, "Not like that, Emmy – you'll break it," and went to take the bed (it was a kind of lazy-tongs machine) out of her hands. No one can say that Jim, jealous and reckless as he was, did anything to cause the final "Palm Cottage scandal".

122 And my plan, too, worked very well. On the next day, when Chester still insisted on palpitations (but he had the letters brought to him in bed and kept me beside him to discuss them), Bootham also transferred his guard post from the Manor to a room in the Longwater Hotel. He came every day before breakfast and did not go till late in the evening.

Either Sally or Bootham was always on the watch and often both. When, after three days, Chester got tired of bed and began to move about the front drawing room in his dressing gown, they set up the typewriter there to take his dictation. The room was like an office; but I was glad of it since it meant that I was not responsible for the "chief".

The understanding was that he would leave as soon as he

had made the extracts from the letters. But we soon found that this was going to take a long time, as long as Chester chose. After a week we were still at the first bundle. And already I had discovered how foolish I had been to set my wits against the man. For on the very first occasion that we were alone together (Sally had stepped into the passage to answer the telephone) he made an attack upon me.

This happened so suddenly, so unexpectedly, that I was taken completely by surprise. His whole proceeding was astonishing. I was going to say that he treated me as if I were still his wife, but this is not so; he treated me (and this is what was so unexpected and shocking) as he had never done before.

For, as I say, however sudden and passionate Chester's action or inspiration as a husband, there had always been something "spiritual" about them. He had never forgotten (even when he was "punishing" me – the punishment itself was a religious thing to him) that that love was for him (and should be for me) a sacred and mysterious thing; or, at least, that even if we sinned (I think he never quite got rid of the feeling that it was wrong to enjoy it so much) we were, on the whole, not forgetful of what we owed to God.

But now he attacked me in quite a different way, as I suppose unfortunate girls are attacked in trains or on lonely commons.

And I was helpless with fright. For Sally was not three yards away in the hall through a half-open door. I could only point at this door and make a face meaning, "For heaven's sake take care." But he paid no attention whatever and did not jump away from me until Sally hung up the receiver.

I was so furious (and frightened – I was shaking all over) that I went out at once, muttering an excuse to Sally. And I wrote Chester a note to tell him that I could not come near him again.

MY DEAR CHESTER,

You must understand how wrong and dangerous it was to behave like that this morning. I'm afraid I won't be able to come to you again. And I do really think you should go back to the Manor. All we need to do with the letters can easily be managed by writing or telephoning. My dear Chester, I hate to seem fussy, but I'm sure you can see that this time it is for your sake and Sally's quite as much as mine.

Your affectionate

NINA.

I sent this to him by Emmy and received not even an acknowledgment. Probably he did not even read it. He never read any of the notes with which Aunt bombarded him (after that one tremendous effort of his reception, she had, to our relief, gone back permanently to bed); one might say that, from this time, nothing at all from the outer world reached Chester across the no man's land of his isolation.

And if one pities him in that appalling solitude (as I had pitied him) one is forgetting perhaps the furious sense of urgency and power (for he still thought of himself as the chosen leader) which had made the solitude. I doubt if he had a moment, in those last days, for self-pity, for any kind of "selfish" consideration.

And when, next morning, I did not come at the usual time, he was so enraged at this interruption to his work that Sally, whom he sent to fetch me, could barely hide her impatience at my excuses (housework and Robert) – for her,

too, Chester's book was all important. She could not dream
that I had any "real" reason for staying away, for she knew
very well that I had never been alone with him for more
than two minutes.

And I had to go back. I only made Sally undertake that
the whole party should leave at the end of that week, and
arranged that, whatever happened, I should do so. And I
made Jim promise (he did so with great readiness) to take
me and Robert and the nurse to London for a week's
shopping.

Chester, of course, having brought me back by Sally's
own intervention, was even more enterprising. Within
twenty-four hours, he had misbehaved in exactly the same
way, and actually in the presence of Bootham, typing at the
table. True, he was out of sight round the pillar dividing the
front from the back drawing room, but he had only to have
pushed back his chair a foot to have seen us.

And now this was always Chester's plan. He would
dictate a long rhetorical sentence (full of the most lofty
sentiments), and while Bootham was typing he would
suddenly stoop over me so that I was imprisoned in my
chair. I could not avoid his hands or his lips; and all the time
he would stare at me with an extraordinary expression of
defiance and fierceness, if that is the right word for the look
which you see on a man's face when he is at a climax of
excitement.

You say I should have turned him out of the house. But I
was extremely anxious to avoid any kind of contretemps
which might upset Jim; and for another, I had Sally's firm
promise that the whole miserable situation would come to
an end that week.

I did indeed struggle with him (risking Bootham's hearing
us), but the only result was to make him angry. He actually

exclaimed aloud, "We haven't time to waste on this nonsense," and before Bootham could crane his neck backwards to see what he meant, he was ten feet away, dictating again about the "true spiritual roots of the British Liberal tradition – the veritable Protestant succession of the free soul". And though I wanted to laugh (I was much too angry at his "hypocrisy" to let myself *be* angry), I felt, too, that his impatience with my "nonsense" was quite real; he thought that my complaints were truly contemptible beside the tremendous ideas and anxieties which filled his mind night and day, until perhaps he simply had to let down the pressure by those sudden attacks on me.

I remembered all I had heard of other great men (and no one who knew Chester can deny that he had something of greatness about him) who in their old age seemed to forget the most elementary conventions (falling in love with little girls, like Goethe, ceasing to wash themselves, or talking, like Tolstoy, so coarsely that the roughest men blushed for them) simply because they were so overwhelmed by the fearful tragedies and perils of humanity, at last made plain to them, that they could no longer give much importance to rules of "mere" propriety. Old age had not so much made them wicked as changed the balance of their moral ideas.

I dare say you will think (as Aunt would have thought if she had taken, any longer, the least interest in the matter) that I am making excuses for Chester simply to hide from myself my own weakness of character and love of peace, but I am not pretending that the man had lost his moral sense; he knew quite well that he was doing something wrong and dangerous.

I think this was even part of his pleasure (I am sure Tolstoy loved to shock the "rough and candid" Gorki). Just as he had revelled, as a young man, in defying a whole town full of enemies (one might say at one time it was a whole nation), now it gave him some mysterious delight to overcome me and to take the risk (quite a serious risk for a famous man and a peer) of being caught in a vulgar and petty "crime" which would be all the more shocking to the public because it was so "low".

And I noticed that after one of these successful assaults – (and now I did everything possible to give the man what he wanted as quickly as possible, simply to get it over) he would seem ten years younger, his eyes would sparkle, he would thrust out his chest and strut about the room with that air (allowing for his shaky legs and shrunken body) which had caused the papers, thirty years before, to describe him as something of the buccaneer. Looking at him then (while still trembling at the danger just escaped and at what he had done to me) I was ready to laugh as well as rage.

And again, when I wrote of his "hypocrisy" in turning straight from one of his buccaneering raids on me to utter most idealistic and noble speeches about freedom, I think now I am probably being unfair. For it really seemed to me that the excitement of the exploit with all its audacity and risk overflowed into all his energies, and so he quite truly felt renewed and inspired by his vision of a free world.

In fact, whether he "needed" a wife or not, as Daisy had suggested, there was no doubt about the improvement in his nerves and even his general health. He had become a different man – the doctors were so impressed that they were all for his continuing in "the sea air of Palm Cottage, bracing, but warm and sheltered".

Aunt Latter, too, would never have agreed to putting Chester out. Indeed, his arrival had had an extraordinary effect on her. She had stopped drinking and spent all day

413

with her files. And though no one paid any attention to her notes (which were hopelessly beside the point), composing them (what she called her dispatches) made her forget her grievances against us all.

I suppose Aunt was born to be a very unhappy woman. Her immense feeling of responsibility, her "busyness" in other people's affairs, her inability (as in my case) to let things "drift", were bound to bring her every kind of disappointment – quite as much as her bitter tongue.

But at least her final enterprise (and as we now knew she had been in the plot of Chester's famous escape – it was she who had arranged the details for him – telephoning for the baker's van that picked him up) had been a success. She was able to feel that she was once more among the people of "character" who did things – the "strong souls" who take upon themselves the responsibility (and the guilt) of managing the world.

It was, I think, this unexpected refreshment (but she had always had great powers of recovery) that encouraged her to begin her memoirs which, among the half-dozen or so now being written round Chester and his career, may well be the most damaging of all. For Aunt, with all her courage in taking decisions for other people, has never understood just how complicated they are.

My greatest fear, of course, was that Jim would catch us. But Jim from that first evening, when in the actual crisis of Chester's arrival he suddenly restrained himself and did *not* make a scene, had been extraordinarily considerate. He never came near the drawing room when I was at work with Chester there, and, indeed, it gradually came about that Chester sent for me usually at times when Jim was out on estate business or down at the yacht club.

Of course, it was obvious that Jim was suffering – he had

suddenly been brought into a situation quite inconceivable to his idea of what was possible for himself. When Chester had stayed week after week, he even changed in appearance. He looked at me sometimes with so haggard and wondering an expression that I was ready to weep.

He knew as well as I did that the whole place (in fact the whole country) was sizzling with gossip and curiosity; newspapers as far away as Aberdeen had paragraphs to say that "Lord Nimmo was staying with Captain and Mrs Latter at Palm Cottage (Mrs Latter was formerly Mrs Nimmo)." To a man like Jim who felt dirtied by such publicity, the position was agonizing, and every day I expected him to burst out and say that it must stop.

But when I realized that he actually did not want to make a discovery, I felt such relief that I was, if possible, in greater love than ever with the man who could sacrifice his enormous pride (but Jim was perhaps too proud to admit that any such vulgar situation could hurt his pride) to his love for me. I knew then, in fact, that Jim did truly love me and could not bear to lose me.

So I had quite good reason to hope that an arrangement which had been established and suited us all would last safely for a few days more.

123 But, of course, no arrangement, however convenient, ever goes on being established – people get tired of it; and Chester especially loved (perhaps needed) to take risks. He grew more and more reckless every day, in talk as well as action. And on Friday afternoon, when I came into the room for our work together, I found both Sally and Bootham with him. He was obviously in his most excited mood and flew out at once, "What's this about your going away? I heard nothing of it.

Why wasn't I told? I don't think I've deserved this of you, Nina. I did not think you would go behind my back in this manner."

Sally was making a face at me over his shoulder and I said, of course, that I had not liked to worry him. "Worry me?" he exclaimed. "It's not a question of being worried – I simply feel let down. I thought you were interested in the work. I thought you had some feeling for its timeliness. I have been relying on you to put smaller matters on one side!"

Sally now intervened for me, saying that I had the house to look after, but Chester had already pulled out a file (I noticed it was not the file we had been working on) and said shortly to me, "At least we can get on now. This is the Tarbiton speech – after I was elected to the council." And then, instead of handing me the file, so that I could make any comment, he began to read it.

I knew then at once why he had taken this file out of its turn and said, "I thought you weren't going to use any of those early speeches." But he only gave me another angry glare, turned his back on me and said to Sally and Bootham, "That was at the big meeting of welcome after I was elected to the county council, my real beginning, and it was the first time I felt the power, that the spirit descended upon me – I speak in all reverence. It was not I who found these words." And he began suddenly to declaim, "Are we then to believe that man is entirely a beast – greedy, selfish, cruel? So our present rulers teach us. It is their faith – the only ground of their despotism – and, to be just, the only excuse for their trickery and their crimes. They may be right – only God can answer such a proposition of the devil. And if they are right, then let them continue in their evil power for the world would not be worth saving.

"But for myself" (and here he laid his hand on his chest, as if he were really on the platform) "I cannot breathe that stifling air of the prison house; I must see sky even if it be but a rag between the storm clouds; I must follow that gleam. Let it be a phantom as they say – a dream – I must pursue. I can no other; for me there is no life but in freedom."

He rolled this out with all his old play of voice. But his voice was growing thin, it cracked on the rising notes, and the whole effect was so like Tom's caricature (the words were even more high-flown) that I felt again that hysterical impulse to laugh and cry.

For though the speech itself (one of his famous orations of those ancient days) seemed now as ridiculous as Jim's old hats and pipe-stem trousers (and perhaps, too, as Jim's notions of honour), yet it brought back to me a confused feeling of excitement, wave on wave; not perhaps that which I felt years before at that meeting, but a quite new one. I was recalling not only the old thrill of Chester's voice and a packed meeting (which was disturbing enough for those old excitements seem to grow inside one as one gets older), and certainly nothing to do with freedom (though it was always an exciting word in Chester's mouth), but something that belonged to the time, to my life with Chester; that started up in me like a spring in dry ground.

In fact, much to my surprise and embarrassment tears came to my eyes, and to save myself from a disgraceful exhibition I quickly took the file out of Chester's hands and said, "But you have two speeches already for that chapter."

He explained in the same excited indignant manner, "You thought that my best at the time – you copied it out for me. Look at it – it's in your writing. And I rehearsed it to you, every word. But I suppose you *want* to forget that

time – when you worked so hard for me – and shared my
success; it was you who called it a triumph. And when we
got away at last in old William's cab – do you forget that,
too?" He turned his back on me and spoke to Sally and
Bootham. "The people wanted to take the horse out and
pull us home five miles along the Queensport Road – and
all this for a county council election, because I was the first
radical to get in. But you young people can't even imagine
what life was like in those days – days when even the
simplest could feel the greatness of a cause; when no one
was ashamed to have enthusiasm and to show it, to confess
a real faith, something to live and die for. What has
happened to you all? Why do you leave your souls to die by
the wayside? Is it lassitude, ignorance – or treachery?" And
he said the last word in a deeper, louder voice which I had
heard very often in his great days. It expressed his utmost
contempt and disgust.

Both Sally and Bootham were well aware that all this was
aimed at me, and Sally said to me, so as to cover my
embarrassment, that she would put the speech on one side
for consideration.

124 And I was very much startled by this deliberate
and angry reference of Chester's to that cab ride.
For what had happened in the cab was that we had both
been fearfully excited, and also fearfully tired, and I had
been drinking champagne, and I was thinking that now
Chester was really a great man (as I thought then, and he
had certainly become a local hero) our life would somehow
be changed into a delightful experience; above all, into
something easy to enjoy (which was, of course, nonsense, as
I knew quite well, but it was also a very strong feeling). And
Chester suddenly proposed that we should offer up thanks

for God's mercy to him – actually kneel down in the cab. But I said no, it would make me laugh, which would be a disgrace. I said that I didn't need to offer thanks – I was all thanks, all over. And he said, "Are you really glad for me?" And I said, of course I was (which was true – I was always delighted by Chester's successes, because he was so wretched and unhappy when he failed in anything) – all the thanks were for him. And he said that I must thank for myself, too, because I had given him everything he had. So I said, of course this was nonsense; he knew perfectly well he couldn't have succeeded without his brains and his talent for speaking, and his very good voice. Then he had said, as usual, that all these would have come to nothing without my encouragement and my goodness. And I had said, "Goodness gracious, any ordinary nice woman would have done for what you call my goodness." And he had been shocked as I had meant, for I was afraid of his getting too serious and religious, and he said that I did not know my own heart. And I had said no, but I knew about the rest of myself, and he had got very passionate, and said that even if I chose to belittle our marriage it was a grand and noble thing for him; and that it was not he but I who was talking nonsense, because I knew perfectly well that God had often sanctified it for me, too, even in what I chose to speak of so carelessly (he meant crudely) and that was what he meant by my goodness, and he begged me not to shut myself out from the joy of the Lord and spoil a lovely thing by my perversity of self-depreciation.

This phrase, "the joy of the Lord", seemed still more comic to me in such an application; and yet he was so excited and earnest that I could not laugh, so instead I wanted to cry (in fact, what with everything that had been happening all day I had been a little hysterical then, and it was that very memory which was making me a little hysterical now) and I threw myself into his arms (just to stop him saying such things and upsetting me even more) and said that the last thing I wanted to do was to spoil anything for him after he had worked so hard and waited so long, and I was very glad he had such a high opinion of me, and hadn't I said I was all thanks – indeed, I was simply aching with thanks.

And he misunderstood me (that is to say, he took my meaning in rather too crude, or perhaps only too masculine, a sense) and was quite astonished, and then carried away, and he tried to pull down the cab curtains, but one of them stuck and the other had an enormous tear.

And I simply could not believe what these precautions seemed to mean, because I hadn't discovered then that all Chester's feelings and energies seemed to run into each other; his religion stirred up his politics and his politics stirred up his religion, and both of them stirred up his affections and his imagination, and his imagination kept everything else in a perpetual turmoil. And now when I asked if it was safe while every now and then people from the meeting were going by on ponies, he said he did not care, he loved me too much, he adored me. I was the soul of his life and the life of his soul. And then he got more and more excited and perfectly reckless and took the most enormous risks. Also, of course, we were fearfully cramped and uncomfortable, and the whole affair – what with my being so tired and excited, and rather drunk with tiredness and champagne, and Chester himself being rather crazy with his triumph and his grand ideas and this special inspiration – was very muddled and desperate, and in fact, rather a failure.

But in spite of that (or because of it; because it was so unexpected for Chester, at that time, to do such a thing at all in such a place, and both of us were so anxious not to spoil it for the other) it was extraordinary and unforgettable; so that we really did feel that we had been carried off into a kind of sacred exalted region, where everything was truly a spiritual revelation (and I may say at once that the cab smelled of mould, and the springs squeaked all the time, and the horse sounded rather lame, and there was a frightful draught through both windows, which wouldn't close properly, and made a most dismal rattling; and there was something sharp in the edge of the cushion which cut right through my dress, and was giving me agony, when we were both at our most exalted moment, and the moonlight kept shooting through the hedges like a searchlight and revealing pictures like something in Cousin Slapton's most curious French books), so that afterwards, when we were at peace in bed, we fell asleep in each other's arms, still feeling that at last we had been admitted into wonderful secrets and mysteries.

Of course, when we waked up in the morning the wonders had vanished; I had a fearful headache, and a pain inside, and a great jagged cut behind, which was sore, and which I was afraid might be infected in some way by that horrible cab. And Chester was fearfully worried in case the cabman had noticed anything, or anyone had looked through the windows at us. Also he was extremely full of plans for beginning his career as a county councillor and making a tremendous rumpus in the shortest possible time.

125 And this act of Chester's in calling up such recollections (under the very noses of Sally and Bootham) alarmed me very much, for I saw that Chester's behaviour to me was not just the ailment of an old man – he really did regard me as still belonging to him. It was "treachery" on my part to try to leave him even for a day. But now, when I looked at the clock and said that I must fly, he suddenly became charming and thanked me for my patience, and said, "Yes, you must go – it will only take five minutes to check these page numbers." He picked up a list.

And I think Sally was shocked, seeing him so "reasonable", when I said no, I hadn't a moment, and went out. I said to myself with delight that I need never see Chester again.

But that afternoon, while I was sitting in the kitchen writing down the list of meals (Aunt Latter's meals), in our absence, and having just ordered our lunch for the train (a cold lunch – cook had just run into the yard to catch a chicken), Chester darted in and thrust me back into the chair.

I had never seen him so angry or felt him so urgent. He was punishing me. "You are like the rest of them," he muttered. "You think of nothing but yourself – rottenness – rottenness everywhere."

"Chester!" I implored him. "Cook is just coming – she'll see us." And in fact the squawking of the chicken which cook had grabbed by the wings had come to a sudden end as Chester spoke. But in the same moment I heard a sound which turned my eyes from the window to the door, and there was Bootham, standing and gazing at us.

The man was absolutely thunderstruck. He could not get out a word, and one saw again, under the large pompous flesh, the timid awkward youth who had failed in the grocer's shop. That youth had been very proper, and the solemn important man was horrified. He turned quite ruby and muttered at last, "Please, please!" actually wringing his fingers together. He seemed to be begging for mercy.

Chester (he did not know that we were being watched and was furious when I tried to thrust him away), hearing these words, was not at all disconcerted. He whisked round, pretended to be in a rage, and shouted, "What do you mean? What are you talking about? Why have you left your work?"

He seemed quite astonished when the poor man stood his ground, wriggling his legs, and making extraordinary faces, and at last got out, "But I saw – I couldn't help – I can't – "

"Am I in a madhouse," Chester exclaimed, "where idiots see visions?" And then suddenly he made a dart at Bootham and waved his hands. "Go away, sir. I don't know what you are insinuating – I will not even guess at it before a lady. But it fits in with your conduct for some time past. A conduct, if I may say so, of a low mind, and I am tired of it; I will not be spied on. You have made yourself impossible in my household. Go, sir. I say get out – get out of my house."

And when Bootham, with the obstinacy of a stupid man, stayed where he was, still wriggling and mouthing, Chester made me a little bow as if to a lady chairman on a platform, and touched my arm to make me get up and guided me out of the room. So that his retreat was full of dignity. It did not even seem like a retreat – it wore the appearance of a considerate act to save me from annoyance.

And, in fact, he did actually turn Bootham out of the house. Of course, there was a great turmoil; no one could understand exactly what had happened, and Chester never stopped talking, throwing such confusion into all our minds, that even I began to wonder if Bootham could have seen anything that would justify his being so shocked. Only Sally stood up for him. But, of course, she did not blame Chester. In her view the whole trouble was due to me – in the first place because of the divorce, and in the next because (and I suppose most young women would take the same view) I shouldn't have "allowed such a thing to happen".

She gave, therefore, an ultimatum – Chester must return at once with her to the Manor. And this Chester refused absolutely and rather rudely.

This astonished poor Sally so much that I was very sorry for her. She had never realized how little her "devotion" meant to a man who was himself "devoted" – not even to a human being but to something that seemed to his imagination (which had done so much to create it) infinitely more beautiful and worthy – the Cause.

In fact, I think that the real reason for the breach between Sally and Chester (and perhaps her bitter indignation against me) is due to this quarrel and Chester's remark that he was not going to be "held in bondage" even by the "most well-meaning of his henchmen".

Sally, too, therefore, shook off the dust of our wicked household – she left in the same cab with Bootham.

126 I thought then, "At last this fearful tension is over." But it is nearly a year since Bootham and Sally left and the tension is very much worse. They are writing a book together (they were married five months ago – or, as Aunt Latter puts it, joined in the love of Nimmo) – revelations – which will tell the "true" story of Chester Nimmo and present me as the cause of their separation from the great man and of all the scandals which have "fallen on his name at the end of a life which should have nothing but honour from the people to whom it was devoted". I quote from Sally's farewell letter.

And Chester, so far from learning decency or at least caution from experience (and rejoicing in his freedom from Bootham's watchfulness), is even more enterprising when the fit takes him. I am in continual terror, for Jim is no longer tactful and accommodating. On the very day of

Bootham's discovery, he came to me in the bedroom where I had taken refuge from the turmoil downstairs, on the excuse of Robert's bedtime.

I was glad to have Robert to play with while he tried to walk, staggering from one chair to another and then sitting down heavily with a shout of laughter. We were laughing together, when Jim came in and said, "So they're going at last?" I said that Bootham and Sally were going, but I knew that the question really meant "Is Chester going?" Jim, still hovering about the room in the background, answered promptly, "Does that mean that you're proposing to let Chester stay?"

I began to say that just at the moment the book wasn't finished and Chester had nowhere else to go and no one to look after him – it would not be safe for us even to go to town in case he was taken ill. But Jim interrupted me. "We can tell the doctor to get a nurse. What I'm asking is if you're going to turn him out?"

I was so frightened by his savage tone that I tried to say yes, but the word would not come.

And I knew then that I should never get rid of Chester, that I dared not do so. And I saw that it was no good pretending that I merely tolerated an old man's whims because he was pitiful – I did not love Chester and I had never loved him, but now, more than ever, at the end of his life, I was in his power. When he fixed his eyes on me (it was perhaps the only time in a week that he even thought of me as a human being) and I felt myself shrink, I knew that he held me still with a thousand ties that I should never break – ties from a marriage of nearly thirty years that was all the more "part of me" because I had suffered in it.

When Jim found that I did not mean to answer him, he locked the door and I felt sure that he meant to kill me. I was not so much frightened as stupefied. I leaned back in my chair and it seemed that I had no bones.

Jim came in front of me and looked down at me for a long minute with a strange expression of hatred and also indecision. I thought he was even afraid. Then he took me by the wrists quite gently and lifted me up. I was so feeble that I could not stand properly and leaned back against the bedpost.

"Tell me the truth," he said in quite a soft voice. "What have you been up to?"

My mouth was so dry that I could only whisper that I had done nothing.

"You mean absolutely nothing? You mean that Bootham is making it up?"

I nodded my head; and Jim shook my wrists as if to bring me to myself, but without hurting me.

"I want the truth this time," he said. "You've got to tell the truth. Do you mean that there's nothing in it – on your soul and honour?"

I nodded again, but Jim shook my wrists and told me to say the words, "I swear – by Almighty God – that this is the truth."

So I said the words, and then Jim, all at once, appeared at a loss. He stared at me for a long time, and I suddenly became faint and collapsed into the chair. Then he brought me some water, and I kissed him and held him for a long time.

He helped me then to lie down on the bed and went out without saying another word. I don't know yet if he believed me, which seems impossible, or if he simply deceived himself, because he could not bear, after all, to "face the facts".

But soon after that afternoon (about a month later, when he had turned the matter over in his mind) he changed his tactics of avoiding the drawing room when I was at work with Chester. He suddenly appeared there one morning on the excuse of looking for the ink. And after that, he often comes upon us with no warning (but you can see by his face that each time he is in terror of what he may find – he will look round with his jaw set as if expecting an ambush) and with no excuse – simply to say good morning to Chester or to remark that I am not to forget some engagement. It is as though he said to himself, "I am not going to accept happiness from that woman at the cost of my honour. I know she is lying and deceitful, but I'm not going to connive at her tricks. I shall behave exactly as if she were honest, and if I catch her out, so much the worse for all of us."

So that the life which was going to be so simple and restful, my "retirement from politics", is more difficult and complicated than ever, and also, of course, more "political". I have to consider every word I say and everything I do. The tension is like a perpetual crisis. I notice that my hair is turning white and I am so thin that my frocks hang on me. But what is strange is that I have never had so much happiness because Jim has never before been so much in love. You would say that neither of us has known till now what is meant by a grand passion – I suppose Jim, like me, feels that every day may be the last.

But how could I make him understand that it is because that happiness is so precious to me I dare not turn Chester out. For I should know that I was committing a mean crime against something bigger than love.

I should despise myself, which is, I suppose, what Chester means when he says that such and such a "poor devil" is "damned". And I am terrified of "damnation", for it would destroy my happiness and all the joy of my life, and Jim can only shoot me dead.

Joyce Cary

The African Witch

Aladai returns to his village in Nigeria after an English education, a candidate for the succession of the old Emir. He finds the village filled with intrigue and shifting alliances but he has an ally in Judy Coote, a friend from Oxford. Both of them discover that prejudice is not the prerogative of one race.

Aissa Saved

The first of Cary's African novels. Aissa, a charismatic young Christian convert, has a high fever and only Christian medicine can heal her despite the claims of the native doctor.

Written with great power and psychological insight the novel gives a fascinating picture of the native mind with its superstition and cruel logic.

Joyce Cary

The Captive and the Free

Cary's last novel (he was working on it when he died in 1957) is about the power of religion and the press. Its galaxy of characters includes the faith-healer Preedy, the journalist Hooper and Alice Rodker who, seduced by Preedy, threatens to denounce him.

Castle Corner

A panoramic novel whose sweeping narrative centres on members of an Anglo-Irish family, the Corners, in late nineteenth century Ireland, England and West Africa.

Joyce Cary

Except the Lord

Chester Nimmo's account of his childhood in the West Country. In this fine portrait, Cary shows the origins of Nimmo's complex personality and leftwing political ideals. We come to understand him as a man dependant on and racked by his love of strong women, with his eyes looking ever toward heaven.

Not Honour More

It is 1926, the year of the General Strike. Jim Latter, now head of the emergency civilian police, opposes Nimmo, whom he sees as an unprincipled manipulator; their uncompromising struggle brings disaster to both, and to Nina.

OTHER TITLES BY JOYCE CARY AVAILABLE DIRECT
FROM HOUSE OF STRATUS

Quantity		£	$(US)	$(CAN)	€
☐	The African Witch	8.99	14.99	19.49	15.00
☐	Aissa Saved	8.99	14.99	19.49	15.00
☐	The Captive and the Free	8.99	14.99	19.49	15.00
☐	Castle Corner	8.99	14.99	19.49	15.00
☐	Except the Lord	8.99	14.99	19.49	15.00
☐	Not Honour More	8.99	14.99	19.49	15.00

ALL HOUSE OF STRATUS BOOKS ARE AVAILABLE FROM GOOD BOOKSHOPS OR DIRECT
FROM THE PUBLISHER:

Internet: **www.houseofstratus.com** including author interviews, reviews, features.

Email: **sales@houseofstratus.com** please quote author, title, and credit card details.

Hotline: UK ONLY: **0800 169 1780**, please quote author, title and credit card details.
INTERNATIONAL: **+44 (0) 20 7494 6400**, please quote author, title, and credit
card details.

Send to: **House of Stratus**
24c Old Burlington Street
London
W1X 1RL
UK